WETHERING THE STORM

D1115334

Also by Samantha Towle
The Mighty Storm

WETHERING THE STORM

Samantha Towle

Text copyright © 2013 Samantha Towle

Published by Montlake Romance

P.O. Box 400818
Las Vegas, NV 89140

ISBN-13: 9781477805053
ISBN-10: 1477805052
Library of Congress Control Number: 2013930036

For those of you who read The Mighty Storm, *loved it, recommended it to your family and friends, wrote reviews, sent me wonderful messages…this is for each and every one of you.*

TRU...

CHAPTER ONE

Pushing my sunglasses from my eyes to rest on top of my head, I tilt my face toward the still-hot early-evening sun. Letting my leg dangle off the edge of the lounger, I push my toes into the soft white sand. Jake is beside me on his own lounger, his hand in mine, fingers laced together, as he talks on the phone to Stuart.

"Just tell them to do the job I pay them to do. If they have a problem with that, then remind them they are not irreplaceable...I know. Fuckin' idiots...oh, you know that thing I asked you to do for me...you did? Good, thanks."

With a sigh, Jake ends his call and tosses his iPhone onto the side table.

"All okay?" I ask, turning my head to look at him.

God, he is beautiful. I don't know if I'll ever get used to how breath-stealing Jake truly is.

He looks even more stunning here, with his skin sun-kissed, causing the freckles on his nose to show more prominently. He looks yummy delicious.

"Hmm? Yeah, everything's fine," he answers, sounding a little distracted. "Just people not doing what I pay them to do."

"You want to talk about it?"

"No." He lifts my hand to his mouth and brushes his lips across my knuckles, placing a specific kiss on my ring.

"There are a lot of things I want to do with you while we are here, Tru, and talking about work is not one of them."

Ignoring his desire to not talk about work, I say, "Do you need to get back to LA early to sort the problem out?"

Jake shifts onto his side to face me. "No. You and I are spending time together here, alone. Nothing and no one will get me off this island and away from you. I plan on spending the next five days keeping you in the minimal amount of clothes possible, if not none at all, and spending most of that time fucking you senseless."

A shiver runs down my spine.

I love it when he talks to me like this. Dirty and domineering. It's incredibly hot.

"You're such a romantic." I roll my eyes playfully.

"You wouldn't have me any other way."

I let my gaze drift to serious. "No, I wouldn't."

I reach over and grab my bottle of water off the table and take a drink, letting my eyes drift over the beautiful scenery before me.

We're on a private island in Fiji. More specifically, we're staying on Turtle Island, one of the Yasawa Islands in Fiji. It's where *The Blue Lagoon* was filmed. It's private and exclusive and has only fourteen villas on the whole island, but Jake being Jake, he has rented out the whole island for a week. A week of total isolation for him and me. Dave and Ben, Jake's bodyguards, are with us, of course, staying separately in one of the other villas at the far side of the island. I've barely seen them since I arrived here. And aside from the staff who live on the island, it's just Jake and me.

That's how it's been for the last two days, and it is heaven. Absolute heaven.

After the show at Madison Square Garden, when Jake did his stage dash to come after me and ask me to marry him, things got a little crazy...well, *crazier*, as life with Jake is always crazy.

Basically, I wasn't thinking straight after everything that had happened that night, and I wasn't as smart as I should have been. I didn't hide my ring. As Jake and I entered the hotel after leaving the show, a member of the waiting press spotted it, and all hell broke loose.

For the next two days we were literally confined to the hotel. Press and fans gathered and hollered outside. It was suffocating. When Jake suggested we get away and leave the country for a while, I was fully on board.

I left all the travel arrangements to Jake. I didn't care where we went, just as long as we were alone.

And alone we are.

I love being here with him. It's the first time since we got together that it's been just him and me.

I know I just offered to go back to LA, but in all honesty it was a halfhearted offer. I don't want to let this go—what we have here right now—the complete solitude to do what we want, when we want.

But I know there's something bothering him workwise. The tone of his voice when he was talking to Stuart was clear enough to tell me that. Even now, I can tell his mind is elsewhere as he stares out at the ocean, his fingers tapping restlessly against my hand.

I hate that he won't share with me what it is. I know it's because he doesn't want to burden me, but I want him to burden me. I want him to share everything with me. Our lives are entwined now, and I don't want him carrying things alone anymore. The last time he did that, he fell off the wagon, and we lost each other as a result of it.

Jake is still only a few weeks' clean, and I, for one, want to keep him that way.

I'm glad he's here, away from all temptation at the moment. Well, all temptations except me, that is. I do worry, though, how things will be for him when we eventually go back to the real world.

"You fancy a swim before the sun goes in?" I nod in the direction of the water lapping the white sand, deciding not to push the subject further. I'll tackle his communication issues later, when he's more relaxed.

Jake's eyes set on my body, his gaze roaming every curve, causing all the muscles in me to involuntarily clench. Especially the ones between my legs.

"You're asking if I want a chance to see you wet, wearing that bikini?" A grin curves his gorgeous mouth as he lifts his brow in question.

I glance down at my favourite and most recent bikini purchase. It's white with pink flowers and has tiny diamantes sewn in. I picked it up from the airport. It was love at first sight.

"How do you manage to turn something as simple as my request to swim, into sex?" I ask, chuckling, as I climb up from my lounger.

I pull my sunglasses off my head and drop them onto my towel. Hands on hips, I stare down at him.

Jake's eyes skim my curves again. "When you're in the equation, sweetheart, everything is about sex."

He slides off his lounger, rising to his feet in one graceful move, and comes over to me.

My whole body suddenly aches for his touch. I feel hungry for him.

I simply cannot get enough of Jake. And I don't want to. Ever.

Jake presses himself against me. My hands instantly go to his hard stomach, fingers pressed against his rigid muscle, as I stare up into his beautiful blue eyes. Eyes I could spend a lifetime staring into.

A devilish smile curves his lips as two large hands reach down and cup my behind, urging me to lift and wrap my legs around his waist.

Of course, I happily oblige his unspoken request.

Snaking my arms around his neck, I wind my fingers into his lush black hair and kiss his lips, feeling his instant erection press against me.

"You're hard?" I smile.

"Well, you're hot," he says with a shrug.

Jake puts his lips against my neck, sliding the tip of his tongue over my skin as he starts the short walk down to the water.

He wades us into the sun-warmed ocean until we're chest deep.

The long length of my hair is already wet, so holding on to Jake's shoulders, I tilt my head back, wetting the rest.

As I right myself, I meet Jake's stare again. "How did I get so lucky to have you?" he asks. His eyes suddenly look unsure.

Whatever anxiety is in his mind right now, I want to ease it, reassure him.

"I ask myself the same question every day about you," I murmur. I need Jake to realise I am no better than he is. He has his faults, but so do I.

Jake exhales, closing his eyes briefly, then leans in and kisses me. His kiss takes my regret with it.

Losing myself in him, I part my lips, letting his tongue into my mouth. His tongue caresses mine with slow, deliberate movements.

Knowing where this kiss is heading, I whisper, "You want to go back to the villa?" I'm so ready to get naked with him.

"No. I want you right here, right now." The command in his voice equals the command in his hands as they grip my ass tighter, pulling me hard onto his erection.

"You into exhibition sex nowadays, Wethers?"

He lets out a deep, throaty laugh. "No, I'm just into you. All. The. Fucking. Time." His words come out staccato with each kiss he places upon my shoulder.

I feel his teeth graze over my skin. My nipples tighten in response, leaving my breasts feeling very heavy in my bikini top.

I cast a quick glance around. "What if someone sees us?"

Jake glances around, eyes glittering. "We're in the middle of nowhere. In the ocean, no less. Who the fuck is going to see us?"

"The people who work here. Or Dave. Or Ben."

"Then they'll get a good show."

"Jake!" I slap his shoulder with my hand.

Bringing his face before mine, he rests the tip of his nose against mine. "They know to stay away. It's just me and you out here, baby."

Feeling uninhibited, as I can only with him, I murmur, "If that's the case…" I press my lips to his neck, kissing him. I run my tongue over his skin, to the sensitive part just below his ear that I know drives him crazy.

Jake shudders and tightens his hold on me, grinding his hips into mine.

Moving my hand down, I submerge it into the water and reach into Jake's swim shorts.

I'm instantly met with the silky, rock-hard feel of him. I slide my fingers down the shaft, stroking just as I know he likes.

Jake's mouth searches for mine, groaning; he kisses me like he's starved for me.

I love how Jake's hunger for me is never sated. We've made love countless times since we arrived on the island, him devouring and depleting me every time, but each time is still as intense as the first.

Jake runs his hand over my breast, cupping it. Tugging my bikini top down, freeing my breast, he traces his thumb over the tip of my already erect nipple. His other hand is busy working its way into my bikini bottoms from behind.

His fingers find my entrance, and he slips one inside me.

I let out a moan of pleasure into his mouth.

"Fuck," he groans. "I can't wait. I need to be inside you. *Now.*"

I love it when he gets demanding and greedy for me.

Loosening my legs from around him, I shimmy his swim shorts down over his hips, then I move my bikini bottoms to the side.

Jake positions the head of his cock at my entrance, and very slowly, he eases a little of himself into me. Jake usually prepares me for his size with his fingers and tongue, relaxing me, readying me for him, but I'm so turned on right now, doing it out here, I don't care if it does hurt.

I need him inside me. Apparently, more than I have the need for self-preservation.

So does Jake, as his hands go back to my ass, grabbing me firmly, pulling me onto the full length of him.

"Shit," I hiss, between my teeth, as he opens me wide, to painful pleasure.

"Are you okay?" he searches my eyes.

"Yeah…" I shift my hips around him "Yeah, I'm good… great," I breathe as I hit onto the amazing feeling of him inside me.

"Sorry, I was being selfish…but…fuck, Tru," he groans softly. "I don't think I'll ever get over how incredible you feel around me. You're so fuckin' tight. So fuckin' hot."

"Ahh," I moan as Jake tilts his hips, hitting that sweet spot inside of me.

"You're gonna come for me," he breathes over my skin. "Right here in the Pacific Ocean. You're gonna scream my name as I bring you to orgasm." He licks my lower lip, then plunges his tongue deep into my mouth with each hard thrust into me.

His movements increase in tempo, and I hold on tight to him, fingernails digging into his skin, the wash of the salty water slick between us.

"I'll never get enough of you, Tru. *Never*," he growls into my ear, hitting me with hard, sure thrusts, penetrating me deep inside.

And he makes sure he doesn't as he continues to make love to me in the swell of the Pacific Ocean, while the sun descends, making its effortless journey behind the water.

* * *

Dusk has settled, and Jake and I lie together in the four-poster bed of our villa.

It's a tasteful, modest villa. Not flashy. It's us.

The whole place is open, each room flowing into the other. It has a free feeling about it. The type of freedom Jake isn't usually granted.

I wonder if that's one of the reasons he chose this place for us.

The bedroom is light and airy, the bedsheets a clean, crisp white. Even though it's a haven many celebrities choose for a getaway, it's not overdone. It's understated.

It's perfect.

The sheets are kicked back because of the insane evening heat. Our legs are tangled together, our bodies touching, sticky from the sea salt and sand coating our skin. I'm draped across Jake's chest as he absentmindedly plays with my tangled hair, quietly humming a song.

I listen intently as he starts to softly sing the words.

He sounds beautiful. I love listening to Jake sing. Especially a cappella.

"What song are you singing?" I ask, lifting my head.

"Our song."

"I didn't know we had one." I smile. Jake and I have lots of songs that remind us of our childhood, but none that are just him and me, that symbolise us as a couple.

"It's called 'You Started,' by Ou Est Le Swimming Pool." At my puzzled expression, he says, "You never heard it before?"

I shake my head.

"And you call yourself a musical journalist." He clicks his tongue in mock reproof. "They were a band from the UK as well. Poor showing on your part, baby."

"Shut up." I stick my tongue out at him.

He catches it lightning quick between his thumb and forefinger, giving it a gentle tug before letting go.

"So why is it our song?" I rest my chin on his chest.

"Because it's us," he replies simply.

"Okay…," I say, needing more. "And just when did you decide it was our song?"

I see a flash of pain cross his face. I don't like the way it makes me feel.

"The first time I heard it was the day after you left me in Boston." With his words comes a fierce pain in my chest as I remember our time apart. "I was in the car with Denny. He'd forced me out of my hotel room to get some food, and he had the album playing in his car. When I heard the song, it was just like listening to the story of us, Tru." He focuses his gaze in on me, staring deep into my eyes like no one else can. "If I didn't already know at that point that I had to win you back, then that song made me realise even more that I…" He pauses, blowing out a breath.

"Realise what?" I urge.

"That I had to fight for you. That I had to do whatever it took to get you back. Even if it meant playing dirty." He runs his rough fingertips down my cheek. "There is no one else for me. I begin and end with you."

Reaching for my hand, he lifts it to his and places them palm to palm.

"Can I hear it?" I ask, feeling choked up. "Do you have it?"

"It's on my phone. It's your ringtone, in fact," he adds, reaching for it.

"How do I not know that?" I narrow my eyes at him.

"Because when you ring me, you're usually elsewhere."
He gives me a dumb face.

"You're such an idiot," I say with a laugh, shoving him
in the chest.

Chuckling, Jake presses a button on the screen of his
phone and sets it down on his chest between us. A few seconds later, I hear light synth piano keys start to play.

The sound fills our villa. The only other sounds are the
washing waves outside and the thudding of my aching heart.

The singer begins, and goose bumps shiver down my
arms as I listen intently to every word. Hanging on them.
Then it hits the chorus, and I can't stop the tears that fill
my eyes.

I know exactly what Jake is saying. It is us. Him. Me.
Everything. The good, and the bad.

The second chorus breaks, and violins strum in the
background, setting the tears to spill over and run down my
cheeks.

"Hey, don't cry," Jake says, soothing me, brushing away
my tears with his fingers.

"I'm sorry. I can't help it. It's stunning. And it's us, completely. You're right."

"You did...start my life," Jake says, referring to the song
title, pushing his fingers into my hair, cupping my cheek.

"And you mine," I utter, climbing on top of him. I crush
my lips to his.

His hand goes to the back of my neck, holding me to
him as his tongue gently strokes over mine. He sucks my
bottom lip into his mouth, exhaling a gentle breath over
me. "You don't complete me, Tru. You make me who I am.
You make me better. I'd be nothing without you. *Nothing.*

I've been there once before, and I'm never going back. I'm never losing you again."

I get chills at his words. "Good, because I'm going nowhere."

"No regrets?" he asks.

"Never. I'm right where I'm meant to be—where I was always meant to be."

Reaching between us, he moves his phone away, placing it on the bed, as the song comes to a close.

I lie against his chest, closing my eyes. I breathe in the essence of him as he wraps his arms tightly around me.

"We've got dinner plans," he says after a moment, picking up his phone and checking the time.

"We do?"

"Yep, and we should get moving if we're going to make them."

Jake rolls me off his chest and gets up.

"The staff will wait, Jake. It's not like they're booked up or anything. Come back to bed." I pat the empty space beside me.

I really can't be bothered to get up. I'm happy to stay here, wrapped up in him.

He stretches his arms over his head, giving me a full, unadulterated view of his luscious body, then leans down and places a chaste kiss on my lips.

"Just humour me for once," he says, then retreats to the bathroom, leaving me behind to ponder.

Humour him? What the hell is he talking about?

I hear the shower turn on.

"You've got half an hour to get ready, so get that sweet ass of yours moving," Jake calls from the bathroom.

He's so bossy.

With a huff, I swing my legs over the edge of the bed and head into the bathroom to join him in the huge twin shower.

* * *

"You look beautiful," Jake says, coming up behind me, wrapping his arms around my waist.

I'm in front of the large bathroom mirror, putting the finishing touches on my outfit. I fasten my locket—the one Jake bought me in Paris—around my neck and smile back at his reflection.

"So do you. I love how your freckles stand out when you've been in the sun."

He scrunches his face. "They make me look like I'm fourteen."

I turn in his arms and run my fingertip down his nose. "No, they make you look *hot*. Hotter than usual." I reach up on my tiptoes and kiss the tip of his nose.

I'm struggling on Turtle Island without my heels—I miss my heels a lot. I'm either barefoot or in flip-flops, which I'll be donning tonight with my white strappy shift dress.

I step back, leaning against the sink, appraising my man, who is wearing cutoff jean shorts and a sleeveless Pearl Jam tee, looking the epitome of a rock star, with his tattoos exposed. You can take the rock star out of LA but never the rock star out of Jake.

"You ready?" he asks, fingering my locket against my chest.

"I am."

Jake takes hold of my hand, linking our fingers, and leads me out of the bathroom, through the villa, and outside into the moonlit night.

It's amazing here. I can see every single star in the sky. No smog shielding them from view—just clear skies for as far as the eye can see.

We walk to the beach, taking the short path to the main house, where the restaurant is. When we reach the turnoff, I start to head that way, but Jake tugs on my hand, pulling me back. He shakes his head.

I tilt my head, intrigued, but I let him lead me onward, no questions asked.

As we round the curve of the island, I catch sight of a table on the beach a short distance from the shoreline, set up and ready for us.

"Dinner on the beach?" I beam at him.

"Only the best for my girl," he says, then kisses my forehead.

There are hanging lanterns, attached to sticks driven into the sand, surrounding the table. But it's not the lanterns that catch my eye—it's the lights just beyond the table.

Dropping Jake's hand, I walk to the candles in the sand.

Marry Me

It's spelled out by tea-light candles that have been worked into the sand, centred in a heart.

With my heart in my mouth, and my head a little dizzy, I turn to him. "You're asking me to marry you?"

Staring steadily at me, he says, "I am."

"Didn't you already do that?" I offer a confused smile, holding up my left hand, displaying my very beautiful engagement ring.

Jake walks over to me. I don't know why, but my heart starts to beat faster. My insides tremble, almost as if this is the first time he's asking.

Reaching for me, he takes hold of both my hands. "Tru, I asked you to marry me backstage at Madison Square Garden in the midst of a show. Hardly a romantic setting and not how I ever envisioned it actually happening." He takes a fortifying breath. "So this is me asking you the right way, the way I always wanted to."

"Jake, I didn't care how or where you asked me…only that you did ask."

He rubs his thumb over my engagement ring. "I want you to have the best of everything I can give you. And I'm not talking money here, Tru. I'm talking memories. Our life together. I asked you to marry me straight after we had both just dragged each other through an emotional wringer. Now things have calmed and we're good—"

"Great," I add.

"*Great.*" He smiles. "I'm asking you again so your mind is clear on the fact that asking you was no knee-jerk re-action on my part. *You*, forever, is everything I want. And I guess, well…" He looks down, shifting uncomfortably, before meeting my eyes. "I guess I want to know for me too. I want to know that marrying me is exactly what you want. That you didn't just say yes because you felt pressured into doing so." His hands tighten around mine to almost the point of pain. "I wasn't exactly taking no for an answer that night, was I?"

"No, I guess you weren't." I smile, shaking my head, remembering Jake's words that night. "But I'm not exactly a pushover either. I wouldn't have said yes if it wasn't exactly what I wanted. I love you. I've *always* loved you," I add, surprised by the tears that fill my eyes.

"I love you too, baby." He takes my face in his hands and kisses me gently on the lips.

"So is that a yes?" he asks against my mouth.

"It's a yes." I grin, happiness bubbling up in me. "Now we have two marriage proposals to tell the kids about one day."

I feel him stiffen up against me. And not in a good way.

Tilting my head back, I catch something in his eyes that sets unease rolling around my stomach.

Not good. Not good at all.

"I don't mean we'll have kids now, of course," I hasten to add. "Not for ages. Like, a really, really long time." *Three, four years max.*

Jake remains quiet, continuing to stare at me, his face an unreadable mask. But even in this low light, I can tell the colour has drained a little from his face.

And now I feel inclined to ask the question, "You do want kids, don't you?"

I do. I couldn't envision a life not having them.

He clears his throat. "I...um...well, I don't know." He shrugs. It's an awkward, jerky kind of shrug. "I mean, it's just not something I ever considered. I guess I just never saw kids as part of my future. They're not an investment I ever considered making."

An investment? Since when did kids become a commodity?

This really is not good. It's so far from good, it's replaced whatever the word for that would be.

"Oh," I say.

What else can I say? A sudden chill settles over my skin, and it's got nothing to do with the night air. I take a small step back from him.

"Look, Tru." He lifts his eyes to mine. "You know I didn't have the best role model growing up."

Jake's dad was an abusive, poor excuse for a man, who went to prison for his treatment of Jake and his mom.

"I wouldn't know the first thing about being a dad," he continues. "And babies…Christ, they don't exactly fit into my world, do they? I mean, I wouldn't have a clue where to start. Music is my thing. You, and music."

I don't know if it's the look on my face or my body language or the complete bloody idiot inside of him possessing him to the point of maximum stupidity that prompts him to say, "But, hey, if kids are what you want, then sure, we'll have kids." He kisses my forehead. "Whatever you want, sweetheart. It's no biggie. Come on, let's eat."

Stunned to silence, I let Jake lead me to the table, never actually saying the words I want to say. The ones that are stuck in my throat, choking me to death.

It's no biggie, he said. No biggie.

He's right, it's not big. It's huge. Fucking ginormous, in fact.

And right now my heart has dropped straight through that fucking ginormous fact and is hurtling somewhere toward oblivion.

You don't have a child with someone because it's what the other person wants, because it will keep them happy.

Especially when that something—as big as having children—is something you clearly do not want. You have a child with someone because it's what you both want, together.

It's most definitely what I want in the future. Apparently, Jake…not so much.

How did I not know this?

A hollow feeling takes up residence in my chest.

Jake doesn't want kids. And I do.

This puts us on very different pages.

Fuck.

How did I go from a second marriage proposal and blissful happiness to a possibly empty future in the space of a few minutes?

Screw me and my goddamn big mouth.

CHAPTER TWO

I wake in the dark to the feeling of my stomach roiling.

I'm going to be sick.

Clamping my hand over my mouth, I scramble out of bed and run for the bathroom.

I make it just in time. Tossing up the toilet lid, I throw up.

The next thing I know, Jake is beside me, gathering my hair back from my face as his other hand gently soothes my back.

When my stomach is empty, Jake reaches over and flushes the toilet while I rest my head on my forearm, sweat trickling from my face and down my neck.

Jake reaches over and gets a tie for my hair off the sink and puts my hair into a loose ponytail for me.

I hear running water and then feel a cool flannel against the back of my neck.

"You're sick?"

"I woke up feeling like I was going to throw up. And then I did, obviously…" I trail off.

Jake puts his hand to my forehead. "You feel really hot."

"Everything here feels hot," I mumble.

"Let's get you back to bed." Jake scoops me into his arms and carries me to the bedroom.

He lays me down on the bed. My sweaty skin instantly sticks to the sheets.

I feel so uncomfortable and very sick.

I hear Jake moving around the bedroom, and then he sits beside me, holding out a glass of water. "Try some water. Just sip it."

Propping myself up on my elbow, I accept the glass from Jake and take slow sips.

I've only just put the glass down on the bedside cabinet when the wave of nausea hits again.

"Sick again," I gasp, putting my hand over my mouth.

I'm back in Jake's arms in an instant, and he strides to the bathroom, placing me beside the toilet, kneeling beside me, once again rubbing my back as I retch up the water I just drank.

"I'm calling for a doctor," Jake says, once I've heaved myself dry.

He disappears for a moment to get his phone, then he's back beside me. I curl up in his lap on the bathroom floor, listening to him barking orders down the phone as he gently strokes wisps of hair from off my damp face. And I begin to feel worse and worse with each passing moment.

* * *

"Ugh," I groan, blinking my blurry eyes against the daylight.

Rolling over, I find Jake beside me wearing his boxer shorts, propped against the headboard, his laptop on his knee.

Glancing at the screen, I see a spreadsheet filled with numbers.

Minimising the spreadsheet from my view, he sets his laptop on the bed and scoots down to face me.

"How you feeling?" he asks. Lifting a hand to my face, he runs his fingers gently over my cheek, brushing my stray hair back.

"Like I spent the whole night throwing up. What time is it?" I croak, rubbing my sore eyes.

"One p.m."

"Christ, I slept the whole morning away."

"You needed it."

"Yeah, I guess. I'm so thirsty," I say, turning my head, looking for the glass of water I'd left on the bedside cabinet.

"I got rid of it," Jake says. "It was warm. I'll get you something fresh." Before leaving the bed, he kisses my forehead, then gets up and heads for the minifridge.

He opens a bottle of water. Helping me to sit, he hands the bottle to me.

I still feel so weak. My limbs are like jelly. I lean back against the headboard and gratefully gulp the water.

"The doctor left you some medication to take once you'd stopped throwing up. You still feel sick?"

Still drinking from the bottle, I shake my head.

Jake grabs a pill bottle from my bedside cabinet, opens it up, shakes two tablets out, and hands them to me.

I pop the pills in my mouth and quickly wash them down with water.

I gag at the harsh taste the pills leave on my tongue. "I hate taking pills."

"Poor baby," he soothes.

"Remind me never to eat prawns again." *Ugh, just the thought of them turns my stomach.*

When the doctor arrived by seaplane a few hours after I'd started throwing up—dragged from his bed due to Jake's incessant demands that I be seen by a doctor straightaway—he checked me over and concluded I had a mild case of food poisoning.

We figured it was the prawns. Jake doesn't like them, and they were the only thing he hadn't eaten.

"Do you want me to have the chef fired?" he asks.

If I thought he was joking, I'd say yes, but knowing Jake as I do, I know he would have the poor guy fired. I don't want that to happen. It's not his fault I ate a dodgy prawn.

"No." I smile, and reaching my hand to his face, I rest it against his cheek.

Closing his eyes briefly, he presses a kiss to my wrist. "Do you want to try and get some more rest?"

"No, what I really want to do is get clean and brush my teeth. I feel skanky."

"Skanky?" He grins, glancing at me through his dark lashes. "Do you just make these words up?"

"No." I stick my tongue out at him. "You've just forgotten how to be British."

With a chuckle, he rises from the bed. "I'll get the shower ready for you."

Jake disappears into the bathroom, leaving me sipping my water.

I rest my head against the headboard and close my eyes to the sound of the water turning on in the bathroom.

Jake doesn't want children.

It's like a whisper in my mind, coming from out of nowhere.

My stomach clenches. I can't think about that now. I'll think about it later.

One thing it does remind me to do is take my contraceptive pill. A pregnancy is not something I want happening right now. Or ever, as the case may be.

Reaching down, I grab my bag off the floor and get my pill out.

I'm just swallowing it when Jake reappears from the bathroom. Moving across the hardwood floor, he comes over and takes the water bottle from my hand, putting it down.

"You ready for your shower?"

"Yep." I slide my jelly legs to the side of the bed to stand, but before I get a chance, Jake picks me up, lifting me into his arms.

"I could have walked," I say, resting my head against his chest.

"No point testing out the theory while I'm here to take care of you."

Jake steps into the huge double-headed shower and sits me down on the wide ledge at the far side.

The steam from the water soothes me instantly.

Jake hands me my toothbrush; it's ready with toothpaste on it. Smiling at his preparation, I start to brush my teeth while he kneels before me and sets about removing my shorts and panties.

When I've finished brushing my teeth, I spit into the running water, rinsing my brush under the shower, and set it on the ledge beside me.

Standing, Jake leans down and takes hold of the hem of my vest and eases it up. I lift my heavy arms, allowing him to pull it over my head. He tosses it to the floor outside the shower, along with the rest of my clothes.

I see his eyes sweep over my naked body. And I don't miss the erection he's sporting when he removes his own shorts. Well, the size of it would be hard to miss.

I love that even sick, I can still turn him on.

"Even sick and skanky, I can still turn you on." I smile up at him.

"Even sick and skanky," he murmurs, cupping my face. Leaning down, he presses a soft kiss to my lips.

Jake reaches for the sponge and shower gel and gently begins washing my skin.

The feel of his hands on me is insanely arousing. I really wish I weren't sick right now.

"This would have been so much easier if this villa had a bath," I muse, thinking how nice it would have been to sit in a tub together. "But you do make a great nurse."

"This is just an excuse so I can touch you," he says, his voice sounding hoarse.

"You can touch me whenever you want," I reply, voice serious.

"Mine," he murmurs, sweeping a soapy hand between my legs, cupping my sex.

My body instantly reacts. Desire pools between my legs. My mouth waters at the thought of tasting him. Even sick, I crave him.

After Jake is done cleaning every part of me, kneeling in front of me, he says, "I need to rinse you off and wash your hair, sweetheart, but these damn shower heads are fixed to the wall. Here, wrap your legs around my waist and put your arms around my neck and hold on tight."

Not wanting to argue, knowing I probably could manage to stand—but honestly just enjoying the attention he's lavishing on me—I do as he says.

Jake stands with me wrapped around him like a koala bear and puts us both under the running water.

I feel so safe and loved here in his arms.

He reaches for the shampoo bottle and begins washing my hair. The feel of his fingers on my scalp is like pure heaven.

"Tilt your head back under the water," he instructs.

I do as told and let the water wash the shampoo away. Without even being asked, Jake applies conditioner to my hair, knowing my thick hair needs it.

He combs the conditioner through my long hair to the ends with his fingers.

"I love you, totally and completely," I say, looking at his perfect face. "Thank you for taking such good care of me."

"No need to thank me, baby. I want to take care of you. I kind of love you totally and completely too, you know." He gives me one of his trademark beautiful smiles. Not the one for his adoring fans. No, these smiles are reserved for me only. As he is. Mine, and mine alone.

How did I ever get so lucky to get this beautiful man back in my life? He is everything that means perfect to me.

"I'm sorry I'm sick, spoiling our holiday," I say.

"Hey." He chucks my chin with his finger. "It's not like you asked to be sick. I came here to spend time alone with you, sick or not. That's what we're doing, right?"

"Right," I say with a smile. "You know..." I continue softly, adding a touch of seduction to my tone. "If I weren't sick, I would so absolutely be on my knees right now, taking you in my mouth, sucking this water off you."

I feel Jake tense, his grip on me tightening. "And I would have been so totally on board with that. When you're better?"

"Absolutely."

After our shower, Jake wraps me in a soft bath towel and carries me to the bedroom. He dries my skin with tenderness and precision, then dresses me in clean shorts and a vest and puts me back to bed and climbs in beside me.

Suddenly exhausted, I shuffle over, resting my head against his hard chest and closing my eyes. Jake's arms wrap around me. Kissing my damp hair, he whispers, "Sleep, baby."

And I do.

* * *

I wake to the sound of Jake's hushed, angry voice coming from somewhere nearby.

"This is a fuckin' joke. I can't believe this even happened. What are we paying these fuckers for? Aren't they supposed to notice shit like this early? I can't believe it slipped through."

Then I hear another male voice I don't recognise.

"I know. I thought they were reliable. They've worked for us for years. Never missed a thing. I take full responsibility on this, Jake. I was the one who hired them."

"No, it's not your fault, Zane. It's the shit who's been skimming for the past six months. I swear, when I get my hands on that fucker…"

Glancing around, I see it's 7:30 a.m. on the clock. I can't believe how long I've slept.

Feeling a whole lot better than yesterday, and wanting to find out what's making Jake so angry, I climb out of bed and make my way to the living room.

I find him sitting at the dinner table, taking a video call on his laptop.

He looks up, his face taut, his eyes piercing blue, but they instantly soften.

Zane is still talking. "The accountant is still working on getting the exact amount, but he figures it sits around five hundred. When he gets back to me, I'll call you straightaway."

I see Jake's jaw tighten. His eyes flicker from mine back to the screen. "Okay. I'll speak to you later."

Jake closes the laptop. "What are you doing out of bed?" he asks in a soft voice. Much softer than the tension lines around his eyes.

"I missed you." Padding across the floor, I walk over to him.

He pushes his chair back, allowing me to climb in his lap. I snuggle my head into his chest. He smells of everything Jake—shower gel, cigarettes, and mint. I never thought I could love such a combination until him. But then I didn't think I was capable of a lot of things until Jake.

"How are you feeling?" he asks.

"Better than I did."

"Are you hungry?"

I shake my head. The thought of food still makes me want to gag.

"Baby"—he presses a kiss to the top of my head, his hot breath blowing through my hair—"it's been ages since you last ate; you really should try something. How about some toast?"

I tilt my head back, looking at his face. "Are you going to bug me until I eat something?"

"It's quite likely."

"Okay," I say with a sigh. "I'll try some toast."

Jake picks his phone up off the table and calls through to the restaurant.

* * *

After eating breakfast on the terrace, Jake and I go down to the beach for a walk. The food has perked me up a bit.

I know he still has the call with Zane on his mind. He was notably quiet over breakfast, and he still is now.

I figure it's something to do with the label. Something is going on there, and I want to know what.

"Are you ever going to tell me what that video call was about?"

Jake's hand tightens around mine. "It was nothing."

"Jake…," I push.

"Look, it's nothing big. We'll talk about it later. You're only just recovering from food poisoning, and we're still on vacation."

Stopping him, I come around and stand before him, wrapping my arms around his waist.

I tilt my head, looking up at him. "Nothing big, right? So why did you sound majorly pissed off when you were taking to that Zane guy?"

"I always sound pissed off when talking to the staff," he says with a grin.

"Stop it," I snap, taking a step back.

His brow furrows. "Stop what?"

"Stop shutting me out, Jake. I wish you would just talk to me. Tell me when something is going on. I might actually be able to help."

Moving closer, he rests his arms on my shoulders, running his fingers into my hair. "I'm not trying to shut you out. I just don't want you worrying about unnecessary things. There's no point when I have a handle on it."

"I worry more when I don't know what's going on. My imagination takes over, and you know how wild that can run."

"I do," he says tenderly, running his thumb down my cheek.

"Look, Jake, I just don't want…" I let out a sigh. "I just don't want things getting too hard for you, and for you to then…fall off the wagon, and for us to end up back where we did in Boston."

His body stiffens. His eyes darken. "It won't happen again. I already told you that. I'm not losing you again. I can't."

"I know. And I believe in you, I do. I just know I'd feel a whole lot better if you shared more with me, instead of keeping me out of the loop. I know you're doing what you think is best for me, but you are what's best for me—you happy and healthy."

He leans down, hands holding my face, and presses his forehead against mine, closing his eyes.

For a moment, I stay still, just listening to his deep, contented breaths.

Sometimes I feel like Jake breathes through me. Because of me. That I'm the air he needs. And I breathe in the knowledge of his contentment within me.

31

"Someone's been stealing money from the company."

"What!" I lean back from him, air whooshing out of my lungs.

Jake sighs, then, taking my hand, he encourages me to sit down beside him on the sand.

"Someone's been skimming for the past six months. And it's not the money, Tru," he says, exhaling. "I can take the hit for the cash. It's just the fact that someone has fuckin' stolen from me. Stolen from what Jonny and I created." He drags a hand through his hair. "It just feels like they're pissing on his memory, you know?" He shrugs, then his shoulders hang heavily forward.

The pain in his voice slices through me.

I hate that after everything Jake has been through in his life, just when things are getting straight for him, someone does this to him. Anger burns in me, but I hide it. I don't want him to know it's affecting me. I want him to keep talking to me.

"I know, baby," I say, taking his hand, trying to ease his pain and frustration. "Do you have any idea who it might be?"

"Not yet," he says with a shake of his head. "We're keeping this on the down low, not letting the staff know, so we can catch the fucker out. With Zane on the case, it won't be long before we know. That guy could sniff out shit in a garbage dump."

"Who is Zane?" I ask.

He glances at me, confused. "Zane Fox. He's the VP at the label."

How do I not know this? I should know this. I'm soon going to marry this man, and I know so little about his business and the people who work for him. The knowledge makes me feel like crap.

"How long has Zane worked for you?" I trace my fingertip over his rough, calloused fingers.

"From the start. Jonny and I hired him when we set up the label. This is stinging him as much as it is me."

Okay, mental note. Spend time getting to know Jake's employees better. Except the one who's ripping him off. That one I'll happily kick the shit out of.

"You definitely think he'll be able to get to the bottom of the theft without you there?"

"Yes." He digs a finger into the sand and draws a deep line in it.

He doesn't sound sure. I don't think it's because he lacks confidence in Zane. I think it's because he feels like he's somehow failing Jonny by letting this happen in the first place. He's not there now sorting it because he's here with me.

He's been so tied up lately with me, with us, that his mind has been off his business. I know right now his loyalty is torn between me and his company.

I hate that more than I can express.

"We're going back to LA," I say.

"No, we're not." His tone is resolute.

Changing tack and looking for some leverage in my argument, I ask, "How much money has been taken?"

He shifts before he speaks, and looks out over the ocean. "The accountant figures about five hundred thousand dollars. I'm just waiting to get the exact figure from Zane once he's spoken with the accountant again."

"Five. Hundred. Fucking. Thousand. Dollars!" I gasp. "Someone has stolen five hundred thousand dollars from you?"

If I was angry before, I'm bloody raging now.

He slides me a look. "From the business, but basically, yes."

"We need to go back to LA, Jake. You need to get back and sort this out."

"No, we're—"

"No," I say firmly. "This is huge. This is fraud we're talking about here. Fraud against *your* company. A huge amount of fucking fraud! When did you find out about this?"

"Yesterday."

I give him a pissed-off look. "You should have told me yesterday."

"Tru, don't be ridiculous, you were sick. Look I'm telling you now like you asked." He brings my hand to his lips and kisses it. "I know you're worried, which is exactly what I didn't want, but here we are. No fuckin' way are we leaving this island for another three days. I'm on vacation with my girl—and no, you're not keeping me from my business obligations," he interjects, cutting me off with his finger to my lips when I open my mouth to protest. "Yes, the label is having some problems. Problems that Zane is more than capable of handling for another three days until I get back."

Staring into my eyes, he traces his fingertip over my lower lip, tugging it down ever so slightly.

I watch his pupils dilate. And I feel the air instantly shift between us.

My nipples harden. I'm not wearing a bra under my vest, so they put on an obvious show to Jake.

34

His eyes darken further as they move downward, over my breasts.

"If you want to help me, Tru, then give me this time with you," he says, his voice rough. "It's what I need right now. *You* are what I need right now."

Knowing exactly what Jake needs, and more than willing to give it to him, I climb onto his lap, straddling him. "Okay," I say. "We'll do this your way."

Giving me a sexy smile, he rests his large hands on my behind. "What do you want to do today?" he asks with blatant sex in his voice.

I reach between us and palm him through his shorts. "I want you inside me—"

Apparently I don't need to say anything more. Jake is on his feet in one swift move, taking me with him, and he carries me back to our villa in record time.

The instant we're inside, he sets me down and tears my vest off. And yes, I mean he's ripped it off.

Fuck, he's strong, and it's so totally hot.

My shorts and panties are next. Thankfully, they avoid a tearing, as he whips them down my legs in one go.

I've been stripped bare in a matter of seconds. Only Jake could make tearing my clothes off a show of how strong his love is for me.

I love that he can make me feel so wanted and cherished.

"Fuck, I've missed this…you." His eyes devour me for long seconds, then his mouth is on mine. Taking me with him in a few strides, he has me flat on my back on the bed.

Moving down my body, he takes my nipple into his mouth and runs his tongue around it. Heat pools in my core, leaving me wet and wanting, and I moan with need and desire.

He grazes his teeth over my nipple, then moving down and off me, he kneels on the floor by the bed, grabs me by the thighs, and yanks me forward.

I gasp.

My legs are set to rest on his shoulders, and he slides a finger over my sex.

"So wet," he rasps.

Knowing what he's about to do, I close my eyes and let my head fall back into the comfort of the bed.

"Watch me," he commands.

Inclining, resting up on my elbows, I look at him.

"I want you to watch me...make you come."

Jake's never asked me to watch him before. I don't really care what's made him ask—I'm just glad he did, because it's so fucking sexy. He's so fucking sexy.

Doing as he asks, I stay inclined and keep my eyes fixed on him.

I watch as he runs his tongue over his upper lip, like he tastes me already. His bright blue eyes darken to inky as he leans forward and puts his mouth close to my sex. Then he very slowly licks his tongue over my sensitive bud, all the while not moving his eyes from mine.

"Mmm, so sweet," he murmurs.

I'm riveted.

Watching him tend to me in this way is mind-blowing. It elevates the sensation of his touch to a level I didn't even know existed. It's insanely sensual watching as Jake's tongue moves over the most intimate part of me, in the most intimate way. What makes me nearly lose control is seeing the pleasure on his face while he's doing it.

My hands fist in the sheets when he blows over my already sensitised clit, driving the sensations higher and me wilder.

I want him inside me now.

Jake pushes a finger inside me as he continues to lick me to crazy with his tongue, and I instantly clench around it.

"You want it...my cock inside you?" he murmurs, sending vibrations humming over my sex.

"God, yes," I moan.

His blue eyes flicker to mine, hitting me with his sex-hot gaze, as he pushes another finger in me and starts to fuck me with them. Then he continues his sweet assault of my senses with his tongue.

"Ah, yes," I breathe, clutching my own breast, the tension inside me building to insane. My core tightens in response to his maddening licks. "Yes, Jake...oh, please... right there...holy fuck, I'm coming!" I suddenly cry out.

Like a bolt of lightning searing through me, the orgasm tears through my body, arching my back off the bed. Jake pins my hips down with his free hand, continuing to draw the orgasm out, while I move under him as he climaxes me to epic proportions.

I've gone two days without this, without him, and apparently I was ready. More ready than I had realised.

As the sensations ebb, I sag into the bed, replete and boneless.

In my hazy orgasmic vision, I see Jake peeling off his T-shirt and reaching for his shorts.

Forcing myself up, I stand on wobbly legs and stop his hands with mine.

"Let me."

Jake is always pleasuring me. Now it's my turn to please him.

I hook my fingers into the waistband of his shorts. Pulling them down, I follow them on their journey, my knees hitting the floor the moment they do. Jake kicks them aside, while my gaze alights on his thick cock.

Without hesitation, I take him in my hand and place my lips over his crown, drawing him into my mouth.

"Jesus," Jake groans, his body jerking at the feel of me around him. He grabs a fistful of my hair, steadying himself. "The feel of your mouth gets me every time, Tru, it's so fuckin' warm…so soft."

The silk and steeliness of him makes me moan.

I feel a shudder move through him.

I flicker my tongue on the underside, pull back slightly, lick the tip, then take him back in my mouth. I feel a burst of pre-cum hit my tongue.

Greedily swallowing it, I start to fist him farther into my mouth, sucking hard, taking in as much of him as I can.

"Tru, your mouth…so hot…you suck me so good."

Pleased that I'm pleasing him, I brace my hand against his hard thigh, relaxing my jaw, taking even more of him in my mouth.

"Fuck," he growls. Taking hold of my head with his other hand, knotting his fingers into my hair, he starts to fuck my mouth.

"God…Tru…ah, we need to stop…I'm, ah, Jesus… I'm gonna come." He starts to pull back, trying to remove himself from my mouth. But I want him to come in my mouth. I've missed the taste of him.

I tighten my hold on his thigh, removing my hand from his cock, gripping his other thigh, trying to keep him in place, letting him know my intention.

"No, baby, you've been sick, you don't need me coming in your mouth."

I glance up at him.

He shakes his head gently, running his fingers down my cheek. "Next time. Right now, I just want to come inside that gorgeous body of yours."

I give him one last remembering suck, then let him guide me to my feet.

Jake's eyes are blazing. I know how hard it must have been for him to stop.

I run my tongue over my upper lip. Jake's eyes follow it.

"Where do you want me?" I whisper.

He inhales sharply. "Bend over and brace your hands against the wall." There's no conversation in his tone.

Loving the command, legs trembling, I do exactly as he says. I bend over and place my palms flat against the wall by the bed, more than ready.

I feel Jake move behind me. He nudges my legs farther apart with his knee, then I feel the head of his cock press against my entrance.

"I'm gonna fuck you, baby. Hard. You ready?" I don't have to see him to know his teeth are gritted together, that his restraint is almost gone.

Keen, I push my hips back against him. "What are you waiting for?"

Jake grabs hold of my hips and slams into me in one swift move, jolting me forward.

"Fuck," he bites out.

I steady myself against the wall as Jake pulls my hips back.

He eases out of me, then drives into me again with a long, hard thrust. I can't help the loud moan that escapes me.

Jake's grip on me tightens to near pain, holding me in place, but I don't care. I need this. I need him.

"Talk to me in Spanish, sweetheart," he growls.

A smile sweeps my lips. Knowing exactly what this does to him, I comply readily. "*No me jodas más,* Jake. Harder!"

Jake loves the Puerto Rican in me, and the sound of me speaking Spanish drives him crazy.

Any reserve he had left is gone, and he starts fucking me hard and ruthless, talking sex to me. "Jesus, Tru, you're so fuckin' sexy with that dirty mouth of yours. You feel so fuckin' tight and hot. I'm so hard…fucking you deep…"

I can feel him growing even bigger inside me, hitting that spot, the one hidden deep within me. It's only ever been touched by Jake, and I know he's getting near.

He moves his hand around to my sex and rubs my clit with his finger, urging me on to another orgasm.

My muscles start to tighten and spasm as he thrusts his big cock in and out of me.

"Come, Tru. *Now.*"

My body bows to his command, and I climax in a lust-fuelled haze of his dominance, my core tightening around him.

I feel him shudder. "Fuck, Tru!" he cries out, and I feel the heat of him spurt into me, his hips jerking, ramming into me, as he fills me with his semen.

When he's given everything to me, Jake brushes my hair aside and lays his chest against my back, resting his hands over mine against the wall.

"You okay?" he asks softly, kissing my shoulder, his teeth gently grazing my skin.

"I'm better than okay."

He shifts his hips, and I can feel that he's still semihard inside me.

"You're not done?" I push back against him, smiling.

"I've not even started. I've gone two days without being inside you." His arm comes around my waist. Sliding out of me, he spins me around to face him, yanking me up hard against his body. "I intend to make up on that time and spend the rest of the day inside you, fucking you senseless, until neither of us can walk."

"Is that a promise?"

"You bet your sweet ass it is," he growls as he picks me up and throws me down onto the bed, climbing on top of me.

CHAPTER THREE

I look down at the lights of LA as the jet heads for LAX.

Jake is sleeping beside me. I reach over and brush his fallen hair off his forehead. He looks so peaceful. I hate to wake him, but we'll be coming in to land soon.

I glance down at my friendship bracelet on his wrist. Shifting it aside, I see where his skin is lighter underneath, where it's been hidden from the sun. The same as mine. We never take them off—a promise made to each other to always wear the reminder of our childhood connection—the bracelets I made for us both all those years ago.

I can't believe our holiday is over. The best holiday of my life. Now we're heading back to reality.

Well, Jake's reality.

Which is so far from any reality I could have ever imagined.

An ordinary girl in a far-from-ordinary world.

I wish we could have stayed on the island indefinitely, because I have a feeling that coming back here means things are about to get very real, very quickly.

Curving my fingertips around Jake's ear, I tickle the sensitive skin behind it. The spot that drives him crazy when I kiss him there.

He catches my wrist, surprising me. "Don't start something you can't win," he says with a sexy growl to his voice.

"Who says I can't win?"

"Me."

"That right?"

"Hmm." He moves in closer, revealing his stunningly blue eyes. "You forget I know *exactly* where all of your sensitive spots are, Bennett."

Heat floods me and I squirm. "I thought you were asleep."

"I was until some little minx started tickling me."

"Minx?" I let out a laugh.

"Yep, that's you. A minx. Cunning and flirtatious."

"Flirtatious?" I scoff.

"Yep, flirtatious and irresistible."

"Meant for you," I add.

"Fucking right, meant for me."

His gaze pins me to the seat, possessing me, owning me.

Holding back a gulp, I say, "Well, python, we're home." A light smile settles on my lips.

Home.

LA is my home now. It feels strange to say.

The last time I was in LA, the story of Jake's dad had just broken in the news.

I shudder at the memory.

Jake sits up in his seat, stretching his legs out, his arms go over his head, then one comes down to rest on my shoulder, pulling me to him. "You okay?" he asks.

"Yeah, just wishing we'd had longer together on the island."

"Me too," he murmurs, resting his chin on the top of my head. "We'll go back there again one day real soon."

"We could take our honeymoon there," I suggest, optimism filling me, as I look up at him.

"That's a great idea." He smiles.

"Guess I need to start planning our wedding, then…or did you want a long engagement?" I bite my lip.

"Fuck no! Baby, we can get married tomorrow if you want. You just say the word and I'll tell the pilot to take us to Vegas."

I let out a laugh. "My mother would have a seizure if I got married in Vegas, and my dad would kick your ass for taking away his chance to walk his only child down the aisle."

"Point taken. I really don't want an ass-kicking from Billy."

"Where do you want to get married? Here or the UK?"

"I don't mind." He shrugs. "I guess it would be easier to get married here because we live here, but honestly the choice is yours. If you want to get married in Manchester, it's cool with me. You just tell me the time and the place, baby, and I'll be there."

"Am I to take it you'll be having absolutely no input in this wedding whatsoever?"

"Of course I will," he says, grinning. "I'll be organising my bachelor party. No, scrap that. I promised Tom he could do it."

Tom is the bassist in TMS, one of Jake's closest friends, and renowned player. The same as Jake was before we got together, but now he's with me and that's all behind him. Thankfully.

"Oh God," I groan. "It'll be a shagfest, filled with lap dancers and hookers. I'm envisioning *Hangover 2* right now."

Jake laughs. "Ah, give him some credit, baby. It won't be that bad."

"If you turn up with a tattoo on your face, telling me you've shagged a lady boy, I'm definitely not marrying you."

He fixes me with a stare. "Sweetheart, if I have to tell you I shagged a lady boy, I'll be telling you from prison."

"Why?"

"Because I'll have fuckin' killed Tom for letting it happen."

We both start laughing, as the pilot comes on the inter-com to tell us to buckle up because we're coming in to land.

* * *

Dave pulls into the drive outside Jake's house. I mean our house. I still haven't gotten used to saying that. And I would never say this to Jake, but it doesn't feel like my house.

Because, well, I kind of hate his house...okay, maybe *hate*'s too strong a word.

I intensely dislike Jake's house.

Don't get me wrong, it's beautiful. Not overly flashy. Modern. It has three bedrooms, three bathrooms, a music studio, and a gym.

But it's a bachelor pad. And that's the problem.

It was Jake's bachelor pad that he brought countless women back to.

God, just thinking about it makes me want to hurl.

I've never had sex with Jake at his house before. During the short stay we had here between tour dates, sex wasn't exactly on either of our minds.

But now I live here, and Jake's going to want to have sex—a lot—and I know I'll be thinking of the countless other women here before me. In Jake's house. In his bed.

The bed that I'm going to share with him.

I hate that more than I can express.

Ugh.

I know I'm being overly sensitive, and I know Jake has never lived here with a woman before. That counts for something.

This is his home. My home now. I'm going to have to get used to it.

How? I'm not entirely sure, because currently I feel like the memory of his old life lingers like a bad smell when I'm in his house.

My house.

Crap.

I really need to get used to referring to it as "my house," otherwise Jake will notice, and I don't want to upset him. I don't need to be stirring up any of my issues with his past.

"Just drop the cases in the hall and get yourselves home," Jake says to Dave and Ben, unlocking the front door, letting me in first.

I see the light is on in the kitchen, and hoping that one of my favourite people in the world is here, I say good-bye to Dave and Ben and head straight for the kitchen.

"Chica!" Stuart beams at me as I enter through the archway. "Aren't you just a sight for sore eyes? Look at you, all tanned and beautiful. What I wouldn't give for your colouring."

"The perks of having a Puerto Rican mother." I walk into his open embrace, planting a kiss on his cheek. "I missed you."

"What? You had time to miss me? You're telling me the infamous snake over there didn't keep you busy while you were away?" Stuart nods in Jake's direction. Jake is leaning against the archway, watching us.

His face looks blank. Sometimes I have a hard time assessing Jake's mood. It's only his eyes that have the ability to give him away. Not this time, though.

"Oh, he kept me plenty busy." I share a secret smile in Jake's direction, one that flickers in his eyes, bringing them to life.

I can almost see what he's thinking, and my cheeks flush at the memories of the many things we got up to on holiday.

"But I still found time to miss my favourite guy," I add, turning back to Stuart.

"I thought I was your favourite guy?" Jake says with mock annoyance, coming over, taking a seat at the breakfast bar.

"Get in line, man. Hos before bros." Stuart clamps his arm around my shoulder.

I snort, then clamp my hand over my mouth.

Not attractive, I know. Snorts just happen sometimes, unexpectedly.

"God, I feel like I'm in an episode of *One Tree Hill*," Jake complains.

"You're such a moody bastard after a flight." Stuart waves him away with his hand. "So you guys had a good time?" he asks, directing his question at me.

"The best! You'll have to come next time, Stuart. It's amazing there, you would love it."

"You want Stuart to come on our honeymoon with us?" Jake raises an eyebrow.

"Oh, right, of course. Okay, so the next time after that."
I smile.

"It's that good that it's going to be the honeymoon destination?" Stuart questions, a glint in his eye.

"That good." I nod, smiling at the memory of the island.

"So you guys have set a date?" Stuart releases me and leans up against the counter.

Taking off my jacket, I hang it on the back of the stool across from Jake and hop up onto it. "Not yet, but I'm going to start planning tomorrow…well, start figuring out how exactly to plan a wedding and set a date."

"If you need a hand, gorgeous, just let me know," he offers.

"I might just take you up on that. Ooh, you made tea."
I smile, noticing the brewing pot on the side. "Could I love you any more?" I jump down from my stool and nudge Stuart with my hip.

"Not too fuckin' much, I hope," Jake mutters, reaching over to get a biscuit out of the barrel.

"Don't worry, baby. I love Stuart in a purely platonic way. He's like the brother I never had."

"Aww, honey, that's lovely." Stuart smiles at me, nudging me with his hip.

"I thought I was the brother you never had all those years growing up." Jake's brow furrows.

"Jake, if I had ever looked at you in a brotherly way growing up, then we would never have ended up having sex in our adulthood."

"Shame I didn't know how you felt back then." Jake's face relaxes into a sexy grin. "Just imagine all the things we could have gotten up to in your bedroom instead of doing our homework."

My eyebrow lifts, and my panties nearly drop of their own accord.

"Still here," Stuart says, cutting into the spell Jake's put me under. "And I'm suffering from a long dry spell, so please cut out the sex talk. Right, let's get to the important matter," Stuart adds, rubbing his hands together. "One of you give me my gift already. I'm dying here!"

"Gift?" I give Stuart a puzzled look, then direct one to Jake, who shrugs. He's in on my little bit. "We were supposed to get you a gift?"

I start to pour tea from the pot into three waiting cups, suppressing a smile.

"Don't fuck around. Come on, duty-free purchases are part of my contract. Gimme." He proffers his hand, curling his fingers up in an impatient gesture.

I put down the teapot. Holding a steady face, I bite my lip for effect. "I'm really sorry, Stuart. I didn't realise we were supposed to get you anything."

I see the light disappear in his eyes. His face drops. "Oh, it's okay, honey, don't worry…"

"I mean, I didn't realise gifts were part of your contract, so I guess it's a good job I got you these Oliver Peoples aviators," I say, reaching over and pulling them from out of my jacket pocket.

Stuart's been hankering after a pair of these but they've been sold out everywhere—I didn't even know sunglasses could sell out—so I asked Jake to pull some strings and get a pair directly from the designer. Which, of course, he did. The perks of being Jake. They were waiting at LAX for me to pick up.

"Holy fuck!" Stuart says. "How did you...? Never mind. These are so totally fucking awesome! You are so totally fucking awesome!"

He picks me up and spins me around, then sets me back on my feet. He takes the sunglasses from my hand and puts them on.

"How do I look?"

"You look amazing. They totally suit you. You know, with those sunglasses on, you look a bit like that model. You know the British one, David Gandy."

"More like Gandhi," Jake quips.

I can't not laugh at that.

"Fuck off!" Stuart says, admiring himself in the glass of the oven door. "You're just jealous you wouldn't be able to carry off something so stylish."

"Um, hottest male two thousand and twelve here, as voted by the great American public."

"I think they were voting for the snake, not you." Stuart smirks, inferring to the nickname for Jake's huge...anatomy. The one he regularly uses on me.

"So anyway, chica, this David Gandy dude...is he hot?"

"Oh, so totally and completely hot." I nod enthusiastically.

"Uhum," Jake clears his throat loudly.

"But not as hot as you, baby."

"Damn straight," Jake mutters.

"On that note, I'm going to bed to spend the rest of the night looking at myself in the mirror and researching pics of this hot Gandy dude."

Stuart picks up his tea and heads out of the kitchen with a wave of his hand. "Good to have you back," he says to us both.

"It's good to be back." *I half mean that.* "Sleep well," I call after him.

"You too, chica."

"You know..." Jake says, pouring milk into the two remaining teas. He picks one up and hands it to me. "Stuart is the only man I will tolerate mauling you. And that's only because he's as gay as they come."

"Stuart doesn't maul me." I laugh. I take a sip of my tea, then set it down. "He's just a tactile guy. I like tactile people," I add, positioning myself between his legs.

"Yeah? Well, if any man ever touches you here"—he brushes his finger over my lips—"I'll kick his ass."

"What about here?" I point to my breasts.

"Hospitalised for sure," he replies, eyes now glued to my boobs.

"What about here?" I point to the V between my thighs.

"Stone-cold fucking dead. You belong to me, Tru." He lifts my skirt and puts his hand to the very place I just pointed to. "No one touches you but me."

He presses his fingers into my panties. Into me.

Heat consumes my body, firing through me.

He's fucked other women here.

I step back, letting his hand fall away.

"What's wrong?" He looks confused.

"Nothing..." I glance around, looking for my excuse. "It's just...Stuart might come back."

I wonder if he's ever had sex in the kitchen. Probably. Knowing Jake, he'll have utilised every room in this house.

The very thought makes me want to throw up.

My fingers curl into my hand, my nails biting into my skin.

"He won't come back." Jake hooks his fingers into my T-shirt and reels me back in.

He starts to kiss my neck, his other hand grabbing my ass, pulling me closer to him.

Crap, he's hard. But then, Jake's always hard.

I close my eyes and try to get into it. The feel of him pressed up against me. His hard body. His masculine scent.

But all I can see in my mind is a preconceived image of Jake with another woman. Him doing exactly what he's doing to me, to her, right here.

I wriggle out of his embrace.

He sighs, and his darkened eyes meet mine. "Okay, what the fuck's going on?"

"Nothing." My voice has gone squeaky. Traitor voice.

"Tru?"

I glance down at my feet. "I just..." I bite my lip.

"You just, what?" There's no happy in his tone.

"I just feel weird having sex in your house."

"You mean *our* house." His eyebrow lifts. "And why? Because Stuart lives here?"

"No. Because of all the women you've fucked here." Okay, so that didn't come out *exactly* as I had intended.

I look up, meeting his eyes, biting my lip, hard.

Jake's face is a mask.

I also note he doesn't deny that he's screwed other women here.

I know it was a long shot, but I was harbouring a tiny flicker of hope that maybe he'd never brought a woman back here.

Stupid, right?

Sighing, he shoves a hand through his black hair.

I move farther away, increasing the gap between us, and lean against the counter. "How many women have you had here?"

"Do you really want me to answer that question?" His eyes burn into mine, waiting.

Looking away, I focus on the wall. I fiddle with the hem of my T-shirt.

Do I really want to know?

The sadistic side of me does. Thankfully self-preservation wins out.

"No." I shake my head.

Pushing off the counter, I start to walk away. I just want to go to bed, sleep, and leave this conversation behind.

"Where are you going?"

I stop by the archway and turn back to him. "To bed. It's okay, Jake. I get your past, I do…sort of." I drag my fingers through my hair. "And I know there's nothing you can do to change it, no matter how much I may wish it. But I can't pretend that at times it doesn't bother me…affect me." I point. "Out there, I can cope with it, mostly…but in here, our home…just knowing that you've been…with hundreds of women…here." I try to shake the sick-inducing images out of my mind.

"It's not hundreds."

"What?"

"I haven't brought hundreds of women here."

"Thanks for the clarification." My tone is sharper than I mean it to be. "Look, however many it is, it's more than one, and that's enough to have me feeling like this. I just need a little time to figure out how to get around it—being here, knowing that. And don't think I'm punishing you because of your past, because I'm not. It's just my own jealousy and insecurities getting the better of me. Just give me time to figure out how to get past it, okay?"

I can see his hands curled around the edge of the stool, knuckles white from the intensity of his grip. He looks like he is having to physically restrain himself from coming over to me. I can almost smell his need to touch me in the air, floating around me like a physical presence.

I need to touch him too. Just without these images in my head.

"Okay," he sighs. He sounds defeated. "I'll follow you up to bed in a minute."

Leaving him where he sits, I go upstairs, get dressed for bed, and brush my teeth. When I reemerge from the bathroom, there's still no sign of Jake.

Turning off the light, I climb in bed, and for the first night in a long time, I fall asleep without Jake beside me.

CHAPTER FOUR

Y ou promise you can't see anything?" Jake asks for the
tenth time.

"I promise I can't see anything." I sigh, feeling a little
exasperated and a lot blind.

I'm currently sitting in the passenger seat of Jake's treas-
ured Aston Martin DBS, aka the James Bond car.

Jake's driving, and I'm wearing a blindfold.

Yes, a blindfold.

A makeshift one, made from the silk scarf I was wearing.
Why?

Because Jake has a surprise for me. A surprise that apparently requires me to be blindfolded to get it.

We've been back in LA for five days.

Jake has spent most of that time at the label, dealing with
the accountants, trying to sort things out with the fraud. It's
definitely five hundred thousand dollars stolen, but they are
no closer to finding out who took it.

It's consuming all of his time. He is literally getting
home as I'm heading to bed, and he's gone when I wake.

Am I worried about the strain this will be putting him
under?

Absolutely.

Am I checking for visual signs of him using again?

Definitely.

I hate that I am, but he's not long clean. I would be stupid not to be a little worried. I don't want either of us to go through what we did before.

It's not that I don't trust him, I do. I just know how easily a slip can happen. I watched it happen to him before and I was blind to it, and it got too far too fast.

I won't let that happen again.

Have I checked the cisterns in the toilets and other hidey holes in the house for drugs?

Yes.

I know it's horrible, checking on him like that, and I know he would be really angry if he knew. But when Jake's life is in play, nothing is more important.

I know he went to a meeting with his drug counsellor on our first day back, and I heard him on a call with someone I think is his sponsor late the night before last.

It's natural that he'll still be struggling, especially now back in the real world, surrounded by temptation. I'm just glad he's making use of the professional support he has to help him get through it.

And I'm here for whatever help he needs.

In my heart I don't think Jake will ever go back to drugs. I saw what the last episode did to him, losing us because of it.

It nearly broke him.

But it also doesn't hurt for me to keep alert for any signs of trouble.

Of course I ask him how he's doing, but I haven't asked directly about his recovery steps, because I know if he wants to talk to me about it, he will.

I've missed him like crazy this last week. But the time apart has had its benefits. Now I'm back from holiday, it's back to work, and I'm glad for it, even if I am working from home. It's allowed me to get on with my work writing Jake's bio, and I've also been working on my column for *Etiquette*.

Etiquette is the magazine I work for. Vicky, my boss and close friend, is the sole reason Jake and I came back into each other's lives. She landed an exclusive interview with Jake and sent me to do it.

I've really missed my job, and the bonus of working means I need to talk to Vicky. Which is fab because I've missed her tons as well.

God love Skype is all I can say.

I called my folks too on the telephone; apparently Skype is just too technological for my mum and dad.

But mostly, I miss Simone.

I'm used to seeing her every day, and it's taking some time getting used to not living in London with her anymore.

I may have called her multiple times over the last few days. And maybe I cried a few times while on the phone too.

I'm just so glad I have Stuart, my only friend in LA. Aside from Jake, of course.

The downside of Jake not being around this week, apart from the obvious, is that we haven't talked about the "no sex in his house" issue since that night. Just like we never talked about the "not having kids" issue on the island.

It seems Jake and I are really good at ignoring things and avoiding discussions on important matters.

I wonder if that's partly why he's spent so much time at the label this week.

This is the longest Jake and I have gone without having sex since we got together. We've gone from multiple times daily while on the island to nothing at all.

I know this is my doing, but I'm starting to worry big-time, because Jake is a highly sexual man. For Jake, having sex is as essential as breathing, and the fact that he's not even trying to get it from me is worrying the shit out of me. I'm scared that if he's not getting it from me, he'll start to look elsewhere. Or maybe he already has.

"You know, we could get pulled over by the cops. They might think you're kidnapping me, having me blindfolded like this," I say.

"The windows are tinted, sweetheart."

"Of course they are."

I fold my arms over my chest at the sound of Jake's soft laughter.

"Well, with the speed you drive at, we'll probably get pulled over for a ticket. Then what will you tell them?"

"That my fiancée is kinky, and she gets her sexual kicks from me driving her around blindfolded. Then, and only then, will she let me fuck her."

"Jake!"

"That, or we're into BDSM, and you're my submissive. And seeing you like this is how I get *my* kicks." I feel his hand go to my leg, his rough fingertips gently stroking the skin just above my knee.

This is the first time in five days that he's touched me intimately. My pulse jumps and my whole body responds.

"Do you realise how hard my dick is right now, just look-ing at you sitting there in those fuck-hot boots, that short skirt...blindfolded."

Holy fuck.

"And what do you plan on doing with it?" My voice has taken on a husky tone all its own.

"Something which will mean you being naked very soon, wearing only that scarf over your eyes and those come-fuck-me-now boots wrapped around my waist."

Sweet baby Jesus.

I wonder if he's taking us to a hotel for sex.

My insides pool at the thought of Jake naked and inside me. I have to suppress a moan.

His hand leaves my leg, and I hear the indicator *tick-tock*ing a turn. Then he stops the car, lowers his window, and talks to someone. A man.

I'm blindfolded here, and Jake is talking to some guy.

Where the hell is he taking me?

"Good to see you again, Mr. Wethers. I'll open the gate for you."

"Thank you."

I hear Jake's window close, and he starts to move the car slowly forward.

A thought thuds into my head.

Oh my God, what if he's taking me to some kinky sex club?

He was just talking about BDSM, and he did say I'll be naked soon, wearing only this scarf and these boots.

Oh, holy fucking mother of God.

I'm not into that kind of stuff. I'm a straight-up-sex type of girl. A little dirty talk, sure. Maybe Jake tying me up...I'd happily give that a try. But not outright kinky stuff.

I didn't think he was either, to be honest. I know he's a little dominant in the bedroom, which is really sexy, but I didn't think whips and chains were his kind of thing.

Maybe this is just another thing I didn't know about him.

Fuck.

"Where are we going?" My voice comes out small.

"You'll know in about two minutes. Think you can hold on that bit longer?"

"Are you taking me to a sex club?" I blurt out.

I hear choked laughter. "Do you want me to be taking you to a sex club?" I can feel his body shaking next to me.

"God, no!"

"Good, because I'm not into sharing you with anyone." He takes hold of my hand, sweeping a kiss across my knuckles. "I've already told you, Tru, you're mine, and mine alone."

Jake stops the car and turns off the engine.

Releasing my hand, he says, "Wait there, I'll help you out of the car."

Doing as he asks, I wait until Jake gets out of the car, then opens my door.

Taking hold of my hands, he guides me out. With his arm around me, he walks with me. "Okay, stand right there," he says, positioning me in place. "You ready?" I can feel his warm breath on my face.

"I'm ready."

I'm actually not. I'm really shitting it now as to what I'm going to be revealed to.

I hate surprises. Why does he insist on surprising me all the bloody time?

God, what if I don't like whatever it is he wants me to see?

Crap.

Jake's hands reach around to the back of my head, and he unties the knot holding the scarf in place.

Loosening it from my eyes, Jake removes the scarf and stands aside.

Blinking rapidly, I let my eyes readjust to the bright sun. Then I see a house.

A huge house, situated about fifty feet before me.

It's single-story. Concrete, stucco, and wood—the combination is incredibly striking. It's modern and stunning, and it's instant love.

If I could marry a house, this would be the house I would marry and have minihouse babies with.

"What's this?" I ask, pulling my eyes from the house to Jake.

I find his eyes already on me. Nervous eyes. "A house." He smiles tentatively. "Our house if you want it."

I turn from the house to face him. "You bought a house?"

"I bought *us* a house. I put an offer in and they accepted. But if you don't like it, I can pull out and we can find something else."

"No." I glance back at the house. "It's just…"

"Tru, if you don't like it, honestly, it's fine."

"I *love* it." I look back to him. "*Really* love it. Well, what I've seen so far, but if the outside is anything to go by, then…wow. Seriously, wow. But…it's just…I imagine it wasn't cheap." I smile, uneasily. It feels clumsy and awkward on my lips.

Couples buy houses together, share the mortgage. Jake buys a house outright. A house that I'm guessing cost millions of dollars.

One that I have no chance of being able to contribute toward.

"Call it birthday present number five."

I let out a high-pitched laugh. Since we came back into each other's lives, Jake has been buying me special gifts to make up for the missed birthdays in the twelve years we were apart. "This is a little extravagant for a birthday gift, even for you."

"You can call it two birthday gifts in one if you want." He moves closer and tucks my hair behind my ear.

"More like a hundred in one. Wow, Jake. I'm just... speechless. Seriously bloody speechless. I just wish I had something to contribute."

"What do you mean?" He frowns.

Looking down, I scuff the toe of my boot against the concrete. "Well...you know, normal people get a mortgage together, pay half each for the house. That kind of contribution."

Lifting my chin, he says softly, "We're not most people, Tru. I told you when we were on the island that I want you to have the best of everything. This house is part of that. I want us to have a home together."

I know why he's bought this house. Because of how I feel about his place. Jake has shopped for a new house and spent an inordinate amount of money, all because of me. As if he hasn't got enough to deal with at the moment.

I'm such a selfish bitch.

"Jake...I'm sorry." I drop my gaze. "I know why you bought this house. And I didn't mean for you to sell your home and buy a brand-new house."

"Look at me." His tone is firm, causing my eyes to lift to his. "You have *nothing* to be sorry for. And I had a house, Tru. It was never a home. *You're* my home. I want you happy. And you're not happy at my place, and honestly, I don't fuckin' blame you. Christ, if it was me, I'd have been climbing the goddamn walls if I had to live permanently in a house that you'd shared with—" He cuts off. He doesn't say his name; he doesn't have to. I know he means Will.

Will, the man whose heart I broke when I had an affair with Jake. Will, whom I left so I could be with Jake. But it still didn't stop me ping-ponging between the both of them in the beginning. I hate so much that I did that.

And I hate the pain it still brings to Jake's eyes. It's like a blow to the gut. A reminder of how badly I handled everything. How much I hurt him.

"You bought us a brand-new house so you could have sex with me again?" I smile, trying to ease the atmosphere. "You do realise getting us a hotel room would have been much cheaper."

He runs his finger down my cheek. "Sweetheart, I would give everything I own to be able to fuck you again." He returns my smile with his sexy grin, and I know I have him back to good.

"Well, it's one hell of a shag-pad-to-be." I tilt my head in the direction of the house.

"Tru." He grabs my face, trapping it between his hands. "I want to make love to you in every single room in that house. But it's not just that. I want a fresh start for the both of us. This place is brand-new. It was completed a few months back. No one has lived in it before. It's ours to fill with memories."

Tears well in my eyes, and one escapes, running down my cheek, trickling onto Jake's hand.

"You're crying—good or bad?"

"Good," I reply as he wipes the wet away. "Really, *really* good."

Jake smiles, and it's so beautiful it makes my heart ache.

I wrap my arms around his neck and reach up on my tiptoes to meet his face. I kiss him gently on the lips.

"I love you," I whisper over his mouth.

"I love you too, baby. Now come on," he says, releasing me, sounding suddenly excited. "Let me give you the tour."

Jake opens the huge wooden front door to reveal an open-plan living room with high ceilings. Across from me are floor-to-ceiling windows that span the whole of the back wall, offering a panoramic view of LA.

Holy fuck, it's breathtaking.

"Jesus," I whisper, walking farther in, my eyes glued to the view.

"What do think?" Jake asks beside me.

Closing my mouth in attempt to form words, I utter, "It's stunning."

"The view is spectacular at night," Jake says, moving through the living room toward the window.

I follow him, dazed, trying desperately to take in my surroundings. It's decorated throughout, finished with two huge light grey sofas, a glass table, and modern art hanging on the walls. There's also an open fireplace—one of those trendy ones with the artificial flames.

"The furniture is just for show," Jake says, as if reading my mind. "You can decorate however you want."

"However *we* want," I correct.

"Right." He smiles.

"This is one of the best features in this place." I watch with interest as Jake flips open a little panel on the wall beside the glass. He presses a button and the huge glass wall starts to slide open, disappearing into the far wall, opening the living room onto the patio.

My jaw drops.

"Holy fuck," I whisper, stepping through. "That's awesome."

"I know, right?" Jake's grinning like a boy with a new toy.

I glance over the huge plush patio area, my eyes locking on the swimming pool. It's massive. The size of the ones you find at the local swimming baths, but way, way nicer.

I move closer and discover it's an infinity-edge pool.

Moving from the pool, I approach the seating area, which is decked out with an L-shaped wicker sofa, padded with thick white cushions and centred around a gorgeous fire pit.

I glance out again at LA. "Whereabouts are we?"

"In the hills."

My eyes nearly pop out of my head. "Hollywood Hills?"

"The very ones."

"Holy fuck."

I can't stop saying holy fuck. But really, this is a "holy fuck" moment in my life if ever there was one.

I'm in a house in the Hollywood Hills. A ginormous house that Jake wants to buy for us.

I may just have a panic attack. Or faint. Or maybe both.

Fucking fuckety fuck.

I don't know much about property prices, but I'm figuring this one costs a lot more than Jake's place in Pacific Palisades.

I wonder who the neighbours are.

"How much is this place going for?"

Jake leans back against the seating area. He eyes me carefully for a long moment before answering. "Thirty."

I have to steady myself on the table, as I'm guessing he doesn't mean thirty thousand.

"Thirty million dollars!" My voice has reached maximum pitch. I'm expecting to hear glass shatter any moment now.

I know Jake has a lot of money, but holy fuck.

Holy fuckety fuck!

"I know it seems like a lot...okay, it is a lot," he adds at my pained expression. "But it's not like I can't afford it. And I don't plan on us moving again. I wanted the best place for us, equipped with everything we need for now and for the future. This place is as good as they come."

Future. Kids? Kids he doesn't want.

Swallowing down on that heart-wrenching thought, I ask, "How many bedrooms?"

"Five."

"Five! Jesus Christ, Jake! There should be at least fifty for that price!"

Snuffling a laugh, he comes over to me and wraps his arms around my waist, pulling me close.

"Baby, there's plenty enough here for the price, trust me. It's a gated community. The house itself is surrounded with gates, and that guy you heard before, he's the security for the house. It's manned twenty-four hours."

"To keep your legions of female fans out?"

"I was thinking more about keeping the legions of admiring men away from my girl." He squeezes me tight. "It's a great place, baby. A great neighbourhood. It's got a huge garden," he says, nodding to the right. "There's a two-bed guesthouse in the garden, which is where Stuart will live."

"Stuart's not going to live with us anymore?" I pout.

"Well, we talked, baby, and we decided it was time he move out and get his own place. He's all grown up, ready to face the world. We have to let him go sometime. We can't keep him forever." Jake gives me a grave look, clearly taking the piss.

"You're an idiot."

"Takes one to know one."

"That it does." I smile warmly.

He rubs his nose against mine, Eskimo-style. "I just thought it would be good to have our privacy, and Stuart gets his too. Also, I no longer have to run the risk of catching him making out with a dude."

"You love it really."

"What? Catching Stuart making out with a guy?"

Pressing my lips together, suppressing a smile, I nod.

"Sweetheart, nothing could kill my hard-on quicker, believe me. I like the person I'm with to be soft and warm." He runs his fingertips down my bare arm. "I want her made to fit around me."

"Like me?" I scratch my fingernails over the denim covering his pert behind.

"Exactly like you."

Jake bends his head down to mine and kisses me softly.

"Will you miss him?"

"Are we still talking about Stuart?"

"I'm just worried he'll think my being here is pushing him out."

"Sweetheart, he works for me, and it's not like he's going far."

"I know he works for you, but he's your friend too. You guys have lived together for such a long time. You're like Joey and Chandler. Except you'd probably have been Joey, and Chandler was never gay. Oh God, would that make me Monica or Rachel?"

"What the fuck are you talking about?" He laughs.

"*Friends.*"

"I'm gonna have to watch this show, aren't I, just so I can figure out what the fuck you're talking about half the time."

"Yes, Pervy Perverson, you are. Honestly, I have no clue how you haven't. I'll buy the first season on Blu-ray and we can watch it together."

"Can't wait."

"Sarcasm doesn't suit you, Wethers."

"No, but you wrapped around me does."

"Later," I say, pushing back from him, grinning. "Because right now you have the rest of this place to show me."

* * *

Half an hour later, the tour of my new home is complete. Jake and I are back in the living room, looking out at LA.

I've discovered this place has a gym, a cinema room, an office, a wine cellar, a library, and a games room. There's another guest section that has two rooms, which Jake said he'll turn into a studio like the one he has at his house. I also discovered this house has the biggest kitchen I have ever seen, complete with a separate utility room, a dining room, and of course the five bedrooms, complete with en suite bathrooms.

It's so big I actually fear getting lost in here. And I have no clue how the hell I'm going to keep it clean. It'll be a full-time job in itself.

I've decided that aside from the living room, my favourite room is the master bedroom. Obvious reasons aside, it has the same breathtaking view of LA as the living room, with the same floor-to-ceiling windows.

"So…do you want me to go ahead with the offer on this place?" Jake asks from behind me, resting his face against the side of mine, his arms moving to tighten around my waist.

I have a vision of Jake and me standing here like this late at night, his arms wrapped around me, as we stare out at nighttime LA.

I feel such an intense wave of contentment that I know unequivocally that I want this house to be our home.

"Yes," I say, unable to keep the happiness from my voice. "I absolutely want you to go ahead with the offer."

"Thank fuck," he says, his hand slipping inside my top to cup my breast, making me gasp at the contact I've been so badly missing these last few days. "So can I make love to you now in our new home?" His breath is hot against my ear.

Swallowing, I reply, "Yes," with a breathy moan.

Jake spins me around, and my mouth hits his at exactly the same time, with the same hungry need.

"I can't wait," he growls. "I need to be inside you now."

The urgency and command in his voice soaks my panties.

"I thought you were gonna fuck me blindfolded and in my boots?" I whisper across his lips.

He groans. "Next time, because right now I just need to bury my cock deep inside you."

"Where do you want me?"

Jake's eyes hit the couch. My back does a second later. A few more seconds, and I'm shirtless and skirtless, my panties torn off.

Jake has barely gotten his own pants off before he's thrusting his insatiable cock inside me.

"Eager much?" I breathe, lifting my hips.

"Too fucking right I am. Jesus Christ, Tru, I am never going that long without being inside you again."

I know it's a stupid thing to ask, but I still have to, because this is me. "Why haven't you been near me?" I ask quietly.

He pauses, staring down at me, a look of confusion on his face. "I was trying to be respectful. I knew how you felt about my house."

I nod, feeling relieved that was his reason why and loving him so much more for it.

"It was really damn hard keeping my hands off you, you know. Why do you think I bought this house so quickly?"

The grin he wears makes me giggle and brings me back to the now and the feel of him inside me.

Taking hold of my hips, he kneels, lifting my lower half with him, giving him the access he wants to get deeper inside me.

"At least I got to wear the boots." I tap the heels of my ankle boots against his back.

"Fuck," he groans, rocking into me. "You're gonna be the death of me."

"Maybe we should stop. I don't want you dying on me."

"No fuckin' way," he growls, burying himself deeper inside. "You're not going anywhere until we've both come."

"Yes, sir."

"Say that again in Spanish."

"Sir?"

"Yes," his voice is strained.

"*Sí, señor*," I whisper. "*No me jodas, por favor.*"

"I fucking love you, Tru, so damned much."

I'm struck by the depth of his need for me, what I can do to him with my words alone, and the total control he takes over my body. And my heart. He owns me. It leaves me breathless.

"*Te quiero*," I whisper.

He shudders, a deep sound escaping his throat. "Keep talking Spanish to me, sweetheart," he groans, thrusting harder, in and out of me, chasing his need for orgasm, never forgetting mine as he presses his fingers against my bud and licks his cock against that sweet spot deep inside me.

Lost in him, wanting to please him, I whisper words of Spanish, heated praise I would never dare say in English, until my orgasm tears through me, pushing Jake over the edge.

I watch in awe as he throws his head back, the muscles in his neck tightening, straining, as he growls out his orgasm, pumping his hips hard into mine.

When he's done, he falls onto me. Brushing my hair from my face, he tenderly kisses my lips, then rests his head beside mine.

I turn my face to his. "So that's the living room christened. Only sixteen more rooms to go, excluding bathrooms, of course."

"Well, I'm good for a few more rounds," he says, grinning. "Where next?"

CHAPTER FIVE

Today is moving day.

We're leaving Jake's old house behind; it's on the market now.

We've been back in LA two weeks now, and I'm really starting to like it here.

I still miss Simone and London like crazy, though. The one thing I miss most is our girls' night out on Friday nights.

I'm constantly surrounded by men here, so any girlie nights are pretty much out of the question.

I really do need to try and make some new girlfriends here. It's just not so easy to make new female friends when you're Jake Wethers's girlfriend.

Half the women here hate me because they want to sleep with Jake. The other half hate me because they have slept with him and they want round two.

I'm currently not liked amongst my gender in LA. Well, worldwide, I'd imagine, because I'm the one who took Jake off the market.

So you see my problem.

Even though I miss London with all my heart, LA has one great perk: the clothes shops.

Stuart's been giving me the guided tour of the best shops here. The man is a maniac when let loose around fabric, credit card in hand. Therefore, he encourages me to buy way too much. Stuart's a hard guy to say no to. Pretty much like Jake in that respect.

I'm near to maxing out all my credit cards with my purchases. But they are all so completely worth it. Especially the new underwear I bought from Agent Provocateur, if only for the look on Jake's face when I modeled them last night.

My modeling debut ended up turning into a marathon lovemaking session. I cast aside my self-imposed sex ban at his house, knowing we were leaving.

I also put a no-ripping ban on the new underwear. After his initial disappointment, Jake removed them the old-fashioned way, quite slowly in fact. And there were certainly no complaints coming once he got in the rhythm.

Jake and I also spent time this past week furniture shopping. I've loved every minute of it.

First item on the list: a new bed.

We bought a custom-made Parnian bed at Jake's insistence, which is being delivered today.

Don't get me wrong, it's beautiful and supercomfy, but I did initially suggest that we could get one equally as good from IKEA. I thought it was such a large amount of money to spend on a bed. I know money is no issue to Jake, but it's still taking a little time for me to get used to that fact. Jake's argument was that if he's going to spend most of his time in it, on his knees making me come, then he wanted the best bed money can buy. Got to love his crass. And really, what could I say to that?

Between bouts of fun and crazy spending, and keeping on top of work, I've started planning our wedding. Well, kind of. I bought some bridal magazines and looked at wedding dresses.

It's the best kind of start, if you ask me.

I still haven't yet decided whether we will get married here or back home in the UK. Mama is naturally pushing for the UK, but I'm just not sure.

One thing Jake and I did do was decide on a date for the wedding.

I will become Mrs. Jake Wethers on 21 July 2013.

Trudy Wethers.

It's so weird. And I so can't bloody wait!

The reason we picked 21 July is because it's the date I went to interview Jake. We'll be married a year to the day we fell back into each other's lives. I still can't believe how much has happened in such a short time.

So I've got a little over nine months to plan our wedding.

Plenty of time. I think. I don't know. I've never planned a wedding before. To be honest, it kind of hurts my head when I think of the enormity of what I have to do.

Jake suggested I hire a wedding planner, but I don't know if I want a complete stranger organising my wedding. It feels like it's something I should do with the help of my mum and girlfriends.

Honestly, though, I have been secretly considering taking Jake up on his offer of Vegas.

The only thing stopping me is the fact that my mother would quite likely never speak to me again if I got married standing before a guy dressed as Elvis.

On the other big news front, Jake and Zane, who I'm still yet to meet, discovered who was stealing from the label.

The A&R director. No one I've ever met. His name is Scott Speed.

Scott has worked for Jake pretty much from the beginning, like Zane.

Apparently Scott is a gambler, and he had run up some pretty big debts. He stole the money to pay the not-so-nice people he owed.

That was his excuse, anyway.

For me, there is no excuse for stealing.

I saw how what he's done has affected Jake, and that's what really pisses me off. I get that Scott may have been in a tight fix, but there are other ways out.

Jake even said that if Scott had just told him what was going on, he would have helped him pay off the debts and gotten him the help he needed with his addiction.

Jake above anyone knows what it's like to deal with an addiction.

The worst thing for Jake was that he had no choice but to report it to the police, and now Scott has been charged with fraud.

It's sad, but Jake's hands were tied. Scott had committed a serious crime, and if Jake hadn't reported it, he would have been in trouble himself.

One good thing is Jake has managed to keep it out of the news. The last thing the label needs right now is any negative press.

But that's all behind us now, and today we start our life together in our humongous new house.

Our $30 million humongous house in the Hollywood Hills.

I still cannot get over how much this house is worth. Or that I'm going to be living in such an amazing house in Hollywood.

It's all still a little surreal.

Currently, I'm standing outside my amazing house, in my surreal moment, feeling a little redundant.

The movers are shifting all our belongings into the house for us, and Stuart is at the helm directing. I currently have nothing to do and no clue where Jake is.

He was here a minute ago but vanished, leaving me here looking like a lemon.

Almost all of the stuff being moved in is Jake's. What little stuff I have, which Simone kindly boxed up for me, was shipped from London. It consists of clothes, shoes, makeup, accessories, handbags, and photos and mementos I've collected over the years.

Not a lot, really. It makes me a little sad that I have so little to show for my life in London.

Making my way past one of the movers, through the front door and living room, I go out onto the patio area, where it's quiet.

Thankful I'm wearing denim shorts, I kick my wedges off and sit down at the edge of the infinity pool and immerse my legs in the water as I stare out at the skyline.

Suddenly awash with homesickness, I decide to call Simone.

"Hey, gorgeous!" comes her chipper voice down the line.

Hearing Simone's voice, and London in the background, causes my throat to thicken.

"Hey," I say, forcing my voice out.

"How's moving day going?"

"Ah, you know."

"You don't sound very excited. I would be bouncing off the bloody walls if I were moving into that house!"

I e-mailed Simone photos of the house last week, and she was, let's say…mega impressed to say the least. She screamed down the phone—a lot.

"Maybe Denny will buy you one," I say, deflecting the conversation from me to her and Denny.

"Yeah, I'd be so bloody lucky!" she laughs.

Denny is the drummer in TMS and one of Jake's closest friends. Simone and Denny met when I was on tour with the band. They've been together ever since, and are managing to successfully maintain a long-distance relationship.

How long they'll stay long distance, I'm not sure.

I can't see Simone giving up her job and coming over here anytime soon, even though for purely selfish reasons I wish she would. And Denny has commitments here with the band.

"I wish you lived here so we could see each other every day like we used to," I murmur.

"Me too."

"So why don't you just move here?" I say. "Move in with Denny."

"Tru, for starters, I don't even know if Denny would want to live with me. He's never mentioned it."

"I bet he would. He's crazy about you."

"Yeah," she sighs. "But I also love my job too, you know. I'm doing so well at work right now that I'd be crazy to throw it all away."

"I guess," I sigh.

Unlike me, who moves halfway around the world to be with the man she loves. But then, that man is Jake. The person I have loved for my whole life. And I guess I didn't have to give up my job either. I'm lucky enough to have the best boss in the world, who's letting me work transatlantic. Thank God for Vicky—and technology.

"Anyway, why are you on the phone with me in the midst of your move? It is still happening, isn't it?"

"As we speak. I'm just...not needed. The movers are putting everything away, and Stuart is making sure everything runs smoothly, which I don't mind, because it's his job to do that kind of stuff. I guess I just..." I let out another sigh, kicking my leg against the blue. "Ignore me, I'm just being silly."

"Not how us normal folk move, eh, babe?"

"Nope." I love how I don't have to say the actual words to Simone. She just gets me every time.

"You remember when we moved into the flat?" I say, the memory tickling me. "Just me and you, lugging furniture and boxes in. And oh my God! That bloody van we hired that kept breaking down!"

"Sodding thing kept cutting out when I was driving it!"

"And on our first night in the flat we ate Indian takeaway straight from the containers, using plastic forks, and drank the wine straight from the bottle because we couldn't be arsed to unpack any plates or glasses!" I'm really laughing now.

"God, we used to have such a laugh!" Simone crows, sounding a little breathless.

"A lot's changed since then," I muse, my laughter quickly dying as I stare into the water.

"For the better," she says. But it actually sounds like a question.

She loves Jake, but he is who he is, and he has the problems he has. I know Simone worries for me.

"Definitely for the better." I smile, the thought of Jake instantly bringing it to my lips.

I hear movement behind me. Turning, I see Jake making his way toward me.

"My absent fiancé has just reappeared," I say to Simone. "I'll call you later, once we're all settled, okay?"

"Okay, honey, speak to you later."

"Simone?" Jake asks, sitting on the edge of one of the chairs.

"Yes." I nod, pushing my phone back into the pocket of my shorts.

"What you doing out here alone?" he asks.

Looking away, I shrug. "Just taking in the scenery."

"It is beautiful."

When I turn back to him, I find his eyes on me.

"Come with me," he says, standing. "I've got something I want to show you."

* * *

Jake pushes open the door to the library and leads me through.

In the centre of the room I see a piano. A stunningly beautiful black piano.

"Is that a Bösendorfer?" I ask, taking a tentative step toward it.

Owning a Bösendorfer was my ultimate dream when I used to play. Jake knew that.

"It's a 290 Imperial," he says softly from behind me.

"Wow, it's beautiful." I run my fingertips over the casing.

"It's yours."

I step back, away from the piano.

"I thought you could start playing again."

"No…I, um…" I shake my head. "I haven't played in a really long time, Jake."

"Your dad said you stopped playing right after I left."

He did?

"My dad talks too much."

"Why, Tru?"

"I dunno." I shrug. "He just does."

"No." Jake smiles, coming over to me. "Not why does your dad talk too much. Why did you stop playing after I left?"

I feel a flood of emotion rush through me, all that bottled-up pain I've carried around for all these years hitting the surface, causing my skin to prickle and my mouth to work of its own accord.

"Because your leaving broke my heart, Jake, and when you cut off all contact, what was left of my heart shattered. Music was always our thing, and it just hurt too much to play without you. And then one day, not long after you were gone, I just couldn't bring myself to touch the keys. When you left…I guess the music left with you."

Jake wraps his arms around me, crushing me to his chest. "Fuck, Tru," he chokes out. "I'm so sorry I left you."

"You were fourteen, it's not like you could have stayed."

I'm seriously fighting back tears here. One wrong word from him, and I'm envisioning a teenage-style sobbing session.

"No, but I could have kept in touch. I *should* have kept in touch. I was such a stupid, selfish fucker back then, so fucking angry, and I couldn't see past my own pain at losing you. I never thought how cutting you off would affect you. I should have come back to you the moment I turned old enough to leave home, and all those years since."

"If you had, then the world would have missed out on the Mighty Storm. Everything happens for a reason, Jake."

"I just wish that reason hadn't meant twelve years without you. I fuckin' hate that you stopped playing the piano because of me. I want you to have this back, Tru. I want you to start playing again."

"I don't know." I shake my head, moving from his tight embrace. "It's been so long since I last played, I might have forgotten how."

"You couldn't forget. You'll be rusty, but it'll still be there. You are an amazing player, Tru. Natural talent like yours doesn't just disappear."

I gaze up at his face.

"Try, for me? *Please.*"

How can I say no to him? Especially when he's giving me the puppy-dog eyes.

"Okay," I concede.

The smile he gives me nearly cracks me wide open.

I take the seat at the piano and let my rusty fingers hover over the keys.

"I don't know what to play," I say, feeling self-conscious, pulling back my hands.

"I bought you some sheet music," Jake says, retrieving some music books off a shelf. "You know, just in case you needed them," he adds, handing the books to me.

"Any of yours in here?" I tilt my head toward the books.

"No." He grins, leaning against the piano. "I made sure they were clean before I bought them."

"What if I wanted to play one of yours?"

"Then I'll teach you. First, play me something from one of these."

I sift through the books and opt for the modern music one.

Opening up the pages, I flick through to the first song and almost laugh. My Adele ringtone.

I wonder if he knew that was in here.

Setting the book up on the piano, I read over the music, refreshing my memory with the notes. I surprise myself at how easily I can read the music.

Jake was right when he said I wouldn't have forgotten.

I position my left hand over the keys, reading to play a C minor for four beats, then G minor with my right for two beats, then shifting to B-flat and G minor.

Okay, deep breath…here we go.

Crap, I'm playing and…it feels surprisingly good. Great, in fact.

I close my eyes briefly, just feeling the keys beneath my fingers, and in that brief moment, Jake starts to sing quietly along, and I'm transported back to a whole other time and place.

Opening my eyes, I see him smiling at me. He's wearing the kind of happiness I haven't seen on his face for twelve long years. Seeing him looking at me this way makes me fall into the music even more, and then it's like I never stopped playing.

* * *

"I'm going to have a bath," I holler down the long hall to Jake, who is in the living room.

"You want some dinner ready when you're done?" comes back his reply.

"You gonna cook?"

"I'll order in, smart-ass."

Holding back a laugh, I reply, "Then, yes, please."

I head into our bedroom, then the en suite, and turn the taps on our new, never-before-used bathtub.

Searching through the cupboard where all my toiletries have been stored, I find my bubble bath and pour some under the running water.

The movers finished a few hours ago and have long since left.

Stuart's in his new abode, getting himself set up. So it's just Jake and me in the house together, all alone.

Being alone with Jake is a big thing for me, as it doesn't happen often. Now that we're living together, though, just him and me, T&J alone time is going to happen often.

The thought sends a thrill through me.

Turning the taps off, I set the music system in the bathroom, selecting the new Killers album. I'm currently having a love affair with it, especially the song "Miss Atomic Bomb." I pull my clothes off, dropping them into the hamper; tie my hair into a loose knot; then submerge my body in the bath.

The scent and heat envelop me.

Heaven.

I close my eyes and rest my head back.

* * *

I wake with a start. Glancing at the clock, I see I've been asleep for just over half an hour. Figuring dinner will be here by now—and I'm more than ready to eat, according to my rumbling tummy—I let the water drain and climb out of the bath.

Wrapping a fluffy bath towel around myself, I turn off the music and go into the bedroom to change.

I put on my favourite pair of comfy jogging bottoms and my TMS T-shirt that I got from the European leg of the tour.

Making my way down the hall, I hear music. Jake's listening to our song, "You Started."

I turn into the living room and find him waiting for me.

He smiles, getting to his feet. I glance at the scene around him.

My skin tingles. The sensation vibrates through to my heart.

Set out on the coffee table are open cartons of Indian takeaway food. No plates or cutlery, just plastic forks. A bottle of white wine is open and waiting. No wineglasses.

Scattered all around the room are empty cardboard boxes.

"Did I get it right?" he asks, tilting his head to the side.

"You heard what I said to Simone?"

He shrugs. "I know things in my life are a little different from what you're used to. I thought because you didn't get a normal moving day, I would give you a normal first night in our new home."

"And the boxes?"

"For effect." He smiles, and his eyes sparkle under the lighting. "They work?"

"Absolutely."

"You hungry?"

"Very."

But now I'm not so hungry for the food, just hungry for him.

"You wanna try that new bed out?" I suggest.

"Abso-fucking-lutely."

The next thing I know, Jake's body is slamming into mine, picking me up, carrying me down the hall to our bedroom.

He lays me down on the bed, hovering over me, propped up on his hands.

"I love you," I whisper to him, in the dark. "Thank you for what you did out there. And for the piano. Thank you for all the wonderful things you do for me."

He stills for a long moment, staring down at me, a blank expression wearing his face. I wonder what's going through his mind.

"There isn't anything I won't do for you, Tru. Nothing I won't do to make you happy. What I feel for you…it's limitless. There is nothing before or after you. There is only you."

I choke up with emotion.

I lift my hand to his face, tracing my finger over his cheek. "When we get married, say that to me as your vow."

He nods, and leaning down, he presses a light kiss to my lips.

A sigh escapes him. "I know I'm not the best choice for you." His words move over my lips. "I know I fuck up a lot, but I promise I will do everything in my power to make you happy."

"You already make me happy all the time. Are you happy?"

Lifting his head, his dark eyes stare at me. "Like I never knew possible."

Then he closes his eyes, almost as if he's in pain. Like at some level, it's actually painful what he feels for me. I understand that, because I feel it too.

"Jake?"

His eyes open to meet mine.

"Make love to me?"

Fulfilling my request, he does just that. Making love to me like tonight is the start. Like Jake and I have finally started.

CHAPTER SIX

I'm at the point of banging my head against my laptop screen when Adele starts singing to me.

Glancing down I see Jake's name flashing. The smile it brings to my lips stays there as I answer it. "Hey, baby."

"How's it going?"

"Not good. You're incredibly hard to write about, you know."

"But incredibly easy to love."

"Well, yeah, but that's only because you have a big willy," I joke.

"Cock, baby. Call it cock, or dick. I'll even swing for snake. But not willy. Willy just sounds so wrong, on so many levels."

"No it doesn't! It's a British term. Have you forgotten those altogether?"

"No, but that's one I will gladly forget."

I hear voices in the background.

"Are you with someone?"

"I'm in the studio with the guys. Zane's here."

"You just said 'cock,' 'dick,' and 'willy' in front of them." I groan.

He lets out a loud laugh. "They've heard me say worse, baby, trust me."

"Hmm," I murmur, cheeks flaming. Jake may have no problem talking sex in front of his friends, but I do.

"Anyway, I was just calling because Zane has managed to fix up a spot for Vintage supporting Raine tonight. Their support pulled out on them last minute. I wondered if you fancied going to watch them?"

Raine is a hugely successful indie band in LA with a massive local following. Vintage is the band who supported TMS at Madison Square Garden, the ones who won the radio contest. I really love their sound, and I mentioned to Jake that I thought they definitely had something. He listened to some of their stuff—he hadn't been paying attention at the show for many reasons—and liked what he heard, so he sent Zane to New York to check them out while we were on holiday.

Zane loved them and offered them a deal on the spot. They are now signed to the label and are in LA recording their first album.

I like the fact that I pointed out their potential to Jake, and he listened to me. I love that he cares about my opinions on these things.

"You're asking if I want to watch a live band I encouraged you to sign? Hmm, let me think…"

"Pick you up at seven?" he says, chuckling.

"Are you not coming home first?"

"No, we've got a good flow going at the moment, getting some new stuff down. I'll shower and change at the studio, and then I'll come by and pick you up."

"Thinking on it, why don't I just ask Dave to bring me to the show, and I'll meet you there. He'll be coming anyway, won't he? So it just makes sense."

Even though things aren't as "follow Jake around" crazy fanwise in LA, he still has Dave or Ben with us when we go out. I get the feeling they're around more for me than him, though. I think he worries about my safety.

"Yeah, okay, good idea," he agrees.

Jake tells me where the show is, so I jot the address down and hang up. I stare at my computer screen for a few more minutes, then close it with a sigh. I head into my dressing room area to figure out what to wear tonight.

* * *

I'm seated in the back of the car and Dave is driving us to the venue. The show is at some hip club in downtown LA.

Getting my mirror out of my clutch, I check my hair and makeup. I opted for hair down and curly, dark smoky eyes, and pink lip gloss. I thought the makeup should match the outfit. I'm wearing my new black knee-length stretch-leather skirt and white off-the-shoulder sheer silk crepe top.

As the top is sheer, I avoided wearing any of my new lacy bras, instead going with my white bra with gentle detail on it, which covers all the important bits. On my feet I'm wearing my new Christian Louboutin peep-toe studded black heels. They are sexy as hell. I know Jake will totally approve of them.

Dave pulls the car around the back of the venue, into the reserved parking area. I see Jake's Aston Martin.

I climb out of the car and follow Dave to the metal door, leading into the back entrance of the club. He bangs his fist on it a couple of times.

A burly guy opens the door and greats Dave like they know each other well.

Dave gestures me through the door first, then I wait to follow him.

He leads me down a corridor, through a door, then another, and then we're in the club.

Looking to the left I see people setting up the stage, preparing for Vintage, who are due to play their set in just under an hour. There's music playing provided by the resident DJ, and people are on the dance floor already.

I spot Jake standing at the bar, drinking a bottle of beer, looking his ever-gorgeous self, wearing his blue Led Zeppelin "Song Remains the Same" T-shirt, slim-fitted bleached, ripped jeans, and black motorcycle boots.

He looks as hot as hell. And he is all mine.

Ben's standing off to the side by the bar, with what looks to be a soft drink. Leaving me, Dave goes over to join him.

At the bar with Jake is a blond guy. A very good-looking blond guy. He looks to be about the same height as Jake, and he's wearing a white Oxford shirt, which he fills out with no problem, and gunmetal grey trousers. He screams urbane sophistication, the complete and utter contrast of Jake's bad-boy rock-star image.

Jake's face lights up at my approach. Then I see his eyes move down my body, and a frown mars his perfect face.

Oh no. He hates my outfit.

Feeling instantly self-conscious, tucking my clutch under my arm, I run my hands down my skirt and pick up my pace to him.

"Hey," I say when I reach him.

He slides his hand around my waist. Pulling me close, he plants a kiss on my lips.

"You hate my outfit," I whisper under his mouth.

"No, I just hate that every man in this place can see your tits through it," he growls, kissing me one more time before releasing me.

Shit. I thought I looked nice. I guess not.

Turning to the man beside him, Jake says, "Tru, I'd like you to meet Zane. He's the VP at the label. Zane, this is the future Mrs. Wethers."

Zane smiles. Smoldering chocolate-brown eyes meet mine. "Great to finally meet you, Tru." He offers his hand. "I've heard a lot about you."

Taking my hand, he lifts it to his lips and kisses it.

"I hope he was saying mostly complimentary things," I say through my now-dry mouth, sliding a glance in Jake's direction.

"All complimentary." Zane smiles, releasing my hand. "You're just as beautiful as Jake described."

Just not in tonight's outfit, apparently.

Zane's smooth. Very smooth. But not in a slimy way. More in an "I'm well practiced at getting women into my bed and they leave *very* satisfied" kind of way. The guy screams confidence and awesome sex. Just like Jake.

"Where the fuck have you been, ass-face?" Jake says over my head.

Turning, I see Tom sauntering toward us.

"Nowhere. Hey, Tru," he says, turning his eyes toward me. "Nice top." His eyes flicker down to my chest, lingering longer than necessary.

"Stop staring at my fiancée's tits," Jake growls.

Fuck. Thanks, Tom.

"Hey, I'm a guy...," he protests, "and they're just there on display, what do expect me to do? Awesome rack, Tru, *seriously awesome.* I'm real glad you decided to put them on show tonight. You really should show them off more often."

"Do you want me to break your face?" Jake says, half joking.

At least I think he is.

Pulling my clutch up to cover my chest, I say, "Haven't you got better things to be doing, Tom? Like finding your next doggie bag to take home, rather than staring at something you can never have?"

"Ooh, harsh!" Tom slaps his hand over his heart.

"I like you more and more by the minute, Tru." Zane grins at me. "What are you drinking?"

"I'll get these," Jake says. "Your usual, baby?"

"Yes, please."

"Tom, you want a beer?"

Tuning out the guys, I glance around the club. It's a nice place. A little grungy, but definitely somewhere I would have hung out back home.

I notice many eyes looking in our direction. Mostly at Jake. Well, all at Jake. Most of them don't even have the decency to look away when they see I've caught them staring at my husband-to-be.

Nice.

"Thanks," I say as Jake hands me my margarita.

"So she blew you out?" I catch Zane saying to Tom.

"No."

"The fact you went back there to try your luck with her, and you're out here with us, definitely says she did, man," Jake says with a smile.

"I never said I went to try my luck. I went to offer my support."

Jake laughs. "The only support you would have been offering her was up against a wall."

"What's this?" I say, taking a sip of my drink. "Tom got rejected by a woman?" I give Tom a mock look of shock.

"Yep," Jake replies, flashing wide eyes at me. "He tried to get into Lyla's pants, and being the smart girl she is, she blew him out like a candle."

Lyla is the ridiculously pretty lead singer of Vintage, and apparently, a very smart girl indeed.

"Shut up, fuck-face, she didn't blow me out. I would've had to try something for that to happen. Not that it ever would. Women can't say no to the cat."

"Wow, man, in all the years I've known you, you've never had a girl say no to you," Jake says, ignoring Tom's defensiveness. "Wait 'til Denny hears this." Jake laughs. "Actually, I might ring him now." He reaches for his phone.

"For fuck's sake!" Tom groans, grabbing his beer.

Zane pats him on the back, keeping a straight face. "Don't sweat it, man, it happens to the best of us. Never to me, but I totally feel for you." Zane cracks up laughing.

"I like Lyla," I pitch in. *I'll get the twat back for the top comment before.* "She seems like a great girl. Really attractive. Smart. Shame for you, Tom, being blown out like that." I smirk at him.

"Jesus Christ! The lot of you are doing my fuckin' head in! She was a nonstarter. I don't put the effort in for a woman. I don't need to. There are plenty more willing to step up to the plate." He nods in the direction of some open gawkers. "On that note, I'll catch you fuckers later. Tru," he says, eyes going straight to my chest, "a pleasure as always. I hope to see you in that top again soon."

"Fuck off, Tom," Jake snaps.

Backing up, grinning, Tom winks at Jake and heads in the direction of the waiting girls.

Needing a reprieve, I ask Jake, "Where is the bathroom?"

"Through the archway." My eyes follow his pointing finger.

I put my drink on the bar, place a loving kiss on his lips, and head to the bathroom.

I've just sat on the toilet to take a pee, when I hear them come into the bathroom, laughing and talking.

"Oh my God, did you see what she was wearing?"

"I know. She looks like a hooker. A see-through top! And what about that skirt? I thought leather skirts went out with *Pretty Woman*."

I glance down at my leather skirt, which is currently sitting around my thighs, and my face starts to prickle.

"She is so totally batting out of her league with him. How the fuck did she ever manage to get a rock on her finger? I'll never know. Definitely not because of her dog-ugly face. Maybe she's got a magic vagina!" She laughs loudly at her own joke.

I twist my engagement ring around my finger.

"I heard they grew up together," the other girl says, "and that he's apparently into her big-time. Always has been. She's the love of his life, and that's why he never settled down with anyone. Or so I heard."

"Yeah, well, whatever. This is Jake Wethers we're talking about. He might be tripping on the English bitch now, but give him a few more weeks, and she'll be gone."

"You think?"

"Yep. If Jake was going to settle down, it wouldn't be with someone like her."

"You?" The second one giggles.

"He kept coming back for more, didn't he? Told me I was the best fuck he'd ever had. Coming from him, I took that as a big compliment. I bet he'd still be good for a go now."

"You think so? From what I hear he's playing the monogamous card nowadays. Never looks at any other women. He knocked Cherie Walters back the other day and was none too polite about it, from what I heard."

"Yeah, well, Jake never could say no to me. Especially when I was on my knees in his office, sucking him off."

I'm going to throw up.

"I knew you were fucking him, but sucking him off in his office? Class!" She laughs.

"I turned up to see him one day at his office, wearing only my underwear under my trench, and I sucked his cock while he sat at his desk. Then he fucked me senseless over it."

Oh God. I close my eyes and put my head in my hands.

"You're so bad." The other one giggles.

"Maybe I'll go offer my services to him now if that British twinkie isn't around." I hear her slap her lips together and then the click of a purse closing. "I'm sure he'll be up for a quickie in the back. If not, I might just pay him a visit at the label tomorrow."

Heels click away from me; then I hear the door shut with a bang.

My whole body is shaking. My head prickling. Why didn't I just burst out there and make my presence known?

Now she's going to go out there and proposition Jake while I'm here like an idiot with my panties around my ankles.

Hot tears sting my eyes.

Don't cry. Don't you dare bloody cry, Trudy Bennett, over a couple of nasty bitches.

It's at times like this I wish Simone were here. I know she would have marched out there and slapped them stupid.

Normally I would have said something.

But I know why I didn't.

Because what could I say? *Yes, Jake was a whore of the worst kind, but he's not like that anymore!*

They'd have laughed me out of here.

Honestly, part of me fears it's still in him. That one day soon, I won't be enough to keep him.

Forcing back the tears, my face burning with the shame of my cowardice, I finish on the toilet, wash my hands, straighten myself out, and head back into the club.

As I come from the archway, I spot Jake across the room still at the bar. Zane's nowhere to be seen, and Jake is now talking to a stunning blonde. Legs up to her neck, skirt there to meet them.

Bile rises in my throat, alongside an intense shot of rage.

I'm just about to march over there and give the blonde tramp a move-along speech, when I hear my name called from behind.

Turning, I see one of my old journo buddies from the circuit back in the UK, Jefferson Dunn. I'd heard he had come to America to work for a magazine.

Even though I'm pissed right now, a smile still crosses my face to see someone from back home.

"Jefferson!" I beam.

"Trudy Bennett," he says, smiling. "Look at you. How the hell are you?" He envelops me in a hug. I instantly get a whiff of strong alcohol on him.

"I'm good. Great, actually, thanks. How are you?" I say, stepping back from his embrace.

"I'm great. All the better for seeing you. I heard you'd moved out here—with Jake Wethers, of all people."

"Yes." I lift my shoulders lightly, lips remaining in a smile.

I really don't want to talk about Jake right now.

"Where is the rock star?" Jefferson asks, looking around. "I'd love to meet him."

Not wanting to point out Jake and the fact that he's at the bar with a leggy blonde—especially to Jefferson, who's always on the tout for a story—I say, "Oh, he's busy right now. Business, you know."

"Sure...you'll have to introduce me to him later." He takes a sip of his drink, which looks to be whiskey. "What brings you here tonight?" he asks.

"The support act is signed to Jake's label. What about you?"

"Work. I'm doing a piece on Raine."

"Right, cool." I shift on my feet, distracted.

I want to go over to Jake and the blonde, who, from what I can see in my glances over Jefferson's shoulder, is shamelessly flirting herself all over him, but I don't want to come off as rude to Jefferson.

"If Jake's busy with business right now, how about I keep you company until he's done? You want to dance?" He tilts his head in the direction of the dance floor. I see his eyes flicker to my chest.

I'm throwing this bloody top in the bin when I get home.

"Um…"

I really don't want to dance. I would actually quite like to go home, to be honest.

I sneak another glance over Jefferson's shoulder at Jake. Jake says something to the blonde, and she throws back her head and laughs, putting her hand on his chest.

I have a flashback to Paris and the redhead. The redhead Jake kissed in front of me, to get back at me for not breaking up with Will, after he'd begged me to.

Jealousy sears through me like a red-hot poker. I grit my teeth.

"You know what? I would love to dance," I say to Jefferson through my teeth.

Screw Jake and his blonde…and all of his fucking conquests for that matter.

Pulling out the strap on my clutch, I hang it over my shoulder. Jefferson downs his drink, and, taking his offered hand, I let him lead me through the crowd to the centre of the dance floor.

We start off dancing separately, but it's not long before Jefferson moves in closer.

"You look great tonight," Jefferson says, leaning in to my ear. "But then, you always do."

I feel his arm go around my waist.

Fuck.

I stiffen in his embrace.

Jake won't be happy if he sees this.

Isn't that the point?

"Thanks, you too." I pull away from him, but I feel his grip on my back tighten, holding me in place, and he starts to dance into me, grinding his hips near mine.

Ugh.

He's not even a good dancer.

Trying not to cringe at his awkward hip movements, I scrunch my eyes tightly, trying to figure a way out of this.

I'm such a bloody idiot at times.

I'm on the dance floor with Mr. Bean's version of *Saturday Night Fever*, in a lame attempt to make Jake jealous, while Jake is probably none the wiser and off screwing the blonde bitch in the back room, not even giving a toss about me.

Now I feel sick, and I just want to go get drunk and kick the crap out of Jake and his whore. I'm just not sure in which order.

I'm about to wriggle out of Jefferson's hold and make my excuses, when I feel him suddenly wrenched away from me.

My eyes shoot open to find a very angry-looking Jake staring down at me, and a very confused Jefferson trying to straighten out his shirt.

"What the hell!" Jefferson says, then I see his face change to awe when he realises it's Jake who just pulled him off me.

"I thought you were in the bathroom," Jake says to me, ignoring Jefferson. He sounds royally pissed off.

Standing tall, I say, "I was. Then I decided to come and dance."

"And you didn't think to come see me first?"

"What? I need to ask your permission to dance nowadays?" I narrow my eyes at him. "And anyway, you looked *busy.*"

"I'm never too busy for you. You should know that by now." There's no nice in his tone.

It's at this point Jefferson decides to pipe up.

"I meant no disrespect," Jefferson says. "I've known Tru for ages. We knew each other back in London."

Jake stiffens. He turns to him and stares down the couple of inches to Jefferson's face. "You meant no disrespect, but you had your hands all over my girl?"

Jefferson raises his hands in defence. "We were only dancing." But the smile on his face says something else entirely.

It makes my body stiffen.

Jake's face hardens. I worry for a second that he's going to do something stupid.

"We're leaving." Jake grabs my arm and starts to pull me away.

"Hey, man, take it easy," Jefferson puts his hand on Jake's shoulder.

I know instantly he's done the wrong thing.

Quick as lightning, Jake grabs Jefferson's arm, twisting it back and under, forcing Jefferson to bend under the strain. Then Jake shoves him away, all but tossing him across the dance floor.

The crowd quickly parts, people shifting out of the way, watching as Jefferson lands hard on the dance floor.

Dave and Ben are beside us in a flash. Ben is quick to get Jefferson off the floor and to his feet.

"I was just dancing with her!" Jefferson shouts, clearly not having learned when to stop talking. Then I see a near smile on his face. Like he's actually trying to antagonise Jake. "She's an old friend."

"She *was* a friend," Jake says, hard and cold, taking a step toward him. "Not anymore. You keep your fuckin' hands off my girl, and if I ever see you near her again, you won't be getting up from the floor the next time."

A grin tilts Jefferson's lips. "Is that a threat?"

Jake's jaw clenches, and his fists ball at his sides. "More like a promise."

Dave stands between Jake and Jefferson, which I couldn't be more thankful for.

"Go," Dave urges, pressing his hand against Jake's arm.

I start to back up, wanting out of here.

Jake takes a step back, moving with me, when Jefferson says loudly, "Call me, Tru."

Jake moves so quickly, he's almost a blur. Luckily, Dave is faster and catches hold of Jake before he can do any damage. I've seen what Jake can do when he loses it. And someone like Jake cannot be pummelling guys in clubs.

Especially journalists.

No longer wanting to be party to the scene I've caused, I turn, and putting my head down, I start to move quickly, weaving through the crowd, heading for the exit.

Jake catches up with me near the door.

Grabbing my arm, he yanks me back, turning me to him. "Where are you going?" He sounds out of breath and angry.

"Home," I state harshly. I'm still pissed off with him for flirting with the blonde and for what I had to hear in the bathroom. And also for the scene he caused with Jefferson. I know I was wrong to dance with Jefferson for the reason I did, but he didn't have to react the way he did—making a show of us.

I try to pull my arm from his hand, but there's no give.

"What the hell is wrong with you?" Jake states angrily in my face.

"Me? What the hell is wrong with you? I was only dancing with him, for crying out loud!"

"Dancing?" He lets out a caustic laugh. "It looked like he was getting ready to fuck you right there and then on the dance floor. And you weren't exactly pushing him off either."

"Screw you, Jake! You can bloody talk with your whores scattered left, right, and centre, in my face all night! Then I'm privy to the absolute displeasure of hearing a conversation about how one of your whores sucked you off in your office. Oh yeah, then you fucked her over your desk!"

He looks confused. It, marred with his anger, makes for a scary-looking Jake.

"I got to hear the full lowdown while I was sitting on the toilet, about your activities pre-me. They didn't know I was there," I add for clarification. "But I got to hear how I'm not good enough for you, and how she was going to go to the label tomorrow to offer her services to you."

"Who?" he asks, voice hard.

"Have there been that many you've screwed in your office that you don't know who it would be?"

"Yes." His tone is low and cold and absolutely heartbreaking.

"You make me fucking sick!" I cry, my eyes filling with tears. "What about the blonde? Is she one of your office conquests too? Or did you just screw her at the house?"

He looks confused again.

"The blonde at the bar I saw you flirting with! Have you shagged her too?"

"I wasn't flirting with her. That's Dina. She works for me. She manages Vintage."

"You didn't answer my question."

"Do I have to?"

"Yes!" I shout at him. I'm past caring who hears me. "I want to know if you've fucked her too!"

His eyes darken. "No, I haven't."

"Just everyone else in LA, then."

He takes a step back, leaning against the wall. "You knew how I'd lived my life when we got together, Tru. Don't act like this is a surprise now." He rubs his face hard. "Are you ever going to be able to get past this?" he asks. His voice is softer but serious.

My anger wilts.

I wrap my arms around myself. "I don't know." I shake my head, looking down. After a beat, I say, "And if I can't, where does that leave us?"

"Right where we are but having to find some way for you to be able to cope with my past mistakes."

Moving away from the wall, he steps closer to me. "I've never given you any reason to doubt my faithfulness to you."

"Aside from the girl I found in your bed in Boston."

Shit.

I shouldn't have said that. But it's too late. I know I've pushed the wrong button.

His face darkens, taking me back a step.

"Out of the two of us, I think I'm the one with more cause for concern—you didn't exactly have any trouble jumping straight from Will's bed into mine. So who's to say you won't do the exact same thing to me?"

I feel like he's just slapped me. Hard. Repeatedly. Over and over.

My face burns. My eyes sting. I can't stop the tears leaking from them.

Without another word or look, I make for the exit.

"I'm sorry." He takes hold of me from behind. Wrapping his arms tightly around me, his chest presses up against my back, and his lips are against my ear. I freeze in his hold.

"I'm so sorry. I shouldn't have said that. I didn't mean it." He blows out a breath, and I feel it rush over me, momentarily heating my chilled skin. "Just seeing you, dancing with him to that song, of all songs."

My ears instantly become alert to the song playing in the club coming to finish—Beyoncé's "Sweet Dreams." The song Jake and I danced to in the club in Copenhagen. The night that was the start of us.

Did I subconsciously dance to this song on purpose to hurt him?

"I want to go home," I say quietly. Shame and embarrassment course through me. And in this moment I'm not really sure which home I'm referring to.

His body stiffens. "I'll take you," he says, releasing me.

CHAPTER SEVEN

We've been driving for a while, not speaking, with only music for company. Jake's not heading in the direction of home. I want to ask where he's taking me. I've wanted to ask for a while now, but I don't want to be the first to break the silence.

I hate when we fight like this.

We didn't even get to see Vintage play. Or say good-bye to Zane. I bet he thinks Jake and I are crazy together.

In many ways we are.

Jake takes a sudden turn down an unmarked treelined track and presses a call into his phone, which is nestled in the hands-free.

Dave's voice fills the car. "Everything okay?"

"Wait at the top. Make sure nobody comes down here."

Jake clicks the phone off.

I hadn't even realised Dave was following us. It makes sense; he's only ever a step behind Jake.

We reach a clearing that opens out to a cliff-top panoramic view of LA. Even better than the view at home.

All the glittering, twinkly lights of the city of angels are before us. Or more like Jake's city of sin.

A city I'm not wholly sure I belong in.

Jake kills the engine but leaves the music playing.

"I come here when I need to think," he says without looking at me.

"Do you need to think now?" I ask, turning my head in his direction, my heart beating a hard rhythm.

He meets my eyes in the dark. "No. But we do need to talk."

Jake climbs out of the car without another word, and I follow suit.

I meet him around the front of the car, where he's leant up against it, legs crossed in front of him, arms folded over his chest.

I set myself beside him, leaving a gap. The gap of our fight. I wrap my arms around myself. "What happened at the club will be in the news tomorrow." It's not a question, I already know the answer.

"Yes."

Crap.

"And I'm pretty sure I'll get a call from the cops soon too."

That gets my attention. "Why?"

"Because he'll file a charge for assault."

"But you didn't hit him."

"No, but I threw him to the ground."

Jefferson was after a story. That's why he kept pushing Jake. It's my fault. That's probably why he asked me to dance in the first place. I'm such an idiot.

"I'm sorry," I whisper. "What will you do?"

"Pay him to drop the charges."

"Seriously?" I gape.

"Money makes everything go away, Tru."

"Except our problems." I sigh.

"Yeah, everything but those." He unfurls his arms, resting his hands on the car.

I want to touch him, hold him—it's killing me not to—but I feel like I can't at the moment, and I'm not entirely sure why.

"Why didn't you take us home?" I ask, quietly.

"Because I want our home to be full of happy memories, not memories of us fighting. I grew up in a house where arguments were a daily occurrence, and trust me, fights stick to the walls of houses like fuckin' glue. I don't want that for us." He drags his hands through his hair, hanging them off the back of his neck, letting out a sigh.

"I thought getting the new house would make things easier for you, but this place is covered in every single fuckin' mistake I made before I got you back." He gestures his open hand to the city below. "And aside from leaving LA, I don't know what else to do to make it easier for you."

He sounds hopeless. Defeated. I hate to hear him like this.

But now, after tonight's events, leaving LA is one thing I would happily do. Move away from Jake's past, go back to the UK together, and build a life together there...but his business is here, and I can't ask him to leave that behind.

"I don't either," I mumble in response, chewing my thumbnail.

"I don't want to lose you because of who I used to be." His voice is barely a whisper.

"I don't want to lose you either."

Without looking at me, he reaches over and takes the hand at my mouth. Holding it, he intertwines our fingers.

My skin burns at his touch.

"The irony," he says, "is that we're both jealous because we love each other so much. God, Tru, when I saw that guy's hands on you, my head went. Just the thought of another man near you, touching you...it drives me fuckin' crazy. I can't see straight when it comes to you. It's not rational, I know. But it is what it is, and I can't change it."

"Just like I can't change that whenever we go out, I'm looking around the room, wondering which, if not all, of the women you've had sex with." My breath catches hard in my chest. Just saying the words cuts me to the bone. "Honestly, I don't know how to get past it," I add quietly.

Leaving me, Jake pushes off the car and walks toward the edge of the cliff top.

I stare at his silhouetted form, and for that moment, Jake cuts a solitary figure.

I wonder what he's thinking.

God, I hope he isn't thinking the only way is for us to break up. I know he just said he doesn't want to lose me, but what if he feels it's all too much for him? That there's no other way?

We can't break up. We can't.

"Where do we go from here?" My voice is quiet, knowing we've reached a crossroads. One I didn't see coming.

The pain in my chest is unbearable. I feel like I'm crushing under the weight of my worst fear realised.

If he says we're over, I will beg him.

Jake turns back to me, a determinedness set in his face. "Well, breaking up isn't even an option, if that's what you're thinking."

I shake my head. Tears are starting to blur my eyes.

He walks to me. Taking my face in his hands, staring down at me, he whispers, "I'm not losing you, *ever*. I know I fuck up regularly, but I can't fuck us up."

"You don't fuck up regularly."

"I made a mistake tonight."

What? Oh God. No.

I don't want to know. I don't want to know.

"You did?" I swallow.

"Yep. A big fuckin' one. I didn't tell you how amazingly beautiful you looked the instant I saw you tonight. I was so damn worried about other men looking at you, that I spoke before I thought and I made you feel self-conscious instead of making you feel as beautiful as you are." He strokes his thumb over my cheek.

I let out the breath I was holding.

"I'm sorry I was a bitch tonight," I whisper, pulling my eyes from his. "Just hearing those women talking about you like that, it threw me off guard. Then I came out of the bathroom and saw you talking to Dina. I just felt all torn up inside. I guess I did dance with Jefferson to piss you off." Biting my lip, I look back to him. "I am sorry. Really."

He presses his lips to my forehead. "I wish I could take all those years back so you weren't having to live them now," he says over my skin, his warm breath soothing me. "But I swear to you, I'm not that person anymore. You have me, like no one before. You have me where it counts." Taking my hand, he rests it over his T-shirt, over his heart. "You hold this in the palm of your hand. You are the only woman who has ever had it, and ever will. You own me, Tru."

"You own me too. Completely."

Jake stares down at me, his eyes flicker to my lips, and I feel a sudden heated charge ignite between us. Like the anger of tonight has flared up and turned into raging sexual tension. I don't know who moves first, but suddenly we're kissing, like we've never kissed before.

It's uncoordinated and desperate. No tenderness. This is hard, starved-for-each-other kissing.

Mouths slipping over each other's, Jake's hand takes hold of my neck. Thumb against my throat, he tilts my head back farther, giving him better access. His tongue is plunging deep into my mouth, practically fucking it, and I love it.

I'm all but climbing his body trying to get closer to him. My hands are everywhere.

Jake's mouth moves from mine, down my neck, biting and sucking. I moan and grind myself against his erection, wanting him badly.

His hand moves down, tracing the cup of my bra through the sheer fabric of my top.

I reach my hand lower, cupping him through his jeans. Jake groans and pushes himself into my hand.

I'm just about to open his zipper, when he steps back, breaking contact.

My heart is beating out of my chest and nearly leaps from it when he says, "Lose the clothes, sweetheart, and sit up on the hood."

My eyes are fixed to his. I'm lost in him totally and completely. We are outside, and Jake wants us to have sex on the hood of his car.

Honestly, I can't wait to sit myself up there.

I lose all my inhibitions around Jake. There is nothing I fear doing when I'm with him. Or fearing doing for him.

I pull my top over my head, dropping it on the car, then unzip my skirt at the back, pushing it down over my hips.

I watch Jake watching me, loving the way his eyes devour every naked inch that I reveal to him.

No one has ever looked at me before the way he does. Like I am the only person in the whole world. That having me—being inside me—is the only thing that will ever matter to him.

Stepping out of my skirt, I pick it up and drop it on the car.

I'm about to kick my shoes off, when Jake says in a rough voice, "Keep the heels on."

I step back, letting my ass meet with the car. I sit up on it, hooking my heels into the bumper, the paintwork warm on my skin from the heat of the engine.

Now I'm closer to the car, I can make out the song that has just started to play. "Pour Some Sugar on Me" by Def Leppard.

Jake obviously registers the song too, because the tilt of his head and the inferred smile he gives practically has me wetting my panties.

Holy fuck.

Jake approaches, removing his T-shirt as he does. He tosses it onto the car and moves past me. My eyes follow him as he leans in through the open window.

I hear the music grow louder.

Then Jake is back, coming to stand between my legs, he leans against me, chest on chest, reaching over my shoulder, he grabs for something, and then I feel the silky fabric of my top brush over my skin.

"Do you trust me?" he murmurs.

My body starts to tremble, knowing where he's going with this.

I nod slowly, my eyes captivated by his.

I watch as Jake twists my silk top into a thin strip of fabric. He brings it to rest over my eyes, tying it in a tight knot at the back of my head.

"Lie back," he whispers in my ear.

I do as he says, my whole body quaking with nerves and sexual excitement.

We're out in the open. Dave is at the top of the track, playing guard. I'm blindfolded by my own top, and Jake is about to make love to me on his sexy Aston Martin with "Pour Some Sugar on Me" playing in the background.

Could he be any fucking hotter?

Jake kisses me once on the mouth, and then I feel his body move down mine.

All I can hear is Joe Elliott's rough vocals in my ear. I feel the heavy drum and electric guitar pumping through the metal of the car, vibrating against my skin, and Jake's mouth on me.

He frees my swollen breast from my bra and runs his tongue around my nipple, taking my breast into his mouth.

I groan, feeling it between my legs via the tethered line to my sex. I push my fingers into his thick hair, winding them into it.

Jake repeats the motion with my left breast, while his hand caresses the right. He rubs the peak of my nipple between his thumb and forefinger almost to the point of pain. Pleasure pain.

It feels even better in the dark. Feeling, not seeing. And it's so very fucking hot.

Jake kisses down my stomach, I feel his tongue and hot breath moving over my highly sensitised skin. He dips his tongue into my navel, and then I feel his fingers tracing the line between my panties and skin.

"New ones?" he asks.

"No." I shake my head.

Jake rips them off, and I swear to God I'm sure I feel his teeth against me when he does.

Did he just tear my panties off with his teeth?

Holy fucking hotness!

I honestly don't think I've being as turned on as I am right now.

I'm about ready to jump up, tear his clothes off, and shag him senseless, when I feel Jake's finger touch my sex. My hips jerk in response. Holding me down with one hand spanning my stomach, he moves his finger between my cleft, stroking gently, then up over my throbbing clit.

"So wet," he murmurs.

I so absolutely am. And I'm so absolutely desperate for the feel of his tongue on me that I'm getting ready to beg if he doesn't put it there in the next five seconds.

He removes his finger from me, the loss of momentary contact almost painful.

Then I feel his tongue on me, and lights explode behind my eyelids.

"Ah," I moan in absolute pleasure, relaxing into the feel of his mouth on me.

I feel Jake's finger enter me slowly, as his tongue teases and explores. In goes another finger, stretching me, readying me for his huge cock.

This is going to be over very quickly. It's just so insanely erotic that I can't even find the will to want to hold off.

"Oh God, Jake…I'm gonna…I'm gonna…"

My whole body is trembling. The sensation and rise working higher and higher. Jake's fingers move harder, in and out, his tongue mercilessly taking me over to complete bliss.

My fingernails scratch over the paintwork as I try to find something to cling to. Sweat mists my skin. My body writhes from the torturous pleasure Jake is giving me.

"Come," he commands.

A lick, a stroke, and…

"Fuck, Jake!" I scream his name out as the most mind-blowing orgasm tears through my body, literally lifting me up off the car.

After very long moments of intense, serious pleasure, I drop back down to earth, my limbs gooey, relaxed. The tension of our earlier fight very much forgotten.

I hear the zipper on Jake's pants open.

I love that sound.

Jake moves between my legs, nudging them farther apart with his hips. I can feel the denim of his jeans against my thighs. I love that he hasn't even waited to take them off. He wants me so badly that the longest he can wait is to get it out of his pants.

I feel the head of his cock pressing at my entrance.

He pulls the blindfold off my eyes. Staring down at me with a blazing gaze, teeth gritted, he says, "I'm going in hard, baby. I need to fuck you raw. You ready?"

I know he has barely any control right now, I can see it in the clench of his jaw, the dark of his eyes. The only thing on his mind right now is the fighting need to come, fucking me until he's dry.

"I'm so ready," I breathe.

Jake slams into me.

I cry out at the feel of him filling me, exquisitely stretching me to the extreme like only he can.

"Jesus," he groans, stilling momentarily.

His hands grip my hips, fingers digging into me, and then he starts to move hard and fast, pounding into me over and over.

Grunts and groans emit from Jake, the scent of our unrestrained sex flowing into me with every ragged breath I take, driving me closer to the edge of another orgasm.

Jake drives into me with a deep-seated force, his fingers finding me, spreading me, aiding to drive my second orgasm to the brink.

"You're mine. Say it, Tru."

"I'm yours," I cry out.

"You'll always be mine," he growls. "God, you're just so fuckin' sexy, so hot...I need...I need..."

I know what he needs.

"*Córrete para mí, cariño!*" I say in a commanding tone.

Jake yells out an expletive, and then I feel him pumping his sweet liquid into me.

My own orgasm takes over, my muscles tensing and contracting around his cock.

When Jake is empty of everything he has, he leans over me, still inside me, resting his chest heavily against mine. Our slick skin sticking together, he kisses my lips gently.

"I'm sorry I was a jealous ass tonight," he says against my mouth.

"Were those orgasms part of the apology?"

"Did they work?"

"Oh, absolutely." I smile. "I'm sorry I was jealous too."

"All forgotten, right?"

"Right. I guess we make a good pair. A good jealous pair."

"The best jealous pair ever," he murmurs, squeezing me tight.

After a moment, Jake eases himself out of me, and I sit myself up, hair ruffled and thoroughly fucked.

"So you finally got to do the blindfolding thing." I grin.

"I told you that you were kinky." He smirks at me.

"Me? You were the one fixing me up with it!" I say, throwing his T-shirt at him.

He catches it, laughing, and pulls it on.

As I'm sliding on my own, now severely wrinkled, top, I add, "Saying that, though…I wouldn't say no to you doing it again. Maybe tying me up one time too." I bite my lip.

Jake inhales sharply and his eyes darken like I've never before known.

He picks my skirt up and thrusts it into my hand.

"Get dressed." His tone is urgent.

"What's wrong?" I look around, expecting to see someone coming. Maybe Dave.

"Nothing's wrong. Far from it. Sweetheart, you have just given me the green light to tie you up and fuck you. I've wanted to do that to you for a *very* long time. Now I just want to get you back home to our bed, so I can tie you to it and fuck you senseless, again, before you change your mind."

Hopping off the bonnet, pulling my skirt on, I zip it up at the back and make my way toward the passenger side.

Opening the door, I glance over the car at him. "Don't worry, baby, I won't be changing my mind. I've wanted you to do it to me for a while now too."

"Why the fuck didn't you say so before?" He grins, hopping in the car and firing up the engine.

Jake has us out of there and back home in record time. Before I know it, I'm naked again. My wrists are bound to the bed with one of my silk scarves while Jake makes both our fantasies come true.

JAKE...

CHAPTER EIGHT

"I say we wrap it up for today; I don't think we're getting any more down."

"Yeah," Denny says through a yawn from behind his drum kit, stretching his arms over his head. "My head's mashed now."

"Bunch of pussies, you've got no fucking stamina," Tom pipes up, strumming his bass.

"You done?" I ask Smith.

Smith is the lead guitarist we brought on board as an unofficial replacement for Jonny. Jonny, my best friend and band member, who died in a car accident a year and a half ago.

"Yeah." His eyes flick to the clock. "I need to get home anyway."

"Home to the wifey," Tom says, grinning. "I was gonna suggest we all go out for a beer."

"No can do." Smith unplugs his guitar from the amp and puts it in its stand. "My folks are down from Tennessee for a few days, and we're taking them out for dinner."

Tom shrugs, then turns to me and Denny. "What about you two fuckers? You up for a drink?"

"Sure," I say with a nod. "Just let me call Tru." I pull my cell out of my back pocket.

"Are you calling for permission? You do realize that you are officially more pussy whipped than lover boy over there." He nods in Denny's direction.

"Yeah, but Simone is in London, so he's not hard to beat. And no, I'm not calling for permission, fuck-wad. It's called being in a relationship."

"I never thought I would see the day that Jake Wethers would be bending over for a woman." Tom grins, putting his bass in its case.

"Love, man. It'll get you one day," Smith says.

"Not fuckin' likely!"

"Smith," Denny says, "aside from the fact there is no woman stupid enough to want to settle down with Tom, do you really think we'll ever see the day he'll be satisfied with sticking his dick in one chick for the rest of his life?"

"Point taken." Smith grins in Tom's direction. "I take it back."

"Damn fuckin' right! There's more than enough of the cat to go around. Why deny all of those women the pleasure of Tom? I'm generous to a fault, and I share myself around accordingly. And since the snake took himself off the market, the demand on my cock has doubled. Someone's gotta keep all the chicks happy now that he's a one-woman man." He grabs his crotch, grinning.

I let out a laugh. "You're more than welcome to them, man."

Tom pauses and looks at me like I'm some fucking puzzle he can't work out. "Seriously, dude. Tru must be an awesome lay to keep your interest for this long. That or the rack. It's the rack, isn't it? It's gotta be the rack." He puts his hands to his chest, sizing out a pair of tits. "I've never seen a pair that big that are actually real. They would seriously keep my attention for a long time. Not as long as you, but fuck...do you just sit and stare at them all day? I seriously would."

"You're obsessed with tits!" Denny laughs, tapping his drum with the stick.

"I appreciate great tits, and Tru has great tits. I'm also enjoying winding up pussy fucker over there."

I'm taking it he's referring to the scowl on my face. I give him a look and reach over to switch off the amps. "Keep talking about my girl's rack like that, and you'll need an expensive fuckin' dental surgeon after I've knocked all your teeth out."

The motherfucker winds me up to no end when he talks about Tru like that. He's right—she has got great tits—but I don't want him going on about them. He is the only one I would let get away with comments like that for this long. I'd have knocked anyone else out by now.

"Don't get your panties all in a twist, I'm just yanking your chain." Tom pats me on the shoulder. "Den, you up for that beer?"

"Got nothing better to do." He climbs out from behind his kit.

"I'm out of here. Catch you fuckers later," Smith says, heading for the door. "Oh, Jake," he adds, turning back, "my old lady asked if you and Tru want to go out for dinner after my folks leave on Friday."

"Sounds good. I'll check with Tru and let you know."

"Cool, I'm outta here. Catch you all tomorrow."

I'm real glad Smith's wife suggested a night out. I know Tru is missing Simone, and I know she'd never say it, but she's lonely for female company. I think she'd get on real well with Carly; she's a cool chick.

"I'm gonna call Tru. I'll meet you two idiots in the car in a few."

I head out of the studio, walking toward my office, calling Tru as I go.

"Hey, baby," she coos down the phone.

God, she sounds so fucking sexy. I love her voice. Especially when it's screaming out my name while I'm inside her.

"Hey, beautiful. Before I forget, Smith's wife invited us out for dinner on Friday. You up for that?"

"Sounds like fun. I'm in. So when are you coming home?" She turns the sexy voice on, and I feel it all the way down to my cock. "I bought this tub of cookies-and-cream ice cream earlier, and I was thinking when you get home, we can take it to bed, and you could maybe…eat it off me. You can blindfold me again too, if you want."

If I want. Is she serious? Right now, I want nothing more.

I groan in my pants. Walking into my office, I close the door behind me and readjust my cock. "Fuck, baby, you've made me hard."

"That was kinda the point." I can practically hear her salacious smile.

"Good job I'm alone, then."

"That as well," she says, giggling. "So how long will you be?"

Staring down at my hard-on, I'm torn between that and going out with the boys. I blow out a breath, letting my head fall back against the door, knowing Tom will never let me live it down if I blow them off to go home to my girl. "That's why I was calling. I just said I'd go out with the boys for a beer."

"Oh."

I hear her disappointed tone loud and clear. It cuts me.

"If I don't go, I'll never hear the end of it from Tom," I explain.

"It's okay, baby, I understand. You should go out with the boys. I take up too much of your time as it is. I'm just disappointed I have to wait a little longer to see you is all."

"I want you to take up all my time."

I hear her breathing down the line. "Me too. Now go have fun with the guys. I'll be here waiting for when you get back."

"With the tub of ice cream?"

"Most definitely."

I smile. "What will you do while I'm out?" I hate to think of her there, all alone.

"I might call Stuart, see if he's free to watch a movie."

"Call? He lives a fucking stone's throw from us, lazy-ass." She giggles. I fucking love that sound.

"I'm lazy and proud of it! What can I say?"

"Say you love me."

"I love you," she breathes. And I feel it everywhere, almost like her pretty little hands are running all over me right now.

"Love you more."

"Not possible."

"No?" I smile. "I'll show you later exactly how much I love you."

A bang on the door frightens the shit out of me, and then Tom's loud voice booms. "Come on, motherfucker!

Stop whispering sweet nothings to Tru and get your tardy ass out here and in the car. I'm fuckin' dying for a drink!"

Shaking my head, laughing, I say, "Gotta go, baby, the boys are waiting. I'll see you later."

I hang up with Tru, and when I get to the car, Tom and Denny are in the back waiting.

"Where to?" Dave asks, pulling out of the parking space.

I look over my shoulder at Tom and Denny.

"Déjà-fuckin'-vu!" Tom grins.

"No fuckin' way, man! I'm not going to a strip joint. If Tru finds out, she'll kick my ass."

Tom rolls his eyes. "Okay, Crazy Girls."

"I said no strip joints."

"It's not a strip joint. It's a respectable establishment."

"It's a bikini bar."

"Exactly. Tits and ass all covered. Tru can't get pissed about that."

"No way." I shake my head.

"Stop being such a pussy!" Tom exclaims. "You do still have a dick in there, don't you?" He nods in the direction of my pants.

"I'm with Jake on this one, man," Denny chips in. "No strip joints or bikini bars," he adds just as Tom opens his mouth to start up again. "Let's just go to a normal club."

"For fuck's sake! You're a right pair of boring bastards! I expect this shit from him"—he jerks his head in Denny's direction—"but you, man," he says to me, "I'm disappointed, and also a little gutted. I've well and truly lost my wingman. I might as well be on fuckin' date night with Stuart, being with you two. Next thing you'll say is let's go to a gay bar because there're no women there."

"There're usually more women in gay bars than normal bars," Denny adds.

Tom's eyes light up.

"No fuckin' way!" I cut him off before he can speak. "We are not going to a gay bar."

Turning to Dave, I say, "Take us to Graphics."

* * *

Dave pulls up outside Graphics and climbs out with us, giving the valet the keys to the car.

Graphics is a celeb haunt that used to be a favourite of ours. Especially Jonny. I have a lot of memories of this place.

Good and bad.

"Mr. Wethers, it's been a while, good to see you again," the host says as we approach the door. "You should have called ahead and we'd have secured your booth for you."

"It was a last-minute thing."

"Let me see what I can do for you." He starts speaking quickly into his headset.

I hate this shit. It used to be cool when these idiots wanted to pander to me, but it got old, real fast. Now I wish I could hit a club without having to announce my arrival first, so that it doesn't become some major fucking issue if I don't.

"Look, don't sweat it," I say, when I see him talking into the headset. "Just sit us anywhere. The boys and me just wanna have a quiet drink."

He looks at me, unsure, then nods. "Okay, we have a table ready for you now, please follow me."

We follow him through the club to the VIP section.

I nod to a few people I know as I pass through.

I slide into the booth, and the waitress is at our table a second later.

She's all tits and ass. The outfits here leave little to the imagination. I forgot that.

I used to like this shit. Used to love seeing women wearing as little clothing as possible.

Now with Tru, I get just as turned on seeing her in a pair of jeans and T-shirt as I do those sexy miniskirts she wears.

She always looks hot to me.

I order a round of beers for us and settle back in my seat.

Tapping my fingers on the table, wishing I'd had a smoke before I came in here, I see Jase Collins heading toward our table.

Jase Collins. Small-timer in the music industry. Big-timer in the drug scene. And once upon a time, one of my regular dealers.

Fuck.

"Been a while," he says, leaning up against our table.

"Not long enough," I reply dryly.

He laughs.

Does he think I'm joking or something? Fucking idiot.

"Tom, Den." He nods at them.

The best they offer back is a couple of grunts in his direction.

I have to suppress a smile. To say they don't like him is putting it mildly. He's a cocky little fucker who once served his purpose of scoring the best coke around for me.

Not anymore.

Right now, I want this fucker as far away from me as possible. Just knowing what he'll have in his pocket is scratching at my skin like sharp fucking needles.

I flick a glance in Dave's direction. He's at the bar, watching Jase like a hawk.

Meeting my eyes, Dave gives me a silent nod. If I need to get rid of him quick, Dave will see to it for me.

The waitress reappears with our beers. Stepping around Jase, she puts our drinks down for us.

"Thanks," I say. I return my focus to Jase. "What can I do for you, Jase?" I ask, getting straight to the point. No sense beating around the bush, wasting my time on a piece of shit like him.

"Heard you're getting married. Wanted to offer my congratulations."

"Received, and thanks."

He stares at me for a long moment, then, resting his hand on the back of the seat, leans over and says in my ear, "The boss is missing your business. I got some real good shit on me tonight that has your name written all over it."

I push him away from me with a firm shove to his shoulder. "Not interested."

"You sure about that?" He smiles. It's a cocky smile. One that I want to wipe off his face.

"Never been more so. Now will you fuck off? I'm trying to have a night out with my buddies." I pick my beer up, tipping my head back. I drink it, but I don't move my eyes from his.

"I saw a picture of your girl in the papers. Trudy Bennett, right? A real English beauty you got yourself there, Jake. I hear she's living over here now."

Slamming my beer down on the table, I stand up, the force shoving the table forward into Jase. Tom and Den are on their feet in an instant.

I see Dave moving toward us, but I put my hand out, telling him I got this.

"Don't talk about her, motherfucker. Your mouth is nowhere near clean enough to speak my girl's name."

"I meant no disrespect," he says with a smirk, and steps back. "Just letting you know I think your girl is pretty. Real pretty."

"I know exactly what you're doing, motherfucker. And I think you've forgotten who you're talking to." I round the table, squaring up to him. "You know what I'm capable of, so don't fuck with me," I hiss in his face. "Forget you ever heard my girl's name, let alone saw her face. You fuckin' read me?"

"Loud and clear." He lifts his hands, backing off. "Like I said, I meant no disrespect, Jake. Enjoy your night."

I watch him go, blending back into the crowd. My body is thrumming with absolute fucking anger.

"You all right, man?" Denny asks as I sit back down.

I shake my head, taking a pull on my beer.

I'm smarting. Jase fucking Collins, laying a threat near my girl. Fucking bastard. I'll take his head off.

Tru. She's at home alone.

I motion Dave over.

"Send Ben over to the house to watch Tru," I say quietly to him.

"He threaten her?"

"No, just being a clever bastard. But I don't take any chances where she's concerned."

"I'll call Ben now, and I'll call the house security to tell them to turn it up a notch."

Taking my phone out, I'm ready to call her, but then I decide against it. I don't want to frighten her.

"Let me know when Ben's at the house," I say to Dave before he walks off to make the call.

"Was that fuck-wad laying a threat near Tru?" Tom asks me.

"No, just being a cocky fucker." Even as I say the words, I still feel twitchy as hell. I know his threat was empty, but it still makes me anxious.

"I hate that little shit. You should have kicked his ass years ago, man. Hell, you should kick his ass now."

"He fuckin' mentions Tru one more time and I will. Motherfucker," I utter, taking another swig of my beer.

The downside of being an ex-user is knowing scum of the earth like Jase Collins.

I'm real glad Den and Tom never got mixed up in that shit. Even with the life we lead, and the people we're around, they've managed to never touch drugs. They had the odd joint in college, sure, but they've never dabbled in the harder stuff. It's especially amazing considering how much Jonny and I used to hit it.

I'm glad for it. I got too fucked up on the stuff. I never want that for either of them.

They tried to intervene when I was at my low point, but back then I didn't want anyone's help except from the likes of scum like Jase Collins, who could provide me with exactly what I needed.

I never ever want to go back there.

I'm lucky Tom and Den stuck with me. Even more lucky that I have Tru back in my life.

Draining my beer and needing the buzz of more alcohol, I call the waitress over.

It's a different waitress, I notice. Tits even bigger than the last one's, and they're about as fake as her blonde hair. I get a pretty close look as she leans over our table to clear the first round, practically sticking them in my face.

Ignoring her as best I can, I avert my eyes and say, "Bottle of Jack, and another round of beers."

"I'll be right back with your order, boys," she says in a Southern drawl.

Leaning back, hands pressed flat on the table, coming to my eye level, she gives me a "fuck me now" stare, pressing her red lips together. Then turning, making sure I get a good view of her ass, she slowly walks away.

"Now you're fuckin' talking with the Jack, man!" Tom bangs his fist on the table, getting my attention. "You up for getting hammered?"

"Abso-fucking-lutely." I'm still feeling wired and twitchy after Jase Collins's visit, and I need something to take the edge off.

There are only three things that can take the edge off for me—alcohol, cigarettes, and sex. Considering I currently can't do two of them, I'm hitting the one I can do, hard.

The waitress returns and puts our drinks down on the table.

I let out a laugh at Tom, who's staring down her top—if it can be called a top. It's more like a piece of fabric covering her nipples.

He just shrugs and grins at me.

Before leaving she tucks her tray under her arm and runs her fingernails down my biceps in an intimate way.

It pisses me off. I give her a less-than-amused look.

She smiles, apparently not reading my look correctly, then blatantly focuses her stare on my cock, licking her lips, before leaving.

"I fuckin' love the outfits here," Tom says, watching her as she walks away. "And the girls in them."

"Outfits?" Denny laughs, gesturing at the belts as skirts and the half-cut tanks. "What fuckin' outfits?"

"Exactly." Tom grins.

I used to think like Tom. It was one of the many reasons I would come here. The waitresses are always half-dressed, and most of them are as easy as fuck.

They're no different than groupies. They all want on a celeb's cock in the hope it will lead to more for them. Get them out of those tanks and into designer threads, walking the red carpet.

The reality is less than that. Much less. Most of the guys who come here usually have a girl at home and are looking for an uncomplicated fuck on the side. No strings attached.

It was the same for me, except I had no girl at home waiting for me back then.

If I wanted to get laid and high when I was in LA, Graphics was the best place to come.

Honestly, I don't know what made me suggest coming here tonight.

"She's after getting on your cock." Tom nods in the direction of the blonde waitress who currently has her eyes pinned on our table. More specifically, pinned on me.

Picking my fresh beer up, I say, "She can want on it all she likes. Fact is, it's not happening."

"No?" Tom raises his eyebrow.

"No."

"Gotta say, man, you're being real faithful to Tru. I couldn't do it."

"That's because you haven't got her."

When Tru first came back into my life, it wasn't that I stopped wanting other women for fear of losing her. The simple fact is I stopped wanting anyone else full stop. I'm not interested in anyone but her. It was weird to me for a long time, but now it makes absolute sense.

She is all I want.

No one gets me like she does. And I love her like I never knew possible.

Sex became about love for me the first night Tru gave herself to me in that hotel room in Copenhagen. I don't ever want to go back from that.

Don't get me wrong, I'm still a guy. I know a hot piece of ass when I see it. The difference is, now I don't want to tap it.

All I want to do tonight is have some drinks with the guys, then go home to Tru, climb in bed with her, wrap my arms tight around her, and kiss her until I can't breathe.

That, and lick ice cream off that hot fucking body of hers.

Of course, I'd never say any of this shit out loud. Tom would have my balls checked for me if I did.

Dave comes over to me. "All's good. Ben's at the house. Stuart's there with her watching a movie. She's fine. No need to worry."

I feel myself relax. I was considering blowing the night off real soon, but she'd know something was wrong if I did. She's as sharp as a tack. And to be honest, I just need to be out with the guys for a while.

I get my phone out and type a quick text to her while those two talk shit.

Can't wait to see you later, beautiful. Keep that ice cream on chill ready for me. x

It beeps back a few seconds later:

That's not all I'm keeping ready for you ;)

Fuck me. I tap out a response, smiling to myself:

You're making me hard again.

Another text back:

Keep that ready for me and I'll see to it later. x

I cast a quick glance at the guys, then reply:

I fuckin love you, hard. x

She responds seconds later:

Love you too, baby. x

"Stop texting Tru, or I'm gonna throw your fuckin' cell out of the window," Tom jokes.

"Okay." I shove it back in my pocket.

"What's Tru doing tonight?" Denny asks.

"Watching a movie at home with Stuart. She's missing Simone and their nights out."

"Simone was saying the other day how much she misses Tru. She's trying to book a few weeks off work in a month or so to come for a visit. Don't tell Tru, though. She wants to surprise her."

"Won't say a word." I take another pull on my beer and realize it's nearly empty. Fuck, these are going down easy.

I line up the glasses the waitress brought with the Jack and pour out three whiskeys.

As I'm pushing the glasses across the table, Tom says, "Been a while since we've all been out together like this."

He sounds so fucking nostalgic. I feel the instant hit of the empty seat in this booth.

Jonny.

"Yeah, it has been a while. Too long." I stare down into my glass. "You remember how we used to be out every night when Jonny was still here?" I say, lifting my head.

Surprising myself as I say it, I realise saying his name doesn't hurt as much as it used to. There was one point where I couldn't even finish a sentence if his name was in it.

"Yeah." Tom laughs lightly. "Jonny wouldn't give us a fuckin' reprieve back then. He had us out every night, tapping ass and drinking hard liquor. That's why we can all hold our drink so well now. Taught by the best."

"You still can't hold your liquor." Denny laughs at him.

"Fuck you! I could drink you under the table any night of the fuckin' week!"

"Bring it on," Denny challenges.

"You are so fuckin' on." Tom waves the blonde waitress over.

Here we go.

"Can we have three Flaming Sambucas, sugar, and a line of tequilas, and keep 'em coming 'til I say stop," Tom orders.

"Sure thing, darlin'. Anything else I can get you?" She turns to me, leans over, puts her hand on my shoulder, and says into my ear, "Maybe me, *again?*"

Again? Shit, have I fucked her before?

I give her face a quick glance. No recollection whatsoever.

I don't know whether to be relieved or shit scared at that realization.

Truth is, I don't think I would recognize near to half of the women I've screwed.

To remember I would've had to have cared, and I never cared.

One in, one out. Those girls were just nameless faces.

Until Tru.

She changed everything. She changed me.

"Sorry," I say, ducking my shoulder out from under her hand. "If it's a quick fuck you're looking for, I'm not your guy. I'm getting married."

"So I heard." She runs her tongue over her lower lip, then tugs her lip between her teeth. "But you're not married yet, Jake, so technically you're still single, and I'm more than willing to get you off real good without a word to your girl. Right now, I want you to come with me on my break, and I'll put my mouth to real good use. A little reminder of what I can do." Moving closer again, she whispers in my ear, "I'll blow you so good, honey, you won't ever want me to stop."

Nothing. Not even a twitch in my dick.

Before Tru, I wouldn't have hesitated. I'd have pushed her under the table and gotten her to blow me right here.

Right now all I want to do is laugh.

Struggling not to be a bastard and hurt this chick's feelings, even though I'm really tempted to tell her she can't have been that fucking memorable the first time around, I laugh and say, "I'm far from single, honey. My girl gets me off just fine. More than fine, she's fuckin' amazing. You're not a patch on her—no offense. You wanna get laid, you're gonna have to look elsewhere. Like I said before, I'm not your guy."

Her gaze practically burns a hole in me.

Okay, so maybe I wasn't as kind as I could have been.

"Hey, sugar, if you're up for a fuck, I'll happily step in where he's lacking," Tom says, catching her attention.

She pulls herself away from me and focuses in on Tom.

I nearly breathe a sigh of relief to have her and her cheap perfume out of my face.

"Bound and chained Jake is, but I'm as free as a bird," Tom says.

"Tom Carter, right?" she says, straightening up, pushing her chest out.

"The one and only."

"I've heard great things about you." She shifts her gaze downward on him. "A few of the girls have been to your place, right?"

"Right." He grins.

"I'm taking my break now." She tilts her head for him to follow her.

"Boys, I'll be back in half an hour."

Tom gets up and grabs the waitress by the hand. I watch him lead her off through the crowd.

I shake my head, laughing.

"Skank," as Tru would say.

At least Tom's getting his rocks off for a few. I'd say he has no shame, but then, there was a time I would have done exactly the same. And really, I should thank him for taking her heat-seeking-missile gaze from me and focusing it straight onto him.

"Ah shit, Tom's just fucked off to the bathroom with our easy access to shots," Denny complains.

"We've got the Jack," I say, picking it up. I pour Denny another, then myself.

"So you off to London in a few days?"

"Yeah, and I can't fuckin' wait." Denny leans back against the seat, resting his head on the top as he takes a drink. "Feels like it's been fuckin' ages since I last saw Simone. Well, it has been fuckin' ages," he adds.

"I don't know how you do it, man. I couldn't be away from Tru like you are with Simone. Just a night away from her does my head in."

I can talk to Denny like this and know he won't bust my nuts because he knows where I'm coming from. Tom, on the other hand, will never understand.

"It's hard fuckin' going," he says. "But it's just the way things have to be at the moment. Her work's there and mine is here."

"Couldn't she get a transfer out here?"

"Nah." He shakes his head. "Her company doesn't have an office out here. It would mean her having to get a new job, and I know how much she loves working at that place."

"You want her to move out here, though?"

He takes another long drink, then, leaning forward, puts it on the table. He cups the glass in his hands, swirling it around.

"Yeah, I do."

"So tell her." I pour more whiskey into my glass and gesture to Denny.

He moves his hands, allowing me to pour it in.

"I told Tru how I felt, asked her to move in with me, and she did. You've got nothing to lose by asking Simone."

"I guess." He shrugs. "I'll talk to her about it when I see her." He throws his drink back in one. "Fuck this, I'm getting hammered." He gestures for a waitress and puts in another order of shots for us. "Hey, what happened at that club the other night? Zane said you knocked some dude on his ass."

"Some dickhead who Tru knew from London had his hands all over her, so I knocked him on his ass. Wish I'd done a lot more, to be honest."

Like broken his fucking nose. Motherfucker filed an assault charge just like I knew he would. Then I got served from his lawyer.

I just gave my lawyer the nod to pay him off. I can do without the hassle of little fuck-wads like him. Honestly, to keep his hands off Tru, it's worth every cent.

"Sounds like he deserved it," Denny muses.

"Too fuckin' right he did."

Denny and I have just knocked back our first round of tequila shots when Tom reappears at our table.

"Dude, that was quick," I say as he lands back in his seat. "Fifteen minutes—must be a fuckin' record for you."

"It was long enough. Just a quick blow job; then I banged her, and I was more than ready to come by that point. Not the best blow job ever, or fuck, for that matter. She's been rode too many times, so I just visualised fucking Maxine Halliday and I was coming in no time."

"Maxine Halliday from college?" I ask, grinning.

She was hot as fuck, and one girl I never nailed. That was only because Tom was fucking her. We didn't share back then.

Not that I share now. No one touches my girl but me.

"The very one. Man, you remember her? She was hot as sin. I screwed her all over campus. I even fingered her during a lecture once, had her coming all over my hand."

"Thanks for the visuals," Denny says.

"You're very welcome." Tom pats him on the shoulder. "And go easy on me. I was taking one for the team, banging that waitress. She wasn't gonna let up on Jake, so I diverted her attention from his cock to mine. And you can thank me now." Tom looks in my direction. "I call it a bottle of the most expensive champagne they have here, and I'm being generous at that."

"You want me to buy you an expensive bottle of champagne for fucking some cheap waitress in the bathroom?"

"Absolutely," he says, grinning.

I shake my head, laughing. I've known this guy nearly ten years, and even now, he still never ceases to surprise me.

"I don't know how you do it," Denny says.

"Den, has it been that long since your dick saw action that you've forgotten how to use it?" Tom takes a slug of his whiskey. "Do I have to get that waitress I just banged over here to teach you the basics?"

"You do remember I have a girlfriend? Anyway, you just said that waitress wasn't even that great. What the hell's she gonna teach me?"

"Ah, she wasn't bad. I've had worse. And dude, you're in a long-distance relationship. Your dick needs daily action, and not just from your hand. Let me get that chick..." Denny stops Tom's waving hand, the one trying to get the waitress's attention.

"Seriously, man, sloppy seconds are not my thing." Denny shakes his head, grinning at him. "And I'm pretty sure she's had her fill from you."

"She did. Best fuck of her life." He gives a self-satisfied grin. "Even if it was just mediocre for me."

"She had the time of her life in fifteen minutes?" I raise my eyebrow, picking up my tequila.

"Yep. My dick has magical powers."

"Maybe you should get 'Rub the Lamp' tattooed above your dick." Denny grins, throwing back his second shot.

Tom's face lights up.

I've seen that look before. The last time Tom looked like that, I ended up in bed with three strippers.

"I was kidding!" Denny raises a protesting hand.

"That's probably the best idea you've had since you suggested I get my tongue pierced."

"I was kidding then as well!"

"No, that was a fuckin' brilliant idea, Den! The women love it, especially when I'm giving them head. Right, I'm definitely on for this tattoo. Come on, we'll blow this place, find a tattoo joint, get inked, and then hit another club."

Tom picks up his two sitting tequila shots and downs them, slamming the glasses on the table.

I throw mine back.

"I'm not getting another tattoo done," Denny says, getting to his feet.

"Come on, man," I say, throwing my arm around his shoulder. "I'm up for getting one done."

"You're getting another?"

"Yep."

And I know just exactly what I'm having done.

Standing, I throw a couple of hundreds down on the table to cover the bill and tip, gesturing for Dave to let him know we're leaving. I pick up the bottle of Jack to take with us.

We load into the car. "Where to?" Dave asks me.

"Shamrock's."

"We're getting inked," Tom says from the back. "I'm getting 'Rub the Lamp' above my cock."

Dave gives me a raised eyebrow.

"Don't ask," I say, shaking my head, laughing.

"Wasn't gonna." Dave pulls out into traffic, heading for Sunset Boulevard.

* * *

"Ah fuck! My jeans keep rubbing against it. It's hurting like a motherfucker!"

"You should learn to wear underwear, then, fuck-face," Denny replies. Tom is in the backseat, rearranging his pants around his new tattoo.

"No fuckin' way! I'm not caging the beast up. I might take my jeans off." He reaches to undo them.

"Don't you fuckin' dare!" Denny yells. "I'm not sitting back here with you bare-assed!"

"But I'm in pain," Tom moans.

"Tough. You are not getting your cock out while you're back here with me."

"Stop being ridiculous. It's not like I'm gonna try and fuck you. Not unless you ask nicely." He laughs.

"Can we swap seats?" Den asks me.

"No fucking way! He's all yours. I still can't believe you got that tattooed above your dick," I say to Tom. "You're officially a fuckin' idiot, you know that?"

"Nah, the women will love it!" He grins. "Anyway, soft cock, why won't you let us see your tattoo?"

"Because it's not meant for your eyes, fuck-wad."

"Ah fuck! You didn't get 'Tru's bitch' tattooed on yourself, did ya?"

Denny snorts.

"No, I fuckin' didn't." Even I can hear the defensiveness in my tone.

"You so fuckin' did!" Tom says, leaning forward. "You got yourself branded with your chick's name."

"Did you really?" Denny says, joining him.

"Might have," I say with a shrug.

"There is officially no fuckin' hope for you." Tom sighs, falling back against his seat, opening his pants to reveal the gauze covering his tattoo. He takes a drink of the last remaining Jack from the bottle. We drank most of it in the shop. "You are officially turning into a woman. Next thing I'll hear, you'll be baking."

"Fuck off! Just 'cause I got my girl's name tattooed on me, doesn't mean I'm whipped. I just kinda love her."

I'm officially hammered if I'm admitting shit like this to Tom.

"Oh God. Hold my hair back, Den, while I hurl." Tom sticks his fingers in his mouth and rubs his shaved head with his other hand.

Even I can't not laugh.

"Cut him some slack. We all have to grow up one day and fall in love, Tom."

"Not me. I'll be riding a different pussy every night of the week 'til the day I die."

"One of them will catch you soon, man, and then you won't know what fuckin' hit you," Denny says.

He's right about that. Except Tru caught me a long time ago. I just wasted too much time screwing around before I tried to get her back.

"Where to now?" Tom asks.

"Home."

"Fuck, that! It's still early, and I need more alcohol to numb the pain of my tattoo and the fact that both my boys are whipped good and proper."

Looking at Dave, I say, "Take us to the next decent bar you see."

* * *

I let myself in, trying to be quiet so as not to wake Tru. The house is in complete darkness.

Staggering around, I make for our bedroom, pulling my T-shirt off as I do, careful of my new tattoo. Tossing the shirt aside, I stumble into our bedroom, trying hard not to make a sound. When I see my girl asleep in bed, she stops me in my tracks.

She's wearing a satin nightgown, the pale pink one that I like with the lace on the hem. She's got the sheets kicked back, and the nightgown has ridden up her thighs.

She's so fucking beautiful. And she looks so very fucking sexy.

Her hair is all mussed up, spread across the pillow. Inch upon inch of her soft olive skin on show, just waiting for me.

My dick instantly hardens.

I need to taste her. Be inside her. I hate to wake her, but not enough that I'm not going to. I've got a raging hard-on the size of Texas, and it's going nowhere until my girl has seen to it.

She loves midnight sex, and she has been really horny lately. Even more so than normal. Not that I'm complaining. When Tru is eager for the snake, you'll hear no complaints from me.

Shucking out of my jeans and boxers, I kick them aside and climb up the foot of the bed.

Starting at her ankle, I run my hand up her smooth skin and keep going until I reach her thigh.

Stirring, she groans and rolls onto her back. "Hey, baby," she says, sounding sleepy.

My dick gets even harder at the sound of her voice.

She fucking owns me, completely.

"Hey," I reply, kissing her shoulder, grazing my teeth over her skin, my hand still moving higher.

"You have a good night?" she murmurs, but I can hear the sex in her voice. She's so fucking responsive, and always so ready for me.

"Hmm," I reply.

My fingers find her pussy, wet and waiting. No panties. God, she is so fucking hot.

"And it just got a whole lot better," I whisper in her ear.

She sucks in a breath when my finger rubs over her clit.

I push a finger inside her while I keep working on her swollen bud.

She's so tight. The way she clenches around my finger, I know she's desperate to be fucked by me. About as desperate as I am to fuck her.

"I missed you," she whispers, her hand reaching for my cock.

"Shit." I wince when her fingers graze over my stomach, catching the gauze.

"What's that?" she asks, sounding worried. Sitting up, she turns the bedside lamp on.

Her eyes hit my stomach. "What the hell happened?" Her eyes are wide. "Did you get into a fight? Jesus Christ, Jake." She leans in closer to look at it, her fingers reaching, wanting to touch.

"No, baby, it's nothing like that. Don't worry."

Fuck, I feel really nervous now. What if she thinks I'm a dumb fuck for getting it done?

Raising her eyebrow, she says, "You have gauze covering your stomach and you're telling me not to worry?"

"I got a tattoo." I smile awkwardly.

"You did?" She looks confused. "You never said you were thinking of getting another one done."

I shrug. "I've been thinking about it for a while as a surprise for you. Getting it done tonight was more of a spur-of-the-moment thing."

"You got a tattoo, drunk?" She raises her eyebrows.

God, she looks so fucking sexy right now. Hair all tousled, falling over her shoulders. The strap on her nightgown hangs low, her tits nearly falling out of it, practically begging me to release and suck on them.

I'm just about to throw her down and screw her senseless, tattoo forgotten, when she says, "Can I see it?"

I hesitate.

She glances up at me.

"Are you blushing, Jake Wethers?" She touches my cheek with her fingers.

"No," I say, defensive.

I so totally fucking am. My face is as red as a fucking beet. Jesus Christ! What does she do to me?

"Why don't you want to show me it?" she asks softly.

"I do. I just…look, I know I should have probably spoken to you about it before, but it just seemed like a good idea at the time."

"Jake?"

"Yeah?"

"Will you stop talking and just show me the bloody tattoo? I'm all intrigued now."

Sucking in a breath, I take the corner of the gauze and lift it. I peel it back, revealing the tattoo.

I hear her sharp intake of breath, and I risk a glance at her face.

Her hand is covering her mouth, her eyes wide, as she lets out a small laugh. "You had my name tattooed on you?"

"Kinda," I say, scrunching my face, looking down at it.

Tru Love

It's across my stomach in arched script. God, I'm such a lame fucker.

"You hate it. It's lame, I know."

"No." She cups her hands around my face. "I love it. I love you. Jake Wethers, you are the sweetest man I've ever known."

"I don't want to be sweet," I groan. "I want to be hard and hot."

"Oh, you're definitely those too."

She kisses me, gentle at first, and then her kisses deepen. I part my lips, and her sexy little tongue slips into my mouth.

I grab a handful of her hair, holding her to me, and meet her tongue with mine, stroking it.

"Can you still...fool around?" she says into my mouth.

"Sweetheart." I grab her ass, hard. "It'll take more than a tattoo to stop me from getting inside you. Death, maybe."

She giggles in my mouth, which pulses all the way down to my dick, and it throbs in response.

"I suppose I should go on top. Can't have you in pain, can I?"

I stare down at her. She's biting those sexy plump lips of hers, and I have the urge to bite them myself—and a whole lot more. Then she pushes me down on the bed and straddles my hips.

I feel her wet pussy against my dick, and it feels so fucking good. She shifts, and starts to move up and down against it, creating friction, rubbing her sweet self all over me.

"Jesus Christ," I groan. "You are so fuckin' sexy. You keep doing that and I'm gonna shoot my load any second."

"Can't have that," she says, slowing. "You want me to get that ice cream?"

"Later, baby." *I'm practically salivating.* "Right now I just need to be inside you."

Smiling that sexy smile of hers, she rises up on her knees. Taking hold of my dick, she positions it at the head of her entrance.

She slides down onto me with a gentle moan, and I swear to God, I enter a state of nirvana for a moment.

I've never felt anything like her before. I'll never get used to how fucking amazing she feels around me. She was made to fit me.

I stare up at her, watching as she pulls her nightgown off over her head, her long hair loose down her body, looking so fucking incredibly beautiful, and I wonder how the fuck I got so lucky.

She's the girl of my dreams, and more.

Glancing down, she looks at my tattoo and grins. "Tru love, eh?"

"Damn fucking right," I growl. "Now love my cock, will you, sweetheart, before I die a death here?"

Grinning, she rises up on her knees, then slowly slides back down my length.

"You know I like to play slow, but right now, I need you to ride me good and hard, because you look way too fuckin' hot up there to hold out."

She looks for somewhere to rest her hands for support, so I offer her my hands.

Lacing our fingers together, my girl starts to move up and down, riding my cock fast, and I'm so close to coming it's ridiculous, but I need to get her off first.

Freeing a hand from hers, she drops it down onto my chest and keeps going.

Putting two fingers together, I offer them to her mouth. She puts her pretty little mouth around them, sucking them, and then I move them to her clit and start working her up more.

She must be as turned on as I am, because it's less than a minute later when I feel her start to tighten around my dick. Then she's crying out in a string of Spanish, and I'm a fucking goner.

I come inside her, hot and hard, spurting everything I have, while she tightens around my dick, squeezing it.

When she's done, she falls forward, head on my chest, but keeps her back arched up, keeping her stomach from touching my tattoo.

After a moment, she moves off me, and my dick slips out, falling heavy against my stomach.

Fuck, I needed her.

Tru reaches over and turns the lamp off, and then snuggles up to my side.

I put my arms around her, pulling her closer. I stroke her back.

Pressing a kiss to my chest, she says, "I can't believe you had 'Tru Love' tattooed on your stomach."

"Could be worse," I say. "Tom got 'Rub the Lamp' tattooed just above his dick."

She sputters out a laugh, tilting her head to look up at me. "You're kidding?"

"Nope. I just wish I was there tomorrow morning to see his reaction when he wakes up and sees it sober."

"What about Denny? What did he get?"

"He wimped out."

"So how come you got a sensible one done?"

"Because unlike Tom, I can handle my drink, baby."

She rests her head back down on my shoulder, fingers tracing close to the tattoo, and whispers, "I love it, Jake."

"I love you, baby."

More than you'll ever fucking know.

TRU...

CHAPTER NINE

Tea or coffee?" I yell to Jake as he showers.

"Coffee," he calls back.

I climb out of bed, giving morning LA a quick glance through the windows. Another beautiful day. Along with the shopping, I've discovered an additional perk to living in LA—the sun is pretty much always shining, even in November.

I head into the kitchen, scoop some coffee into the coffeemaker, fill it with water, and turn it on.

I grab a chocolate biscuit out of the jar and lean against the counter, nibbling it while I wait for the coffee.

I see the pile of pizza boxes on the counter near the sink that I had asked Jake to take out to the bin after the guys left last night. He's such a lazy bum.

We had Tom, Denny, and Stuart over for dinner. Well, saying we had dinner may be glamming it up a bit.

We ordered pizza and ate in the living room while the guys watched football. As expected, I was ignored for the TV, and I ended up bringing my laptop through and sitting at the table, Skyping with Simone, until Denny butted in.

He's flying to London to see her. I wish I were going. I've been thinking of asking Jake when he can next take some time off work so I can visit my folks and London and see Vicky and Simone. I know things are busy for him at the moment. He's spending a lot of time in the studio record-ing new stuff, which is great.

This is their first time recording an album without Jonny.

Jake seems to be doing okay with it. If he's not, then he's hiding it really well.

I pick up the boxes and take them through the utility and out the side door.

The warm California air embraces me.

I might bring my laptop outside and work on the patio today. My column is due in three days, and I haven't come up with anything yet. Last-minute, that's me.

I finish breaking the boxes down and push them in the bin, then head back inside.

The coffee is just finishing when I get back. I get two cups out of the cupboard and reach for the milk in the fridge.

Realising I haven't bought any recently, I check the date on it: 3 November.

I check the calendar pinned to the wall: 2 November. *Still good for today.*

I unscrew the cap and I'm just about to pour the milk, when it dawns on me.

Setting the milk down, I step back and look at the cal-endar again.

Today is the second. Next to the second, marked on the third, is "start pill." That's my reminder to start my contra-ceptive pill after my break.

The break in which I have my period.

The period that hasn't started.

I step back from the calendar.

Fuck.

My chest starts to tighten. My head starts to buzz.

No, it'll be fine. I've just been under a lot of pressure lately, feeling stressed with one thing and another. That's what it is. That's why I haven't started.

Going back to the counter, I attempt to pour milk into one of the cups, but my hand is shaking so badly I have to put it back down.

The tremors are running all the way down my body. My heart is beating so wildly, I can hear the pulse beating in my ears.

I rest my hands on the counter and close my eyes, taking a deep breath.

I've never been late before. Never. The pill keeps me regular as clockwork.

I can't be pregnant.

I can't.

Jake doesn't want kids.

As if hearing my silent call, he walks into the kitchen.

"Can I take that coffee to go, baby? Zane just called; he needs my help with something at the label."

"Sure." Forcing my body to work, I reach up for a thermo cup and fill it with coffee and milk, desperately trying to keep the tremor in my hand from showing.

Turning, I see Jake, perched on a stool, reading something on his phone.

I watch him for long moment.

I can't be pregnant. This can't be happening. Things are going so well between us. If I'm pregnant, it will break us.

You can't have a baby when only one of you wants it.

He glances up at me, catching me staring. A sexy smile spreads on his face. "You enjoying the view?"

Forcing a smile, I walk toward him. "As always." I put the cup down before him on the counter.

He catches hold of my retreating hand and pulls me into his embrace.

Nuzzling my neck, he says, "I love the smell of me on you."

We had sex first thing this morning. We always have sex. And I'm pregnant. Maybe. Possibly.

Fuck.

"I need a shower."

"Thanks." He chuckles.

"No, I didn't mean it like that."

"I know what you meant," he says, lifting his head to stare into my eyes.

I suddenly feel exposed. What if he can see it in my eyes. Closing them, I lean in and kiss his lips.

I'm going to lose him when he finds out.

Don't panic until you know for certain.

Jake's hands start wandering, and I can feel his kiss deepening, his erection growing through his jeans.

Catching his hand on my ass, breaking the kiss, I say, "I thought you needed to get to the label."

"I need you more," he growls, lips attacking my neck, hand going straight to my breasts.

I can't have sex right now. Anything but sex.

"You had me half an hour ago, and isn't Zane waiting for you?"

He pauses and looks me in the eyes.

I never dissuade Jake from sex. Never. He'll know there's something wrong with me. But right now I can't find the will to care about that.

"Am I wearing you out?" he asks, softly, stroking his fingers along my jaw.

"No, I'm fine." I smile. "I like you wearing me out. I'm just trying to be the level-headed one out of the two of us, and you've got to get to work."

I move away from him under the pretence of getting my coffee. The truth is I can't even stomach the thought of drinking it. My stomach is roiling with fear.

I hold the cup in my hands, resting it against my chest.

Jake gets to his feet, picking up his to-go cup. "Don't forget, we've got dinner with Smith and Carly tonight."

Crap. That's the last thing I want to do tonight. Not with what I have on my mind.

"Sure." I smile. "Looking forward to it."

"I think you'll get on well with Carly. Be good for you to make some girlfriends here, right?"

"Right," I say, smiling again.

These smiles feel so insincere, I'm pretty sure my face is going to crack under the strain of them.

"I've been talking to Tom and Denny these last few days," Jake says, coming around the counter, "about asking Smith to become a permanent member of TMS."

"Really?" I say, totally taken by surprise. I never thought Jake would consider it. I'm so happy he has.

"He won't replace Jonny, of course. But Tom and Den are on board with it. He's a great guy who fits in well with us, and I hate to lose him to another band."

"Is someone trying to poach him?"

"Not that I know of, but he's making a name for himself in the music world now, so it's only a matter of time. What do you think?"

He wants my opinion. I love that.

Walking to him, putting my arms around his waist, I say, "I think it's a brilliant idea. Smith will be over the moon when you ask him."

Brushing my hair back, he tucks it behind my ear. "You don't think I'm being disloyal to Jonny?"

I see the downturn of his lips, and it makes my chest hurt.

I shake my head. "No, I don't. I don't think Jonny would either. You're doing what's best for the band. TMS meant everything to Jonny. He would want you guys to carry on, and do what you felt was right."

He closes his eyes briefly and presses a kiss to my forehead. "I guess I'll speak to him today," he says against my skin.

"So we'll be celebrating tonight?"

"If he says yes."

"He'll say yes."

Putting his fingers under my chin, tilting my head back, he presses a firm kiss to my lips.

"I'll be home at seven, so make sure you are well on your way to being ready. I know how long it takes you to get dressed for a night out."

I muster up the energy to give him a look.

He laughs. Making for the door, he looks over his shoulder at me. "Later. Love you, beautiful."

"Love you too."

The instant he's gone, I sag back against the counter, gripping it for support.

What am I going to do if I'm pregnant? A termination isn't even an option for me. But Jake won't want the baby.

He'll say he does for me. Or maybe he won't. Maybe when reality hits, he'll realise just how much he doesn't want a baby and he'll leave me.

Oh God.

I need to know if I am pregnant. Today. Now. I can't keep running the maybes around in my head.

I'm so overtaken with nervous energy and the need to know, I don't even bother to shower. I pull on a pair of jeans and a T-shirt.

I grab my sunglasses and one of Jake's baseball caps and put them on. I look a complete twat, but I don't want to get recognised buying a pregnancy test, so the twat look it is. Unfortunately, being Jake's wife-to-be gets me recognised a lot lately.

I grab my phone and handbag, the keys for Jake's other car, the Vanquish, and I head for the garage.

When I reach the gates, Henry, our on-site security, stops me to ask if I need accompaniment on my outing.

"I'm just going for a drive. I've got writer's block," I say. "Thought the drive would help clear my head."

No way in the world do I want security coming with me on this journey.

"Sounds like a good idea," he says with a smile.

"I've got my phone with me in case anyone needs me."

"Okay. Enjoy your drive, Ms. Bennett." Henry opens the gates, allowing me out.

I've told him a million times to call me Tru. He still calls me Ms. Bennett every time.

I turn out onto the street and start driving toward the exit of the gated community.

I need to find a chemist (or *drugstore*, as they're called over here), but one that's not local. Too many people know we live around here.

I start fiddling with the built-in satellite navigation, but unfortunately it doesn't offer the feature "here's your local chemist to buy pregnancy tests at." I decide to drive until I spot one.

I end up driving for forty-five minutes before I find a chemist that's a decent distance from home.

I'm in and out in a flash, thankfully unnoticed, thirty dollars lighter and three pregnancy tests heavier. One to find out. One to make sure. Another to make doubly sure.

I drop the bag on the passenger seat, fire up the car, and tap the address in for home.

For the whole drive, every time I catch a glimpse of the bag sitting on the seat beside me, it makes me want to throw up.

Once I'm back in the safety of the house, I head straight for our en suite, clutching the bag to my chest like it's a bomb about to go off.

That's probably quite an apt description, because if I am pregnant, I foresee explosions of the gigantic kind.

Locking the bathroom door behind me, I drop the toilet lid and sit down.

I pull a test from the bag.

Swallowing back a huge lump of fear, I stare down at it.

My future with Jake depends on what this will tell me.

Oh God.

Fear seeps into my bones like poison.

Deep breaths. It's going to be okay.

With shaky fingers, I open the box. Briefing over the instructions, I tear the protective seal on the test and, thanking God that I need to pee right now, I do as it says and pee on the stick.

I put the cap back on the test and place it on the top of the toilet.

I wash my hands, then come back and kneel on the floor just in front of the toilet.

I pick up the instructions to read again.

Okay, so this is simple. Three minutes I have to wait and if I'm pregnant it will read: "Pregnant."

If I'm not: "Not Pregnant."

Easy, right?

Well, no, not if I'm pregnant. It'll be so far from easy, there won't be a word that exists to cover it.

How can my whole future ride on what the outcome of a tiny piece of plastic tells me?

It feels like it should be more epic than this. Especially if I am pregnant. Something so wonderfully and terribly life-altering as this should have a bigger moment than sitting alone on my bathroom floor, waiting for a little piece of plastic to tell me my future.

How am I going to tell Jake?

I just can't even begin to think how to broach the subject with him.

I squeeze my eyes shut. *Don't think of that now. When you know, then think of it.*

How long has it been? *Two minutes,* I think. I should have brought my phone in with me to time it.

Should I look now? It might be ready.

I rise up on my knees to take a look, but fear sits me straight back down.

I can't do this.

I drop my head in my hands.

I'm just so fucking scared. I know I have to know, but I don't want to know.

No, come on, Tru. Woman up.

Taking a few deep breaths, figuring it must be three minutes by now, I close my eyes as I slowly get to my feet.

Okay, just open your eyes. Deep breath. One…two…three…

I flick my eyes open.

Pregnant

Fuck.

CHAPTER TEN

I'm sitting by the pool on a lounger, lost in my painful thoughts, when I hear Jake's voice. "I thought you'd be getting ready for dinner."

Instantly tensing, I turn to see him with his shoulder leant against the wall, watching me.

He looks so beautiful. Achingly so. It makes my chest tighten and hurt so badly I feel like I can't breathe. Like I'll never be able to breathe right again.

"Sorry, I lost track of time," I murmur.

"Staring out at LA?" He smiles, with a forward tilt of his head.

"Something like that." I get to my feet.

"Hey, you okay?" he asks, eyeing me as I approach.

No, I'm pregnant with our baby, Jake.

"I'm fine," I hear myself uttering.

"You don't look fine." His eyes search mine. "You look… have you been crying?" he asks, straightening up. "Has something happened?"

Yes. I'm pregnant.

"No, I'm fine. I just saw one of those starving-children-in-Africa commercials, and it had me in tears by the end," I say.

His head turns toward the blank screen of the television.

"You should donate to those charities," I say, trying to distract his quickly working mind.

"Already do."

How do I not already know this? Sometimes, I feel like I know everything and absolutely nothing about Jake.

His eyes meet mine. He looks nervous. Shy. I love shy Jake.

"You really are wonderful, you know." I stroke my fingertips gently down his cheek. "You should let everyone see this amazing, caring side of you."

"Baby, this side of me is reserved for you only."

Overcome with love and fear, it's quick to consume me. I can feel it spreading across my face, I wrap my arms around him, hugging him tight, pressing my face into his chest.

Jake holds me equally as possessively, resting his cheek against my hair. "Are you sure you're okay?" he murmurs.

I nod, afraid to talk for fear of breaking down.

"I hate to know you've been crying here alone. I hate to think of you crying, period. No more sad commercials for you, okay?"

I swallow past the pain engulfing me. "No." I shake my head gently.

"I spoke with Smith today," he says, caressing my back with his fingers.

"And?" I lean back, looking into his face.

Holding my gaze, I see something shift in his eyes, and then he smiles and says, "He's in."

I know he's happy. But he's conflicted too. Feeling guilty because of Jonny.

I want to soothe his guilt in this moment, but I'm afraid if I stay in his arms for a moment longer that I'll crack. And right now, just before we have plans for dinner, is definitely not the right time to tell him. We need time to talk this through, not a quick, *By the way, Jake, I'm pregnant. Let's go to dinner.*

Later. I'll tell him later.

I release myself from his hold. "Guess I better go get ready for dinner."

As I'm about to leave, he catches my hand. "Tru, you would tell me if there was anything else bothering you, right?"

"Of course," I say, swallowing past the lie.

I squeeze his hand, forcing a smile, then I walk into the living room, but I can feel Jake's eyes on me the whole time.

* * *

"What're you having, baby?" Jake asks.

Baby.

I'm pregnant.

Oh God.

My worry and fear have grown exponentially as the night has progressed. Being alone earlier, knowing what I know, was hard enough. But being around Jake, holding the truth in, is killing me. I feel like I'm lying to him every second I don't tell him I'm pregnant.

I fear I'll just blurt the words out any moment now. Focus is the key.

I will tell Jake, I just need to find the right moment, and right now is not it.

I glance up to see the waiter standing at our table. "Oh, um, I'll have the mushroom ravioli, please."

"Would you like wine with dinner?" the waiter asks Jake.

"Which wine, sweetheart?" Jake asks.

Crap. I can't drink. Not now that I'm having a baby.

But I always have a drink with dinner when we eat out. He'll know something is off if I say no.

But then I think you are allowed a glass of wine every now and then when you're pregnant, aren't you?

Afraid to say no, for tipping him off, I say, "Smith should choose. We are celebrating his acceptance into the band, after all. I'm really glad you're an official part of TMS now."

"Me too." Smith smiles. "As for the wine, anything with a high alcohol content works for me," he says to Jake.

"We'll have a bottle of the Montrachet," Jake orders.

"Good choice." The waiter takes the menus from our table and departs.

"I love your dress," Carly says to me over the table.

"Thank you." I'm wearing the Pucci print jersey dress I treated myself to on one of my shopping trips with Stuart. He picked it out for me. He has amazing taste. And I might as well get some wear out of it while I still have time.

I'm pregnant. And I have to tell Jake.

Fuck.

"I love your dress too." I force a smile.

I actually do like her dress, I'm just forcing all my smiles tonight.

Carly is wearing the Marc Jacobs Night Bird dress. I was eyeing it last week. It's gorgeous. But Stuart talked me out of it. He said my boobs would have looked more stacked than the New York skyline.

Looking at it on Carly, I know he was right. She's a little lighter than me in the chest department, and it suits her just right.

Oh God, don't a woman's boobs get bigger in pregnancy? Christ, they're big enough as it is.

I look over at Carly, with her lovely blonde hair, golden skin, and slim figure and remember how I always used to want to look like that growing up. I used to hate being the foreign-looking girl in a sea of blonde hair and blue eyes. Now I'm comfortable with myself mainly because of Jake. Because of how he looks at me. The way he adores me with his eyes.

But not for much longer, because I'm going to get fat and bloated, and Jake won't want me anymore.

I'm going to lose him. He's going to leave me for some thin, blonde goddess who doesn't want to tie him down with kids.

Panic grips a strong hold of me.

"So you're a writer, Tru?" Carly asks.

"The best." Jake smiles, putting his arm around the back of my chair, fingers resting lightly on my shoulder.

I freeze under his touch. Thankfully he doesn't seem to notice.

Composing myself, I say, "I wouldn't go that far, but yes, I write for a magazine. And I'm currently writing a book."

"That's right, you're writing the band's bio from the tour. That must be kind of cool, writing about the guy you're living with. I guess you just need to remember to leave out the bad habits, like leaving the toilet seat up or wet towels on the bed." She raises an eyebrow in Smith's direction.

"I try to remember." Smith raises his hands in defence. "I just slip up every now and then."

"Every damn day is more like it," she says, laughing. "Six years married, reminding him more times than I care to mention, and the man still can't remember to hang his bath towel up! I'm sure he just does it to drive me crazy."

"You know me, darlin', I live to drive you crazy." Smith puts his arm around her neck. He pulls her to him and presses a kiss to the top of her head. Giggling, Carly chastises him with a hand to the chest for ruffling her hair.

Their love for each other is so obvious, it's infectious. I hope Jake and I are still that much in love six years into our marriage.

The thought escapes me, paining me, because I know when I tell Jake I'm pregnant, we probably won't even have six more minutes together.

Especially when I tell him I'm keeping the baby.

"I'm just using all my notes from the tour," I say, answering her question. "So Jake's bad habits, like never cleaning out his stinky ashtray that he leaves out on the patio, are sure to be left out." I slide him a look.

"You just clean them so much better than I ever could, baby," he says, giving me a doe-eyed look.

It hits me right in the chest with a sharp twist, leaving me feeling breathless.

"Yeah, that works." I give him a mock-stern look, forcing my façade back up.

Jake gives me one of his sexy smiles, the ones that let him get away with anything, as he leans over and plants a kiss on my cheek. My skin burns long after his lips have left me.

"What do you do for a living, Carly?" I ask, putting my focus on her.

"I'm an interior designer."

"Best damn interior designer California has," Smith says, proud.

"Do you have your own company?" I ask.

"I do." She smiles. "It's small, but I do okay."

"We've just recently moved into a new house, and I could really use some help decorating it. If you're not too busy, I'd love to hire you to help me. I haven't got a clue where to start. That's okay with you, isn't it?" I ask Jake.

Why am I making plans to decorate?

I suppose the baby will need a nursery…

What the hell am I doing, getting all moony-eyed over this when I don't even know if Jake wants this baby? He won't, I know he won't. I remember the look on his face when the subject came up on the island.

"Of course. I think it's a great idea," Jake answers, bringing me back to the present.

"Then I would love to." Carly beams. "How about I come round to your house on Monday, and we can start from there?"

"Sounds great, I can't wait." *If I'm still living there, that is.* I force another smile.

"So you guys have been married six years," I say, needing the subject change.

"Yep, and together for ten," Carly answers. "We are the stereotypical high school sweethearts."

"Maybe 'stereotypical' is pushing it a little far, darlin'. I was the lame grungy emo kid, and she was the hot cheerleader," Smith explains. "It took me five years to get her to notice me; then, once I had her attention, I lured her in with my wit and charm, and we've been together ever since."

"It was the persistence," she says, laughing. "I figured a guy who had kept at it for that long must have some serious stamina."

"So it was my persistence and stamina, not my hot body and charm?" Smith says, feigning shock.

"No, those are what got me to marry you." She grins at him.

As I watch them interact, it warms my unsteady heart, and I feel Jake take hold of my hand under the table. When I look at him, smiling, he smiles back, but there's something off about it.

Or maybe that's just my own paranoia setting in.

"Have you guys set a date for the wedding?" Carly asks.

"July twenty-first," Jake answers, beating me to it.

"How's the planning going?" she directs her question to me.

"Slow," I say with a grimace. "I just haven't got a clue how to get started. So far, I have some wedding magazines, some dresses highlighted as maybes, and a drafted guest list."

"Well, I've planned a wedding before, so if you need a hand at all, you let me know."

"I might have to take you up on that offer." I smile.

"Just call me interior designer and wedding planner extraordinaire," she jokes with a flourish.

I laugh.

It's easy to laugh when, for that moment, I've forgotten I'm pregnant. Then I remember I have our baby growing inside of me, and my mood drops like a rock in water.

The waiter comes over with the bottle of wine, and it's at that moment Jake brushes my hair back revealing the nape of my neck. Leaning over, he whispers into my ear, "You look so sexy. If I could, I'd take you on this table right now. Dining table, later, at home?" He moves back, staring at me. His eyes are dark and fixed.

I nod mutely, forcing another smile.

He presses a soft kiss to my lips and moves back in his seat, then starts talking to Smith.

He wants to make love tonight.

Of course he does. We have sex every night. And morning.

But I can't. Not with this on my mind.

I'm going to have to tell him before we get home.

Fuck.

* * *

We've said our good-byes to Carly and Smith and have just gotten in the car when I blurt out, "We need to talk. And it's not something we can talk about at home."

Pausing before he starts the car, he turns his head to look at me, his face full of myriad questions. "Why not?"

I know how important it is to Jake that our home remains untarnished by fights. And I feel this conversation isn't going to be a happy one.

"Just because," I reply. "Is there somewhere private we can go to talk?"

"*Just because?*" He frowns. "You think that's a fuckin' answer, Tru?"

"I don't want to talk about this in the car, Jake." I wrap my arms protectively around myself.

"But you don't want to talk about it at home. So I'd say here is as good a place as any." He turns his body toward me, bending his knee to rest on the seat.

Shaking my head, I stare out the passenger window. I can feel the fear trembling through my body, the words clotting in my throat.

"Is this what was up with you earlier? Why you were crying? What I've felt simmering under the surface all night?"

I feel my eyes swell with tears.

"Will you fuckin' answer me?" he demands. His tone is so sharp, it turns me to face him.

"Are you leaving me?" He looks in pure pain. It's like a blow across my face.

"No," I say in a rush. "Why would you think that?"

"Because of the look on your face right now, Tru. You look like you're grieving. Like you've lost something big. Everyone you love is safe and well, so the only thing you could be mourning right now is the death of our relationship."

"No, Jake, no." I shake my head. A tear rolls down my cheek, and I brush it away. "I would never leave you. *Never*. But…you might leave me when I tell you what I have to tell you." I clasp my hands in my lap.

I see a mix of anger and pain flash across his face, tightening his beautiful features.

After a beat, he says, "Have you—" He pauses. Turning from me, he grips the steering wheel, looking out the windshield. When he speaks, his voice is so low, so heartbreakingly low. "What you have to tell me…if it'll break what we have right here, this love between us, then don't tell me. I don't want to know. I want you, Tru, and anything that could for one second make me feel like I don't...then...just don't tell me."

My heart shatters into a million tiny pieces. I know what he's thinking. I hate that he thinks that.

"I'm pregnant." The words fall from my lips. For a moment it feels like all the air has been sucked out of the car. My world pauses. I wait. Wait for him to say something. Anything.

But he doesn't.

And when he starts the engine, putting the car into drive, and pulls out onto the street, I feel my world slip from my grasp, bottoming me out hollow.

A tear escapes. A whole lot more want to follow, but I hold them back. Brushing the stray one away discreetly, I stare out the window.

* * *

It's a long fifteen-minute drive back home. In all that time, Jake says nothing and neither do I.

I feel a distance settling between us, widening with each passing minute, to the point where there may as well still be twelve years and an ocean between us.

Jake pulls up on the drive. I get out and slam the door.

I fumble to get my keys out of my clutch as I approach the front door. I wrap my fingers around them, shove them in the lock, and let myself in.

I slam this door too. I'm angry and hurt that he's said nothing. I want him to know.

I take a step forward, and that's when I hear his car reversing out.

Moving quickly, I yank the door open and catch sight of the taillights speeding back down the driveway.

Pain tears through me, so fierce that my legs buckle. I fall back against the wall, clutching my chest. I feel wide open. Broken. Devastated.

He's left.

Hot tears sting my eyes like pokers.

Don't cry, Tru. Keep it together.

I press my palms to my eyes, forcing the tears back.

He's supposed to love me. So much so that when he thought I had cheated on him he didn't want to know.

But I tell him I'm pregnant and he hotfoots it out of here like his ass is on fire, without so much as a word.

Bastard. Motherfucking bastard.

Then I get angry. Really fucking angry.

Fine, he doesn't want this baby. Then I don't want his sorry ass.

I march to our bedroom. I grab one of Jake's holdalls and some jeans, T-shirts, pyjamas, and underwear. I stuff them in the bag.

I get my passport from the safe in our walk-in wardrobe. I get my phone from my clutch.

I need a cab.

I do a quick web search for local cab companies on my phone and call the first one that comes up.

They tell me it'll be fifteen minutes for the cab.

I go to the foyer, take the handset off the wall, and dial through to the main gate to let them know I have a cab coming.

Ready to leave, I stand a moment, holdall at my feet, handbag on my shoulder.

I'm not really sure what I'm doing right now.

Twisting my engagement ring on my finger, I pause. I lift my hand to look at it.

"Trudy Bennett, I love you beyond any lyrics I could ever write or any words I could ever say. I always have, and I always will. Marry me?"

A tear slides down my cheek, and I pull my engagement ring off.

Taking a slow walk back to our bedroom, I place the ring on Jake's pillow.

Then I head straight to the foyer, pick up the holdall, swing it over my shoulder, and let myself out into the warm California night.

I lock the front door, and keeping the keys in my hand, start the walk down the long driveway.

Jackson, one of the night security guards, jumps out of the booth when he sees me.

"Ms. Bennett, is everything okay?" I see his eyes go to the holdall on my shoulder.

"Could you give these to Jake when he gets back, please?" I hold out the keys.

His eyes flicker to them, then back to my face. "Are you sure you don't want to keep hold of them?"

"No." I shake my head. "I won't be needing them anymore."

Reluctantly, he takes them from me.

I start to walk toward the gates, when he says, "If you need driven somewhere, Parker can take you wherever you want to go." He thumbs back to Parker, the other security guard, who is standing by the door, watching our interaction.

"No, it's okay. Thanks. I've got a cab coming." It's at that moment the cab rolls up.

"Bye, Jackson. Bye, Parker." I give a small wave.

Jackson gives me a sad smile as Parker opens the gates, letting me out.

Without a backward glance, I climb into the cab, settling my bags beside me.

"Where to?" the driver asks.

"LAX, please."

JAKE...

CHAPTER ELEVEN

I'm pregnant.*"

Tru's pregnant. With my baby.

But she's on the pill. How can she be pregnant?

Jesus fucking Christ. She's pregnant. With my baby.

I can't be a dad. I'm not dad material.

I get a smoke out of the pack and realise my hands are shaking.

I clench my hands into fists, trying to ease the tremors. I put a cigarette between my lips, light it, and take a long, slow drag.

Lowering the window, I blow the smoke out into the night, and stare out at LA.

The last time I was parked here, I was seeing to Tru on the hood of my car, and now I'm here after finding out I'm going to be a dad.

Fuck.

I know without a doubt that Tru will want the baby. An abortion won't be an option for her.

Now I feel like the worst kind of bastard for even thinking it. Thinking of getting rid of a part of myself and Tru.

But what the fuck do I know about being a dad? Nothing. I know absolutely nothing. I didn't exactly have the best teacher growing up. I may have had Dale for the last part, and sure, he's a good guy, but the damage was done by that point. I was well beyond repair by the time Paul was gone.

He fucked me up. And I can't screw a kid up like he did me. Not my own flesh and blood. I'd never forgive myself.

Taking another drag, I rest my elbows on the wheel and put my head in my hands.

"You're a fuckin' waste of space, Jake…Can't you ever get anything right?…Take after your mother, you do, fuckin' useless…I wish you'd never been born, I never wanted saddling with a kid—especially not a whiney little shit like you…You'll never amount to anything…What the fuck are you crying for? If you don't stop crying, boy, I'll give you a fuckin' reason to cry…"

I bang my palms against my forehead, trying to get the sound of his goddamn voice out of my head.

He's dead, and he's still here, fucking with me. Still taunting me.

I need to drown the dead motherfucker out.

I turn the music on, quickly search through to Linkin Park, and press Play on "Numb." I crank it up loud, until the song bleeds through every sense.

I always listen to this song when I need to clear my mind. My drug counsellor said to find something to focus on when I feel like everything is slipping away from me. Music is my life, aside from Tru, so I took to this song.

I know this might seem an odd song to calm me, but it works. "Numb" is my comedown song.

I can feel my anger and frustrations already beginning to ebb.

Numb is exactly how I need to feel right now. I don't want to think. I don't want to feel. Because if I do, I'll be turning this car around and heading in the wrong direction, straight to a dealer.

Resting back in my seat, I take another long pull on my smoke, flicking the ash out the window.

I'm going to be a dad.

I don't know how to be a dad. I want to be…for Tru. I want to be everything right for her. But I don't know if I can. I'll fuck it up. I fuck everything up.

The thought of screwing up something as important as having a kid terrifies me beyond words.

I can't be him. I can't be Paul. And I have been, for a very long time.

I would never raise my hand to a woman or a child. Never. But what if we had a kid and something just snapped inside of me and changed me into the bastard he was? It doesn't take just fists to hurt and break a kid. Words do some serious fucking damage too.

I know that all too well.

And I'm like him in so many ways. Too many ways. What's to say that I won't morph into the full shithole of a package that was Paul Wethers once my kid is born?

I might be successful professionally, but behind that façade, I'm a whole lot of fucked up and broken. Tru is the glue that holds me together, and look what I just did to her. She is my whole world. She told me she was pregnant and I just walked away from her. I left her all alone.

What type of man does that? A fucking coward, that's what.

God, when she told me she was pregnant, she sounded so scared. I could hear it in her voice. Almost like she knew what I'd do. That I'd run away. That I'd fuck up.

Didn't I do that so very fucking spectacularly?

It's no excuse, but I panicked. When she said she was pregnant, it was like a fuse went in my head and I couldn't think straight. For the whole ride home, I felt robotic.

I couldn't think or focus on anything.

It was just...*Drive the car, Jake.*

Get home, Jake.

I couldn't get any farther than that. When she got out of the car, I knew she was angry and hurting, but I was frozen to my seat.

I was telling myself to get out of the car, to follow her, to talk to her, but I literally couldn't make my body move.

The next thing I knew, the car was in reverse, and I was spinning it around, driving out of there.

I was just so fucking terrified. I'm still terrified.

Tru is carrying my baby inside of her, and I left them both behind.

I walked away.

I am him.

I'm the legacy he left behind. He got exactly what he wanted. He wanted me just as screwed up—no, more screwed up—than he was.

Well, cheers, Dad. You did a top-notch fucking job.

Taking one last drag of my smoke, I flick my cigarette butt out the window.

I'll never be good enough for Tru or the baby. But I want to be.

I know the baby will be perfect and beautiful, because Tru is. It'll take after her, because it has to. I don't want an ounce of my fucked-up-ness in our baby.

Our baby.

We're having a baby. It's growing inside of her right now. A tiny baby, made from me and Tru. It'll be so small... so tiny, with a little heart beating in its chest.

It'll need protecting, keeping safe for its whole life.

And it's mine to protect.

I'm going to be a dad.

Out of nowhere, I feel a tiny lift in my heart at the thought. A tiny flicker of hope buried deep inside my fractured, fucked-up soul.

Then the realisation slaps me across the face.

I've so completely fucked up. She's never going to forgive me for this.

Fuck.

I need to go back. I need to talk to her. Beg her to forgive me. Tell her I'll make it work somehow. I'll figure something out. I'll figure out how to be a dad to our baby. I want to be the man she believes I can be. I will do anything for her.

I can't lose Tru. She's my reason for being. She's my everything.

And I want to be the same for our baby.

I'm just about to fire up the car when my cell starts to ring.

I glance at the screen and see it's home security.

Tru.

Fuck, no.

"What's wrong?"

"Mr. Wethers. It's Jackson. I, um, I just thought you might want to know that Ms. Bennett just left in a cab. She had luggage, and she, um, left her house keys with me to give to you."

My heart drops through my stomach.

God, no.

"You just let her leave?" I say through gritted teeth.

"I'm sorry, sir. I tried to talk to her, offered to drive her wherever she was going, but she wouldn't have it."

That's Tru. Stubborn to a fault.

"Do you know where she was going?" I ask through my dry mouth.

"No, sir."

"Find out."

"How?"

"Did you see which cab company it was that picked her up?"

"Yes."

"Then fuckin' call them and find out where the driver is taking her! How long ago did she leave?" I drive my hand through my hair.

"The cab pulled away less than a minute ago."

"Call them now. Then call me straight back."

I hang up.

She left. I have no one to blame but myself. I have so totally and monumentally screwed everything up.

Fucking idiot, I'm such a complete and total fucking idiot.

I have to make this right. I have to bring her home. Bring them both home.

I speed-dial Tru's cell.

It's ringing.

Pick up, baby, please.

After three rings, it diverts to voice mail.

She cut me off.

Fuck.

I press redial.

Voice mail.

Fuck. Fuck. Fuck.

I wait for the tone to leave a message. "Sweetheart, I'm so sorry. I screwed up, I know, but don't leave. Call me back, please. We can talk and sort this out. I shouldn't have left when I did. I shouldn't have left you like that. I just panicked. I'm not strong like you, baby. It's no excuse, I know, but please don't leave." I exhale. "I just...I love you so fuckin' much."

I can feel my throat tightening, so I hang the call up before I start crying.

I get out another smoke and light it up and sit and stare at my cell.

Call me back, baby, please.

A minute later, my cell starts to ring, but it's not her. It's security.

"Where is she going?" I ask in a clipped voice.

"LAX, sir."

Fuck.

I slam the car into drive and, spinning it around, I put the pedal to the floor, desperate to get to LAX and stop the only woman I've ever loved from leaving me and taking my baby with her.

TRU...

CHAPTER TWELVE

Adele starts to sing in my bag. I rifle through my bag to find my phone.

Jake.

My heart thumps in my chest as I stare at his name on the screen.

He left me. He just drove away and left me.

The pain, rejection, and humiliation all clusters together and burns straight through my heart.

I reject his call and switch off my phone.

"How much longer to the airport?" I ask the driver.

"About fifteen minutes."

I rest back in my seat. I don't even know when the next flight back to the UK is. I didn't plan that far ahead. I didn't plan this at all.

I'll just have to wait it out at the airport until I can get the next flight out of this godforsaken place.

I expected Jake to react badly to the news of my pregnancy. I expected a fight. What I didn't expect was for him to not say a word the moment I told him, then drive away the instant he got me out of the car.

Just thinking of it makes my chest hurt again. I cross my arms, trying to compress the pain.

"Nice place you were coming from back there," the driver says.

"Yes," I reply, not wanting to get pulled into a conversation with him.

"Worth a lot of bucks, those houses. You live there?"

He keeps flicking glances at me in the rearview mirror.

Oh God, I hope he doesn't recognise me.

"No. I was just visiting." I turn my face away to stare out the window, letting him know I'm in no mood to talk.

Thankfully he gets the message.

Fifteen minutes later, I see the huge LAX sign. I'm so absolutely ready to get out of this cab and out of this goddamn city.

I just want to go home. I want my mama and daddy.

God, I can't even begin to think how Mama will react when I tell her I'm pregnant and that Jake doesn't want the baby. My dad will go ape. He'll probably fly out here just so he can kick Jake into next week.

Crap.

This is all such a bloody mess.

"How much?" I ask when the driver pulls to the curb.

"Seventy-five bucks."

Bloody hell. I'm sure he's taking me for a ride, but I can't be arsed to argue the point.

I pull two fifties out of my purse and tell him to keep the change. I know the fucker is ripping me off already, but I just want out of this cab, not to sit around waiting for change.

I climb out, wobbling on my heels, with the holdall on one shoulder and handbag on the other.

Glancing at the entrance, I take a deep breath.

Securing the strap on my shoulder, I walk toward the doors.

I hear the screeching tires of a car. Turning, I see the James Bond car pulling to a stop in the middle of the road. The driver's door flies open and Jake jumps out.

Horns beep as cars pull around his abandoned car, but he doesn't seem to care.

I see him scanning the area, and then he spots me, so I quickly turn on my heel and make for the door.

"Tru, wait!" he calls.

"Piss off!" I yell back.

I see people stopping to stare, and my face instantly flames.

I hear someone call out, "Hey, man, you can't leave your car there!"

The next thing I know, Jake is in front of me, taking hold of my arms. "Just wait. I'm sorry, Tru. I'm so fuckin' sorry. Don't leave. Just hear me out, *please.*"

"I'm not interested in listening to a bloody thing you have to say!" I yell.

Okay, so maybe I don't care too much that people are watching us right now. I guess I'm too hurt and angry to care.

I can feel tears welling in my eyes, but I refuse to cry. "I understood you loud and clear."

"I fucked up. I panicked and I ran, and I shouldn't have. I'm sorry. Sorrier than I have ever been in my life." He shakes his head. Looking down, he blows out a breath. Lifting his head, he meets my eyes. "It's no excuse, Tru, but I just didn't know what to say or do. I couldn't think straight. I'm so sorry, baby."

"Don't call me that!" I cry at him, his words touching a raw nerve in me. "I'm not *your* fuckin' baby!"

"Yes, you are." His tone is so low, so intense, that all I can do is stare at him. "You will always be mine, Tru. Always."

"Hey, man, didn't you hear me? I said you can't just leave your car there!"

I tear my gaze away from Jake to see an airport employee walking toward us. Young guy, early twenties.

He eyes Jake, stopping in his tracks. "Hey, aren't you... Jake Wethers?" he squints at Jake. "Holy fuck—you are! It's you! Hey, it's Jake Wethers!" he exclaims, gesturing to the people around, bringing all of their attention to us.

We're out here alone, without Dave and Ben, surrounded by about twenty people who now recognise Jake.

Fuck.

I feel Jake tense, his grip tightening on my arms. He moves his eyes from me and says to the guy, "I'm not him."

"You are," he says, stepping closer. "I'd recognise you anywhere! Been to all your shows, man. Got all your albums. I'm one of your biggest fans! Fuckin' love your music! Holy fuck, I can't believe you're here! Wait 'til Marie hears this! My girlfriend—she loves you almost as much as I do! When Jonny died, she cried for weeks. Oh man, I gotta get your autograph and a picture." He starts moving closer, reaching into his pocket.

I can't believe we're in the middle of an argument and some überenthusiastic Jake fan wants an autograph and picture.

I hear the murmuring voices of the people around us, the excitement lifting their tones, and my heart starts to beat uneasily.

We're going to get mobbed.

"We're going *now*," Jake orders in a quiet but firm voice, staring down at me.

I nod once, and then Jake grabs hold of my hand. As quick as lightning, we're moving toward his car.

I hear people following us, voices calling.

"Don't go, man!"

"Sign my T-shirt!"

"Can I get a picture with you?"

"Let me give you my number!"

Jake opens the passenger door and all but shoves me inside, closing it firmly behind me. I watch, uneasy, as he tries to manoeuvre his way to the driver side as people grab at him. Jake shoves people out of the way, the crowd suddenly much thicker than before.

Even if Jake wanted to stop and do autographs, the people are way too excited now, and there are way too many of them to control.

A person is rational. People are just plain crazy.

I'm scared and shaking at the crowding around the car, trapping me in.

Then Jake's in the car. He revs the engine loudly in warning and pulls the car forward, getting us out of there.

Still trembling, I watch him make a call. He doesn't put it on speaker but drives while on his phone. He never does that.

"There was an incident at LAX...I'll tell you later...no, we got mobbed...yeah, we were arguing, people heard. It'll make the news for sure, clean it up best you can...she's fine, we're both fine...no, I'm not being followed...I'm heading home right now...okay." He hangs up. "Are you okay?" he asks.

I nod.

"Don't run like that ever again. I know you're pissed with me right now, but it was a stupid thing to do."

Anger flashes through me. I let out a sharp laugh, turning in my seat to him. "Are you fucking kidding?"

"Do I look like I'm fuckin' kidding?" The look he gives me is harsh enough to make me shrink in my seat. "You could have gotten hurt out there," he says in a low voice. I'm not sure, but I think I see a shudder run through him.

Then I get angry again.

I wouldn't have even been at the airport if he hadn't pulled a Houdini on me. This is all his bloody fault!

I shoot him a look of disgust. "Like you would even care. This is all your fault!"

One hand on the steering wheel, he turns his head, firing such a weighted look at me that I fear I may splinter into tiny pieces under the force of it. "You think I wouldn't care if something happened to you?" His jaw is gripped tight.

I give him a hard stare back and shake my head no.

His face tightens. I can even see a vein pulsing in his neck. I don't think I've ever seen him so angry.

And it's me who he's angry with. Cheeky bastard.

That raises my hackles again. "Let me out of this goddamn car," I demand through clenched teeth.

"No."

"Did you just tell me no?"

"Sounded like it."

"'Sounded like it'! What the hell?" I seethe. "Who the bloody hell do you think you are? You're an arrogant twat, Jake Wethers! I'm not one of your employees you can order around! God, you are just a big fat fucking arsehole!"

And I'm thirteen again, apparently.

"I deserve that," he says. He actually looks like he's holding back a smile, which pisses me off even more. "But I can't let you out, Tru. It's not safe."

"What are you gonna do? Hold me hostage?"

"If I have to."

He sounds so serious that I'm not wholly sure he's kidding.

"I fuckin' hate you," I hiss.

Shit, where did that come from?

I see a flash of pain across his face. It doesn't make me feel good. It makes me feel like a bitch.

"I deserve that as well." He drags a hand through his hair. "Look, just let me get you safely home. Then give me ten minutes of your time, listen to what I have to say, and if you still want to leave, I'll arrange for the jet to take you wherever you want to go. You just can't be out there moving around alone without security. It's not safe for you...or the baby."

I sharp in a breath at the mention of the baby. Tears spring to my eyes, and then a sob escapes me. I clamp my hand to my mouth.

"Tru..." He reaches out to touch me.

I pull back from him. "Don't touch me," I whisper, my words watery with the tears.

"I'm so sorry..."

"Stop it!" I snap. "I don't need your fucking pity or sympathy. Just leave me alone."

Kicking off my shoes, I bring my feet up to rest on the edge of the seat. Wrapping my arms around my legs, I rest my cheek on my knee and stare out the window.

I hear his light exhalation of breath, but he doesn't make another attempt to speak to me.

I hear the quiet sound of Linkin Park fade out in the background. The next thing I hear is Snow Patrol's "Make This Go on Forever."

Bastard.

Mother-crapping bastard.

I hate it when he does this. Plays a particular song to speak to me. To get my attention when I won't listen to him.

But all he's doing right now is just reminding me of how much he hurt me. How much he's still hurting me.

I'm not playing his games. And I am most certainly not listening.

He can piss right off.

Lifting my weary head, I free an arm from around my leg and reach over and turn the music off.

Resuming my position, I spend the rest of the long, silent ride home trying to equal out the pain threatening to crush me to dust.

Jake pulls up on the drive outside our house and turns the engine off, leaving us with only the lights from the dash providing a small glow.

"Are you ready to hear me out, or do you need more time?" he asks quietly.

I lift my tired head and stare at him.

He looks torn and broken. I hate to see him this way. But I'm feeling torn and broken right now too.

"I'm listening," I whisper, putting my feet to the floor, not wholly sure I am ready to hear what he's got to say.

He turns his body toward me. "I'm so sorry for driving away and leaving you earlier." His voice is soft, tentative. "My behaviour was cruel and stupid. Tru, I need you to know I would never hurt you on purpose." He rubs his face roughly, driving his fingers into his hair. "God, the thought of you hurting—knowing I caused it—it's like a knife through my fuckin' heart. Believe me, if I could go back and have a do-over, tonight would go very differently."

Surprised, I look up. "Differently, how?"

He glances down at his hands, and when he speaks, the heartfelt tone in his voice almost breaks me. "To start with, I'd tell you that I love you and that nothing matters to me but you. But I'm afraid. Terrified. God, Tru, the second you told me you were pregnant, my own childhood flashed before my eyes." He breathes in deeply. "That's why I ran: because of my own fears, not because I don't want you or the baby."

He wants the baby?

"What are you terrified of?" I ask quietly.

"That I'm not good enough to be a dad. That I'll screw it up. That I'll fuck everything up. That I'll turn our child into a fucked-up mess like I am. Just like my dad did to me."

I'm just about to speak, to protest, to tell him he's not a fuck-up, that he's not Paul, he never could be, when he speaks again.

"But while I sat there thinking about all the negatives, I realised something."

"Which was?" I'm all but on the edge of my seat.

"That I have you," he says simply. "With you I know I can do it, because you're my strength, Tru. You make me want to be a better man, a good dad to our baby. The best. And I want to spend the rest of my life taking care of you both," I hear his voice break before he continues in a quieter tone.

"I don't want to be him, Tru. I don't ever want our kid to experience what I did growing up, and that's what will keep me straight. You'll both keep me straight."

I see tears staining his cheeks, and my heart shatters.

I choke out a sob. Releasing my seat belt, I throw myself into his lap.

His arms grip me with a vice force, and he buries his face in my neck. "I'm so sorry. Please forgive me for leaving you."

"I do. Of course I do. I'm sorry I said I hated you. I don't. I never could. I was just hurting."

"Right now, I'd deserve it if you did hate me, but it would break me if you did."

Lifting his head, he looks at me, and the force of his gaze hits me straight in the heart.

I trace his tears away with my fingertips and kiss over every inch of his face, moving slowly, until he catches my lips with his.

"Don't ever leave me again," he breathes against my mouth.

"How did you know I was at the airport?"

Moving from me, he rests his head against the headrest. "Jackson called to tell me you'd left in a cab, so I had him call the cab company to find out where they were taking you."

Ever resourceful. That's Jake.

I touch my hand to his face, running my fingers into his hair, gently twisting the ebony strands around the tips, and he closes his eyes, content.

Watching him, I hope that our baby looks just like him. I hope it has Jake's lovely features and beautiful blue eyes and my skin tone. But not my Puerto Rican–size bum.

Then I feel doubt start to creep in again. What if he changes his mind once the baby arrives? I don't think I could bear his leaving then.

"Jake," I murmur. He opens his eyes. "Are you absolutely sure this is what you want? The baby, I mean."

"I'm sure." His gaze drops to my stomach. "This baby will be made of everything I have loved my whole life."

"I'm gonna get fat," I mumble.

"No, you're going to get even sexier." Coming close again, he wraps his arms around me tightly, rubbing the tip of his nose against mine. "How could I not want something made up of Trudy Wethers's DNA?"

"Still Bennett." I grin. "You haven't made an honest woman of me yet."

"You ready to hop that plane to Vegas now?"

"A shotgun wedding. My folks would be so proud." I laugh.

"What do you want to do about the wedding?" he asks. "Move it forward?"

"That would give me a matter of weeks to plan it. Why don't we just wait until after the baby is born?"

I see him quickly do the math in his head. "We wouldn't be able to get married July twenty-first. You okay with that?"

"I'm going to have a mini-Jake soon. Of course I'm okay with that."

"Or a mini-Tru," he says. Then his expression suddenly changes. "Fuck, a girl. We might have to lock her up, Tru."

I scrunch up my face. "Why?"

"Because, if she looks anything like you, I'm one day going to be fighting off horny teenage boys left, right, and centre. I'll probably end up in jail for beating one to death if I find him with his hands on my baby girl." He shudders comically.

I let out a laugh. "Let's hope if we have a boy, he's doesn't grow up to be one of those horny teenagers...or God forbid, as horny as you are. Otherwise we'll have some girl's dad round here kicking his ass."

"Then I'll end up in jail for beating the shit out of the dad—fuck, this is a no-win, sweetheart," he groans, dropping his head back against the rest. "I'm doomed to a future behind bars."

Laughing softly, I say, "Don't worry, baby, we'll figure a way to keep you out of prison." I kiss the tip of his nose, then open the door, ready to get out of the car and into the house to bed.

Once inside, I head to the bedroom, grabbing a glass of water from the kitchen to take with me.

Smiling, feeling a million times happier than I did the last time I was here, I walk into our bedroom to find Jake still dressed and sitting on the edge of the bed, staring down at something in his hand. He doesn't look happy.

"You were really leaving me," he whispers.

My eyes go to his hand, and I see my engagement ring.

Crap.

My face prickles, shame burning it when I see how hasty I was in taking it off.

"I'm sorry." I take a step toward him. "I was angry, and I thought you didn't want the baby. I thought we didn't have a future anymore."

Jake gets to his feet. Coming over to me, he takes the glass from my hand and puts it down on the bedside cabinet.

He takes hold of my left hand. "I can't promise I won't fuck up again, Tru. I've tried and failed so many times. Just know that no matter what, I want you both very much." He slides the ring onto my finger. "I will always want you."

Taking his face in my hands, I pull him down to me and kiss his lips gently.

He picks me up and carries me to the bed. Turning off the light, Jake lies beside me, pulling me to his side, arms tight around me.

We're both still dressed, but I sense that right now, Jake doesn't want to be an inch away from me, just like I don't from him.

In the dark, Jake's hand goes to my stomach, rough fingers tracing over the fabric of my dress. "I love you," he whispers.

For the first time since we got together, I know that declaration isn't meant just for me. It gives me a flicker of hope that maybe, just maybe, things will be okay after all.

CHAPTER THIRTEEN

I wake in Jake's arms, still wearing last night's dress.

"Hey," he says softly beside me.

Turning my face to him, I look straight into his blue eyes.

His black hair is all mussed up from sleeping, but his eyes are wide-awake. He's been thinking.

Not good.

"How long have you been awake?" I ask, my voice wavering slightly.

"Not long." He brushes a stray curl from off my forehead.

There's a moment of still between us.

I don't know what to say after last night, and it seems neither does Jake.

"Are you okay?" he asks, breaking our silent stare.

Do I need a reason not to be?

"Yes." I nod, swallowing.

Are you?

Jake closes his eyes, releasing a breath.

What is he thinking? I'm afraid to ask. Afraid he's changed his mind about the baby.

I watch him, waiting. Opening his eyes, he takes my face in his hand and kisses me.

Deeply. Passionately. Reverently.

It's a kiss filled with unspoken words, promises, and love. Deep love. The love that has bound us together for nearly three decades.

"We're having a baby," I say when Jake's kiss slows.

"We are." He tilts his head back, looking into my eyes.

"You're going to be a daddy." I can't read him right now. He's still holding back from me.

He smiles, but it's tight. I can see the fear in his eyes that he was hiding a moment ago.

It sparks a pain in my chest. An awful, all-consuming pain.

"Jake, are you…okay?"

"Yeah, just a little—"

"Overwhelmed. Scared. Not ready. Changed your mind," I blurt out, cutting him off.

He looks puzzled, and then his eyes firm up, his gaze pinning me. "More like ready. Happy. Wanting our baby more than anything." His hand touches my stomach, and I exhale the breath I was holding. "I'm just worried," he adds quietly, casting his gaze beyond me.

My stomach tenses under his touch. "About?"

"That the baby isn't okay."

"The baby's fine." I relax, putting my hand over his, pressing it to my stomach.

"I want you to see a doctor today, Tru."

"I was planning on going on Monday."

"It has to be today," he says tightly. "I'll get Stuart to arrange it."

He sits up, turning from me, putting his feet to the floor. I follow, sitting beside him. Turning to face him, I wrap one leg around his front and the other around his back, trapping him.

"Why the rush?" I ask, tilting my head to the side, looking into his face.

Sighing, he meets my eyes for a brief moment, then looks away. "Tru, I've spent the last eight years using drugs—the last three, on a daily basis."

"But you're clean now," I input.

"Just over five weeks ago, I wasn't. Even though I wasn't using when you got pregnant, those drugs could have still been in my system, and…" He inhales sharply, driving his hand through his hair. He looks down. "I just need to make sure that the baby is okay, that the drugs haven't had any effect on the baby or caused any long-term damage." His voice sounds pained.

Fuck. I hadn't even thought of that. And if Jake's worried, I need to be too. He never worries unnecessarily.

Afraid but trying to remain positive, I say, "I'm sure the baby will be fine."

His chest expands on a quick, deep breath. "I'll believe that when I hear it from a doctor. I need to know today, Tru. Once I know, then I can relax and enjoy this with you."

I reach over and take his hand, linking our fingers. "Okay," I say, running my other hand through his soft, inky hair.

Reaching to the bedside cabinet for his phone, he says, "I'll call Stuart now to make us an appointment with the best pregnancy doctor there is."

I put my hand on his, stopping him. "They're called obstetricians, baby. And don't you think we should tell my folks, and your mum and Dale first, that we're having a baby, before we tell Stuart?"

"Sure I do, but we're not telling them until we know everything is okay. I don't know of a good obstetrician—do you?"

I shake my head.

"Then Stuart it is."

"How exactly will Stuart know about obstetricians? He might be gay, but he hasn't magicked up a vagina overnight that I know of."

That gets a smile out of him. A small one, but it's a start.

"Because, smart-ass, there isn't anything Stuart doesn't know or can't find out. That's why I pay him so well."

Lifting my hand from his, I say, "Okay, well, just don't tell him I'm pregnant. Tell him I'm having women's problems."

Not only do I want to tell my parents first, I don't want anyone to know about the baby until I know everything is okay.

I wasn't worried before Jake said something. But now... now I'm terrified there could be something wrong with the baby.

* * *

Three hours later, Jake and I are sitting in the office of Dr. Suzanne Kline, doctor to the rich and famous and the best obstetrician money can buy.

Her receptionist let us into her office. She looked less than happy to be working on a Saturday, but the instant she saw Jake walk in behind me, her face lit up like a Christmas tree.

She seated us in Dr. Kline's office, with the offer of a drink, telling us that Dr. Kline would be with us shortly.

I have to say it's the nicest doctor's office I have ever been in.

It's light and airy, all cream and beige. I'm sitting in the comfiest leather chair I've ever sat in, in front of a huge mahogany desk that looks like it cost more than I earn in a year. There's a sofa in the corner resembling the one we have at home, and there are pictures of babies everywhere. I'm guessing famous babies.

My child is going to be famous.

Crap. I hadn't even registered that fact. Sometimes I forget Jake is famous. Even though it's thrust into my face on a daily basis, I still just think of him as Jake Wethers, my best friend and boy next door.

Our child is going to be famous simply for the fact Jake is.

The baby's not going to have the chance for a normal childhood like I had.

It's going to live its life accompanied by bodyguards, safety always a cause for concern.

I'm going to have to talk to Jake about this. I want our child to have as normal a life as possible. I know he'll want that too, so we're going to have to figure out a way to make it happen.

Jake hasn't sat still since we arrived. I can feel nerves and tension radiating off him. I have never seen him this worked up before. It's freaking me out.

I rest my hand on his thigh, settling his jigging leg.

He looks at me, giving me a tight smile.

"It's going to be fine," I say, trying to sound convincing, even though I am less than confident myself. I become even more so as the minutes pass.

"I hope so," he utters. "I really hope so." He takes my hand, bringing it to his mouth, and brushes a kiss over my knuckles.

It's at this point Dr. Kline finally makes her appearance.

Imagine the one doctor you wouldn't want in the same room as your hot, ex-womanising, rocker boyfriend. Well, yeah, that's Dr. Suzanne Kline.

She is tall, early thirties, I'd say, long blonde hair that is tied back in a sleek ponytail. She's wearing high-waisted blue jeans that only stick-thin people can wear, with a button-up white shirt tucked in, which sits just perfectly around her perfect-size chest. No gaping buttonholes for her.

Basically, she's gorgeous. And I hate her instantly.

Remind me to kick the crap out of Stuart when we get home.

She may be the best OB/GYN in LA, but I would have rather settled for the second best, even the third, as long as they didn't look anything like her.

"Sorry I'm a little late," she says, advancing across the room toward us.

Reaching her hand out to me, I spot her perfect mani-cure and cringe at my chipped red nail varnish.

"I'm Dr. Suzanne Kline," she says. "But please just call me Suzanne."

"Trudy Bennett," I reply. *But please just call me Ms. Bennett,* I'm tempted to say just to be a bitch.

I bite my tongue, hard.

Turning to Jake, she releases her hand from mine and offers it to Jake. He takes it. "Jake Wethers," he says.

"I know who you are, Mr. Wethers." She presses her lips into a quirked smile, looking a little shy, and I see her eyes have widened in his gaze. In this instant she looks like one of his groupies.

I hate the effect he has on women. She's a smart, successful doctor, one who comes in contact with celebrities on a regular basis, yet one touch and a look from Jake and she's a teenage girl again.

I think I may vomit.

"Jake, please," he says, and he sounds so smooth that I have the urge to slap him up the back side of his head.

Releasing her hand, he instantly takes hold of my hand again, pulling it to rest in his lap.

I feel like giving a smug smile, but I don't. I know I'm being irrational, I know that Jake only has eyes for me, but I hate the way she was looking at him. I take a quick glance at her left hand as she makes her way around the desk to her chair.

It's a yes on the wedding ring. But when has the little matter of having a husband ever stopped women from trying to get into Jake's pants?

"Please excuse my attire," she says in her sexy American twang, gesturing to her clothes as she sits down. "I came straight from family brunch."

"Sorry to pull you away," Jake says. "But I wanted Tru to see a doctor today."

"No worries. What seems to be the problem, Tru?" She directs her question to me, leaning forward in her seat.

I stiffen a little under her blue-eyed scrutiny. "Well, I, um, took a pregnancy test—three actually—and they all said

I'm, um, pregnant." I have no idea why, but my cheeks are bright red, and I feel flustered.

"This is good news…for you both?" she asks carefully, moving her eyes between Jake and me.

"Very good news." Jake smiles at me, squeezing my hand. "Unplanned but very much wanted."

My heart melts.

"That's wonderful news." She beams, smiling a bright white Hollywood smile. If possible, she looks even more gorgeous.

Ugh.

"Many congratulations to you both," she adds.

"Thank you," Jake replies.

I can't reply because I'm too busy gnawing over the fact that I'm going to get as fat as a house and my baby doctor is a glamazon.

Dr. Glamazon.

There really should be a law against this kind of thing. People as beautiful as her should not be allowed to be baby doctors.

I think I might kick the crap out of Stuart twice now, just for good measure. He's officially off my Christmas list.

He's just introduced Jake to a smart, beautiful glamazon who knows her shit about women's bits, probably men's too, so therefore, she will be awesome at sex. And I'm about to turn into fat, dumpy Tru, who very soon won't have a lot to offer in the sex department.

"I'm taking it from the urgency to see me today, you have some concern over the pregnancy," Dr. Glamazon states rather than asks, cutting into my bitching thoughts.

"Yes." Jake sits forward in his seat but keeps a tight hold of my hand. "It's public knowledge of my use of drugs and that I was in rehab getting clean." I feel him tense, so I rest my free hand on his knee. He gives me a quick glance and continues. "What isn't public knowledge is that a little over seven weeks ago, I started using again."

"Are you still using now?" she asks.

"No." He shakes his head vehemently. "I used for two weeks, stopped, and I've been clean for the last five."

"What drugs were you taking?"

"Cocaine."

"I take it you're worried you might still have had drugs in your system when you conceived?"

"Yes." His grip on my hand tightens to near pain, but I don't say anything. I'm as anxious as he is to hear what she has to say.

I'm watching Dr. Glamazon, trying to gauge her reaction to what Jake's asking, but there's not a shred of emotion in her face.

Poker face. I bet she's had Botox done.

She leans back in her chair, elbows on the rests, fingers steepled.

"I understand your concern, Jake, but honestly, there is nothing for you to worry about. There's been a lot of research done about the possible side effects on sperm from recreational drug usage, and to date there is nothing to prove that drugs cause any long-term side effects on a developing fetus."

I feel Jake relax beside me. And me too. It's such a relief to hear.

"The only known side effects are significant reductions in sperm count," Dr. Glamazon continues, "sometimes resulting in infertility—which obviously hasn't been a problem for you." She gives him a hinting smile, which raises my hackles.

I know she's a doctor, but she seriously shouldn't talk about my man's virility like that.

I clear my throat and raise my eyebrow at her.

She breezes a look to me, composing herself, and says to Jake, "Most commonly, the issue we see from drug usage and a developing fetus comes directly from the mother. If a woman uses drugs when pregnant, the drugs will pass through the placenta and directly to the baby. That's when we have issues such as deformities and long-term health problems."

Ooh, you bitch.

I'm seriously getting a new baby doctor.

"I have never touched drugs in my life," I state, probably a little too loudly. I dig my nails so hard into Jake's hand, I hear him wince. "I don't even smoke cigarettes, let alone joints!"

"That's really good to hear, Tru." She smiles pleasantly.

Now I just want to slap her. Hard. A few times.

God, what the hell is wrong with me? Is this what pregnancy does? Or have I always been this jealous?

I guess I'm just jealous when it comes to Jake.

He runs the pad of his thumb across the palm of my hand.

I know he's trying to settle me, but I'm a riled right now and in no mood to be settled.

"I was still on the pill when I got pregnant," I blurt out.

Crap, how did I forget that? Actually, how the hell did I manage to get pregnant while on the pill? It's never failed me in all the years I've been taking it.

"You were taking the pill when you got pregnant?" Dr. Glamazon asks, her perfectly shaped brow raised.

Does she think I'm lying or something? Or that I've trapped Jake by getting pregnant on purpose?

Does he think the same?

I sneak a quick glance at him, but his face is impassive as he looks at Dr. Glamazon.

I wish I knew what he was thinking right now.

"Yes, I've been on the pill for a really long time, and it's never let me down before—obviously," I mutter, not helping my case at all.

I start to chew on my free thumbnail, killing all hope for my nail varnish.

"Have you missed taking any pills this month?" Dr. Glamazon asks.

"No." My face is bright red, like I'm guilty of something. I hate it when that happens. "I never forget. I've always been methodical about taking it."

"Have you taken any other medication lately?"

"Yes she has," Jake answers. He removes my hand from my mouth, stopping me from biting my nails. "Tru was sick while we were on holiday. She had food poisoning, and the doctor prescribed her some medication."

"Did he advise if there would be any interference with contraception from taking the medication?" she asks.

"No," Jake answers again before I get the chance to. "Tru was too sick to be asking or answering any questions at that time, so it was on me, and honestly it wasn't something

I even considered asking the doctor. The fault lies with me on that one."

I feel him talking to me in that last sentence.

"There's no fault," I whisper to him. "I'm happy to be having our baby."

He smiles. One of those special, reserved-for-me-only smiles.

Dr. Glamazon starts talking, interrupting our moment. "The medication you took, combined with the sickness, possibly will have made the contraceptive pill ineffective. The prescribing doctor should have advised of this."

"Will my being on the pill while pregnant have harmed the baby at all?" I turn to her, shifting forward in my seat, changing the direction of this conversation.

Between the two of us, Jake and I don't seem to have been aiming to give our baby the best start in life.

She smiles, and this one actually appears genuine. "It's a common thing that happens among women, so no, I don't think there will be any side effects from it. Just to give you both total peace of mind, I'll do a scan now and take a look at your baby to make sure all is okay."

A scan? Now? I'm going to see my baby right now? My heart practically pole vaults out of my chest.

I don't miss the way Jake's hand tightens around mine either.

I risk a look at him, but his face is impassive. A mask. The one he wears when he doesn't want people—mainly me—to know what he's thinking.

Standing and moving around her desk, past us, Dr. Glamazon asks, "When was the last day of your last period, Tru?"

I cast my mind back. Turning in my seat, I say, "The third of October, I think."

"Okay, can you undress your lower half and hop up on the bed?" She points to the sterile-looking bed at the far side of the room she's walking toward. "You can cover yourself up with this." She places a drape on the bed.

With nerves fluttering in my tummy, I go over to the bed, leaving Jake in his seat. Dr. Glamazon pulls the curtain, giving me privacy.

It's not until I'm actually on the bed that I wonder why the hell I need my pants off if she's going to scan my tummy? Unless she's going to do an internal examination first.

Oh God, she's going to do an internal in front of Jake. I know he's seen everything I have to offer, but I really don't want him here while the doctor pokes around my lady bits. I wonder if I could ask him to leave without offending him.

"All ready?" Dr. Glamazon asks from behind the curtain.

"Yes," I reply, my voice sounding a little strangled.

Pulling back the curtain a little she walks in, followed by Jake.

He looks uncomfortable. Then I see his eyes instantly go to my lower half, which is covered by the drape, and a sexy smile flirts across his lips.

Only Jake would see the sexy side of this current situation. He's such a perv. But I like that no matter what circumstance I'm in, I can still get him that way.

I reach for his hand, smiling up at him. I mouth, *Perv*.

His eyes twinkle, and he grins, lips pressed together. He flickers a glance to Dr. Glamazon, who has her back to us, getting something from a cupboard. He mouths to me, *You look so fucking sexy right now.* He traces his finger along my jaw.

I roll my eyes at him and mouth back, *Yeah, sure I do.*

Another glance to the doctor and he mouths back, expression firm and serious, *Yes, you do. You always do.*

Okay. That's me told.

I smile softly at him, and then Dr. Glamazon appears beside me.

"Okay, Trudy," she begins, while fiddling with a monitor she's pulled over beside me. "Because you're so early into your pregnancy, I'm going to do a transvaginal ultrasound."

"A what?"

"A transvaginal ultrasound. I'll place this inside you." She lifts up what can only be described as something that looks exactly like a handheld blender. "It will show us your baby. It's the same as a sonogram, only done internally."

"You're going to put *that* inside of me?" My lungs seize up for a few held breaths.

"Don't worry, it's perfectly safe and pain-free."

I look at Jake, worried. He smiles and smooths my hair back from my forehead, but I can see in his eyes that even he's a bit freaked.

"You'll be fine," he says. "Having this done means we're going to get to see our baby."

Yeah, well, that's easy for him to say. He's not getting a huge handheld blender stuck up his vagina. Of course I want to see our baby and know it's okay, but holy fuck, that thing looks painful.

"I would normally do a sonogram for the first scan," Dr. Glamazon explains, "but they're done at twelve weeks. As you're so early into your pregnancy, the baby won't show on a sonogram. This is the only way I'm going to be able to see the baby to check that all is okay."

Guess I don't have a choice, then.

She retrieves a pair of surgical gloves from a box and puts them on.

"Don't worry, Tru. In a few moments you're going to see your baby on this screen here." She nods in the direction of the monitor beside me.

"Okay." I swallow.

I'm going to see my baby in a few moments. Wow. This is getting real now.

"If you could just bend your knees up for me. Perfect. Now just relax," Dr. Glamazon says, resting her hand against my knee as she starts to insert that god-awful thing inside of me.

Wincing, I scrunch up my face, squeezing Jake's hand.

Oh, okay, actually it's not as bad as I thought it would be.

"There we go," she says. "This tiny little thing here is your baby."

I flick my eyes open and come face-to-face with a little blob on the screen.

My baby. Our baby.

My heart lifts into my mouth, and tears prick my eyes.

I notice Jake's grip on my hand has tightened along with my own, and when I turn to look at him, I see his eyes fixed on the screen. Glittering and filled with awe. My heart trembles, lifts, and then flutters daintily out of my chest.

"Jake?" I whisper.

His eyes move to mine, and in their meeting, a heartbreaking smile sweeps over his face. A smile I will remember for the rest of my days.

Leaning down to me, he presses a kiss to my forehead.

"Thank you," he whispers against my skin, and I almost crack wide open on the spot.

A tear slides from my eye, and I discreetly brush it away.

"Everything looks absolutely fine to me," Dr. Glamazon says, looking at the screen, moving a mouse around, clicking little markers around my tiny baby. "We have a good, strong heartbeat. Baby is growing nicely. I'd say you're coming up to about six weeks along."

Staring at my tiny baby, I feel all kinds of emotions I've never felt before. I can't even begin to form words to express them.

Then Dr. Glamazon is removing the wand from me, and my tiny baby disappears from view.

"I'll run off some prints for you." She smiles at both Jake and me, and I'm guessing it's because of the mirrored expressions of disappointment on our faces.

Leaving me to dress, Jake sits back in his seat while the doctor sorts out our baby pictures.

I dress, feeling happy and excited. We're having a baby. A real honest-to-God baby.

Seeing the pregnancy tests made it real, of course. But in a surreal way. Seeing our baby up on that screen made it real in the best possible way.

I slide my shoes back on and return to my seat beside Jake.

He takes hold of my hand the moment I sit down, linking his fingers with mine. He kisses my hand.

The love and emotion moving between us right now is palpable. I can't wait to be alone with him and talk to him about the future we're going to have with our baby.

"I'll write you up a prescription for some prenatal vitamins," Dr. Glamazon says, scribbling on a prescription pad. "And I'll have my receptionist make an appointment for your next checkup so we can order some bloodwork."

She tears off the prescription and hands it to me. "Don't forget the pictures of your baby," she adds, handing me a white envelope.

My baby. I'm going to be a mum.

Taking that as our cue to leave, I rise from my seat. "Thank you, Doctor. And thanks for seeing us on your day off."

"I was happy to. If you have any other questions, please don't hesitate to call me."

"I have a question," Jake adds, still perched on his seat, long legs stretched out.

I pause and look down at him.

"Sex," he says to the doctor.

"Sex?" Dr. Glamazon repeats.

Sex?

"Yes, sex. Can Tru and I still have sex while she's pregnant? Is it safe for the baby?"

She smiles. I do too. I actually have to stop from giggling. He is so bloody cute to me right now.

"It's absolutely safe," Dr. Glamazon says, nodding. "You can continue to have a healthy and active sex life throughout the whole pregnancy."

Jake scratches his forehead. "Yeah, I know people generally have sex while pregnant, but it's just that I, um…well, I have…" He thrusts his hand through is hair, and I can't help but smile at his struggling, wondering where on earth he's going with this.

"Look, I have a huge penis," he states, looking Dr. Glamazon dead in the eye.

I burst out laughing, quickly clamping my hand over my mouth.

Dr. Glamazon looks shocked. Can't blame her. Jake Wethers just said "penis" in her office. Specifically, "I have a huge penis."

My smutty, tattooed, sexy rock star Jake just said "penis." It just sounds so very, very wrong.

I start laughing again.

Jake turns his head, giving me a pissed-off look. Okay, so he's not amused.

"I'm sorry," I say, moving my hand from my mouth. "I've just never heard you say that word before." I snort. "Okay, I'll shut up," I add at his hardening expression. I press my lips together, twisting the grin off them. It's harder than you'd think.

"Look, what I'm trying to say is…" Jake thrusts his hand through his hair again. "Is that I'm bigger than the average man. A *lot* bigger. And I just want to know I won't hurt the baby when Tru and I have sex."

I look at Dr. Glamazon and can see her eyes are flicking to everything but Jake. I know she's desperately trying not to look at his crotch. Honestly, I can't blame her. The curiosity would be killing me too.

She clears her throat. "Um, Jake, the baby will be fine during intercourse. Honestly fine. It's really well protected. There is no way you can hurt it, no matter how big you… um, are." She looks so uncomfortable right now that I actually feel for her.

But I still want to laugh. I bite down hard on my lip.

I see Jake's face relax. "Cool, that's really good to know," he says, getting to his feet.

He sounds like he's just finishing up a conversation about the weather, not one about his huge penis.

Penis.

I snuffle another laugh, and Jake fires me another pissed-off look as he turns my way.

I'm so in trouble when we get out of here.

CHAPTER FOURTEEN

"Will you stop fuckin' laughing?" Jake growls.

He's not amused that ten minutes later, I'm still laughing about the penis comment.

"I'm not laughing." I suck my bottom lip into my mouth, staring out the passenger window.

"Sure you're not," he mutters. "Look at me."

I try to compose my face before turning to him, but it betrays me. I scrunch my features up.

"You are so fuckin' laughing." He scowls.

"I'm sorry." A laugh slips out. I try to cover it with a cough. "I just can't believe you of all people just said the word 'penis.'"

"What did you want me to call it?" he bites out.

"I would have preferred it if you hadn't said it at all to Dr. Hot back there."

He slides me a "let's not go there" look. Taking a left turn, Jake takes us into the hills toward home.

"Look," he sighs. "I just wanted to make sure I couldn't hurt our baby when we have sex, which you know with you, I want to do often—multiple times daily, in fact." He runs his hand up my thigh and my sex quivers, suddenly desperate for his touch, needing to feel him inside me.

"It's not like I'm going to say to the doctor, 'I have a huge *cock*,'" he adds, and that's like a bucket of cold water over my libido, setting my laughter off again.

"I'm never going to live this down, am I?" he grumbles, taking hold of the gear stick.

"Nope." I slide him a humoured look.

"You're going to tell everyone we know, aren't you?"

"Not everyone. Maybe just Stuart. And Simone. And my dad."

My dad would find it hilarious for sure. He has the same warped sense of humour as me.

"If you tell Billy that I said penis to the doctor, then I'm going to tell him exactly what you do to my *penis* with that hot, dirty mouth of yours."

"You wouldn't dare," I gasp.

"Try me." He narrows his eyes, challenging.

"You're such a child," I huff.

"Says you, who's been laughing about the word 'penis' for the last ten minutes."

Penis.

I look at him. I'm grinning. Then Jake's smile cracks, and we both start laughing hard, and it feels good. For a moment, it feels like we're those carefree teenagers we used to be.

We're still laughing when Jake pulls up at our gates and Henry lets us in.

Parking the car on the drive, we go inside, and I kick my shoes off and flop down on the sofa.

I pull the envelope containing the baby pictures out of my bag. I've been dying to look at them, but I wanted to wait until we were home so we could look at them in private together.

Another happy memory to coat the walls of our home.

Jake sits beside me, taking my feet in his lap. "Can I?" he gestures to the envelope.

I hand it to him and watch as he takes the pictures out.

I move closer to him, sitting beside him, my thigh pressed against his. Jake's arm goes around me and I rest my shoulder against his chest as we both stare down at the black-and-white picture of our baby. Our tiny, tiny baby.

Jake is so still. All I can hear is the sound of his gentle breathing. I steal a glance at his face, and the emotion I see steals my own.

"It's really ours," he says, fingertip touching the image of our baby. His voice is so soft.

"It's really ours," I utter, my voice cracking.

"Who knew I could contribute to making something so perfect?" Jake glances at me through his long lashes. "Thank you." This is the second time today he's thanked me, and this time I have to ask why.

"For being with me. For giving me a chance at getting my life right. Only with you would I ever have a chance at having a family. You're everything to me, and now you've given me so much more with our baby."

Tilting his face to mine, I kiss his lips tenderly.

He wraps his arms around me, taking me with him back into the sofa, his lips pressed to my forehead.

I love feeling Jake this way. Contented and at peace with himself.

I trace my finger over the detailed tattoos on his arm. "Life's good, huh?" I murmur.

"Life's great." I feel his smile against my skin.

"You hungry?" I ask.

"I could eat something. You want to order in?"

I shift back from him so I can see his face. "We could cook something once in a while, you know," I tease.

"You in the mood to cook?"

Too comfortable to consider moving right now, I shake my head.

"Ordering in it is, then." He chuckles deep. It vibrates through his chest. "What are you in the mood for?"

"Chicken Caesar salad with Parmesan and a crusty roll."

"Nothing specific, then," he teases.

"Hey, I'm eating for two here, you know."

Smiling, Jake gets his phone out and orders my salad and a grilled cheese for himself from the local deli.

While he's on the phone, my thoughts drift to the scan and how it felt seeing our baby. Then my thoughts move to Dr. Kline and how attractive she is. I wonder if Jake thinks she's good-looking. Before I can think it through, in usual Tru style, I'm saying, "Dr. Kline is really pretty."

He shoves his phone back in his pocket. "I hadn't noticed."

"Sure you hadn't." I roll my eyes.

Jake lifts my leg off him. He leans over me, forcing me to lie back, and places his hands either side of me, pelvis pressed hard against my sex. He rests the tip of his nose against mine. "I hadn't noticed," he repeats. "When you're in the room, sweetheart, I don't see anyone but you."

A shiver runs down my spine, and I start to hum with desire.

"I'm going to get fat," I say, pouting.

"No, you're going to have my baby growing inside of you, and right now I can't think of anything sexier."

Jake slants his mouth over mine, kissing me leisurely. I part my lips with a moan, and his tongue moves inside, stroking mine.

Right now, I would like nothing more than to have Jake inside me, but our lunch is on its way, and I have this nagging worry about calling my parents to tell them about the baby. Mainly my mum. I'm worried how she's going to take the news. I'm already well aware of her concerns over my relationship with Jake and my moving here after such a short time together. Plus the engagement, coupled with the problems Jake's had—we've had. I fear this may push her over the edge.

"Speaking of the baby," I say, as his tongue trails over my lower lip.

"Were we? I thought we were heading more in the direction of doing what created our baby in the first place." He puts his hand up my top, pulling back the cup on my bra, and gently rolls my nipple between his thumb and forefinger.

My body instinctively arches into his touch.

"I need to call my folks and tell them about the baby," I utter, breathless.

"Soon," he groans, pushing his erection against my sex. The seam of his jeans works through my own, rubbing against my throbbing clit.

"I can't call my parents straight after we've made love."

"So call them tonight. That's if I'm done with you by then," he breathes, nipping my earlobe with his teeth. "I'm desperate for you," he groans.

Aching from his promise, but worry claiming me more, I put my hands to his chest. "I want you too, Jake, but right now, I need to call them."

Stopping his assault on my earlobe, he moves back and looks me in the eye. "You're worried they won't be happy about the baby, aren't you?"

I bite my lip and shake my head.

He sits back on his heels, staring down at me, and I see a darkness take his eyes. "Sorry, I'll rephrase that. You're worried Eva won't be happy about you having a baby with me."

I sigh and push my hands through my hair.

"You know Mama thinks we've moved too fast together. She worries for me—a lot—and she lived this life with my dad, having a baby with a musician, on the road, and…" I trail off, struggling to find the right words. "I guess I'm just worried she'll…"

"What? Want you to go back to England to live? Make you choose?" He frowns.

"No. I don't know." I shrug. Sitting up, I wrap my arms around his waist, resting my cheek against his chest. "I just don't want her to be angry with me."

"Tru." He rests his hands on my shoulders and moves down to my eye level. I can see that his hardened expression has softened. "You just said yourself that she's lived this life." He tucks my hair behind my ear. "But remember, we are more financially secure than they were back then. I'm not just some singer in a band."

"But when she gets something in her head, Jake, it's hard trying to change it."

"Reminds me of someone I know well," he implies with a smile. "We'll call them now and settle your mind, and I'll screw you mindless later."

Getting his phone back out, he dials my parents' home number, putting it on speaker, and sets the phone on the coffee table before us.

"Hello," comes my dad's deep voice down the line. Just hearing his voice causes my heart to beat faster.

"Hey, Daddy."

"Baby girl!" I can almost see his big, bright smile. I miss him so much. "How are you?"

"I'm good, Daddy. Um, is Mama there?" I swallow.

"Yeah, you want me to get her? Your old man not good enough to talk to nowadays?" he teases.

"Actually, I need to talk to you both. Can you put me on speaker?"

"Everything okay, darlin'?"

"Everything's fine, Daddy. I—*we*—have some news."

"Okay, let me get your mum."

I slide a look at Jake, desperately trying to swallow down my nerves.

Jake rubs my back. "Don't worry, it's going to be fine," he whispers.

"Tru, is everything okay?" My mum's worried tone comes on.

"Yes, everything's fine. Great, in fact." I run my tongue over my dry lips. "Is Dad still there?"

"I'm here," he says.

"Okay. Jake's here too, and, um, we've got some news. We're, um...we're having a baby."

There's utter silence. For a really long time.

Then my dad breaks it.

"That's great news, honey. Really, really great news. Isn't it, Eva?" I can practically feel him elbowing my mum to respond.

"*Cómo pudiste permitir que esto suceda?*"

My face heats and prickles.

"*Que esto suceda?* Let this happen, Mama?" I repeat in English, as I don't want to hide anything about this conversation from Jake. "I didn't let anything happen. We didn't intend to get pregnant, obviously. But it's something that has happened, and we are both extremely happy about it. I was hoping you would be too."

"We are happy," my dad insists.

"Mama?" I press.

"Are you going to give the band up, Jake?" she asks him directly.

"No, he's not," I say before he gets a chance to speak.

She sighs loudly. "So he will be on the road touring, and you will be home alone in America with a baby."

"No," Jake butts in before I get another chance to speak.

Probably a good thing because I'm so bloody rattled right now.

"We haven't worked out the fine details yet, Eva, but Tru won't be home alone with the baby. I'm going to be the biggest part of our baby's life. I won't have my child raised the way I was." The harshness of his tone surprises me, but I can't blame him. "I see your concern, really I do, but it won't be that way. I will always be here for them both. I don't want you and Billy to worry."

My mum is silent for a tense moment.

"I want you to be happy about this, Mama. This isn't like you and Dad on the road. Jake's life is different—"

"Yes, it's bigger than your father's ever was. Jake is busy and in demand, and his life is pressured. Look at what happened the last time things got hard for him. He was back on drugs and you found that girl in his bed. You were brokenhearted."

"Mama!" I cry, devastated she's bringing that back up.

"Enough, now, Eva," my dad says. "You know what happened."

It's another tense moment of silence, as tears make their way down my cheeks.

"I know I've screwed up in the past and let Tru down," Jake says, breaking the silence. "Trust me, no one knows that better than I do." His voice is hoarse and it hurts me to hear. "But it won't ever happen again. I know what I stand to lose, *believe* me. I love Tru very much. She's everything to me, and I want her happiness as much as you do."

I reach out and caress his cheek.

I turn back to the phone. "I thought you of all people would understand this, Mama." I rub the tears from my face. "That you would be on my side and support us in having this baby."

I hear her sharp intake of breath. "I am on your side, Tru. I'm always on your side."

"So then be happy for me...for us. You're going to be a grandma, and Dad a granddaddy."

The moment of silence is soft, not sullen. That's when I know I have her.

"How far along are you?" she asks, her voice wavering a little.

"Six weeks." A smile bites my lips. "I have some pictures. I can scan one into the laptop and e-mail it to you."

"I'd love that."

"Okay," I say, wrapping the call up. "I'll scan it in soon and e-mail it over."

"Tru." She pauses. "I'm happy for you...for you both."

Tears prick my eyes. "Thanks, Mama. I love you."

"Love you," Mama says.

"And me!" Dad calls in.

I chuckle past the lump in my throat. "Love you too, Daddy."

"Oh, and make sure Jake doesn't smoke near you now that you're pregnant," Mama starts in, "and you'll need to start taking prenatal vitamins. No caffeine or seafood…"

"I got it covered, Mama." I smile. "Don't worry."

"Okay, we'll see you soon."

We all say our good-byes, and Jake ends the call. I fall back against the sofa.

"Bloody hell, that was stressful," I mutter, driving my fingers over my aching scalp.

Jake lies back beside me. "You can't blame her. She worries because she loves you, and I can see where she's coming from. In her eyes, I'm not exactly ideal husband or father material."

"Well, she's wrong." I turn my face to his and trace my finger over his full lips.

"That may be, but I have to prove it to her."

"You don't need to prove anything to anyone."

"I do. To both your mom and dad. I want them to trust that I can take care of you both." He runs his fingers over my tummy.

"My dad trusts you. He thinks the world of you."

"He likes me, Tru. We get on great. But I don't know about trust, especially not with his little girl."

"Well, I trust you, and that's what counts." I take hold of his hand, bringing it from my stomach to my mouth, and kiss it. "Do you want to call your mum and Dale?"

He shakes his head, chuckling. "No, I think we need a break after that."

"You think she'll be difficult like Mama was?"

"No, but right now all I can think about is getting you naked and finishing what we started before. I seriously need to get inside you after listening to you get all fiery, talking in angry Spanish like that."

Laughing, I say, "The food will be here soon."

"We've got time," he says, taking hold of my legs, pulling me down the couch. He kneels between them and sets to work on removing my jeans and panties, while I remove my top and bra.

Jake takes his T-shirt off, and then we're skin on skin, as he rests his chest against mine.

I wind my fingers into his hair, bringing his mouth to mine. I hook my leg around his hip as his hand slides down my thigh, gripping my butt, and he kisses me like he's starved for me, his tongue plunging into my mouth, deep and hard. His hands take mine, above my head, pinning them to the cushion.

I grind my pelvis into him, groaning in his mouth.

Then the doorbell rings.

"Motherfucker," he growls heavily into my mouth. "Can't a guy get a moment with his girl here?" He grumbles, getting up to answer the door.

I start to sit up to retrieve my clothes. "Don't you dare move," he commands. "I want to come back here and find you exactly as I left you."

"And how's that?" I ask, resting my arms on the back of the sofa and my chin on my arms, looking across at him. God, he looks so totally hot right now. Abs rippling down to his low-slung jeans. My tattoo inked around them. His hard-on so very visible through his jeans, like his cock is straining to get out of them and into me.

"Naked and waiting to be fucked." He grins, walking backward.

"*Sí, señor.*" I salute.

He groans, grabbing his cock through his jeans, then turns and heads for the door.

I lie back down on the sofa so whoever's at the door won't see naked me sitting here.

I hear the door open, then Henry's voice. The door closes, so I sit up just as Jake walks back into the living room with a bag containing our lunch in his hand.

"You want to eat now?" he asks, totally insincerely.

I shake my head. "I want you to get your hot ass over here and use that huge penis of yours on me." I bite down on my grin.

Jake puts the bag of food down on the side table and advances toward me like a panther moving in on its prey.

"With absolute fuckin' pleasure," he says, vaulting over the back of the couch, landing on his feet between my legs, he gets down to his knees, and down to business instantly.

CHAPTER FIFTEEN

I look around at the Christmas decorations adorning the restaurant and I get that giddy, excitable feeling I always get this time of year. Now it's a million times amplified, because this Christmas will be Jake's and my first Christmas together in years, and our first as a couple. A couple who's having a baby.

We're having a baby! I'm still excited about it, if you didn't guess.

It's also Jake's birthday on the twenty-third of December. He'll be the grand old age of twenty-seven. Like our Christmas, this is the first birthday together in twelve years, so I'm making sure it'll be a good one.

That's why I'm out for dinner tonight with Stuart and Carly: we're planning a surprise birthday party for Jake.

I considered spending his birthday with just the two of us, but we have so many people coming for Christmas, that it just seemed right to share his day with everyone we love.

Carly has become a really good friend since I hired her company to decorate our house. She is doing an amazing job. We're halfway through the decorating, but Carly assures me it will be finished in time for Christmas, thank God. I can't think of anything worse than a house full of people in a half-decorated house.

My mum and dad are coming for Christmas. I'm so excited to see them; it's been way too long.

Simone is coming for Christmas too. She'll be staying at Denny's place, but they're coming over to ours for Christmas dinner.

We've also got Tom coming, and Zane too. Apparently Zane isn't close to his family in New York, so I told Jake to invite him. I can't bear to think of anyone alone at Christmas, let alone people I care about.

I invited Smith and Carly too, but they're heading back home to Tennessee after Jake's party.

Of course Jake's mum, Susie, and his stepdad, Dale, are coming.

Jake knows none of this. He knows everyone is coming for Christmas, but he thinks everyone is getting in on Christmas Eve.

It'll be nice to see Susie again. I haven't seen her since Paul's funeral in Manchester. And I haven't seen Dale since I was fourteen.

She was over the moon when we called and told her I'm pregnant. Hers was the complete opposite reaction from my mum's.

I think she's relieved and happy that Jake is finally settling down. That he's found his happiness.

Everyone else was stoked about the baby too. Stuart flipped, in the best possible way. Simone went all crazy too. But the most touching reaction was Vicky's. When I told her I was pregnant, she started crying real, happy tears. I was Skyping with her, and I could see the genuine emotion. It set me off crying too.

I owe Vicky a lot. If it wasn't for her landing the interview with Jake, we wouldn't be together now. I have everything in the world to thank her for.

I was hoping Vicky would come for Christmas too, but she already has plans with her family. But I'm making sure I'll see her real soon.

"So we're really having this birthday party at Pizza Hut?" Stuart grimaces.

"Stop being a snob," I say, laughing. "Pizza Hut is important to Jake and me."

"Ah yes, the teenage-dream years." He places his hand over his heart, teasingly.

"What's this?" Carly asks.

"It was a tradition when Jake and I were younger. We used to celebrate our birthdays at Pizza Hut. When we got back in contact, the first thing Jake did was take me out to dinner at Pizza Hut."

"He hired the whole place out for her," Stuart adds. "It was really sweet. I was genuinely impressed with him." He smiles at me, giving me a secret wink.

"Have you picked out his gift?" Stuart asks, cutting into his steak.

"I have." I smile proudly, biting down on a stick of asparagus.

I was stuck what to buy Jake. I mean, what do you buy the man who has everything?

Then I remembered Jake's old guitar, the first guitar he ever had that my dad bought him.

When he left for the States, he left his guitar behind, and my dad has kept it all these years. It was packed away in the garage, so I asked my dad to get it out and have it reconditioned.

He's shipping it out to me this week, and when it arrives, I'm going to have some artwork done on the back for him.

I definitely think it's thirteen birthdays' worth in the thought alone.

"So we've got the guest list settled, then?" I say, peering down at my notepad on the table, reaching for my water.

"Actually, you need to add a plus one…for me," Stuart says, looking sheepish.

I put my glass back down without taking a drink. "A plus one." I smile. "Might this be the mysterious man you've been keeping from us?"

"Yes, and he isn't mysterious. You know his name."

"Josh the hot doctor!" both Carly and I chime together. "And yes, he is," I add. "You haven't let any of us catch a glimpse of him, let alone meet him."

"Because I didn't want you lot scaring him away. He's shy." He bites the steak off his fork.

"But he's coming to the party?"

Stuart smiles, chewing. "He is."

"Yay!" I clap my hands together.

This guy is important to Stuart, I can tell by the way he is about him. I cannot wait to meet the guy who is putting that gorgeous smile on Stuart's face.

I scribble down hot doctor Josh's name on my list and underline it.

"Are your mom and dad coming for the party?" Carly asks.

"Yes." I press my lips together.

"Your mom is okay with Jake and the baby now?"

Carly has been the listening ear to my venting. Even though Mama has accepted the fact that Jake and I are having a baby, and she's looking forward to being a grandma, she is still somewhat frosty when it comes to Jake. And I know for a fact she thinks I should move back to England to have the baby.

"She's almost there," I say with a nod, picking up my water again. "I think the visit at Christmas will do it. Jake will win Mama over. I'm sure of it."

Okay, maybe not sure—hoping.

Mama can't see past Jake's history. But I'm not perfect either. She doesn't see how I hurt Jake when I was stuck between him and Will, and how he fought for me. How much he loves me.

No matter how many times I tell her that Jake and I have hurt each other enough to last a lifetime and he's not going to hurt me like that again, she thinks what she thinks.

It can take a while for Mama to change her beliefs.

I know deep down she knows Jake loves me, but she's worried Jake will screw up, and I'll be left alone, broken and hurt.

I'm not worried for a moment. I know Jake. I know what us being together, having this baby together, means to him.

I hope that Christmas will make her see this; then all will be good, and she'll relax on Jake.

"I gotta give your mom kudos, though, gorgeous," Stuart says. "She is the only woman I have ever known who Jake can't get eating out of the palm of his hand in five seconds flat. Not only that, I think he is actually scared of her. I think I may be in love with a woman for the first time in my life," he muses, knocking my elbow with his, chuckling.

"That's Mama," I sigh, putting my glass down. "A force to be reckoned with."

I just hope she fully comes around soon. She will. I think.

* * *

After dinner, Dave drops Carly at home, then brings Stuart and me back. Dave is now my personal bodyguard. Jake has gone all superprotective, more than normal, now that I'm pregnant, and I'm to have Dave with me at all times.

Honestly, I can barely pee without him there. Seriously, it's a good job I like Dave, because I'm with him more than I am Jake nowadays.

Jake ramped up my security when the news of my pregnancy broke. I've been receiving hate mail from some of Jake's more "overenthusiastic" fans.

They think I'm trying to take him away from his rock lifestyle by having his baby. Turn him into a family man and away from his music.

Yes, some people are that crazy.

The overall reaction from the public has been really positive, though. I think the normal, sane people are glad to see Jake happy. I couldn't be happier to be the one who brought him to this place in his life.

So now Jake has Ben with him, and I have Dave permanently attached to my side.

Dave pulls up on the drive, and I climb out of the car, saying good night to him.

Stuart sees me to the front door, leaving me with a kiss on the cheek, and heads around to the back to his place. I don't hear Dave pull away until I'm safely inside the house.

He is nothing but thorough when it comes to his job. And currently, for the foreseeable future, I'm Dave's job.

The house is in darkness.

Not bothering to turn on the lights, I head straight for our bedroom, figuring Jake will already be in bed.

When I enter, I find it empty.

He wasn't outside having a smoke, as I would have seen him when I passed through the living room. I wonder if he's in his studio.

I put my purse on the dressing table, kick off my heels, and set about finding Jake.

As I walk down the hall, I hear the piano playing in the library.

The door is ajar.

I push it open and find the room in darkness, lit only by the bright moon coming in through the windows.

Jake's seated at my piano, playing a song I don't recognise, wearing only a pair of black pyjama bottoms.

He cuts a solitary figure.

I listen to the song he's singing so very softly, but I can't make out the actual words. He sounds beautiful.

"He plays piano in the dark," I say, leaning against the door frame.

He instantly stops playing and glances over his shoulder.

"Hey." He smiles. But even from here, I can see something is off in his smile.

He turns from me, back to the piano, and starts to play the chorus from Brenda Russell's classic "Piano in the Dark."

This is my mum's favourite song.

I have so many memories of it from my childhood. I remember listening to Mama sing along to it on her stereo while she was in the kitchen fixing dinner. I wonder if Jake remembers.

I love how music can elicit memories.

And I love how even now it still binds Jake and me together. It's our connection. It's how we talk.

Jake continues to play as I walk across the hardwood floor to him.

I trail my fingers over the back of his neck, running them into his hair, and kiss his temple before leaning over the piano, resting on my elbows.

No matter where we are, or what he's singing, Jake's voice does incredible things to me. It's like pure, hot sex listening to him. His voice touches parts of me I didn't even know existed. Parts of me that belong only to him. That will only ever belong to him.

Watching the way he moves his fingers over the keys makes me want his hands on me so very badly.

I press my thighs together.

"Jake…" I trace my fingertip over the smooth surface of the piano. "Will you ever one day write a song about us? About me?"

He stops playing and stares at me. "Every song I've ever written was about you in some way."

"Really?" My eyes widen.

His gaze is steady on me. "How do you think I wrote about love, Tru? You were the only person I ever loved. Every message of love in those songs came from you…because of you. Every line of loss came from losing you. Listen to them and you'll hear it. I'm surprised you didn't before now."

He glances back down to the keys and starts tinkering with them. I'm getting the distinct impression he's disappointed that I didn't know.

I shift, uneasy. "I guess when I was listening to your music, I thought you didn't care about me." Turning away, I rest my back against the piano and stare across the darkened room.

"I hate that you thought that." His voice is soft behind me. "It couldn't have been further from the truth."

Turning back to him, wanting to stop this conversation before it starts, I say, "I liked the sound of the song you were playing before. Is it new?"

He nods.

"Will you play it for me now?"

He stares at me for a long moment and shakes his head. "It's not finished. I'll play it for you when it is."

"Okay." I reach over and touch his face with the tip of my index finger. I draw a path across his cheekbone, up over his nose, then trace the line of his brow.

Jake closes his eyes, breathing shallow. Then he reaches up, taking hold of my wrist. He draws me to him, putting me between him and the piano.

He rests his forehead against my stomach. I run my fingers into his hair, holding him to me. His deep breaths are hot on my skin through the thin fabric of my shirt. In and out he breathes.

Something's bothering him. I knew it before in his smile, but I know it more so now.

I can see it in the tense line of his shoulders. Feel it with every deep breath he takes.

"How was your night?" Jake asks, muffled, into my top.

"Good, we had fun. How was yours?"

He lifts his shoulders. "Standard."

"Baby, what's bothering you?" I press my fingers into his tense shoulders.

Lifting his head, staring up at me in the darkness, he grips my waist.

Without a word, he stands and picks me up, sitting me on the piano. The keys tinkle as I rest my feet on them.

Leaning into me, he buries his face in my neck. "I don't want to talk." He surprises me by taking a shaky breath. "I just need to be inside you, Tru. Deep inside you."

His words shiver through me. I know that whatever is bothering him right now, he needs to forget, in me.

His hands push my skirt high up my legs. He groans at the sight of my hold-ups and runs a finger around the edge of one, then roughly pushes my thighs apart and grabs my ass, pulling me to him. He kisses me.

My breathing stutters at the intensity of him, the feel of his erection pressing against me, his tongue hard in my mouth. It's a heady combination.

Reaching for my shirt, he rips it open. The buttons scatter, pinging across the piano, hitting the floor.

Jake pushes the shirt down my arms. Taking over, I free it, tossing it aside.

His hand moves over my breast, tracing the edge of the cup of my bra. He runs his finger in and over the tip of my nipple. The gentle contact makes me gasp.

His hand leaves me, only to push his pyjama bottoms down, freeing his erection.

He nudges it against my sex, his eyes burning into mine, filled with a hurt I don't understand.

"Jake…," I whisper, but he cuts me off, crushing his mouth to mine. He tears my panties off and thrusts his hungry cock inside me.

I cry out in pleasure at the sudden invasion. Jake grabs a tight hold of my hips, pinning me where he wants me, and he starts fucking me. His mouth on my neck, teeth biting, tongue licking, soothing.

With each hard thrust, the keys on the piano groan their own frustrated, chaotic chord. I can feel him trying to get deeper in me, pushing against me, almost desperate to find his escape, while my sounds of pleasure echo around the library.

"Lie back," he growls in my ear.

My bare back hits the cool piano at his command. I can barely feel the chill because I'm so absolutely taken with Jake. Watching the hunger and need for me that's consuming him in this moment. There is only him and me. We're our own island, and nothing and no one can touch us. And I know it's exactly where he needs to be right now.

Jake lifts my legs higher, pulling me closer, and the instant he touches the spot in me that only he can, an orgasm tears through me.

But Jake's not done, as he continues to chase his own climax, fucking me, hard and rough. His teeth grit, jaw clenches, eyes burning with hunger, the moonlight silhouetting him, and in this moment he has never looked more sexy to me.

When he meets his moment, throwing his head back, his face tight in release, he drives his orgasm out, hips jerking against me, pumping himself into me, and I come again, pulsing tightly around his cock.

"Fuck," he says as my muscles relax around him, us both trying to catch our breath.

He leans down, resting his chest against me. His head on my breasts, he stays inside me.

I trace my finger around the shell of his ear, listening to his shallow breaths, feeling the lingering frustration in him like it's my own.

"Talk to me," I murmur.

He lifts his head, resting his chin on my breast. He stares into my eyes.

"Let's go to bed." Rising, he pulls out of me carefully.

Jake reaches a hand to me and eases me off the piano. He keeps hold of my hand all the way back to our bedroom.

Removing the clothes I'm left with—my bra, skirt, and hold-ups—I grab one of Jake's T-shirts from the wardrobe and put it on.

When I return, he's already in bed, so I climb in beside him and snuggle up to his warm, hard body.

He exhales heavily, and I feel his hot breath brush over my skin.

"Jonny's mom called while you were out."

So this is what's eating at him. This is why he just fucked me so desperately on the piano.

I tilt my head back to him. "What did she want?"

He rubs his hand over his hair, and stares up at the dark ceiling. "She saw the press release about Smith joining the band."

"Oh."

His eyes meet mine in the darkness. "I hadn't called to tell her it was happening."

"How did she take it?"

"She yelled. She cried. She's hurt, and she has a right to be. I fucked up. I should have told her. I didn't think. I hate that I didn't. I feel like such a fuckin' bastard." He shakes his head. "She said I'm heartless and selfish…"

"No, Jake, no…"

"She's right. I am. But she said…" He takes a shaky breath. "She said I was replacing Jonny. That I'd forgotten about him. That putting Smith in the band is erasing Jonny from it, that I'm acting like he never existed. She said Jonny would never have done that if it had been me who had died. And she's right. He wouldn't have."

"That's bullshit." I move around onto my front so I can talk directly to him. "She's wrong."

I'm trembling on the inside with the anger I feel. I know she lost her son and is grieving, but she has no right to hurt Jake this way.

"I don't think she is, Tru." He shakes his head again, looking away. "But I haven't forgotten him." His voice is so quiet, as his eyes return to mine. "How could I? But I've just been so happy with you and the baby…when I asked Smith to become a permanent member, it was purely a business decision. I wasn't trying to hurt anyone. Least of all Jonny's parents. But I should have called."

Sitting up, I straddle his waist and trap his face between my hands, forcing him to look at me. I can see the hurt glistening in his eyes, and it makes every fibre of me ache.

"You listen to me, Jake Wethers. You haven't got a malicious bone in your body. Yes, you made a mistake by not calling, but I think even if you had called, she would have reacted the same. She lost her son and she's still angry and hurting about that. But she's wrong when she says that you're replacing Jonny. You're not. If you'd forgotten him, then the show you're doing next week to officially bring Smith into the band, well, you wouldn't be donating the proceeds to a charity that provides support to people affected by car accidents, and their families, would you? You're just doing what's right for the band now. That's what Jonny would want, and would have done, if he was in your shoes."

Jake's chest expands on a breath. He closes his eyes, his head gently shaking.

I know I'm not reaching him. This isn't going to fix it for him. I know it'll eat away at him. That's Jake. The Jake only I know.

"Why don't you go see her to talk it through in person? It's always better face-to-face than on the telephone. Sometimes you just need to see the person's face, you know?"

"She's in New York."

"It's a few hours on a plane."

"Six. And I've got meetings tomorrow."

"Rearrange them. Going out there will show her you care. I'll come with you if you want. We can stay in a hotel, spend some time with his mum and dad."

"You'd do that for me?"

I look down at him, surprised. "I'd do anything for you, Jake. Don't you know that by now?"

He presses his hands against my stomach, moving them outward, settling on my waist. "I love you so fuckin' much, Tru."

"I know." I lie down on him and love the feel of his arms as they come around me, holding me tight to him. "I love you too." I kiss his biceps. "So we're going to New York tomorrow?"

"We're going to New York tomorrow."

CHAPTER SIXTEEN

I'm standing side stage at the Wiltern Theater in West LA with Stuart, Carly, and Dave. The guys are onstage playing. This is their welcoming gig for Smith.

It's a small show with only two thousand fans. The tickets were expensive, so this show is seating only hard-core TMS fans. There are quite a few celebrities here as well. Yes, I am feeling starstruck by some of them.

All the proceeds from tonight are going to a charity for the victims of road accidents. It's an important charity to Jake because of how Jonny died.

I think this is his way of letting himself feel okay about Smith being a permanent fixture in TMS now.

We went to see Lyn and Bob, Jonny's mum and dad, last week in New York. I'm so glad we did.

Jake made his peace with Lyn. Their talk was long overdue, and something they both needed.

I spent time chatting with Bob in the kitchen while Jake and Lyn talked in the living room. Such a nice man. He regaled me with stories of the things Jake and Jonny used to get up to when they were teenagers. They were bad boys with good hearts. That's exactly what Jake still is.

Bob also makes the best tea known to man, and he fed me Lyn's homemade biscuits. I have seriously never tasted a biscuit as good.

After we left Lyn and Bob's, Jake and I visited Jonny's grave at Woodlawn Cemetery, at my suggestion.

He was reluctant, but I knew he needed to. The last time he'd been there was for the funeral.

I left Jake alone with Jonny for a time and took a walk. It's a beautiful place. Peaceful, as a place like that should be.

After the visit, I could feel Jake's relief. He seemed freer, and I knew I had done the right thing by encouraging him to go.

We stayed in New York for a few days, shopping and going out for dinner. It was relaxing, and I enjoyed every minute of being there with him. Then again, I could be in a dump with Jake and still be happy.

The only unfortunate thing about our trip was that Susie and Dale were away on holiday, as we could have visited them too. Maybe it was a blessing in disguise. I think the visit with Lyn and Bob was all Jake could handle at that point.

Jake has ongoing issues with his mum, and that's my next goal—to help fix them. I'm hoping Christmas will be just the right time. I want everyone right before our baby arrives.

As it's a special show, the guys are playing a few unreleased songs from the new album, which is scheduled for release next autumn. I know what a new album means: it means touring.

And our baby is due in July.

I don't want Jake to delay the album release. This isn't just about him and me and our life. It's about Tom, Denny, and Smith too. We're going to have to figure out what to do. But something tells me I'm going to be going on tour with a newborn next year.

At the moment, I'm not thinking about that. I'm just enjoying the here and now.

And right now life is amazing.

I scan the packed theatre, watching the crowd singing along as Jake belts out one of their more recent tracks, "Revved."

The crowd is pumped. The guys are bouncing off each other brilliantly. Jake is in top form, vocally. Tom is playing his bass like he's about to have sex with it any minute. Denny is on fire behind the drums, and Smith is finally relaxed. I'm finally seeing that big Southern personality of his, up here on the stage.

Smith has found his place among them now, and I'm so happy for him. He deserves it.

I see how proud Carly is by the look on her face.

I turn to watch Jake sing. He is dripping sex, hands around the microphone, lips singing the words like he's making love to them. My panties are damp just watching him.

He's mine. That stunningly talented, beautiful man is all mine.

I run my fingers over my tummy and whisper to the baby, "You hear that? That's your daddy up there singing."

As I lift my eyes, I catch Stuart watching me, smiling.

He wraps his arm around my shoulders, pulling me to his side. "He's doing good, huh?" He nods in the direction of Jake.

"Yep," I say, smiling. "He's on fire tonight."

I can't wait to get him naked later.

My libido is set to high now that I'm pregnant. We've been having sex everywhere. Whenever and wherever we can.

"I don't mean onstage," Stuart says. "That's the one place you can always guarantee Jake will be okay. I meant with the baby. Jake is one person I never figured for having kids. But that was before you. I thought he was happy when you came back into his life, but this, with your being pregnant, he's like sickly happy."

"You mean like you are with Josh." I poke him in the ribs.

"Exactly." He presses a kiss to my head. "Jake's found his home. And I think…" He looks a little abashed. "Well, I think I might have found mine, chica."

My heart lifts. "That serious, huh?"

"I think so."

I wrap my arms around his waist, hugging him.

I cannot wait to meet hot Dr. Josh at Jake's party. I'm almost as excited about that as I am the party.

"You're wanted, gorgeous." Stuart lifts his arm from my shoulders, nudging me forward with his hip.

I look from Stuart straight ahead, to see Jake walking toward me, grinning, guitar slung around his back, gesturing for me to go to him with his outstretched hand.

No bloody way. Not in a million years am I stepping out onstage in front of two thousand people.

I shake my head a firm no.

Narrowing those bright blue eyes on mine, he gets a look of determination.

I know that look. It's the one that usually means he gets his own way.

Removing my arms from around Stuart, I take a step back, readying for a quick escape, but Stuart catches the small of my back with his hand and gently pushes me forward, straight into Jake.

I give Stuart a "you're in for it later" look. He starts laughing.

Jake wraps a firm arm around my waist and steers me onstage.

"What are doing?" I hiss into his ear, stumbling on my heels.

"Showing off my girl," he says, smiling down at me.

My whole body is shaking. I daren't look out at all the people. I can't believe he's brought me out here. I'm going to bloody kill him.

Reaching the mike, Jake addresses the crowd. "I'm sure you all know my girl, Tru." He gestures to me as some whistles and catcalls come from the audience. My knees start knocking together. "Say hello to LA's finest, baby." He looks at me expectantly.

Seeing no way out of this, I lift my hand and, like a complete twat, wave to two thousand strangers, mumbling hello into the mike.

A round of cheers and whistles comes from the crowd, and my face goes beet red.

He is so fucking dead when I get him home.

Moving the mike back to him, Jake says, "We have another new song off the album that we're going to perform now. Seeing as I wrote the song about my girl, I thought she should be up here the first time I sing it."

My head snaps around to him.

He wrote a song about me?

Jake meets my eyes, but I can't read them.

I start to feel a weird sense of discomfort in my chest.

He wrote a song for me because of what I said that night at the piano. Because I hadn't heard his words for me in any of his other songs.

I don't know whether to kiss him for the thoughtfulness or to cry because he wrote me a song out of pity.

Out of my peripheral, I see a couple of roadies bringing a small piano onstage. Jake leads me to the piano and hands off his guitar. The bench is big enough to seat us both, and Jake pulls me down to sit beside him. The good thing is he's stage-facing, so at least I can hide a little behind his body.

I glance up at Denny behind the drum kit, and he gives me a knowing smile.

I give him a "you're dead next after Jake and Stuart" look.

Denny chuckles, shaking his head at me.

I look back to Jake, just as he leans toward the fixed mike on the piano, and says, in that sexy, throaty voice of his, "Okay, this one is called 'Everything Is You'..." He slides his eyes to me. "This one is all yours, baby."

Pressing down on the keys, Jake starts to play a gentle melody...

I saw her there, standing twenty feet away, feeling like we were still an ocean apart,
But there was no turning back, she had to be mine,
Knew she'd be mine,
I brought her in, chased her for a while, until she broke down,
Tell me you're mine, that you'll always be mine.

Take that chance with me,
I'll let you down, I know,
But I'll fix it too, because everything is you,

Everything is you.
She made her way to my bed, already soul deep inside me,
"It's always been you," I said. "The only one on my mind,"
But still I got wild, I broke the rule,
She left, taking everything with her.

Take that chance with me,
I'll let you down, I know,
But I'll fix it too, because everything is you,
Everything is you.

Like a beggar I pleaded for my home,
Words were the only way I knew how,
Lighting the sky with pink, she turned back and smiled,
I got you, baby, always mine, take me home.

Everything is you,
No matter where we are, with you by my side, I can walk these
    weak white-lined streets blind,
You're my guide. My everything.
Now with that new beating heart inside, you've given me eternity,
Forever is now. And everything is you.

It's the song he was playing at the piano that night.

He didn't write it because of what I said. He'd already written it.

That's why he wouldn't play it for me that night. He wanted to surprise me.

My eyes have not left him, and his have been on mine for most of the song.

My teeth are biting down on my wobbly lip, eyes heavy with tears. For the whole time, it has felt like there is no one else in the theatre but Jake and me.

But for me, there is no one but him. He is all I see, and all I have seen since I walked into that hotel room all those months ago.

The song has touched me so deeply that, not caring where we are, the instant his fingers leave the keys, I grab his face, pulling him to me, and I kiss him with every fibre of my being.

Jake's hand goes around the back of my neck, fingers tangling in my hair, his tongue moving in my mouth, he kisses me back with everything he has.

I'm aware of the whistles and cheering around us, but I don't care. All I care about is Jake. My lovely, sweet, beautiful Jake.

Coming to, we break from each other, eyes locked, panting, Jake wearing that fuck-hot smile of his. I know exactly what he's thinking. I also know exactly what he would be doing to me right now if this place were empty.

"You wrote me a song," I whisper.

He nods. "I wrote it a while ago. But I just made some recent changes to it."

The baby. The line at the end of the song.

Now with that new beating heart inside, you've given me eternity.

My heart swells with happiness.

I never knew happiness existed like I have with Jake. I never, ever want to lose this feeling.

Turning to the mike, his voice decadent with sex, he says, "I think she likes the song. What do you guys say?"

Tilting his head toward me, he grins, eyes alive, and the crowd goes wild.

I can't stop the smile beaming on my face. All I want is for him to play the song again.

Jake stands and offers me his hand. "Take a bow for your audience, baby."

Standing beside him, I give a little curtsey, and the crowd's cheers grow louder.

I even hear a whistle and cheer come from Tom. I glance at him and see he's smiling.

I knew there was a romantic buried deep inside the man whore.

I grin at him, and instead of giving me a sarcastic look or comment like he normally would, he winks and smiles.

As I turn to make my exit from the stage, Jake pulls back on my hand and whispers in my ear, "I meant every word of that song. You know that, right?"

Leaning back a fraction, I meet his eyes. "I know."

And I do. I really and truly do know the depth of his feelings for me. Any tiny remaining doubt I may have had about Jake's feelings for me disappeared with that song.

He presses the side of his face to mine, cheek to cheek. I close my eyes, revelling in the feel of him, intoxicated by his special Jake scent.

"Straight to the limo after the set, sweetheart," he murmurs, breath hot on my skin. Tingling sensations ripple down my body. "In it, on it, anywhere and any way I can have you."

Stepping back, I say, "The limo it is." I give him a sexy smile and slink offstage, feeling more confident than I ever knew possible, to wait for my limo-sex date with my gorgeous, sexy Jake.

CHAPTER SEVENTEEN

You promise you can't see anything?"

"I can't believe you've blindfolded me," Jake complains.

"Makes a change, huh?" I whisper in his ear.

I feel him shiver.

Sliding my hands down his arms, I slip my hands in his and lead him forward as I take a step back, closer to the door.

Releasing a hand, I reach back. Catching the handle, I open the door.

I guide him through the doorway.

"Okay." I stand in front of him, taking a deep breath. "I wanted to give you your present before we go out for dinner, because it's been killing me waiting all day as it is, and I didn't want to wait any longer."

That's only partly true. The other reason I wanted him to have it now is because we'll be at the surprise party late into the night.

"I'm sure I'm going to love it, Tru," he says.

Cocking my head to the side, I say, "How do you know?" He can't have seen it, because I just took it out of hiding and put it in here.

I peer close to his face, making sure he can't see through the blindfold.

As I near, his warm breath blows over my skin, igniting me. He smells so totally divine that I have the urge to kiss him.

Without warning, he grabs my face and kisses me. I melt into him, wrapping my arms around his waist.

Under my lips he says, "I know because I know you. Anything you get me I will love, because it came from you."

"Smooth talker."

"You bet your sweet ass I am. Now can I have my gift?"

"Okay, Mr. Impatient," I say, laughing.

I free the blindfold from Jake's eyes and stand beside him, watching with butterflies as he locks onto his present a few feet away.

He takes a step closer. "Is that…is that my old Strat?" His voice sounds quiet.

He turns to me.

I nod.

"How?" His mouth is open. "I—I thought it would have been long gone. I mean, after—"

"My dad kept it all these years." I run my tongue over my dry lips. "You know what he's like. He never could get rid of a guitar."

"I—I…" He looks back at the guitar. Then he turns back to me, and I see the emotion on his face. It takes my breath away. "My mom wouldn't let me take it…" He starts to tell me the story I already know. "…and everything had already been shipped to New York, and I thought I'd be able to take it on the plane with me, but she said I couldn't and I had to leave it behind…"

"I remember." I bite my lip.

Moving from me, he goes to the guitar sitting in its new stand and crouches down.

I go over and kneel beside him.

"It was a little worn," I explain. "It'd been in the garage at Mum and Dad's, cased up, but the damp gets in, you know, so I had Dad get it reconditioned and put brand-new strings on. Then he shipped it over to me, and then..." I bite my lip nervously. "Well, I had a little artwork done on it." I point to the Mighty Storm's band logo on the face. "I hope that was okay."

Jake runs his finger over the emblem. "It's more than okay." His voice sounds choked with emotion.

Hearing him sound this way sends goose bumps racing over my skin.

"I had a little something else added." Carefully, I lift the guitar from the stand. Resting it over Jake's knees, I turn it over to show him the artwork on the back.

~ Love is just a word until someone comes along and gives it meaning ~

Jake & Tru
August 31st, 1989
July 21st, 2012

"The first date is—"

"The date you moved next door to me," he finishes. "The second, the day we reconnected at the interview." He meets my eyes, and the intensity in his gaze marks me, branding me with the love I know he feels for me.

"I thought we could mark each memorable date we have on it. The next one I thought could be the day the baby's born." I run my fingers over my stomach. "Then our wedding day."

Jake looks down at the guitar and runs the tip of his index finger over the engraving.

"The quote is from *Aleph* by Paulo Coelo." I indicate the worn copy on my bedside cabinet. "He wrote *The Alchemist.* Do you remember when we read it in school for English?"

"I do," he says, nodding. "We worked on the assignment together, and I got an A, thanks to you." He winks, then turns the guitar right side up and starts strumming.

"DRs?" he asks in reference to the strings.

"You know my dad, he likes the best."

"They're all I use," he says, eyes down on the guitar, as he strums the chords from the Rolling Stones' "Honky Tonk Woman." "Your dad was my musical influence, Tru. I listened to everything he said and took it in, because he knows his shit."

"He misses playing. He loves teaching, but he loves being in the thick of it more. He loved being at the concert with you in Spain that day. It's all he's gone on about since."

"My best childhood memories consist of you, this guitar, and your dad..." His thoughts trail, and he starts to hum the lyrics, then stops. "Do you think he might be interested, when I do finally tour again, in coming with us?"

My face lights up as my heart gets all warm and fuzzy. "I think he would love that. My mum, not so much!" I laugh. "But you would make my dad's year if you asked him." I reach out and touch his arm.

His eyes smile. "I'll talk to him at Christmas about it." He puts the guitar back in its stand, and then, resting down on his knees, he pulls me into his lap so I'm straddling him and wraps his arms around my waist. "Thank you for the guitar. It's the best gift I have ever received."

"Really?"

"Really."

"I'm glad." I smile. "Happy birthday, baby." I kiss the corner of his mouth.

"I love you." He shifts his face, capturing my lips with his, and kisses me. "So fuckin' much."

"I love you too," I whisper, running my fingers into his hair. "So I was thinking…when we're in bed later, after you've had your dirty way with me, you could play me some of the old songs you used to play on it."

A wicked grin spreads over his lips, making him look even more edible. "You know I was totally trying to seduce you with some of those songs I played when we were teenagers."

I start laughing. "You were trying to seduce me with 'Honky Tonk Woman'?"

"Maybe not that one." He runs his fingers down my spine. I shiver under his touch. "But definitely 'Touch Me.'"

I laugh again. "And I thought you were just crushing on Jim Morrison."

"Only you, baby. Only ever you." His face goes serious. "You know, back then, this was how I dreamed my life would be, what I have right now with you. Marrying you. Growing old with you. When we parted"—he lifts his shoulders—"I figured that dream was gone forever…I'm so glad I got a second chance at this."

"Me too." I lift my hand and brush the length of his eyebrow with my fingertip, then the bridge of his nose. His eyes close on a soft sigh. I lean forward just a little and kiss his lips gently. "Time for birthday present number two."

Jake's eyes flick open. "I get another present?"

"Of course, silly." I rise to stand and go over to my dressing table, retrieving the gift box. I walk over to the bed, where he's now sitting, waiting for me.

I sit on the bed beside him, facing him. "This is from me and the baby." I hand the small box to him.

Taking it from me, Jake pulls the blue ribbon off the box and lifts the lid. He lifts the box sitting inside and cracks it open.

He smiles. "You bought me a Rolex."

"We bought you a Rolex," I say, tilting my head to my tummy. "It's vintage, nineteen eighty-five. Since I was going for memorabilia, I thought I would get something from the year you were born."

"I love it."

"Do you really?"

"Yes, really." He gives me an encouraging look before he leans in, bending his head down to my stomach. "Thank you," he says to the baby and presses a kiss there.

Touched by his sentiment, feeling like I might burst into tears any second, I add levity to the situation. "Hey, don't be giving the baby all the credit. I was the one hauling ass around the shops to find it." I grin.

"She doesn't mean it," he says to my stomach in all seriousness. "I know it was all your idea."

"You're a geek!" I laugh, pushing his head away.

"Just having a one-on-one with my kid." He smiles, sitting up.

He starts to take the watch out of the box.

"I had it engraved too. I was on a bit of a theme." I bite down on a smile.

He gives me a curious look, and removing the watch from the box, he turns it over.

Everything Is You
J.W.
2012

"For the song," I say.

He nods silently, staring down at the watch.

"I mean, if you hate the engraving, if it's too much, I'm sure I can get it removed…"

"I love it." He presses his finger over my lip. "The watch. The engraving. The guitar. You. I love you more than I knew possible, Tru."

My heart is racing behind my ribs. I take hold of his hand on my mouth and kiss his finger. "I know I didn't buy you a house…" I smile lightly. "But I was hoping these gifts would go to making up for the last twelve years of missed birthdays, like you've been doing for me."

"They surpass them. But like I told you in Paris, I got all my twelve the moment you agreed to be mine."

I slide my fingers between his, linking our hands. I glance at the clock. "We should get going."

"Where are we going?"

"You'll see." I give him a teasing smile, getting off the bed.

"Hold on," Jake says. He takes his watch off—the one that probably cost ten times more—and puts on the Rolex. My heart fills with happiness, fitting to burst in my chest.

"I'm ready now." He stands, taking hold of my hand, and I lead him out of the bedroom.

* * *

"You gave Dave the night off?" He doesn't sound pleased.

I pull out of the drive, waving bye to Jackson. "Yep."

He sighs loudly.

"Jake, I'm out with you. Nothing is going to happen to me. I wish you'd relax on this."

Dave is waiting at the party with everyone else. No way was I having him or Ben working tonight. They are guests at Jake's party just like everyone else. They might work for him, but they're his friends too. More like family at times. They're both bringing their wives, who I'm looking forward to meeting.

"I'll never relax when it comes to your or our baby's safety."

He sounds pissed. I don't want him worked up tonight of all nights.

"I know. I'm sorry." I soften my tone. "In the future I'll consult you about this kind of thing, okay?" I give him a quick doe-eyed look.

"Don't look at me like that," he says, trying to remain pissed off, but I can see him giving in already.

"Like what?" I give him the same look again.

"You know what. The wide-eyed, gorgeous stare. The one you think gets you out of everything."

Grinning, staring out at the road ahead, I say, "It does get me out of everything."

"That's the fuckin' problem," he mutters. Reaching over, he starts fiddling with the iPod.

"Can you put on some of the songs we used to listen to when we were kids?" I'm feeling a little nostalgic after our trip down memory lane.

Jake scrolls through the listings, and then I hear the Doors' "Touch Me."

I can't help but laugh. "Starting the night off as you mean to go on, Wethers?"

"Abso-fucking-lutely." He grins that fuck-hot grin of his, making me squirm in my seat. I want to pull the car over right now and do what we did after the show at the Wiltern. But I somehow refrain from doing so and step on the gas, heading downtown to Pizza Hut.

I see his face light up as I pull into the parking lot at Pizza Hut.

"I've got my old Strat back, a vintage Rolex on my wrist, and now I'm gonna be having Pizza Hut with my hot girl. Could this birthday get any better?"

Turning the engine off, I whisper, "I hope so."

With butterflies swarming my stomach, I climb out of the car, lock it, and put the keys in my purse.

Jake meets me around the front of the car.

Looking at the darkened windows of the building, he says, "Sweetheart, it looks closed. Don't worry, we can go somewhere else."

He starts to turn back to the car.

"No, let's just check it out." Taking him by the hand, I lead him toward the door. "It'll be open. This is Pizza Hut, they never close. Maybe the lights just went out or something."

"Pizza Hut in the dark...I can work with that," I hear him say from behind me, with sex in his voice.

I resist the urge to turn around, knowing my face will probably give me away if I do.

I push open the door and lead Jake through. "Hello?" I call out to let Stuart know to flick on the lights.

On cue, all the lights flash on, and we're met by our family and friends, calling out, "SURPRISE!"

The look on Jake's face is amazing. He looks overwhelmed and surprised, but best of all, happy. He looks so very happy.

The power of a surprise party.

I throw my arms around his neck and hug him. "Happy birthday, baby," I sing in his ear.

"You threw me a surprise party?" His arms go around my waist. "At Pizza Hut?"

"I did." I lean back, staring into his face. "With Stuart's and Carly's help. You like?"

"I love." He plants a kiss on my lips.

I see his eyes lift, and then he releases me. I turn to see Susie and Dale approaching us.

Dale looks the same as I remember, just greyer around the edges.

"Happy birthday, darling." Susie kisses Jake on the cheek. "Tru, you look beautiful tonight." She leans in and hugs me, kissing my cheek.

"Thank you, so do you." I gesture to her gorgeous fitted knee-length black dress.

"Dale, you remember Trudy."

"I do. Hello again." He smiles at me. Turning to Jake, he claps him on the back. "Happy birthday, son."

I feel Jake stiffen next to me. I know Dale didn't mean any harm using the word "son," but it must still feel strange for Jake to hear it.

I exhale in pure relief when I see my mum and dad heading toward us.

"Daddy!" I beam, breaking away from Jake to give him a big hug. "Mama!" I reach an arm out and pull her into the hug.

"Hey, baby girl," Dad says, hugging me back.

"How are you feeling?" Mum asks.

She's always asking since she found out I'm pregnant.

"I'm fine, Mama."

"No morning sickness?"

"No."

"Fatigue?"

"I'm a little tired, but overall I'm good." I smile.

"You're lucky. I was sick as a dog when I was pregnant with you." She tucks my hair behind my ear. "Has Jake stopped smoking?"

Hearing his name, Jake turns to us.

"No, Mama, he hasn't, but he doesn't smoke anywhere near me."

"Passive smoke can be harmful to a baby."

"Mama…," I warn.

"Good to see you, Billy," Jake says. "Eva."

"Happy birthday," Mum says, almost cracking a smile at Jake.

"Yeah, happy birthday, son," Dad adds, putting an arm around Jake.

I notice it doesn't seem to bother Jake that my dad called him son.

"You like the guitar?" Dad asks.

"Yeah, thank you for keeping it all these years."

"Never could get rid of a guitar," Dad says. "We got you a little something. It's not much…"

"Thank you," Jake says.

Dad waves it off. "It's over there with the rest of the presents."

"Dale's and my gift is over there too," Susie says, gesturing to the table. "Do you want to open it now?"

"I'll open it later."

"Okay, no problem," Susie replies, but I see the disappointment in her eyes.

He's still angry that she came to Paul's funeral only after I called her. I really need to fix this rift, and fast.

"Go open your present from your mum." I nudge him with my hip.

Jake stares down at me, giving me a less-than-impressed look, then turns to his mum. "Sure, okay."

I watch Jake follow Susie and Dale to the gift table.

My mum gives me a "what gives there?" look. I shrug.

"I'm going over to see Simone. See you in a bit."

I leave mum and dad and all but run to Simone.

This is the first time I've seen her since New York.

She's with Denny and Tom. Denny has his arm around her waist, and I swear this is the happiest I've seen him in months.

Her face lights up when she sees me coming.

"Look at you, all pregnant and gorgeous!" She throws her arms around me.

"No bump yet." I pat my flat tummy. "Won't be long, though, before I'm big and round like a bowling ball."

"I still can't believe it! I can't wait to be Auntie Simone!"

"I know!" I beam at her.

"It's so good to see you, and you look flippin' gorgeous in that dress." I gesture to her deep-purple silk dress.

"Ah, this old thing? I just threw it on last-minute." She winks.

I know Simone. She'll have spent hours getting ready and changed her outfits about ten times before settling on this one.

"I'm so glad you're here. I've really missed you." I wrap my arms around her again. I feel awash with tears at her being here.

"Me too," she says, sounding equally emotional.

"I hate to break up this reunion of beauties," comes Stuart's voice from behind me, "but I need a quickie with the hostess."

"Cock not your thing anymore?" Tom says, grinning.

"No. I saw the state of yours and it put me off *rubbing the lamp* ever again."

Denny chokes on his drink and starts coughing. Simone pats him hard on the back.

"I got it," Denny says, wiping his mouth.

"Hey, don't mock the genius simplicity of the tattoo," Tom says to Stuart.

"Please tell me girls haven't actually fallen for it?"

"For it...on it." Tom grins.

"My baby can hear this crap you're talking." I lay my hands over my tummy. "I don't want him or her corrupted by you pervy lot. Especially not you," I say pointedly to Tom.

He rolls his eyes. "Number one, this is Jake Wethers's baby we're talking about here. By DNA alone, it's designed to be corrupt. Two, it's a TMS baby and future rock star. Its rite of passage is to be corrupted by us. I'm just teaching it early."

"You will not be teaching my child anything. What if I have a girl? I don't want my daughter corrupted by stories of your pervy indiscretions."

"No way are you having a girl," Stuart pipes up from beside me.

"Why not?"

"Because like pussy cat over there said, we're talking about Jake. With the level of testosterone in him alone, you're definitely having a boy, gorgeous."

I ponder this for a moment. A boy. A mini-Jake. I like the sound of that.

"What did you want me for anyway?" I ask Stuart, turning from the others.

"I just wanted to check that this is all okay?" He's gone light on the decorations, knowing Jake doesn't like too much fuss. There are some lanterns, balloons, and a few banners.

"I think you've done an amazing job. Thank you for doing this." I reach up on my tiptoes and give him a kiss on the cheek.

"No bother." He waves me off. "The cake is in the kitchen, ready for later; drinks on tap; and the pizzas will be out soon."

"What would I do without you?"

"Your life would absolutely fall to pieces."

"Which means you can't ever leave. You're stuck with us forever." I slip my arm through his.

"Works for me. I'm kinda used to having you around now."

"You're so sweet." I squeeze his arm. "Speaking of sweet—sorry, I mean hot—is Dr. Josh here yet?"

"He is. You wanna meet him now?"

"Do I wanna meet him now." I give him a "duh" look. "I've been waiting ages to meet this guy. Lead me to the hotness." I gesture.

"And this is why I haven't introduced him to you yet." He gives me a cheeky grin.

"I'll keep it together for you. I won't geek out on him, I *promise.*" I cross my finger over my heart.

Then I take the promise back almost immediately, as Stuart leads me toward a grade-A hottie. Like seriously hot. Blond hair, chiselled jaw, dark green eyes, golden skin. He's dressed in jeans and a fitted black shirt.

Holy fuck. He is shit-hot.

Now I know why Stuart calls him hot Dr. Josh.

"Josh, this is Tru. Tru, close your mouth, and say hi to Josh."

Realising I'm staring, mouth wide open, I quickly close it, my face going bright red.

"Hi, Tru, it's really nice to meet you." Josh smiles.

Holy fuck, he's got dimples too.

Why are all gay men so ridiculously hot? I remember the first time I saw Stuart, I nearly died of heart failure. Or maybe it's the fact that they're gay that makes them hotter?

Nah, they're just seriously hot. Stuart and Josh together look like an ad campaign for Armani.

"Hi, Josh." I smile, composing myself. "It's great to meet you. And I wasn't staring." I elbow Stuart. "I was just admiring Josh's, um…shirt. It's a really nice shirt."

Josh looks down at his plain black shirt. "Thanks." He grins.

I feel a pair of arms come around my waist, and Jake presses a kiss to my cheek.

"Hey, baby." I turn my head to him. "Jake, meet Josh, Stuart's new boyfriend, who's wearing a black shirt."

Jake doesn't even blink at my introduction. He loosens an arm from around me and reaches over to shake Josh's hand. "It's good to finally meet you, man. Stuart never stops talking about you."

I see Stuart flush beet red and shoot daggers at Jake.

"Excuse us a minute," Jake says. "I've just gotta steal my girl away for a little while."

Taking my hand, Jake leads me through the restaurant to an empty booth in the back, out of sight from everyone else.

He gestures for me to sit, so I slide in the seat.

"Everything okay?" I ask as Jake slides in beside me, but instead of answering me, he takes my face in his hands, leans into me, presses my back up against the wall, and kisses me.

I part my lips, and Jake's tongue snakes out to meet mine. Then he starts to kiss me ravenously. Like he's starved for me. I wrap my arms around his neck, winding my fingers into his hair.

"What was that for?" I ask breathlessly when he finally pulls away.

"I was making the one birthday wish I always had come true."

My brow knits together.

At my confused expression, he continues. "I always wanted to make out with you in a booth at every birthday dinner we had at Pizza Hut, but I never had the balls to do it. I just made it come true."

I stare at him, a little lost for words. Even when he stands and holds his hand out for me, I still can't think of a thing to say.

"Come on, beautiful. Pizza's out, and we've got guests to entertain."

Taking his hand, getting to my feet, I say, "You're totally gorgeous. You know that, right?"

"Oh yeah, I absolutely know that." He winks, walking ahead, leaving me with a view of his very gorgeous ass.

He really is.

And I really am the luckiest girl in the world.

FIVE MONTHS LATER...

CHAPTER EIGHTEEN

Come back to bed."

"I can't," I call to Jake in the bedroom. "I'm picking Simone up in half an hour."

"You mean Dave's picking her up and you're just sitting in the car looking gorgeous."

"Yes, boss," I mutter, giving my eyelashes one last coat of mascara. I put the wand back in, screw on the cap, and drop it in my makeup bag.

I don't know why I'm bothering putting makeup on. It's only going to come off at the spa.

I leave the bathroom in just my underwear, fastening in my earrings. "My shadow will indeed be picking Simone up, while my fat ass sits in the car."

"You're not fat, you're pregnant. Hot, sexy pregnant. Come here." He beckons to me with his finger.

I approach Jake, who's sitting on the edge of the bed in his boxer shorts. I stand between his legs.

He places his hands on either side of my swollen tummy and kisses it.

Tilting his face, he looks up at me. I rest my hands against his cheeks.

"Stay home with me today," he murmurs.

"I can't. Simone and I have had this spa day booked for ages, and she goes back to London in a few days. Anyway, you're going into the studio today."

He turns his face away. Pressing his cheek against my pregnant belly, he lets out a sigh.

I run my fingers through his bed hair. "What's wrong?"

"Nothing."

"Jake…" I urge him to look at me.

"I dunno," he says with a shrug. "I just have a weird feeling."

"What kind of feeling?" I sit beside him on the bed.

I don't like the look in his eyes.

My heart jumps in my chest, making my pulse thrum.

Then, lightning-quick, Jake pulls me down on the bed, trapping my legs with his. He pins my arms above my head and kisses me, his whole demeanour instantly changing to relaxed.

"I just have a feeling you should stay in bed with me." He runs his tongue lightly over my lower lip. "You taste minty," he murmurs.

"The power of toothpaste." I nip his lip with my teeth. I hate when he hides things from me.

"Someone's snarky this morning."

"Someone's evading."

He looks directly into my eyes. Vivid blues burn into my brown.

"I'm not evading." His voice is controlled, measured, but harsh. "I just wanted to spend the day in bed with you. But maybe, snarky, you should go out before we have a fight neither of us wants."

"I'm sorry," I sigh. "I don't mean to be. I'm just tired. The baby is so wriggly. I haven't had a full night's sleep in so long."

Releasing my pinned arms, Jake moves down to my tummy. "Let your mama sleep," he says. "If she's moody and tired, Daddy doesn't get any."

"Jake! Don't say sex things to the baby!"

"Don't interrupt, beautiful. This is a father-and-son talk," he teases.

He glances up at me through his long black lashes. Just like that, the almost-fight is gone.

"You're so sure we're having a boy." I run my fingertips down his cheek.

We didn't find out the sex of the baby at the five-month scan. We both agreed we wanted to wait until the birth.

"Sweetheart, the baby keeps you up all night, it's definitely a boy." He winks.

"You're incorrigible!" I giggle.

"Just how you like me," he whispers over my skin. Moving up my body, he runs his tongue lightly around the edge of my bra and presses a kiss there.

The sensation tickles down my body. Then the baby kicks me, hard.

I wince.

Seriously, it hurts so much sometimes that I expect bruises. I think I'm carrying a minihulk in there.

"You okay?" Jake asks, concerned.

"Yeah fine, the baby's just kicking." I take his hand and place it on the spot where our little ninja is going for it.

Smoothing his hand over my stomach, he rests his cheek against my breasts and starts to softly sing Guns N' Roses' "Don't Cry."

Our baby has a penchant for old rock songs. It's the only thing that settles him.

Him. Jake's even got me saying it.

I've tried playing Jake's music when he isn't around, but it doesn't stop the baby's marathon kicking sessions. Apparently, the baby will only settle for the live, acoustic renditions of Jake singing old rock songs.

Which has made for some interesting evenings.

Jake goes all out, wearing leather pants and playing his old Strat—when Jake does something, he does it to the max. And it always ends in us having seriously hot sex.

We lie together until Jake finishes the song. With the baby now settled, I get up from the bed and go to get dressed.

I'm in the dressing area, tying my black maternity wrap dress, when Jake comes in.

He pulls on his black pyjama pants, then comes up behind me, sliding his arms around my bump. He nuzzles my neck. "You want some breakfast?"

"Cereal."

"Okay." He places a kiss on my neck and gives my bum a gentle slap before wandering off.

I slip my feet into silver ballet pumps, then grab my black Céline Nano tote that Jake bought me for Christmas and hang it on my shoulder.

I grab my lip gloss from the bathroom and put it in my bag. I get my phone off the nightstand and head for the kitchen.

When I get there, I find Jake, Stuart, and Dave around the breakfast bar.

Ah, my men.

My heart. My best friend. My bodyguard. Just missing my dad, and I'd have the complete set of important men in my life.

Stuart's eating toast, Dave's sipping on coffee, and Jake's eating Cocoa Krispies. There's another bowl with cereal and milk in it, waiting for me.

Cocoa Krispies, the American equivalent of Coco Pops. To me, they will always be Coco Pops. The only. The best.

I put my bag down and sit on the stool beside Jake. I lean in, giving him a quick kiss on the lips, but he pulls me in and kisses me harder. Parting my lips with his, he slips his tongue into my mouth.

He tastes of Coco Pops. So fucking delicious.

Even with our audience, a heat still spreads between my legs.

"Please," Stuart groans. "No tongues over breakfast."

Breaking from Jake, my face flushed, I dig into my Coco Pops.

"When's Josh back?" I spoon some cereal into my mouth.

The chocolate hits my tongue and I moan a little sound in my mouth.

Jake's hand slides down my thigh, pushing between my legs, parting them. I meet his eyes, then watch as he readjusts himself in his pants. I bite on my lip as he flashes me a sexy grin.

"This afternoon," Stuart says, cutting in on our moment. "He's got to go to the hospital first, so I'm not seeing him until tonight."

Josh has been away for the last five days at a doctors' conference. It's the first time Stuart and him have spent any real time apart, and Stuart has missed him tons. I know because he's told me so every single day while Josh has been gone.

"So this means you'll finally cheer the fuck up," Jake imparts.

"I haven't been that miserable," Stuart protests.

"You have." I smile, gathering more cereal onto my spoon.

"I need you to come into the label with me today," Jake says to Stuart. "There's some work I need you to do."

"Sure, no probs," Stuart mumbles, biting down on his toast. "It'll keep me busy until tonight."

I glance at the wall clock and see I have ten minutes left before I'm due to pick up Simone.

I shovel the remainder of my cereal in my mouth and put my bowl in the dishwasher.

"You ready to go?" I ask Dave.

"Yep." He takes one last sip of his coffee and goes over to the sink and washes it out.

Grabbing my bag, I lean over and give Jake a kiss on the cheek. "I'll be home at about four thirty, all pampered and smelling pretty."

"You always smell pretty." He stares into my eyes for a long moment.

"What?" I smile.

"Nothing," he shakes his head, breaking his stare. "Have a good day." He kisses me on the lips. "I'll see you at four thirty. We're staying in tonight. Takeout and a movie, okay?"

"Sounds perfect." I peck him once more on the lips.

"I love you," he says as I start to move away.

Turning as I walk, I smile. "Love you more."

"Not possible." He grins, his eyes lingering on me. But there's something off in his eyes, and it makes me feel uneasy, just like before in the bedroom.

His eyes move from me to Dave. "Take good care of my girl."

Dave gives him a strange look. "Always do, Jake."

Letting me through the door first, Dave and I head outside to my black BMW X5. Another Christmas present from Jake.

Except I never get to drive it because Dave drives me everywhere. I've driven it twice in five months. But I swear, once the baby is here, I'm driving this car everywhere. Dave can just sit in the backseat like I currently do.

I climb in my usual place behind the passenger seat and buckle in, setting the seat belt around my bump.

Dave fires the engine up and starts toward Denny's house to pick up Simone.

"Can you put some music on, please?" I ask Dave.

"Anything in particular?"

"No." I shake my head.

Dave starts searching though the radio stations and hits on one belting out Meatloaf's "You Took the Words Right out of My Mouth."

Clapping my hands together, I say, "This! Keep this on!" I start singing along loudly.

Chuckling, Dave turns it up, but I'm sure he's just trying to drown me out.

We reach Denny's house a few minutes later, and Simone is already waiting out front.

Dave gets out and opens the door for her.

Thanking him, she climbs in and pulls off her sunglasses.

"You look tired," she observes.

"Is that code for, 'Tru, you look like shit'?"

"No." She swats my thigh. "It's code for 'You look tired.' Being pregnant is really wearing you out, huh?"

"Yep," I sigh. "I had such an easy pregnancy in the beginning, but now the baby is getting bigger, and I feel uncomfortable all the time. Plus the baby gets so active at night that I'm hardly getting any sleep, and I just feel cranky all the time." Unexpected tears prick my eyes.

I take a deep breath, holding them back.

"Then this spa day is exactly what you need. Some pampering will make you feel tons better."

"I hope so," I utter as Dave heads for the Four Seasons Spa.

* * *

Dave pulls the car up front the Four Seasons. Sitting forward in my seat, I say to him, "You can leave us here, and I'll call you when we're ready to be picked up."

He turns in his seat, not looking so hot about this idea. "I should escort you in."

"Dave, it's a spa that deals with celebrities all the time, and I'm hardly a celebrity—"

"Just carrying the baby of one," Simone inputs.

I give her a "not helping" look.

With a laugh, Simone opens the car door and hops out.

"Just go do something fun, and I'll call you when we need you."

"I'll wait out here in the car."

"I'm here until four." I screw up my face. "I'm not having you sit out here in the car for six hours waiting for me, because…well, it's just plain weird."

"Tru, my job is to take care of you. And believe me, sitting outside a spa for six hours is nothing compared to other things I've done."

A thought flashes through my mind. I wonder if he's referring to what he's done for Jake in the past. Or what he's waited for Jake to do. Things I most definitely do not want to know.

"Leaving you alone is more than my job's worth—so it's either I wait out here, or I come inside with you and wait in the waiting area or, worse, the treatment room."

I frown at him. "Fine," I huff, sliding along the leather seat, "sit out here if you must." Pausing, with my legs dangling out of the car, I ask, "Do you want me to send some food out for you?"

"No, I'm set." He indicates a thermos on the passenger seat. "If you need me at all, you make sure to call me straightaway," he says just before I shut the door.

"Yes, boss," I mutter.

I swear I hear him laughing just as the door closes.

I watch him pull the car into a spot facing the entrance. I link arms with Simone, and we walk toward the doors.

"You weren't kidding when you said he literally goes everywhere with you."

"Nope," I sigh.

"Jake's doing?"

"Oh, absolutely," I mutter as the doorman lets us in.

* * *

I'm in heaven.

Spa heaven.

I'm having a facial, and it may be the best facial I have ever had.

We're into the afternoon. So far I've had a massage, a pedicure, and lunch. After my facial is done, I'm having a manicure.

Simone is on the bed beside me, having a facial too.

"So the book launch is next week?" Simone asks.

"Yep."

"Wish I could be there."

"I wish you could be too."

I finished up Jake's biography two months ago, and it's been with the editor. Then back to me. Then back to the editor.

This went on for a while, until we both settled on the final draft.

The excerpts have already started publishing in *Etiquette*. Vicky said they have seen a 10 percent increase in sales already, which is amazing.

"Is Vicky coming over for the launch?"

"She is." I smile.

The launch is in New York as that's where the publishing house is, so Jake and I are flying over for it. Vicky is meeting us there, and afterward she's coming back to LA to spend a few days with me.

I can't wait.

I haven't seen her since I left London. Of course I've seen her via Skype, but it's not the same.

We have lots of shopping planned for when she's here.

"You really need to get your butt over to London," Simone says. "It's been way too long since you've been home."

"I know." I let out a sigh. "I miss it."

"And London misses you. Maybe you and Jake could come over for a holiday after the baby is born."

"You know what," I say, feeling uplifted at the thought. "We totally should. I could have my hen night in London. Most of my friends I want at my hen are there, and I'm sure Carly and Stuart would come over for it."

Jake and I have set the wedding for December. It won't be the summer wedding we were originally wanting, but neither of us wants to wait until next summer. More than anything I want to be Jake's wife. December gives me just enough time to lose my baby weight.

"Speaking of London," Simone says, her voice sounding tighter, "I saw Will last week."

My heart pauses.

I turn my face to her and out of the therapist's hands. "You did?" My voice wobbles, giving me away.

I haven't thought of Will in a long time. I don't let myself.

Because if I do, I remember how much I hurt him and how things were left the last time I saw him.

"Hmm." She nods, eyeing me carefully.

I compose my features to neutral. "Why are you just telling me now?"

"Because this is the first chance I've had. There's always someone around."

Jake.

"How's he doing? Did he, um, ask about me?" I might have my face under control, but my mouth is set to give me away.

"Do you really want me to answer that?"

I pause.

Do I?

"Yes."

"No. He never mentioned you. But then, he wouldn't have, because, he, um…well, he wasn't alone when I saw him, Tru."

"Oh." Pause. "He's seeing someone?" *Of course he is. Will is a really attractive guy. He's smart and caring. A real catch.*

"Yes."

Is it wrong that I feel a spike of jealousy?

I look up at the ceiling. Gritting my back teeth, I force a smile. "Well, that's great news. I'm really pleased for him."

"No you're not. But I know what you mean. Happy he's happy. But it still stings, even though you feel you have no right for it to."

I love how Simone just gets me. God, I miss not seeing her every day. I'm going to hate it when she's gone in a few days.

I turn back to her. "I'd say that just about covers it." Biting my lip, I ask my next question. "Is she anyone we know?"

"No." She smiles gently.

That clarification makes me feel better. If it were someone I knew, I would have felt weird. Okay, weirder.

"She seemed real nice, Tru," Simone adds. "He looked happy."

This is exactly what I wanted for Will. I wanted him to be happy with someone who deserves him.

"I'm real glad he's happy." I smile. "And I actually mean that."

"I know you do." Simone turns her face back to the waiting therapist.

"What does she look like?" I have to ask. Curiosity gets the better of me every time.

"The complete opposite of you. Blonde, small-chested, tall."

"Peroxide, flat-chested, and lanky. I take it back. She's not good enough for him."

"Bitch." Simone flicks her gleaming eyes to me.

"You expect any less?" I grin.

"No." She smirks, and we both start laughing.

* * *

Dave is standing by the car as we exit the Four Seasons.

"You had a good day?" he asks, opening the car door for us. I let Simone climb in first.

"We had a fabulous day." I beam. "How was yours?"

"Well, the selection of cakes and fresh coffee that was brought out to me certainly brightened it up. Thank you, Tru. You're a special kinda lady, you know that?"

"You're a special kind of guy, Dave. Not many men would sit in a parking lot and wait six hours for me." I smile, giving his arm a pat.

"Jake would." He grins.

"Yeah, but he's just as crazy as you are!"

Laughing, he helps me step up into the car and closes the door behind me with a firm clunk.

I click my seat belt in just as Dave gets in the driver's side.

He glances over his shoulder. "Denny's to drop off Simone, then straight home?" he checks.

"Yep."

I kick my shoes off, still feeling all kinds of relaxed from my pampering, and settle back in my seat.

I tune in to the music Dave is listening to—Pearl Jam.

"Ooh, is this the *Backspacer* album?" I ask him.

"How do you guess the album from just one song?" He gives me a quick look back. "You're a little scary, Tru. You do realise that, don't you?" he chuckles.

"It's a gift." I nod, grinning. "And Dave, a Pearl Jam fan. How did I not know this? Seven months of riding practically every day with you, and you only now reveal your excellent music tastes to me."

"I always wait at least seven months before revealing my excellent music tastes to anyone." He chuckles.

I loosen my seat belt, leaning forward to talk to him.

"Can you skip it forward to 'Just Breathe'? It's my favourite of theirs by far. Oh, and crank it up loud."

"I knew there was a reason I liked you." He winks.

He pulls up at a red light and takes the opportunity to jump the tracks ahead. Hitting "Just Breathe," he turns the volume up loud. For a moment, I stay still, arms resting on the passenger seat, listening as the beautiful guitar melody fills the car completely.

The baby gives me a gentle kick. I rub my hand over my tummy.

A gentle kick, now there's a first.

"You like this song, huh?" I murmur. "I'll get daddy to sing it to you when we get home."

The lights change to green, and Dave shifts the car into drive.

I sit back, setting the seat belt back around my bump, and start singing along. Simone joins in. I reach over and squeeze her hand. She smiles. Then we hear Dave in the front singing.

Simone giggles, and I sing through a smile at his baritone voice.

Life's good.

Life is real good.

I don't think it gets any better than this, does it?

Something from the right catches my eye. Still singing, still smiling, I turn my face to the window.

And that's when I see it.

The smile drops from my face.

They say your life flashes before your eyes in the moment you know you're about to die.

Well, I do see my life. But not the one I've lived: the one I *expected* to live.

Having my baby. Watching him grow. Marrying Jake. Growing old with him. Living with him, loving him. Loving them both until I was old and ready to die.

That's what I see in those milliseconds as that car hurtles toward us.

It's not my time. Save my baby, please.

My eyes lock with the driver's. He looks almost...apologetic. I cover my baby with my arms, and then _____

JAKE...

CHAPTER NINETEEN

I had the worst dream last night.

Well, I think I did, because I woke up this morning with the worst feeling. Like impending doom. And I haven't been able to shake it since.

I'm so fucking ready to wrap this day up and get home to my girl.

I haven't spoken to Tru since she left for the spa. I didn't want to disturb her, but normally I speak to her at least once during the day.

I need my Tru fix, what can I say?

I'll call her now that she should be on her way home to see what she wants for dinner.

While I switch off the amp, I pull my phone from my back pocket and speed-dial her cell.

Voice mail.

Weird. She never turns her phone off.

Maybe she had to at the spa and forgot to turn it back on.

I hear Katy Perry start to sing across the studio. Stuart's fucking ringtone. He really is the epitome of gay at times.

I unplug my guitar and put it in its stand.

"Hey, gorgeous…what?…Wait, what!…Oh God, *no*."

It's the "no" that makes me stop and turn to him, because he sounds…well, he sounds exactly like he did when we got the call that Jonny had died.

My head prickles, and my blood starts to run cold.

I feel the air in the room shift instantly. That fucking crap feeling I've had since this morning starts to turn my thoughts to shit.

"When?...Are they?...She's...oh God, no...no." Stuart's voice comes out a whisper. He turns and locks eyes with me.

And I know. I just know.

Fuck, no.

"We're coming now." I watch the phone slide from Stuart's ear in slow motion.

"Stuart, what's wrong?" Denny comes from around his drum kit.

Stuart casts a glance to Denny, then comes straight back to me.

Stop looking at me.

"That was Josh." His lip trembles. "He was just about to leave the hospital, when..." His voice breaks, and he clears his throat, then continues. "Three people were brought into the ER. A car accident. It's Simone, Dave, and...Tru."

Tru. Car. Accident.

No. God, no.

Denny clasps his hand over his mouth. "Simone, is she...?" Denny sounds afraid.

I'm afraid. Terrified.

I can't breathe. My heart hurts against my ribs. Hurts real bad.

Tom and Smith have drawn closer to Stuart.

He looks at Denny again. "Josh said Simone is roughed up, but she'll be okay. Dave too, but..." He brings his eyes back to mine. "Jake..." He steps toward me.

"*No.*" I step back and bump into the guitar.

I don't want to hear this. I don't want to know.

I shake my head. I try to move away again, to get away from Stuart, but there's nowhere left for me to go.

"I'm so sorry." I watch, numb, as he wipes a tear from his face. "The other car hit the passenger side. Tru took full impact. Josh said she's in surgery now. We have to get to the hospital."

I close my eyes.

"The baby?" The words fall from my mouth. I don't feel like it's me talking.

"I don't know. I'm sorry. We need to go. Josh is waiting in the ER for us. He'll take us to them."

The room is closing in on me. There's no air.

I feel like I'm underwater.

Drowning. I'm drowning.

I had her this morning, in my arms. I should have kept her there, held her tight, and never let her go.

I can't lose her. I can't.

Fuck, this hurts. So much. Too much.

"Jake…," Stuart says.

I lift my head. "I can't lose her." *I can't breathe. I'm gasping for air.* "Not her. Anyone but her."

My eyes meet his.

"I know." Another tear falls from his eye. He wipes it away.

Tears keep leaving his eyes.

I want to cry. *I* want to shout. Something. Anything to get this excruciating pain out of my chest. But nothing's happening.

"Come on, let's get to the hospital. We'll know more once we're there." Stuart urges me to move, and that's when my legs give out on me.

He grabs me, wrapping an arm around my back. "I got you," his voice cracks. "I got you, Jake. It's gonna be okay. They'll both be fine."

Fine. They'll both be fine.

* * *

I'm in a car. My car, I think. Stuart's driving.

Car.

Accident.

Tru.

I can't breathe.

The pain in my chest is unbearable.

I don't know what to do.

I should be doing something. I'm supposed to protect her, protect them both.

"I wasn't there. I should have been there," I choke out. I know it's me speaking, but it doesn't sound like my voice.

"It's gonna be okay, man." Tom's hands come over the backseat, pressing down on my shoulders.

I feel like he's holding me in place. Like he thinks I'm going to lose control any moment now.

I want to lose control. But I can't seem to get this maddening, sickening feeling out of my chest. It's trapped in there, burning every part of me.

"Tru's gonna be fine," Tom continues. "She's a fighter. She'll get through this."

"And what about the baby...my baby?" I choke on the words.

Tom's silence weighs heavy.

"They're gonna be fine, Jake." He squeezes my shoulder.

There it is again. That word—fine.

But that isn't what I want to hear. I don't want to hear any of this. I don't want to be here. I don't want to be hearing *fine.*

I want to be home with Tru, holding her beautiful body in my arms. I want to feel her skin on mine. Her breath mixing with mine as she kisses me in that gentle way she does.

I want to hear her laugh. I want to see her smile.

I want to feel my baby kick.

I want…them.

I close my eyes again.

* * *

I'm in the hospital. I can hear Stuart talking. There are people everywhere.

And white. White walls. White coats.

Where's Tru?

"Jake…"

I turn. It's Josh. He looks sorry. Sympathetic.

I don't want sympathy. I want Tru.

"Jake…," he repeats. "I'm so very sorry…" I hear the break in his voice.

Stuart puts his hand on Josh's arm. I see Josh's eyes go to it.

He looks back at me, and then he sounds very business-like. Like a doctor delivering bad news. "Tru's in surgery. All they're telling me right now is that she suffered a severe head injury as a result of the accident. Dr. Kimble, one of the surgeons, will be out to see you soon. If you'll follow me this way…"

Severe. Head. Injury.

I'm moving. In an elevator. Upward.

The doors open with a *ping*. Then it's like I wake up. I realise where I am. Why I'm here.

Tru. Car. Accident.

Fuck, no.

No. No. No. No. No. No.

No!

I run out of the elevator, sprinting down the hall. I'm not sure where I'm going.

I just need to find her.

Surgery. Josh said surgery.

I can hear voices calling out behind me, but I can't stop.

Tru.

I need to find her.

Where are you, baby?

I'm stopping. Why am I stopping?

Arms around me, stopping me, holding me.

I don't want them touching me. I want Tru. I just want Tru.

"Wait, take it easy, Jake. You're here. We need to go in here." Stuart, with Tom's help, steers me through a door into a room.

A white room.

Fucking white everywhere.

Then I'm sitting in a chair.

I don't want to be sitting.

I stand up.

Everyone stands with me.

Stuart. Tom. Smith. Josh.

"Where's Denny?" *Is that me speaking?*

"He's downstairs in the ER with Simone and Dave," Stuart answers. "Why don't you sit down, Jake?"

I shake my head.

I can't sit while Tru's...what? While she's in surgery? While she's...dying?

Dying.

Is she going to die?

Is my baby dying too?

Am I going to lose them both? Are they both going to die like Jonny did?

Why is this happening?

It hurts. It hurts so fucking much. I feel like my rib cage is being cracked wide open and my life is being drawn out of me, slowly.

The door opens. A man in a white coat approaches me.

White.

Sympathy.

No.

I don't want sympathy. I don't want to be here. I need to get out of here. I need to find Tru.

I just want to touch her. Hold her. Never let her go.

"Mr. Wethers, I'm Dr. Kimble."

My insides start to shake through to the bone.

"Tru...where is she?"

The doctor puts his hands together in front of him, in an almost prayerlike manner, pointing them in my direction.

I don't like it. I want to knock his fucking hands away.

"Trudy is still in surgery." He sounds like Josh did—businesslike. "She sustained a very severe head injury..."

There are those words again. But he said "very." Josh never said "very."

That's worse. *Very* is worse.

God, no.

"...excessive bleeding within the skull...pressure on her brain...swelling...baby...delivery..."

Baby.

I meet the doctor's eyes. "What?" There's my voice again, but it still doesn't sound like me.

Dr. Kimble shifts on his feet. "We had to make a decision, Mr. Wethers. There was no time to waste. The baby was in severe distress. Its heart rate was dropping exponentially. We had no other choice but to perform an emergency caesarean section."

I grip my hand to my chest, digging my fingers into my sternum, trying to relieve the agonising, burning pain inside of me.

"But she was only twenty-nine weeks..." *I can't breathe.*

"The baby's fine." He nods, slowly. "He's having a little difficulty breathing on his own because of respiratory distress syndrome, which is very common in premature babies, but we're helping him with that, and he's responding well."

"Him?" A tear rolls down my cheek.

"Yes, you have a son."

A son.

We have a son, and Tru doesn't know. She needs to know. I need to see her, to tell her.

"Where is he?"

"They'll be moving him to the NICU shortly."

"And Tru...will she...is she...?"

He wraps his arms over his chest. "She's with some of the best surgeons in the world right now, and they're doing everything they can for her."

"Is she"—I take a staggered breath—"Is she going to… *make it?*"

I see the look in his eyes, the one he thinks he's hiding, but I see it clearly.

"The doctors are doing everything they can to help her pull through, Mr. Wethers."

And this is the exact moment that my worst fear is realised.

She might die.

I could lose Tru, with no way back to her.

Lose her. Forever.

Oh God, no.

No. No. No. No. No. No. No. No.

I press my fist into my forehead. "You don't think she's going to make it."

He shifts again, not meeting my eyes. "It's too early to make an appropriate diagnosis of—"

"DON'T FOB ME OFF! JUST TELL ME THE FUCKIN' TRUTH! IS SHE GOING TO DIE?"

"Jake…" Tom's hand touches my shoulder, but I shrug him off.

My chest is heaving, fear driving everything inside me.

I stare into the doctor's face, searching.

I have to know. I have to know if I'm going to lose everything. Lose the only person who has ever mattered to me.

And right now, he is the only one who can tell me.

He exhales, his voice softening. "Right now, Trudy's chances of survival are fifty-fifty at best. When she wakes from the surgery…" He catches himself, and his expression communicates compassion. "If and when she wakes…"

If.

"We have no idea as to the extent of the damage to her brain."

"*No...*"

I don't remember falling. I just know I'm on the floor. Tom's holding me.

And I'm crying.

* * *

There are more people here. More white. More talking. Then they're gone.

Silence. Crippling silence.

I'm still on the floor, but I'm now leant up against the wall. Tom and Stuart are beside me.

I hear the door open again. I lift my gritty eyes, and I see Josh slip out into the hall to talk to a woman in a white coat.

More fucking white.

I close my eyes and let my head fall back against the wall.

"Jake..." Stuart's voice forces my eyes open. I stare blankly at him. "We need to call Tru's mom and dad. They need to know what's happened. The press will get wind of Tru's accident soon, if not already, and they can't find out from the press."

My heart stops.

Billy and Eva.

I can't.

I shake my head. "I don't think I can..."

"I'll call them. I'll get them on the first flight out here." He touches my arm briefly, then stands. "Do you want me to call your mom too?"

My mom? Do I want her here?

I nod, once.

"I'm gonna get a drink." Smith stands. "Jake, do you want me to get you anything?"

Tru.

I shake my head.

"Tom?"

"A black coffee."

The door bangs shut as Stuart and Smith leave.

Then it's just me and Tom.

And silence. More crippling fucking silence.

"What if she dies?"

Tom turns his head and looks me in the eye. "Tru's a fighter, Jake. She kicks my ass daily. She's going nowhere."

"But what if…"

"Don't 'what if.' Don't do that to yourself."

My eyes blur. "I don't know what to do. What to think. What to say." I bury my face in my hands, taking a staggered breath.

A tear runs through my fingers and drips to the floor.

I hear Tom take a shallow breath. "Don't think of the bad, Jake. Think of the good. Think of the moment you get to hold your boy in your arms. Think of the moment you get to put that ring on Tru's finger when she finally sees stupid and marries your sorry ass. Think of all the amazing fuckin' things the three of you are going to do together. And while you're thinking of all that, I'll pray to the big man upstairs. I'll promise to make some serious lifestyle changes in exchange for you to have all that, to have what you were always meant to have."

I feel Tom's hand on my shoulder. He squeezes it.

I start to cry harder.

* * *

How long has it been? Hours…days…minutes.

My eyes are sore. My head hurts.

I hear the door go again. It's Josh.

He comes and sits by me.

"I was just talking to Dr. Fuller. She's the neonatologist caring for your son. She said he's doing good, Jake, real good. You can go up and see him when you're ready."

I turn and look at him blankly.

Go and see him. Without Tru.

But…

I shouldn't see him without Tru.

And I can't leave here. I need to know what's happening with Tru.

I can't. I just…can't.

"I'll take you up to see him, and I'll wait outside. The instant I get any news about Tru, I'll come in and get you, I promise," Josh says as if reading my mind.

"I…" I shake my head. "I don't think I can."

Josh draws his knees up and rests his arms on them, linking his hands together. There's a long pause before he speaks again. But when he does, I hear the intention clear in his voice. "I know you feel like leaving this room is like leaving Tru, but there's nothing you can do for her right now, Jake, no matter where you are. But your son…he needs you. He needs one of his parents."

One of his parents.

I close my eyes.

He's alone up there. He must be so confused and scared. He needs me.

"Okay…," I agree, opening my eyes. "Okay."

* * *

"Your son is right in there." Josh points to the closed door across from us. "There's a nurse with him, and I'll be waiting right out here for you." He indicates a row of three plastic chairs.

Turning to the door, I stare at it for a long moment.

I take a deep breath as I push my hand through my hair, then I walk toward the door.

My body is trembling, and the closer I get, the harder I start to shake.

He's in there. Right behind that door.

I reach for the handle. Curling my fingers around the metal, I push down and slowly open the door.

The room is low-lit. There's no sound except for the beeping of a machine.

The nurse has her back to me, but she turns and smiles at my arrival.

"Mr. Wethers?"

"Yes." My voice is hoarse.

"He's right over there. He's been waiting for you." She smiles warmly.

Turning to my right, I see an incubator. Inside the incubator is my son.

My son.

I can't see him clearly through all the tubes surrounding him, but he looks small. So very small. Fragile. Breakable.

My heart starts to beat hard in my chest.

I want to go to him, but I find myself taking a step back.

I don't think I can help him. I shouldn't be here. Coming up here was a mistake.

I'm just about to turn and leave when the nurse comes up beside me. "Don't let all the tubes scare you, honey. They're just there to help him breathe until he's strong enough to do it himself. Why don't you go say hello?" she urges gently.

I stare blankly down at her.

My mouth is dry. My pulse is thumping so hard that blood is roaring in my ears.

Tru should be here. She should be seeing him with me. It shouldn't be this way.

This is wrong.

I swallow back the tears burning my throat.

Somehow I manage a step forward. Then another. Until I reach the incubator.

I stare down at him through the clear unit.

He looks just like Tru. Exactly like her. Perfect in every way possible.

And it hurts in every way imaginable.

He's even smaller close up. There's a tube taped to his little nose and a little white knitted hat on his head.

"How much does he weigh?" I ask.

"Two pounds, seven ounces."

My heart sinks. *Two pounds, seven ounces.* Jesus, he weighs about the same as a bag of sugar.

My hand reaches out to him before I even realise I'm doing it. I stop myself, clenching my hand into a fist.

"You can touch him," the nurse says. "Just clean your hands with this first."

Coming over, she squeezes some sanitizer into my hand. I rub the cold gel over my hands until it's gone.

"I'll give you a moment alone."

"Is he going to be okay?" My words come out ragged.

"You've got a fighter there, honey. He's gonna be just fine." She touches my arm briefly, and then she's gone. And I'm left alone with him.

My son.

I get down to my knees, putting me at face level with him. His little face is turned toward me.

He's got Tru's full lips.

I reach my trembling hand through the porthole, and resting my palm flat on the mattress, I reach my little finger out to his tiny hand, and I touch him.

In this moment, I've never felt anything like it.

Love.

It's different from the love I feel for Tru. But equally as strong. It's an all-consuming need to protect him forever. To keep him safe from any pain. Like the pain I'm feeling right now.

It chokes me to tears.

I stroke my finger gently along his hand, and as I do, his fingers curl around it, holding on to me.

He needs me.

Salty tears trickle down my cheeks and into my mouth.

Pressing my lips together, I rest my forehead against the incubator.

"I'm so sorry I wasn't there..." I whisper. "So very sorry."

CHAPTER TWENTY

J ake."

Hearing Josh's voice behind me, I pull my head back from the incubator, away from my son. I blink up at Josh.

Tru.

I gently slip my finger from my son's hand and stand up. My legs are stiff and aching. And my heart is painful in my chest.

"Tru's out of surgery. They're transferring her to a private room. You can go down and see her."

"Is she…?" My heart pauses. I swallow past the fear. "Is she *okay?*"

Josh runs his hand over his face. "All I've been told is they got the bleeding under control and managed to relieve the pressure off her brain, but there is still significant swelling. The resident neurosurgeon, Dr. Kish, who led on Tru's surgery, is waiting downstairs to talk to you before you go in to see her."

To prepare me.

Fear slithers down my spine.

I see Josh's eyes move to the incubator. He takes a step closer. "He's beautiful, Jake. Really beautiful."

Just like his mom.

I nod. "Thank you."

"Shall we go?" Josh gestures to the door.

I take a hesitant step forward.

There are so many emotions going through me right now. Mostly fear, but I'm also torn.

I need to see Tru with a desperate, painful ache, but I feel like I can't leave my son alone either.

Seeming to sense my distress, Josh says, "Stuart's waiting right outside. He wants to talk to you before you see Tru. Do you want him to sit with the baby while you see her?"

"Yes," I exhale, briefly closing my eyes. If I was going to entrust my son to anyone, it would be Stuart.

Turning, I reach my hand through the porthole again and touch his tiny arm lightly. "I'll be back soon."

I give him one last parting look, then follow Josh out of the room.

I pull the door closed behind me and find Stuart leant against the wall. His eyes are red and puffy.

Pushing from the wall, he comes over. "How is he?"

"He's…good." I push my hands in my front jean pockets. *Perfect. Beautiful. Everything his mom is.*

"How does he look?"

"Like Tru." Raw, acute pain tears through me. I stare past Stuart, at the wall. Tears push at my eyes. I close them. I never thought there would be a day that it would be painful for me to speak her name. "He looks exactly like his mom— beautiful."

I hear his choked breath.

As I open my eyes, I catch him swiping a tear.

"Tru's mom and dad are on the way to the airport now. I took care of all the arrangements. I chartered them on a private jet. They'll be here first thing in the morning."

"Thank you." I push my hand through my hair. "How did they take it?"

Stuart shakes his head.

He doesn't need to say anything. I know exactly how they took it. I felt it the moment Stuart told me.

Devastation. Complete and utter devastation.

"I spoke to your mom. I got her and Dale a private flight in too. They're coming straight to the hospital as soon as they land."

"Okay. Thank you for calling them." I swallow past the burning in my throat. "How are you doing?" I ask him. "I know how much Tru means to you."

"I'm…" He lifts his shoulders lightly, biting his lip. "You guys are my family." He swipes away another tear. "I'm here for whatever you need."

Sensing rising emotions, something he seems good at, Josh steps in, putting a hand on Stuart's shoulder. "I'm going to take Jake to see Tru now. I said you'd stay with the little guy." He tilts his head toward the door behind me.

"I don't want him to be alone," I add, my voice raw again.

"Of course." Stuart nods. "There's nowhere else I'd want to be right now."

Leaving Stuart, Josh takes the lead and I follow him.

Stopping, I turn back. "Stuart?"

He stops with the door partway open. "Yeah?"

I step forward. "Hold his hand. He likes to wrap his hand around your finger."

He offers a light smile. "Okay, I'll make sure to do that."

"And Stuart." I catch his attention again. "You have to clean your hands with that sanitizer stuff before you touch him, you know, to keep the germs away."

"Sanitizer. Got it." He nods. "I'll take good care of him, Jake."

"I know you will."

I follow Josh down the hall toward the bank of elevators. My heart labours heavy in my chest. Fear roils around me at the thought of seeing Tru.

All I've wanted for the last few hours is to see her, and now I'm so close. I'm so very fucking terrified.

We step inside the elevator. Josh presses the button to take us down a few floors.

The doors slide closed.

"Jake, I want you to be prepared for seeing Tru. She's not going to be—"

"Don't say it. I know. But…just don't say it." I cross my arms, pushing at the ache in my chest.

Josh nods and stares straight ahead.

The elevator glides to a halt, the doors slide open, and I follow Josh out.

With every step closer to Tru, the more panic and terror I feel at what I'm going to see.

We take a right at the end of the hall, into another empty hall, except for a man sitting, writing on some papers attached to a clipboard.

Putting the clipboard down, he stands at our approach and pushes his glasses up his nose.

He's a bookish-looking doctor wearing blue cotton pants and a V-neck top. At least he's not wearing a white coat.

He's wearing scrubs.

Are they what he wore while operating on Tru?

I start to feel sick as unwanted images flash through my mind.

"Josh." He nods.

"Lucas, this is Jake Wethers, Trudy's fiancé. Jake, this is Dr. Lucas Kish."

"Nice to meet you, Jake."

I nod a response.

It's not exactly like I want to shake his fucking hand and say *It's nice to meet you,* because it's really fucking not.

I don't want to meet him. I don't want Tru to be here.

"Okay, so…" He pushes his hands into his trouser pockets. "As Dr. Kimble explained to you before, Trudy suffered a severe head injury as a result of the impact."

I wince at the pain the words bring me.

"From the impact, she hit her right frontal lobe, what we call the emotional part of the brain, causing a severe contusion to the skull. There was internal bleeding and swelling to the brain. We stemmed the bleeding and eased the pressure there. Trudy also suffered other injuries from the accident. Her collarbone was fractured, her right arm broken, and her hand crushed…"

Fractured. Broken. Crushed.

"…but it's the head injury that obviously causes the most concern."

I try to steer my emotions deep inside so I can focus on what he's telling me. But my eyes keep flicking to the door to my left, where I know Tru is.

Taking a deep breath, I force out the words I fear the answer to most. "Is she going to get through this?"

Dr. Kish removes his hands from his pockets, folds them together, and takes a deep breath. I see his eyes sweep the floor before coming back to me.

Nerves crawl around my body.

"The next twenty-four hours are critical. Her vitals are stable but low. She's in a coma and attached to a ventilator. She isn't breathing on her own. With your consent, I plan on removing the ventilator in the next twenty-four to forty-eight hours to see if Trudy responds to breathing alone. If she does, we're looking on the side of positive."

I swallow hard. "And...if she doesn't?"

He looks me firmly in the eye. "We cross that bridge when we come to it. These next few days are critical for Trudy's recovery, but I promise you that we are going to do everything in our power to see her through to the other side of this and get her back home with you and your son."

I push at the ache in my chest with my hand. "When she does wake, could there be long-term damage to her brain?" My mouth feels papery.

He removes his glasses and rubs his eyes. "Possibly, yes. We won't know that until she wakes. The good thing is, the left side of her brain is fine. If it had been the left, her speech, amongst other things, could have been affected. So we have that to be thankful for."

I tense, fist clenching at my side. "I don't see anything to be thankful for right now." My tone is cold, biting.

I see the concern flash over his face. "Of course not, I didn't mean...I'm sorry."

"Jake." Josh's hand goes to my arm, but I can't relax. "Lucas didn't mean anything by it. He's just trying to give you the positive side of the bad. He is one of the best neurosurgeons the US has to offer. You can trust him. He will do everything possible to get Tru through this."

My eyes go to Josh, then Dr. Kish. I swallow past the brick in my throat. "You have to get her through this because… she's *everything*."

He looks at me with understanding, and he nods his head once. "You have my word, Jake."

"Okay, I just…" I rub my hand over my face. "Can I…? I just want to see her."

Dr. Kish steps closer. "You can, but I need you to be prepared. Trudy will look very different right now. There's severe bruising to her face, and her eyes are slightly open, giving the impression that she's awake. It's due to the swelling on the brain, which forces the eyes open—"

"Okay," I cut him off, not needing to hear any more. "I just need to see her."

Leaving them both where they stand, I head straight to the door.

Then I pause.

Turning, I realise I haven't asked before now. "How did the accident happen?"

Josh glances at Kish, then back to me. "A drunk driver. He ran a red light and went into the side of them."

Rage I never knew I possessed strikes me, driving into my head like nails. I grit my teeth together, fists clenched at my sides. "Did he survive? The driver?"

Josh shakes his head slowly. "No. He died on impact."

"Good." *Because I would have killed the motherfucker with my bare hands if he had.*

Turning back to the door, back to Tru, I pull in a deep breath, then push down on the handle and walk slowly into the room.

Tru.

Jesus, no.

Pain digs its ruthless claws deep into my chest.

Nothing could have ever prepared me for this.

She looks broken. Barely resembling the Tru I know.

Everything suddenly seems slow, like I'm moving against water as I take her in.

Her skin is pale. There's a white soft bandage over the right side of her head, and I can see that her beautiful hair has been shaved off in front.

Her right arm up to her shoulder is in a cast. Her hand is swaddled in bandages. Her face is swollen and bruised. Her eyes are slightly open, like Kish said they would be. She looks awake, but I know she's not.

More than anything, I wish she were. I would give everything to have her awake right now.

My skin prickles and my senses go into overload as I take in all the tubes emerging from her body.

The machines keeping her alive beep, echoing inside my mind.

Jesus, no, baby.

Memories of her flash through my mind…

Seeing her again in that hotel room after all those years… Tru lying beneath me as I moved inside her the first time we made love… confessing my love for her… dancing with her at the Eiffel Tower… her agreeing to marry me… us together on that island… her face when she saw our new home… Tru telling me she was pregnant… the first moment we saw our baby on the monitor…

Crossing the room in strides, I fall to my knees at her bedside, hitting the cold, hard tile floor. The bite of pain is barely noticeable to me.

I take hold of her hand, pressing my face against it. I inhale her scent, needing to be close to her. Needing her. But it only makes this hurt so much more.

Tears track painful lines down my cheeks.

"Don't leave me, Tru." I choke on the pain in my throat as tears drip from my chin onto the bed. "I need you so fuckin' much. *We* need you. We've got a son, Tru, and he's so perfect, so beautiful. He looks just like you. I love you so fuckin' much. Don't leave me, baby, *please...*" I close my eyes. "Please come back to me."

CHAPTER TWENTY-ONE

I pace the foyer of the small wing where Tru and my son now are. Security flanks the door behind me.

As I knew would happen, the press are camped outside.

They won't even give me space to figure my way through this. It's all over the news—the accident, Tru's condition, and how my son was brought into this world.

A few hours ago, a reporter managed to sneak his way into the hospital. His aim was to get a picture of Tru in her hospital bed.

What kind of sick fuck does that?

If he had gotten anywhere near her, I would have killed him where he stood.

It turns out the guy never even made it down the hall.

Dave set up residency outside Tru's room the second he was released. With his broken arm, he dragged the reporter out of there. Or so I've been told. I didn't see it myself. I was with my son at the time. I hate that I wasn't there.

For Tru and my son's safety, I had them moved to a private wing. Their rooms are next to one another's, with Dave situated outside Tru's door and a guard outside my son's. Security is covering both entrances and exits.

I haven't spoken to Dave about the accident or the incident with the reporter. I haven't spoken to him at all.

In a brief conversation with Denny earlier, he told me Dave is blaming himself for the accident.

It wasn't his fault.

Have I told him that?

No.

Why?

I'm not entirely sure.

And why am I here pacing the floor outside the elevators and not with Tru right now?

Because Billy and Eva are on their way up.

And I am so very fucking terrified to see them.

I haven't spoken to them yet. Ben picked them up from the airport and drove them straight here.

I haven't spoken to them because I don't know what to say.

Do I say I'm sorry?

Because I am. So very fucking sorry.

I'm sorry I didn't get Tru to stay home with me that morning. Sorry I didn't protect her like I promised I would. Sorry I brought her to LA.

If I had never talked Tru into moving to LA, this never would have happened.

We should have moved to the UK. If we had, she wouldn't be in that hospital bed fighting for her life.

Fighting. For. Her. Life.

I want to fight. I want to fight this fucking pain out of me.

I want to beat the shit out of the motherfucker who got drunk, and then climbed into his car and ran that red light, changing our lives irrevocably. I hate that he's dead, because I want to kill him myself. I want to kill that bastard over and over again for what he's done to my girl.

I feel like I haven't breathed since I saw her. All those tubes were coming out of her body, with the sound of the ventilator's pumping giving me the only sign she's still alive.

I miss her so fucking much.

I miss her voice. Her smile. Her beautiful brown eyes gazing at me in that special way.

If she dies...if I lose her...I don't think I'll be able to go on.

How do you live when your life dies?

The light in the elevator bank signals an imminent stop.

My mouth dries and my hands start to shake. I flex my fingers in and out.

The door slides open. I see Eva first.

I hadn't realized until this moment just how much Tru looks like her mom.

Seeing Eva, her eyes wide with fear and heartbreak, looking like Tru, twists a knife in my heart.

Her eyes meet mine and I see them fill with tears. "Oh, Jake." Her voice breaks. She rushes toward me, throwing her arms around me, and cries into my T-shirt.

I try to hold it together, but then Billy is there. He puts one arm around Eva, the other around me, and I break down.

After a moment, I wipe my face dry on my sleeve. Needing to regain some space and composure, I take a step back from them both. "Shall I take you to Tru?" I ask, my voice hoarse.

Dabbing her eyes dry with a tissue, Eva replies, "Yes," at the same time as Billy.

As we walk to Tru's room, I'm relieved for the space to piece myself back together.

Listening to Billy and Eva cry for Tru was like feeling their heartbreak coupled in with my own.

I know heartbreak. I felt it when Tru left me when I fucked up with the drugs.

But this—it's like my heart is slowly dying, gasping for the fuel it needs to go on. *Tru.* I know, unequivocally, if I lose her, everything that is me will go with her.

As we approach Tru's room, Dave stands.

He's the only one here at the moment. I sent everyone to the hotel across the street.

I needed them all out of here.

I told them Billy and Eva would need space with Tru. But honestly, I just couldn't cope with Simone's constant crying. Stuart's worrying eyes on me. Even Tom was driving me insane. He kept looking at me like he was expecting me to fall over the edge. I know what he was thinking.

What they're all thinking.

Worrying I'll do what I always do when things get hard— run straight to the ready hands of a dealer.

I'm not doing that this time.

Things are bad enough without me being the coward I know I am and erasing the pain with coke.

I knew it was only going to get so much harder when Billy and Eva arrived.

I just didn't realize how much harder.

"Mr. and Mrs. Bennett, I'm so very sorry about Tru." I notice that Dave can't meet their eyes.

I watch Eva's eyes rake over Dave's injuries, then come back to his face. "Dave, you were with Tru…in the accident?"

He nods solemnly, his eyes going to the floor. "Yes. I was driving the car."

"Was she…*awake* after the accident?"

Fear clings to my skin. I hadn't asked this question, because I was afraid of the answer. I can't bear to think of Tru in pain. The thought alone tears me to pieces.

Dave looks up, first at me, then Eva. "No." He shakes his head. "She didn't wake up."

I hear a rush of breath come from Billy, mirroring my own. As I glance at him, I see how very bad he looks.

Unshaven, crumpled, quiet. Not the Billy I know.

She's his little girl. This is killing him.

We need to get this over with. They need to see Tru.

I take the lead, heading for the door, and they both follow.

From the instant they see her, their reaction is no different than mine was.

It hurts so fucking much to hear their pain. Watch them sob over her bedside.

It's crippling.

I feel like I'm drowning again. Fighting against the tide with no way of surfacing. Suffocating under the pressure of the emotions in the room. I know I have to get out of here.

Slipping out of the room quietly, I leave them alone.

Fogged up, my head aching, I take the seat beside Dave.

We sit in mutual silence for a long moment.

"I don't blame you," I finally say. I take a deep breath, then turn and look at him. "I know you will have done everything you could to protect her. I know what kind of man you are."

Dave turns, briefly meeting my eyes. He gives a slow nod, then quickly looks away. I don't miss the tears misting up his eyes.

The door to Tru's room opens soon after, and Billy and Eva emerge.

"Can we see him?" Billy asks.

"Of course." I get up and lead the way to my son's—their grandson's—room.

I push the door open. The nurse is sitting in a chair by his incubator, reading.

Closing her book, she stands at our entrance. "I'll give y'all a moment," she says, exiting the room.

The room is so silent. The only sound is the blipping of the machine.

I walk over and stare down at my sleeping boy. I get a heavy combination of love and heartbreak every time I look at him.

Turning back, I see Billy and Eva still standing near the door.

"He's sleeping," I say quietly.

Billy is first to move. He walks over to the incubator and stands beside me.

I hear his breath catch. Lifting his gaze back to Eva, he says to her, "He looks just like Tru."

I bite my quivering lip, hard, to stop the flow of emotion I feel coming, and I get a sharp taste of blood in my mouth.

Eva comes over, so I stand back to give them space.

I know why they were hesitant to see him once they were in here. They fear he might be all they'll have left of Tru.

I know this because it's what I'm so very fucking terrified of myself.

Resting her hand lightly on the top of the incubator, Eva turns to me. "Do you have a name for him?"

"No." I shake my head. "We couldn't agree on one."

Tru and I had so many disagreements over baby names. But now it all just seems so irrelevant. I would give anything for her to be here with me, naming our son.

"I don't want to name him until Tru wakes up." I clear my throat. "I want her to choose his name."

Eva nods. "I think she'll like that, Jake." She looks back down at my boy. "For now, my little darling," she says, smiling, "until your mummy wakes up, you're Baby Wethers-Bennett."

CHAPTER TWENTY-TWO

Okay, so in the world of music"—I start flicking through the music magazine that Dave brought me—"there is absolutely nothing worth telling."

Closing the magazine, I toss it to the floor beside my chair, and it hits with a loud slap.

Leaning back, I stretch out my aching legs and push my fingers into my hair. "What else is happening? Right, so Vicky's going home today. She's stayed as long as she could, sweetheart, but she has to get back to the magazine, keep it running so you've got a job to go back to. Not that you need to work, but I know how much you love your job. Oh, and don't worry about the book launch. The publishers said it can happen whenever we want, so there's no worry on that score…" Taking a deep breath, I trail off and stare at Tru.

Her eyes are closed like they have been for the past four days.

As the swelling on her brain started to reduce, her eyes closed naturally, and now it just looks like she's sleeping. My beautiful sleeping girl.

The good news is she's breathing alone. Kish monitored her breathing and how much was assisted and unassisted for the first few days. Her unassisted breathing increased hourly, and when she reached 90 percent unassisted, Kish removed her ventilator.

He assured me this was very positive for her recovery.

I want to get my hopes up. But I'm afraid to.

So for those four days, like the three before them, I have sat here waiting for her to open her eyes and tell me to stop boring the fuck out of her with the shit I spout.

Because that's all I do, sit here and talk to Tru, waiting for her to wake.

Aside from the regular visits to my son, I never leave her. My son, who is still waiting for his mom to wake up and name him.

Leaning forward, I reach over and take hold of her soft, warm hand. Her unresponsive hand.

"Our boy is still waiting for his name, Tru, so you need to hurry and open those beautiful eyes of yours so you can choose it. It can even be one of those god-awful ones you were suggesting when we were trying to decide on names—you remember, sweetheart? What was that one you suggested? Skip? Fuckin' Skip Wethers!" Shaking my head, I let out a laugh.

It echoes around the room and hits me back painfully in the chest.

Closing my eyes, I let my head hang back and I release a long sigh to the ceiling.

The ceiling that I close my eyes to every night.

I haven't stepped foot out of this hospital since the day of the accident.

When I do manage to sleep, it's beside Tru on a bed I had brought in for me. The times I do eat, it's in here with her.

I fear wandering too far from this room in case she wakes. I have to be here when she opens her eyes. I have to be the first thing she sees.

I need her to know that I'm here for her, that I will always be here for her.

So here I wait. In a hospital, surrounded by medication.

Drugs.

Do I want a hit?

Yes. So very fucking badly.

I want the fear and pain that's consuming me to disappear.

I fucking hate that I want drugs.

I hate that while my girl is lying in that bed, trying to fight her way back, I'm sitting here thinking about getting high.

I'm a shitty excuse for a human being.

How can I think of drugs at a time like this?

Because I'm a motherfucking bastard.

And I hate that.

But for me, it's life. The addict will always live inside of me.

The only resolve I have is that Tru doesn't know just how much the addict still lives in me. And she'll never know.

I couldn't bear it if she did.

Currently I'm still clean, and I want to keep it that way… but I can feel my resolve slipping.

Only two things are stopping me from taking a hit.

One—my son.

And it's not because I'm father of the fucking year. I wish I were.

No, it's because I'm all he has right now. I know better than anyone what it feels like to be let down by your deadbeat drug addict of a father. I won't be him.

And two—Tru.

I made a promise to her, and I will do everything in my power to keep that promise. I never want her to look at me again the way she did when she found me that morning with that girl in my bed.

So that's what's stopping me from becoming the lowest scum of the earth. How long that will last, I don't know.

Leaving my seat, I walk over to the window.

The city moves below like nothing is amiss. But everything is amiss.

My world has stopped turning.

It feels unjust that people's lives are still moving forward while mine is trapped at a standstill.

I lift my eyes to the setting sun.

Another day will soon be over. Another day without Tru.

Another day without the sound of her voice, her smile. God, I miss her beautiful smile. Her laughter.

Most of all, I miss her touch.

The feel of her in my arms, her warm skin against mine.

I close my eyes tight and let my forehead rest against the glass. "Seven days, baby…" I sigh. "Seven fuckin' days without you. I just…" I bang my forehead against the window. "I need you to come back to me now, Tru. I can't do this without you. I need you so very much. God, baby, I'm losing it without you." Tilting my head to the side, I open my eyes and look at her still form. The empty shell of my girl.

I feel an intense rush of frustration and uncontrollable anger surge into me.

"Are you angry with me because I wasn't there when the accident happened? Is that why you're not coming back? Are you punishing me, Tru?" Leaning back from the window, my muscles tighten as I turn to her. "Goddamnit, Tru, don't punish me, *please*. I can't bear this silence. Not having you here with me…it's killing me."

I let my head drop. Tears burn my eyes.

I rub my face roughly.

Then frustration flares through my veins again.

I snap my head up. "Goddamnit, Tru!" I know my voice is loud, but right now, I don't give a fuck. "Open your eyes and kick my sorry ass for failing you! God knows I deserve it. This isn't you, Tru. You don't give up on anything!"

Moving in strides, I'm at her bedside in a second, I place my hands on the bed.

Looming over her body, I search her face. I can feel all my want and anger and frustration pulsing under my skin.

"Goddamnit, Tru! Wake up!" I stare hard at her face, willing her eyes to open, as though my pain and longing alone will do it.

My fingers curl into the sheets.

"We fuckin' need you! *I* need you!"

The pain hits again. Sharp and sudden.

Exhaling in a rush, I move away from her, walking across the room.

Part of me wants to turn and walk out the door, out of the hospital, and to the nearest dealer I can find.

No.

I won't fall. Not now. I can't.

I just need to find a way to bring her back.

Forcing focus, I start pacing.

She can hear me. I know she can. She's still in there. I just need to figure out what will bring her back.

Stopping, I turn to her again. "I know you can hear me, Tru. I know you're listening."

Then it hits me.

I pull my cell from my pocket, go to my music listings, and start searching.

I've been playing music to her every day. Songs I know she loves, songs we grew up listening to, songs I wrote…the song I wrote for her.

I even sing to her. But none of those songs have touched her, so now I'm last-resorting it.

Now I'm going to play the one song she wanted me to leave behind. I need her to hear me, and this is the last card I've got to play.

I need her to know how desperate I am.

That I'm more desperate than I was that night I sang it to her at Madison Square Garden. At least I knew she was here in the world, vibrant and living.

Now she's…nothing.

I select the live version of Nine Inch Nails' "Hurt," hoping upon all hope that it will evoke the emotion I need her to feel. I press Play and set it on repeat. I then close my eyes under a silent prayer as the song starts, filling every part of the room.

I open up my eyes and carefully climb up on the bed beside her, put the phone between us, while Trent Reznor sings, reminding me of a troubled time, one I would right now give anything to go back to.

I lie beside her, my hand holding hers, as I will my girl to come back to me.

* * *

"*Jake?*" I feel a hand on my hair, fingers gently stroking.

My heart jumps.

Tru.

I flick my eyes open.

No.

My heart bottoms out.

Tru is still sleeping beside me.

Turning my head slightly, I see my mom standing over me.

"Hi, darling." She smiles down at me. It's a careful smile. A smile she's been using around me a lot lately. I don't like it.

"Mom?" I rub my eyes with my palms. "What time is it?"

"A little after eight."

"Where's Eva and Billy?" Picking up my phone, I turn "Hurt" off and sit up, sliding my legs over the edge of the bed.

"Next door with that beautiful son of yours." Pulling a chair over, she sits bedside. "Have you eaten today?"

I cast my mind back. I can't remember the last time I ate anything.

I shrug.

She lets out a light sigh, reaches out, and takes hold of my hand.

I tense up.

This isn't the type of relationship we have. My mom is not touchy-feely with me. She used to be that way when I was a kid, but after that night, the night Paul Wethers changed everything for us both irreparably, a barrier slid down between us and it's been there ever since.

The last time my mom touched me was at my dad's funeral, and that was the first time in a long time. I know she did it purely out of guilt.

Maybe it's guilt now.

"Jake, you need to eat," she says in a quiet voice. "You need to take care of yourself. You never leave this room."

"Yes, I do." My look is as sharp as my tone.

I'm really not in the mood for this. My last hope at reaching Tru hasn't worked, so I'm feeling pretty fucking lost right now. The last thing I need is a lecture from my mother.

She shakes her head. "No, Jake, you leave this room to go to your son's room next door. You shower in there." She jerks her head toward the bathroom. "And the few times I've seen you eat, it's been in here. I can't believe I'm saying this, because you know how much I hate it, but you don't even smoke anymore because it would mean leaving this room. *Believe* me, I'm happy you've stopped smoking, but honestly, if going outside to have a cigarette would get you out of this room for ten minutes, then I'd encourage it."

"Why?" I yank my hand free.

Her eyes snap to mine. "What do you mean, why?"

Getting to my feet, I stand over her. "Why do you even care what I do?"

I see the hurt in her eyes, but she neutralizes it quickly. Pushing the chair back, she stands.

"Because you're my son, and I love you. I might not have given you that impression over the last fifteen years—"

"Eighteen. It's been eighteen years, *Mom*." The disdain in my voice surprises even me.

What the fuck is wrong with me?

I move around her, rubbing my suddenly achy head.

"I let you down, I know that," she says quietly. "But not for one moment did I ever stop loving you."

I hear the break in her voice, and I see that's she crying.

I haven't seen my mom cry in a very long time. The last time was *that* night.

It sparks a pain deep in my chest. One that's been buried for eighteen years.

"I can't do this right now." I start to back away.

"I know." She pulls a tissue from her pocket and dries her eyes. "I just want you to know that I'm sorry I pushed you away." She drives her fingers through her perfectly styled hair. "I just couldn't bear what I'd let happen to you. The look in your eyes that night…it was something I never wanted to see again."

"So you pushed me away?"

What I want to do is yell at her. Tell her that we're not discussing this. But I'm immobile.

"Jake, I didn't know I was even pushing you away until it was too late. I was so consumed with making a better life for you after everything you'd been through because of your dad. With that job at Dale's firm, I was trying to earn enough money to take us away from Manchester before your dad got out of prison. But I was in debt. Your dad had taken a second mortgage out on the house without my knowledge, and when he went to prison, I was left with all of it to pay. I wanted to clear everything up and get you out of there before he came back for you."

"I didn't want to leave, though." I glance at Tru. "But you never asked my opinion, did you, Mom? You just did what suited you." Then the realization dawns on me. "That was why you married Dale, wasn't it? You knew all along he would be transferred to New York."

The look in her eyes tells me everything I need to know.

"You took me away from Tru," I say, pointing in her direction. "The only person I've ever loved. Things didn't get better for me, Mom. They got worse. Yeah, I met Jonny and started the band, but all I did was turn into Dad, and you just stood back and let it happen." I know my voice is getting louder, but I don't care. "If I had been with Tru all along, that would never have happened. She would have kept me straight. *None* of this would have happened." I sweep my hand angrily across the room.

I'm being irrational, I know, but I don't fucking care. I want to hurt her.

"I was doing what was best for you." She reaches for me, but I jerk away.

"No. You did what was best for you, like you always do."

I yank the door open, stepping out into the hall, trying to find my balance and breathe. I shut it behind me, leaving my mom with Tru.

My body is thrumming with anger.

Dave's already on his feet, eyes on me. I'm guessing he heard all that.

"I'm going to get some air. Watch Tru for me."

He gives me a brisk nod and heads for Tru's room as I move past him.

I've just reached the exit door when Dave shouts my name.

Turning, in what feels like slow motion, I catch his eye. And I know.

I don't think I have ever moved as fast as I do now.

Barrelling through the door, I push Dave and my mom aside.

Over the sound of my own heart pounding wildly in my ears, I can hear the monitors attached to Tru beeping loudly.

Falling to her bedside, I look straight into her open eyes.

"Tru?" I almost choke on the word, my voice strangling to get it out. I reach out my shaking hand, wanting to touch her, but fear holds me back. "Tru, baby, I'm here."

Turning to Mom and Dave in the doorway, I yell, "Get the doctor!"

Dave exits the room, leaving Mom.

"Get Eva and Billy!" I yell at her. I'm surprised they haven't heard all the commotion yet.

Mom hurriedly leaves the room.

Turning back to Tru, tears blurring my sight, I touch her face gently with my fingertips.

"I'm right here, sweetheart. I've been here waiting for you. God, baby, I've missed you so much."

She blinks. Once. Twice.

I hold her stare, my heart, and my breath as I wait for her to find focus.

Fear seeps into my stilled heart.

I'm so very fucking scared that this isn't the same Tru. That she doesn't recognize me. Or worse.

Kish had warned me that her memory could be affected. Or there could be irreparable damage to her brain.

Either way, whoever I have here, I'll take her. I'll take any version of Tru I can get.

Her lips part, but the only thing I hear is a light breath escape.

"Shh, don't try to talk, sweetheart." I smooth her hair back. "It's okay. You're okay."

I watch her eyes, waiting. Desperately waiting to see if this is my Tru.

She closes her eyes, and I see a tear trickle from the corner of her eye.

My heart implodes.

When they open, her gaze hits mine, and I see Tru's fire in there, the recognition of me in her eyes, and I know she's back.

I've got my girl back.

TRU...

CHAPTER TWENTY-THREE

Jake, I know you're there, I can hear you talking.

Why isn't he answering me? Who is he talking to? Why does he sound so upset?

I need…

Jake?

I can barely think. I need to open my eyes but…

"Hurt." I can hear "Hurt"…

How long have I been awake? Is that Jake yelling? Who is he yelling at?

God, my head hurts. My whole body hurts, for that matter.

I try to open my mouth to speak, to tell him to stop yelling, but my lips feel like they've been glued together, and there's an intense burning sensation in my throat. I'm so thirsty.

Giving up on talking, I try to move…but I can't. I feel weighted down.

Everything hurts. What's wrong with me? Something's different. Something's wrong. I feel *wrong.*

Oh God, what's happening to me?

Jake, I need you to help me!

I hear a door bang.

No! Don't leave! Please don't go!

Fuck!

I need to move.

I focus with all my might on moving my left hand. There's a pain screaming down my right arm and I dare not attempt to move it.

I'm scared.

No, you're okay, Tru. Just keep calm and you'll be fine.

Maybe I'm just sick? Yeah, that'll be it. I'll have one of those really bad twenty-four-hour flus or something. God, I hope the baby isn't sick with me.

I just need to get a part of me moving; then everything else will follow, and I can get to Jake. Once I get to Jake, I'll feel better.

I focus on moving my index finger. I feel it move.

Thank God.

Gaining confidence, I go to move the rest of my fingers.

Okay, here we go.

Flexing them in and out, I shift my left hand and my arm moves with it.

Okay, I just need to get up now, maybe if I—

"Trudy?"

What?

Who is that? Is that…Susie? Why is she here?

With huge effort, I wrench my heavy eyes open.

Everything is foggy. Dark. I can't get a focus on anything.

Then I hear voices calling out. More yelling.

Dave?

Then Jake…I hear Jake. He's back.

Thank God.

"Tru." He sounds fearful. "Tru, baby, I'm here."

Why does he sound so scared?

Fear starts to prickle my skin. I need my fucking eyes to work! Goddamnit!

Then Jake's yelling again, "Get the doctor!"

Doctor? Where the hell am I?

"Get Eva and Billy!"

Mum and Dad?

I feel his fingers touch my face. "I'm right here, sweetheart. I've been here waiting for you. God, baby, I've missed you so much."

He's missed me?

At the feel of Jake on my skin, my worry starts to ease. That man has the power of touch, I swear.

I blink though the haze, desperate to see him. It feels like ages before my eyes focus.

Then they find his beautiful face.

He looks really tired. Like he hasn't slept for days. Worst of all, he looks afraid. I can see it clear in his eyes.

The last time I saw Jake look like this was when I found that girl in his bed. And that was because he thought he was going to lose me.

Oh God, what's happened, baby?

I need to talk to him.

With every ounce of strength left in me, I force my lips to part.

I try to make the words, but my throat screams in pain and the only thing that escapes is a breath.

"Shh, don't try to talk, sweetheart." Looking at me with love in his eyes, he smooths my hair back with his hand. "It's okay. You're okay."

It's not okay. Nothing about this is okay.

I close my eyes and feel a tear of frustration squeeze from the corner, running down my temple.

I open my eyes and meet with Jake's. I see what I think is a glimmer of relief in his.

Then the ache in my head intensifies. My eyes feel heavy. I'm struggling to keep them open…

* * *

How long have I been awake? God, my head is pounding like a bitch.

I move my tongue around. The inside of my mouth feels like the morning after a really bad hangover, and even moving my tongue takes real effort right now.

Bloody hell, what's wrong with me?

I reach into my memories but don't come up with much, and it hurts my head to try. I remember being in bed with Jake yesterday morning…showering…Jake asking me to stay home. Then…nothing.

If I didn't know better, I would think this is the mother of all hangovers, but there is no way it could be—pregnant lady here.

Well, I might not know why I feel like crap, but what I do know is I really need a drink of water.

With much effort, I force my gritty eyes open.

It takes a moment to adjust to the light.

Ceiling tiles. I can see ceiling tiles. Those really awful ones you find in offices. What do they call them—asbestos ceiling tiles?

Why would I be somewhere with those? Where the bloody hell am I?

I take a light breath. My throat burns again.

Jake.

Jake's here. I can smell his scent close by.

With much effort, I turn my head to the side. *Shit, that hurts.* Jake's sitting in a chair by me.

"Hey, baby." He reaches over and strokes my face, cupping my cheek with his hand.

I can see tentativeness in him.

"Wh-ere…" *God, it hurts so much to get that one word out.* It reverberates around my head, setting the pounding off again. Steeling myself, I finish with, "am I?"

Jake moves closer to me. He leans down and kisses the hand he's holding, then lifts his head and looks at me. "You're in the hospital, sweetheart."

The hospital? Why? Is the baby okay?

"Ba-by?" I exhale, broken. I try to sit up.

"No." Jake gently eases me back down. Not that I had gotten very far. The pain in my head exploded the moment I tried to lift it. "Don't try to get up."

My eyes move past Jake, down to my bump.

My heart drops hollow.

Where my bump was is now a flat, empty surface.

Oh God, no! No, no, no, no, no! Where's my baby?

I want to scream, cry, something…but nothing is working.

I've lost the baby.

No.

The pain I feel is unbearable.

I start shaking my head, uncaring of the pain. Tears run from my eyes, pain pushing them out.

Jake takes my face in his hands, holding me still. He stares into my eyes.

"Our baby is fine, Tru. I swear to you." His voice is filled with so much conviction. Staring into his eyes, my fears start to calm.

Jake wouldn't lie to me.

But if our baby is fine, then why am I not pregnant anymore?

That means my baby was…born?

Jake strokes my hair gently, looking at me like he often does—like I'm the most precious thing in the world to him. But this time, with even more intensity. "Everything is fine now, Tru. You're back and everything's going to be okay." I'm not quite sure in this moment if those words are meant for me, or him.

Jake leans in and kisses my tears away. The feel of his gentle breath against my skin, the warmth of his nearness, is like a salve to wounds I didn't even know I had.

He shifts back, looking into my eyes, but keeping my face in his hands. "You were in a car accident, sweetheart."

Fragments of memories instantly blur into my mind. I was at the spa with Simone…Dave waited in the parking lot all day for us…I teased him about it…we were all driving home, listening to Pearl Jam…"Just Breathe"…then…nothing.

Simone. Dave.

It must be the look on my face that prompts Jake to say, "Simone and Dave are fine. The impact was on the passenger side. Your side." He sounds like he's in physical pain as he says these words. Jake pushes my hair behind my ear using his fingertips. "You were in a bad way. I thought I was going to lose you..." His voice breaks, his eyes filling with tears.

Slowly, with much effort, I lift my good hand and touch his face. "I'm...okay," I reassure him.

He holds my hand to his face, kissing the palm.

A tear drips from his eye and lands on my cheek. I can literally feel the pain it represents.

"You hurt your head real bad in the accident." His eyes flick from mine to my forehead. "You were in surgery. Our baby was in distress. The doctors had to perform an emergency C-section, Tru. He was born before I even got to the hospital."

He.

I watch him, stilled by his words. "We have a son, Tru. And he's beautiful."

A son. We have a son.

"He's doing real good. He's breathing on his own now. It took a while before he could, but a few days ago they removed his ventilator and he did great. God, he's so amazing, Tru. He's growing stronger every day. They said he should be able to start feeding from a bottle in a week or so."

I can't help but cry again. These tears are sheer happiness. Nothing else matters to me right now other than knowing my baby is here and he is healthy.

Then I realise—I haven't been asleep for a day. Everything Jake's said to me, from the way he's talking and the way he's looking at me...I've been away for longer than just a day.

Moistening my lips, I part them to speak. "How...long?"

His eyes dip. "You were in a coma for seven days."

I inhale sharply, causing the burning to start in my throat again.

Seven days. My son has been here all that time without me.

"You first woke up two days ago. But you kept coming in and out of consciousness. Kish told me that was perfectly normal—oh, Dr. Kish. He's the doctor who's been taking care of you," he explains at my questioning expression. "The first time you woke up was for a few minutes, but you didn't talk. For the last two days, you've been here a little. Sometimes you'd open your eyes for a few seconds. Sometimes minutes. You even mumbled a few incoherent words. But this is the first time you've actually talked to me. This is the longest you've stayed awake, so I'm taking this as a good sign." He smiles, but it's not one of my Jake smiles. It looks forced.

"I haven't left you, Tru. I've been here the whole time. The only time I left was to see our boy—and he's right next door." Jake tilts his head to the right.

He's right through there. There's only a wall separating me from my son.

"I want...see him," I force out.

"I know, sweetheart." He strokes my cheek with his thumb. "But I think I should get Kish now that you're fully awake to let him check you over. Your mom and dad—I should call them and let them know you're properly awake now. They're waiting over at the hotel. They'll want to see you."

And I want to see my son.

"No." I shake my head. *Shit, that hurts.* "I want...*him.*"

350

Jake smiles, and this time it's a real honest-to-God Jake smile. The smile he reserves for me only, and I couldn't be more relieved to see it right now.

"Okay," he concedes. "How could I ever say no to you? I'll get him now and bring him through."

Jake leans down and presses his lips gently to mine. "I missed you so much," he whispers over my lips.

Then he leaves the room, leaving me alone.

The silence hits me immediately.

I was in a car accident that resulted in my son's being born while I was unconscious.

I missed his birth. I've missed the first week of his life.

I've missed those important first moments. The moments when a mother bonds with her child and he bonds with her. They were taken away from me. I can't ever get them back.

What if I can't bond with him now? What if he rejects me?

He doesn't understand why I've not been with him for the start of his life. To him, I'll be a stranger.

We don't know each other.

What do I say—do?

I know he's only a baby and won't understand what I'm saying, but these first moments between us now are crucial, and I'm lying in a bed, struggling to move and in pain every time I speak.

I hate that I haven't been here for him. I hate that this is how I'm meeting my son for the first time.

This was not how I imagined it.

I imagined my baby being handed to me, holding him in my arms. Giving him to Jake to hold for the first time. Watching as Jake had his first moments with our son.

Not having my child pulled from me while I was unconscious and Jake was on his way to the hospital.

Loss for what should have been ours overwhelms me. Visions of what happened form in my mind, forcing fresh tears to my eyes.

My son was born alone, surrounded by strangers.

I'm just so thankful he's had Jake with him ever since.

But it makes my heart hurt that Jake has had to cope with this alone—take care of me and become a dad all on his own.

I can't even imagine how Jake felt when he was told what happened. If it were him, I know it would have killed me.

I know without a doubt that Jake and our son will have bonded, and I am so happy for that. I'm just afraid he won't bond with me, that he might reject me.

I don't know how I will cope with that.

And now instead of being excited to meet my son, I'm terrified.

I hear the door open, then the squeak of wheels and two sets of feet.

My body starts to tremble, my heart beats erratically.

I close my eyes, afraid.

I don't think I can do this.

"Put him over by the bed," I hear Jake say.

The squeaky wheels grow ever closer. Then they stop and I hear the sound of a plug being put it in the socket, a switch being turned on, and the gentle hum of a machine.

"Give me a holler when you want a hand bringing him back through," I hear a female voice say. Then the door closes.

I feel the bed dip as Jake sits down by my legs. "Tru." His voice is soft. "Are you awake?"

I know I made him get the baby, but now I'm scared. I hesitate, actually considering faking sleep, and immediately hate myself for it.

I nod.

"Open your eyes." His voice is still soft, but there's a quiet command in it.

Taking a burning breath, I whisper, "I'm...afraid."

I hear a light sigh escape Jake. He takes my hand in his. I curl my fingers around his hand. "I know, baby..." I can tell he's talking from experience. "But I promise, one look at him, Tru...that's all it takes. Trust me."

So I do. I open my eyes and turn my head to the side. There he is, in an incubator pushed up against the side of my bed. I see him, and it's love at first sight.

He is beautiful. The most beautiful thing I have ever seen.

I can't remember ever feeling a love like this before. It's equally as powerful as the love I feel for Jake, but so very different.

A mother's love.

God, I can see so much of Jake in him.

He has the same furrow Jake has in his brow when he's sleeping.

Any worries of not bonding with him are gone. I just love him, completely. And I start to cry instantly.

Jake squeezes my hand. "Hey, don't cry. He's okay in there, really. It's just keeping him warm."

Jake thinks I'm crying because I'm worried that's he's in an incubator. Of course I'm concerned about the incubator, but that's not why I'm crying right now. I'm crying because I'm happy.

"Why don't you touch him?" Jake suggests. "That might make you feel better. It helped me the first time I saw him."

I start to free my hand from Jake's when he says, "Hang on."

Jake releases my hand and disappears into the bathroom.

It's then for the first time that I notice the tubes taped to my arm. I follow them up and see them attached to two different drips.

I glance at my right arm and see a cast covering it, my hand swaddled in bandage.

Jake said I hurt my head in the accident.

I lift my good hand to it and feel a thick bandage on my head.

"I just need to clean your hand before you touch him," Jake tells me, reappearing with a bottle of gel.

I smile at him. He sounds so responsible. In a way, he sounds like my dad would.

That's because he is a dad. He's had over a week learning how to be one.

Today is my first day as a mother.

Forcing back a wave of fresh tears, I chance a quick glance at Jake and see him squeeze some gel out and rub it over his hands. Then he squeezes another blob into his hand, sits back down on the bed, takes my hand in his, and starts gently working the gel into my hand.

It's cold on my skin, but Jake soon warms me.

"You're good to go." He smiles, giving my hand one last rub.

I grin at him.

Taking my hand from his, I slowly put it through the porthole, keeping my eyes on my baby boy.

The instant my fingertips touch the soft downy skin on his tiny hand, sensations explode under my skin, tunnelling straight for my heart.

He is perfect.

I could spend forever here with him like this.

I have so many questions about him that I want to ask Jake, but I don't think my throat will hold out, so I ask the important one.

"Name?"

Jake shakes his head, smiling gently. "I haven't named him. I was waiting for you. That honour is all yours, Tru."

My heart crumbles.

I stare at my son, thinking of all the names I had come up with…all the ones Jake hated.

"He still like…rock songs?" I grate out.

A small chuckle escapes Jake. "Yeah, I sing to him a lot— the old favourites. I think we might have a mini–rock star on our hands."

I shake my head, smiling. A rock star needs a rock star's name, right? A smile curves my lips. "I know."

Jake gives me a suspicious look, humour in his eyes. "It's something crazy, isn't it?"

"No," I croak out, giving him an affronted look. "I thought…" I pause, swallowing through the burning. "Jonathan Jacob."

The look on Jake's face right now is beautiful.

"You're giving him Jonny's name?" I watch him gulp down the words.

"And yours."

Jake bends close and gently kisses my lips. "I love it. I love you."

"Love you," I whisper.

From out of nowhere our little boy curls his fingers around my little finger, the one that was still gently stroking his skin, gripping tightly for his small size.

I laugh softly in surprise, turning to look at him.

"He does that a lot, he likes to hold on to your finger," Jake tells me, running his own fingers along the crook of my arm. "I think he likes his name."

"Yeah?" I smile.

"Yeah…" Moving away, Jake walks around the bed, kicks his shoes off, and carefully climbs onto the space beside me. Lying on his side, his head on the pillow, he says into my ear, "I missed you so much."

His breath tickles my skin.

I turn my face to him and he leans in and kisses me softly on the lips.

Turning from Jake, I move my gaze back to my son. I'm finding it hard not to look at him.

Jake's arm goes across my waist. "He looks like you."

"No, like you." *Beautiful like you, Jake.*

He laughs softly. "No, he definitely looks like you. Everyone agrees with me."

Everyone agrees.

Everyone else got to see my baby before I did. Sadness pokes at my heart.

Brushing over my sadness, I shake my head in disagreement.

Jake chuckles, then presses his lips to the skin between my neck and shoulder blade. It tickles down my spine; even the parts of me that are in pain shiver with delight at the feel of Jake's lips on me.

"He's got your lips and your colouring," Jake says against my skin, still kissing me.

"This…gonna go on for…while," I force out, giving him a quick look, eyes smiling.

"Forever," he replies, and I know he's not talking about the disagreement anymore. Burying his face into my neck, he takes a ragged breath. "I love you so much, Tru. Thank you for coming back to me."

I press my cheek against the top of his head. "I…always will."

He tightens his hold on me. That's how we stay.

Jake's holding on to me, and I'm holding on to our son.

The three of us are together, and nothing is ever going to keep us apart again.

CHAPTER TWENTY-FOUR

It's been three months since the accident. Three months since my beautiful son, JJ, was born.

We called him Jonathan Jacob for a day, and then Jake shortened it to JJ, and that's what everyone has been calling him since.

I spent just over two months in the hospital recovering. Initially it was bed rest, letting myself heal. Then I started daily physiotherapy once my arm and hand had healed.

I also saw a counsellor twice a week. Dr. Kish recommended it. I may not remember the actual accident, but he said I'd been though a terrible trauma, and while I might not remember it on the surface, it's still buried deep within me. Talking about the accident with someone would help.

And he was right.

I went through phases of emotions. One day I'd be on top of the world, feeling extremely lucky to be alive, knowing I could have died. Then the next day, I would be angry. Angry this had happened to me. Angry I had missed the birth of my son.

Then I had bouts of depression.

I wanted to stay positive and happy all the time, but when the black hit, there was nothing I could do about it.

And through all of this, Jake was right there with me.

The day they removed the bandage from my head, I sobbed. The scar on my head was red and angry, running a few inches back from my hairline, over my scalp, and a huge patch of my hair was missing where it had been shaved off for the surgery.

I felt hideous.

When I said this to Jake, he held me in his arms.

"We can always make a fashion statement out of it, sweetheart. I can shave a patch of my hair off too."

"You wouldn't suit the bald look." I smiled through my tears.

"Nah, you're probably right. But you do." He took my face in his hands, brushing my tears away with his thumbs, the tip of his nose resting against mine. "You suit every look, Tru. You are beautiful to me right now. You are beautiful to me always, no matter what."

Jake knew how much it bothered me, so once I was able to, once the scar had near to healed and my hair had grown back a little, Jake had a hairdresser come to the hospital and put some extensions in. Once she was finished, you couldn't tell there was a scar unless you were looking for it.

Jake has done everything possible to help me get back to the person I was before the accident. Because of his help, I'm almost there.

I don't sleep great. I suffer with nightmares. I have blinding headaches to contend with along with shooting pains in my right arm, and my right hand isn't as strong as it used to be. But I'm lucky to be alive, and I make sure to remind myself of that every single day. It doesn't take much, I just look at Jake and JJ and know how lucky I am, that I have everything in the world to be thankful for because I have them.

I haven't spent a night away from JJ since that day Jake brought him into my hospital room.

Jake had JJ moved into my room. Of course, Jake was there with us too.

It became our home away from home. I even spent my birthday there.

Well, it wasn't like I could go out celebrating, so Jake brought the celebration to me, and we had a miniparty with Mum and Dad, Simone, Denny, Stuart, Josh, Smith, and Carly. Even Susie and Dale were there. Tom was away, so he couldn't be.

Jake had Pizza Hut brought in, and he bought me seven gifts to catch up to the twelve missed, then another to mark my actual birthday.

The seven gifts were a charm bracelet. The bracelet was one and six charms made up the others. Each one meant something to us—a slice of pizza, a little Eiffel Tower, a guitar, a cupcake, a piano, and a scroll charm inscribed with "Best Friends."

My present for my actual birthday was diamond earrings from Tiffany to match my locket.

He put so much thought into my gifts. But that's Jake. Where I'm concerned, he puts thought into everything.

The only downside to my party was the tension between Jake and Susie. It wasn't noticeable to the others, but it was to me.

After everyone had left, I asked Jake what was going on.

He told me about the discussion he and Susie had right before I woke up from my coma. When he said "discussion," I knew it was an argument.

It made my heart hurt for him, hearing what was said between them. I told Jake he needs to make some workable relationship with Susie because she's JJ's grandma. Kids are smart—JJ will pick up on the tension between them as he starts to grow, so they need to talk it out sooner rather than later.

I know he hasn't talked with Susie yet, but he will, and soon, now that I'm back on my feet. I'll make sure of it.

I don't care what he says. He needs his mum.

I know that even more, now that I am one.

In the beginning with JJ, it was hard not being able to do the things a mother should for her baby, like change his nappy, bathe him, and soothe him when he cried.

I felt useless. And it frustrated the hell out of me.

I had to watch Jake do it all, but he made sure to include me as much as possible, and in truth, I loved watching Jake with him.

He's so sweet and loving with JJ. He treats him like precious cargo. And no matter how many times I tell Jake not to let JJ fall asleep in his arms, to put him down in his crib, he still lets him. Our boy has Jake wrapped around his finger, and it warms my heart to see.

Jake is everything a dad should be and more. I knew he had it in him, and I made sure to tell him one night in the hospital.

"You're really good at this," I said over the sound of JJ wailing, while I watched Jake give him his first proper bath.

I couldn't help—my arm was still set in a cast—so I sat by the baby bath, watching instead.

"I don't know about that." He gave me a quick panicked look. "I think I might be doing it wrong. He's done nothing but cry since I started bathing him."

"You're doing it right. It's just new to him, that's all. He's just telling you, quite loudly, that he's not sure about this bathing business." I gave him an encouraging smile.

"Yeah, and he definitely gets the loud from your side of the family."

"Ha!" I laughed and gave him the middle finger.

"Did you just flip me the bird?" he asked, deadpan, rinsing the soap from JJ's hair with water from the sponge.

"Looked like it." I grinned.

"I can't ever remember you doing that—what's happened to my sweet girl?"

Getting to my feet, I grabbed JJ's towel and handed it to Jake. *"I don't know if I was ever sweet."*

"You were. You still are." He leant close and kissed me on the lips. *"Except for when you're flipping me the bird, that is."*

I stepped back, my lips still tingling from his kiss. *"It must be all the time I've spent around foul-mouthed rock stars."*

"If you haven't noticed, I hardly curse anymore. Not around JJ, anyway," he said, grinning, as he wrapped the towel around him, swaddling him up in it.

"I've noticed." I smiled, climbing up on the bed.

I've noticed a lot of things about Jake lately. He hardly ever smokes anymore. I think he's well on his way to quitting completely. He never curses while JJ's around, which is all the time.

Jake has always been in control of everything around him, but never relaxed...now he's relaxed.

He has slipped into his dad role with perfection, and he hasn't even realised it.

I watched silently in fascination while Jake dried JJ's skin with care and precision, put his cream on for his dry skin, then put on his nappy, or diaper, as he calls them, and dressed him in the cute blue onesie that my mum bought for him.

Jake then brought JJ over to me with the bottle that he'd put in the warmer right before JJ's bath, and laid him down on the bed beside me so I could feed him.

Like I said, he's the perfect dad.

Jake sat with us, and we both watched in silence while JJ drank his milk. It didn't take him long—he's got a healthy appetite. Then about ten seconds later, with his belly full, he fell asleep.

Jake carefully picked him up and put him in his crib by the bed. Then turned the light out and climbed in bed beside me.

This was one of my favourite parts of the day. Of course, I love spending every minute with JJ, but I loved the quiet moment at night when it was just me and Jake in the dark, together.

"You're so good with him," I whispered. "You're an amazing dad."

"I'm only good because of you."

"No." I turned to him. "This is all you, Jake, and it's about time you realise that. You are everything a dad should be to our son, and more. JJ's lucky to have you."

His arms went around me, and his lips pressed a kiss against my shoulder. "I guess I'm doing okay. But I'm the lucky one, believe me."

Jake hasn't spent a moment away from JJ and me since the moment I woke. He's put everything into us.

He had Zane handle things at the label. What work he could do, he did at the hospital or at home when I was finally released.

The guys put a pause on working on the album, but I want them all to get back to finishing it soon. A world with no more TMS music wouldn't be a world at all.

Tom even pitched in when Dina, Vintage's manager, broke her leg skiing when they were about to go on a six-week tour across the States. That's why he couldn't make my birthday.

I was still in the early days of my recovery at the time, and it was stressing Jake to no end to find a new manager for Vintage he could trust, and Tom offered his services.

He's never managed a band before, but he's spent most of his life on the road touring.

Jake thought it was a brilliant idea. At first I thought it was because Tom was still trying to get in Lyla's pants, but Jake said it was because he genuinely wanted to help. Then I felt bad for thinking it.

In all honesty, I've seen a different Tom of late since he got back from Vintage's tour. Actually, he was a little different before he went away.

It's like something has changed in him. The new Tom is freaking me out—he hardly ever talks about sex or the women he's slept with. He still manages to make a crack about my breasts, though, to wind Jake up, so I know a bit of the old Tom is still in there somewhere, thankfully.

I never thought I'd say this, but I'd miss the old Tom if he changed completely and that Tom making cracks about the size of my breasts is comforting—weird thought, huh?

So anyway, I digressed a little—okay, a lot.

I've been out of the hospital for three weeks now, and we've settled into life at home with JJ, though I'm not actually at home at the moment. I'm at my old home, my first home, the currently blissfully warm Manchester.

Jake, JJ, Stuart, Dave, Ben, and I flew in a few days ago. Jake has some business to do here. It has something to do with the label, and he's been a little vague about it. Why he'd have business in Manchester, I have no clue. It's usually London.

Jake didn't want to be away from JJ and me, so we came along. Not that I needed my arm twisted—I didn't fancy being away from Jake either, and I'd take any excuse to come home, as it means being able to spend more time with my folks.

They came back home once I was released from the hospital. They had both spent so much time off work, and they had to go back.

I got so used to seeing them every day that I've missed them since they left.

But one person I don't have to miss anymore is Simone.

The day after I woke from my coma, Simone and Stuart came to visit me, and Simone had some news.

Simone came bursting into my room, with Stuart close behind. She took one look at me and burst into tears.

"I don't look that bad, do I?" I joked, knowing I actually did.

"No—I," she hiccupped.

"Simone, I'm fine, I promise," I reassured her.

She stumbled across the room, swiping at her tears, and plunked herself down on the bed, then practically threw herself on top of me, wrapping her arms around me. "I thought I'd lost you," she sniffled.

I could feel her tears soaking through my nightie, and she was hurting my C-section scar. I didn't say a thing. She needed to hug me, and I needed a hug from her.

"You don't get rid of me that easy," I said into her hair, holding back my own tears.

"Hey, let a guy in, will you?" Stuart joked.

Giving me one last squeeze, Simone moved off me.

"Hey, gorgeous." Stuart sat on the bed beside me. I could see his eyes shining with tears. Seeing him looking at me like that made the tears I'd been holding in spill over. Stuart took my face in his hands and kissed me square on the lips. "You frightened the shit out of me, chica. Don't ever do it again," he whispered close to my lips.

"Cross my heart." I smiled, making the sign over my chest.

"Good girl." Rubbing my tears away with his thumb, he moved off the bed and sat on one of the chairs.

"Where's JJ?" Simone asked, glancing around the room.

"Jake took him downstairs for his checkup in the NICU."

"The little guy's doing okay?" Stuart asked.

"He's doing great." Without fail, the thought of JJ brought a smile to my face.

"Stuart and I really wanted to come and see you last night, but Jake said you were exhausted from your folks visiting and all the tests, so he said we would have to wait until this morning to see you," Simone said.

"I was pretty zapped," I said.

I was knackered yesterday, but I think Jake put them off because he wanted some alone time with me, after having to share me for the best part of the day. And honestly, I wanted time with him too.

"Did you get the flowers I sent yesterday?" Simone asked, glancing around at the numerous bouquets of flowers and cards around the room.

"I did, and I got yours too," I added, glancing at Stuart. "They're gorgeous. Thank you."

Stuart waved me off, in that way he does.

"Looks like you didn't need any more, though, you've got tons," Simone said, getting up from her seat. She started checking out the bouquets and reading the cards. "Holy fuck!" she exclaimed, spinning on the spot, waving a card around. "Did you seriously get a bouquet of flowers from the president?"

I laughed. That had been my exact reaction when they arrived first thing this morning.

"Apparently, when you're the fiancée of Jake Wethers and you're in a serious car accident, it qualifies you for big-time flowers. I seriously doubt he ordered them himself, but it's still really nice."

"No kidding! Bloody hell," she muttered. "I'd frame this card if I were you."

"Oh, I will. I've already asked Jake to order me a frame." I laughed. But I wasn't kidding, I actually had.

I watched her put the card back in with the flowers and sit down in the chair by my bed.

"So how are you doing?" I asked, looking at the bandage on her wrist, noticing the yellow bruises on her face.

"I'm good." She smiled. It looked a little forced.

"Simone…," I pushed.

"Really, I'm fine. My injuries were minor compared to—"

It was at that moment she chose to brush her hair away from her face.

"Holy fuck!" I said, reaching forward, grabbing her left hand. "Is that what I think it is?"

"Jesus Christ!" Stuart said, pulling her hand from mine to examine the huge-ass rock on her finger. "How in the hell did I miss this? I must be losing my touch!" He scratched his head.

"Oh my God! You're getting married!" I squealed. I didn't even care that it hurt my throat. "To Denny!"

"Yes." She looked a little sheepish. "He asked me last night."

"Arghh!" Stuart and I cried in unison. "This is awesome!"

"Yeah." She looked down at her hands and started picking at her nails. Simone only does that when she's worried about something.

"What's wrong?" I asked, concerned. "You do want to marry Denny, don't you?"

"Of course I do. I just…" She let out a sigh. "I just feel a bit shitty." She looked up at me. "You're here in the hospital recovering after being in a coma for a week, and I come to visit you…I just feel bad being excited about this."

"Don't be soft," I chastised. "This is exactly the kind of news I need to hear right now. And you were in that accident too, Simone— you deserve happiness more than anyone I know. So come on, tell us. How did he ask?"

Her expression turned doe-eyed and I knew I had her. "After Jake wouldn't let us see you, I was a bit bummed, so Denny suggested we go out for dinner." She bit down on a smile, and I could see how happy she was. "We ate at an Italian restaurant near his place, and he was acting a little odd all night, but I just let it go. Then on the way back to his house, he suggested going for a walk in Echo Park. We walked for a bit, and then he stopped me up by the lake, got down on one knee, pulled a ring box out, and said, 'I bought this ring a month ago, and I've been carrying it around with me ever since, trying to find the right way to ask you to marry me. The day of the accident, coming so close to losing you, I wanted to ask you then, but it seemed out of place with everything that was going on. But now Tru's awake, I'm not waiting any longer.' He took a deep breath and said, 'Will you marry me?' Then he popped open the box and pulled the ring out. I cried, and said yes."

"God love that boy," Stuart said as we both let out a dreamy sigh.

"Does that mean you'll be moving here?" I asked, hoping and praying.

She grinned. "We haven't really talked everything through yet, but yeah, I reckon I'll be moving here."

So thanks to the ever-gorgeous Denny, I get to see Simone practically every day.

And thanks to Jake using his contacts, he managed to help get Simone an interview for a top PR firm in LA, and of course she got the job.

She handed her notice in at her old firm and officially moved out here two weeks ago.

She and Denny are getting married this December. A winter wedding. I can't wait! JJ is going to be page boy and I'm the maid of honor.

With the way things are looking, Simone and Denny will be married before Jake and me.

It's funny how things work out.

Jake and I haven't talked about when we're getting married. In all honesty, we've talked about everything but, and I'm not really sure why.

Actually, talking is the only thing Jake and I have done since I got out of the hospital. We haven't made love since before the accident.

Jake hasn't made a move on me. But then, neither have I with him.

I guess I'm feeling self-conscious about my body after the accident and having JJ.

There was no way we were having sex in the hospital. I was healing, for starters, and toward the end, when I was almost better…well, it just wasn't happening there. Now we've been home for two weeks. We kiss, but it has yet to go further than that.

I'm not sure why. Well, I know why on my part, but not on Jake's.

I'd be lying if I said I wasn't worried.

But then, Jake has so much going, taking care of me and JJ.

I'm sure we'll get back to that side of our relationship soon.

I have a lot to be happy about. I'm with the man I love, the man I was always destined to be with, and together we have the most beautiful baby boy this world has ever seen.

Speaking of my baby boy, I'm missing him at the moment.

He's with my mum and dad. And I'm in a car right now, destination unknown.

You see, Jake has a surprise for me, and Dave is driving me to that surprise. You know what that means…yep, I'm blindfolded.

Dave is still my bodyguard and driver.

When I found out that Dave had spent the vast duration of the time I was in the coma guarding my room, I asked Jake to bring him in to see me.

We talked for a long time.

Dave blamed himself for the accident, which was crazy, and I told him so. There was no way he could have prevented the accident any more than me or Simone could have. The only one who could have prevented it is buried in a cemetery right now.

I would, and still do, trust Dave with my life.

That doesn't mean that riding in a car is easy for me now, because it's not.

It's a challenge I face every day.

The first ride I had to take in a car after the accident was horrendous. It was the day I left the hospital. I was shaking with nerves. Even though I don't remember the crash, just knowing I was in one was enough.

It took me nearly twenty minutes before I could muster up the courage to get in.

I sat in the back with JJ, who was in his car seat, while Jake drove us home. I focused on JJ the entire time. It felt like the longest car ride of my life.

I can't remember ever being so afraid.

But I had to do it. I can't spend the rest of my life fearing being in a car.

I'm slowly getting there. Don't get me wrong, I'm still jittery every time I'm in a car. Just like I am now. But it's getting better.

"How much longer?" I ask Dave from the backseat, fingers curled around the edge of the seat, my foot nervously tapping the mat under my ballet pumps. I know I sound like a whiny kid in the back of her parents' car, but Dave is used to my angst. He understands it. He's the only other person aside from Simone who does.

"Another five minutes at the most," he replies.

"How long has it been already?"

"Thirty minutes. We'll be there real soon, I promise. Try to relax. I'm taking it real steady, and I'm sticking to the speed limit. You remember what I told you?"

"That lightning doesn't strike twice." I exhale. It's a motto Dave told me to remember while in the car.

"We're golden, Tru. I promise you."

"Okay." I loosen my death grip from around the seat, trying to relax. "You definitely can't tell me where it is I'm going?"

He lets out a deep chuckle. "More than my life's worth."

"Figured," I grumble, folding my arms across my chest.

I'm so ready to find out what this surprise is and get back to JJ.

I haven't seen Jake all day, or Stuart for that matter. They've both been quite absent since we arrived in Manchester. I've not minded, though. I know Jake is here for business, and I've kept busy with JJ and spending time with Mum and Dad.

I was expecting them back at dinnertime, but then I received this cryptic text message from Jake at three in the afternoon, telling me he has a surprise for me. I'm to leave

JJ with my mum and dad, get in the car with Dave, put on this bloody blindfold, and he'd see me soon.

So here I am, driving to wherever my surprise is.

I lean my head back against the headrest and fold my arms in my lap, fiddling with my engagement ring. "Can you put some decent music on? This song is driving me nuts." It's some annoying boy band I've never heard of before. "Oh, but not Pearl Jam," I add. "I don't want to tempt fate and set that lightning to strike twice."

"See, that was quite funny." Dave chuckles. "You're getting there."

I touch my head where my scar is. "The only way to get through the bad stuff is to laugh about it, right?"

"Right."

I listen as he flicks through the radio stations.

"Go back to one," I tell him.

Dave jumps back a station, and Jake's voice fills up the car.

"Through It All," the song he sang for me in Copenhagen, the first night we slept together.

I always think of that night as the start of Jake and me, but in truth we started a long time ago. We started the very first moment we laid eyes on each other through our shared garden fence all those years ago.

It just took us a long time to get there.

CHAPTER TWENTY-FIVE

As Jake's song ends, I feel the car come to stop.
My door opens. "You look beautiful."

I can't help smiling at Jake's words.

"I'd say the same to you, but it'd help if I could see." I tap my finger against the ever-present blindfold.

"Oh, you know me, baby. I always look hot."

I laugh.

"Come on." I feel his hands take hold of mine, and he guides me out of the car.

I step out into the warm late-afternoon air. The ground is hard under my feet, but I'm definitely on grass. Jake slips his arm around my waist and guides me on.

The sound of running water hits my ears.

I think I know where I am.

I bite down on the smile the thought brings so Jake doesn't know I've figured it out. I know how important the actual surprise is to him.

After less than a minute of walking, Jake stops me. I feel him move behind me and undo the blindfold. I hold my breath in anticipation of whether I'm right or not.

Holy shit.

My breath comes out in a rush.

Yes, I'm at Lumb Falls, but this is…*wow*. Just bloody wow.

No more than fifty feet before me, on the bank overlooking the falls, is a wooden structure that could only be described as an altar.

There are fairy lights woven around it, intricate with white and pink flowers, dressing it up to beautiful.

Dozens of lanterns hang from the nearby trees. A couple of rows of chairs are set on both sides, and down the middle is an aisle covered with pink and white rose petals.

I turn to Jake, my mouth wide in awe and wonder. "Wha…I…you did all of this?"

His mouth lifts at the corner as he pushes his hands into his jeans pockets. He shrugs lightly. "I want to marry you, Tru." He takes a step closer to me. My heart starts to thump. "But if I've got this all wrong and today's not that day—that this isn't how you saw us getting married—then that's okay, I'll wait. If you want a big church wedding, then I want that too. I just want you, any way I can have you. But today…well, I at least wanted to try and see if my girl would marry me in our special place. The girl who, twenty-four years ago to the day, stepped into my life with her big brown eyes, her hair in pigtails, sucking on a lollipop as she stared across at me through the garden fence and said, 'I'm Trudy, you want a lollipop?'"

I let out a laugh as tears fill my eyes, realising what today's date is: August 31. The day Jake and I met.

"So have I got this right? Is today that day?" he asks, cupping his hands around my face.

"Yes," I breathe, leaning forward, pressing my lips to his. "Yes, it is."

I touch his face with my hands. My beautiful Jake.

I can't believe he has done all of this without my knowing. I seriously had no clue this was going on at all.

Excitement bubbles up inside me.

We're getting married today!

I look down at my jeans and T-shirt, which has a stain on it from where JJ spit up earlier.

I'm definitely not dressed to get married.

I don't even know if I've got a dress with me that I could get married in. I start doing a quick mental run-through of the things I brought with me.

Nope, definitely nothing wedding-worthy.

"Jake, I love all of this, and I so want to marry you right now." My lips turn down at the corners. "But I'm not exactly dressed to get married, and I don't have anything I could wear. I could go to the shops in Manchester and pick up a dress real quick, I suppose, but then—"

"Tru, stop talking." He presses his fingers over my lips. "Do you really think I would bring you here and expect you to get married in jeans?" He lets out a soft laugh as he tilts his head back, looking to the left, past the altar. I follow his gaze, but I can't see anything beyond the trees.

"Through those trees, we've set up a place for you to get ready. Everything you'll need is in there, including Simone, who's waiting for you. And when you're ready"—he looks back at me and caresses my cheek with his hand—"I'll be out here, waiting at the altar for you. Your mum and dad are on their way with JJ. Stuart, Ben, and Dave are already here. Tom, Den, Josh, Smith, Carly, my mom, Dale, and Vicky are all arriving soon."

"Vicky's coming?" I beam. I haven't seen her in so long. Jake told me that she came while I was unconscious in the hospital, and we've Skyped since I woke up, but it's not the same as seeing her in person.

"She is."

I press my face into his hand. "I can't believe you did all of this under the radar. How did I not know about all of this?"

"It wasn't easy. You're nosey as hell." He rests the tip of his nose against mine. "But I wanted this to be a surprise, and I wanted our wedding private. No press. Just you, me, JJ, and the people we love."

"I love you."

"And I love you. Now go and get your hot ass ready so I can marry it," he says, giving my behind a gentle slap.

He kisses my lips once, then steers me off in the direction of where Simone is.

I walk past the altar, through the trees. In a clearing is a tall camping tent, the kind you can stand up in and fit a small family to sleep. It's white. Perfect for a wedding.

The door on it is tied open, and I can see Simone inside, sitting on a stool as she tinkers on her phone, by a table filled with what looks to be makeup.

She looks up, and when she sees me, a huge smile appears on her face. She puts her phone down and comes out to meet me.

"You're getting married!" she sings.

"Apparently so," I say with a grin. "How long have you know about this?"

"A little while." She grins sheepishly. "From the minute I moved to LA, Jake's had me shopping for everything you need. He even asked me to pick out a wedding dress for you."

I can tell from her face that Jake's asking her meant a lot. It means a lot to me too.

"You pick something good for me?" I tease, poking her in the ribs.

"Of course." She gives me a look of mock-offence. "I snuck a look at the dresses you'd highlighted in your wedding magazines that Jake gave me, and I bought the three that had hearts next to them. I know what a geek you are. You only heart things when you really love them. You've been doing it for years in our Next catalogue, so I figured I couldn't go wrong."

I didn't even know she knew I did that. I hadn't really registered it as a thing I do.

"Very sneaky. I'm impressed." I grin at her.

She gives a little curtsy. "I have everything in here you'll need—wedding dresses, of course, shoes, veils, tiaras, makeup…underwear." She winks. "It's like your very own personal bridal shop."

"In a tent."

She meets my eyes and laughs.

"I love it, really," I say, wrapping my arm around her waist. I give her a gentle squeeze.

I peer inside the tent, and I can see she really has thought of everything, and it's all laid out for me. I spy a pale pink dress amidst the flashes of white hanging on a rail. It causes excitement to ripple in my stomach.

"You're still going to be my bridesmaid, right?"

"Of course, already got my dress." She nudges me with her hip, grinning.

"Good."

"Come on, then." She links her arm through mine. "Let's get you ready to become Mrs. Wethers."

* * *

I look at my reflection in the mirror. I'm ready to marry the man I love. But then, I've been ready to marry Jake for a very long time.

Simone got me ready. She did my makeup, keeping it natural, with soft pink on my eyes, mascara, and gloss on my lips. She left my hair down. Thankfully it was already clean and curly, so she pinned some tiny diamante flowers in, pulling a few strands back from off my face.

For jewellery, I'm wearing my Tiffany locket and earrings, my charm bracelet, my beautiful engagement ring, of course. But most importantly, I'm wearing my friendship bracelet.

But the prizewinner is the dress.

I knew right away out of the three which one I was wearing. It was the one I had been leaning toward all along when I was looking at wedding dresses.

It's a Jenny Packham gown, white and floaty, with a deep V-neck and crystal beading decorating the waist and shoulder and framing the open back. It's beautiful and the perfect dress to become Mrs. Jake Wethers in.

I can't believe I'm getting married today, here at Lumb Falls. It's so surreal that I have to keep pinching myself. It's so incredibly perfect. I can't believe I didn't think of getting married here myself.

Then Jake is always one step ahead of me, and everyone else. That's what makes him...him.

"Hey, baby girl."

I turn at the sound of my dad's voice. The voice that can always bring a smile to my lips no matter what—not that I need any help today. "Hey, Daddy." I smile, turning.

"You look..." He takes a step toward me, arms out. "You look beautiful, Tru." I can see the pride swelling up his eyes.

"You look real handsome, Daddy." I take a step closer to him and brush a piece of lint off his jacket. He's wearing a dark grey suit, white shirt, and pale pink tie.

"Is Mama still crying?" I ask.

"Of course." He smiles.

Mama came in to see me while I was getting ready, and she kept bursting into tears. Happy tears thankfully. Since the accident, Mama seems to have changed her whole attitude toward Jake. They've bonded on some level. And she's completely besotted with JJ, of course, which helps.

"You ready to go out there and get married?"

"I am. Just let me get my flowers." I pick up the small bouquet that Stuart brought me a short while ago. It's amazing: pale pink roses with two dark pink roses pressed together in the middle. Like they're meant to represent Jake and me.

"How's Jake doing?" I ask, turning back to him.

"He's good. Surprisingly calm for a man about to get married."

"And JJ?"

"Currently asleep on Jake's shoulder."

I let out a laugh. "Knowing JJ, he'll probably sleep through the entire wedding. Not that he'd remember it if he was awake."

"We'll just have to make sure to take plenty of photos for him to look at when he's older."

I lean over and kiss his cheek.

"What was that for? Not that your old man is complaining about getting a kiss from his baby girl."

"Just to say thank you…for everything, Daddy."

He stares into my eyes for a long moment. "You don't have to thank me for anything. You were the best kid a dad

379

could ask for. Really, I'm the one who has everything to be thankful for, to have you standing here before me now." A sob catches in his throat, and he presses his fist to his mouth.

"Don't you go crying on me." I wrap my hand over his. "You'll set me off, and Simone will go mental if I spoil my makeup."

He gives me a gentle nod and lowers his hand from his mouth.

I wrap my arms around him, hugging him.

"You know how much I love you?" he says into my hair.

"I do, Daddy. And I love you the same right back."

He leans back from me, hands resting on my shoulders. "I always knew one day I'd be walking you down the aisle, and that Jake would be the one standing there waiting to marry you."

"You did?" I swallow past the tears creeping in.

He nods. "The way he always looked at you, and you him…it was inevitable." He smiles. "Come on." He holds his arm out for me to take. "Time for me to give my girl away."

I slip my arm through, curling my fingers around him, holding on to the material of his jacket.

We make our way out of the tent, and Simone is there waiting to take her place behind me.

The dusk is creeping into night, but our walk is lit with lanterns.

Simone straightens my dress out from behind. "Ready?" she asks.

I glance back at her, and then to my dad. "For the last twenty-four years." I smile.

Dad puts his hand over mine on his arm, and we start the short walk to Jake.

As we make our way through the trees, I hear "You Started" begin to lilt softly into the air.

We step out of the trees into the clearing. I feel Jake's eyes on me immediately, but I don't look at him.

I want to wait until I reach the start of the aisle, because I want a full, unrestricted view of him. This image of how he looks right now will be etched into my mind forever, and I want it to be perfect.

Daddy walks me until we're ready to begin our walk down the aisle. Then I lift my eyes to Jake.

He looks as beautiful as I knew he would.

He's wearing a dark grey suit exactly like my dad's, except that Jake's tie is dark pink, just like the two roses in the middle of my bouquet.

Then the world melts away, and there's only him. There has only ever been him.

With the way he's looking at me right now, I can see in his beautiful eyes that he feels exactly the same.

My dad gives my hand a gentle squeeze and starts to walk me up the aisle toward Jake, and I don't for one moment take my eyes from his.

"You look breathtaking," Jake says when I reach him.

"So do you."

I can't take my eyes off him. I'm mesmerised.

Jake moves his eyes from mine to my dad's. "Thanks, Billy," he says.

I kiss my dad on the cheek before slipping my arm from his, and take Jake's hand.

Dad leans into Jake and says something into his ear. Jake looks him in the eye and nods. My dad pats him on the back, and then heads to my mum, who has a still-sleeping JJ in her arms.

She smiles proudly at me and mouths, *You look beautiful.*

I smile back and whisper, "So do you."

I look to Jake, and I'm about to ask what my dad just said to him, when the music quiets and the registrar begins to speak.

"I welcome you all here today for the wedding of Jacob David Wethers and Trudy Consuela Bennett…"

I listen as the registrar speaks, my eyes fixed to Jake's, his to mine, neither of us wanting to look away from each other.

"I believe Jake has something he wishes to say to Trudy before we do the official vows. The floor is all yours," the registrar says with a smile to Jake.

My face prickles, my cheeks colouring in anticipation of what he's going to say.

Jake clears his throat, running his finger into his shirt collar. He's nervous. This man can stand up on a stage and sing his heart out in front of a hundred thousand people, but here, before me, he's nervous. I love that.

He steps closer to me. "Do you remember what I said that first night we moved into our house? What you asked me to say as my vows?"

"Yes," I whisper.

"It still stands, Tru. It will *always* stand. My love for you is limitless, it knows no bounds. You're in my veins. I bleed you. I belong to you…I always have and I always will." He takes a deep breath. "You will *always* be my June, Tru."

My mind instantly goes back to that poignant moment Jake and I had, the one that defined us, the one that told me of the depth of Jake's feelings for me, how he'd always seen me.

"Reznor's version or Johnny Cash's?" I asked quietly, trying to conceal the pain from my voice.

"Johnny Cash."

"Why?"

He closed his eyes briefly. "Because I have a few things in common with him," he answered, opening his eyes.

"Like?"

"The drugs...the women...hanging out for the girl of my dreams."

I took a sharp breath in. Tears instantly pricked the backs of my eyes.

He touched my face, his thumb smoothing over my lips. "You're my June, Tru."

With tears filling my eyes, I say to him for the first time, "And you're my Johnny Cash, Jake."

Jake smiles widely, and then I can't help myself. I throw my arms around his neck and kiss him deeply.

In this moment, it's just Jake and me.

When we break away, breathless, I can see the fire in Jake's eyes, and I know where his mind is at right now... because mine's there too.

"Okay," the registrar says, clearing his throat. "Time to say your vows to each other. Jake, if you could present the rings."

Jake reaches inside his jacket and pulls out two wedding bands.

The smaller one is platinum and encrusted with three pink diamonds to match my engagement ring. Jake's is matching platinum, encrusted with three sapphires.

Taking his ring from his hand, I ask, "Why sapphires?"

He pushes his lips together. "Blue. It's more manly than pink, baby."

He raises his brows, and I laugh.

Then I watch, holding my breath, as Jake recites his vows, gently sliding the ring onto my finger, making me his wife.

Then I do the same for him, my hand and voice trembling the whole time.

"I now pronounce you husband and wife. You may kiss your bride—again."

We're finally here. It's taken us a long time, a lot of hard times and work, but we've made it. And it was worth every single moment.

My heart is full of happiness as Jake takes my face in his hands and presses his lips to mine, giving me the most breath-stealing kiss he's ever given me.

My first kiss as his wife.

"Finally mine, Mrs. Wethers," he whispers over my lips.

I stare straight into his blue eyes, the eyes I will spend the rest of my life staring into. "I've always been yours, Jake."

"Yes, you have." He smiles, and kisses me again.

EPILOGUE

Adele starts to ring in my huge bag. I dig around for it. Bloody hell, I have way too much stuff in this bag. I pull some nappies and wipes out and set them on the table, then my makeup bag, one of JJ's rattles, and a juice cup. I finally find my phone as Adele tells me she's "Rolling in the Deep," and I connect the call.

"You took your time answering." Jake's voice comes down the line.

"You're calling me? You're in the next suite, you lazy ass!" I laugh.

"Stop giving me grief," he says, chuckling. "I was just letting you know we're ready to go down."

"We'll be right there." I put my phone on the table and slip my feet into my shoes.

"Hey, gorgeous, come to Mama." I put my arms out to JJ. He reaches up from his sitting position on the floor and I lift him into my arms. "Time to go get Uncle Stuart married," I say, heading for the door.

We're in New York at the moment for Stuart and Josh's wedding. It's one of the few states in the US that performs same-sex marriages. Jake is Stuart's best man, I'm bridesmaid, and JJ is page boy.

Yep, that's right, Stuart and Josh are getting married!

Josh asked him the day after Jake's and my wedding. It was so sweet. We were having breakfast together, when Josh got down on one knee in front of everyone and asked Stuart.

Yes, I cried. So did every other woman at the table. All the men were manly, but I know they were touched, especially Jake.

It was the perfect memory to christen our new house.

Yes, you heard that right, our *new house.*

After the wedding, Jake drove us to Littleborough, which is a fifteen-minute drive from Lumb Falls and a thirty-minute drive from Manchester. He'd bought us a house near Hollingworth Lake. When I say "house," this is Jake we're talking about. It's a seven-bedroom country estate, secure with a gated entrance. It's beautiful.

We had our wedding reception there, which Jake and Stuart had already set up. The house was decorated, courtesy of Carly.

It's a beautiful second home for us. We spent a long wedding night making use of our big new bed, making up for the time the accident took away from us. Jake had told me that he'd been holding back from making love to me since I'd gotten out of the hospital as he'd wanted our wedding night to be special.

And he bought the new house because he wanted us to have a home in the UK as well as LA, so we could all have the best of both worlds.

Could I love that man anymore? He really is my version of perfect.

My mum and dad moved in the new house. They live there permanently, and we go over regularly, but our base is still LA.

We went on our honeymoon two days after the wedding.

Once the press found out Jake and I had gotten married in secret, things got frenzied, as expected, so going away on our honeymoon was a good way to escape the craziness that is Jake's life, and mine now.

Our honeymoon was a long one—we were gone for four weeks, just Jake, JJ, and me. And, well, Dave and Ben, of course.

We changed our original honeymoon plan to go back to Turtle Island, as we didn't think the heat there and JJ would go well together, so we instead travelled to all the sights Jake and I had never seen, the ones he had waited to see with me.

We will go back to Turtle Island one day in the near future, but in the meantime Stuart and Josh are going on their honeymoon there. They don't know yet; it's our wedding gift to them.

Jake, JJ, and I went to Venice to see the canals and take a ride in a gondola. We went to Pisa to see the tower. Rome to see the Colosseum. Barcelona to see the *Sagrada Familia*. You name it, we visited it. It was the best trip of my life, and I will always remember it.

Then we went back to LA. Jake went back to work at the label, and TMS finished their new album. The tour that was scheduled for autumn was pushed back, and they'll be going on tour at the beginning of next year. Of course we'll be going along, as is my dad. He's ridiculously excited about it.

I also went back to work. My book finally came out. The launch was moved to LA to make it easier for me, and it went great. The biography received really great early reviews, and sales went through the roof.

Everyone wants to know and have a little piece of Jake Wethers, written by the woman who knows him best.

I'm fine with that, because I have the real man as a whole here with me.

I'm still working for Vicky, doing my column. The magazine is doing amazingly, thanks to Jake's book.

I know you're probably wondering why I'm still working for Vicky—it's not like I need to work, and I have JJ now. But I love it. I love writing and I love music, and I owe everything to Vicky. There's no way I'm leaving her now, when the magazine is starting to take off.

She keeps talking about making me partner. One day, I think yes. But right now I have my hands full with JJ, and then we'll have the new baby coming too.

Oh, did I not mention that I'm pregnant again? I'm six months gone. We're having another boy. He's our honeymoon baby.

I'm going to let Jake name him.

Simone's pregnant too, which is awesome! Denny is like the cat that got the cream.

They got married on Christmas Eve, and it was magical. I was bridesmaid, JJ page boy—we're doing that a lot recently—and Jake and Tom were best men. Then Simone found out while they were on honeymoon that she was pregnant. They had gotten married while she was pregnant and she didn't even know. At least they can't be accused of a shotgun wedding.

I know you're wondering about Tom: Is he still the changed Tom of last year or is he back to the man-whoring Tom we all knew? All I'll say is Tom is happy right now. The happiest I've ever seen him.

I open the door to Stuart's suite to find Jake and him sitting at the table, sharing a laugh, drinking whiskey.

"Bit early to be on the hard stuff, isn't it?" I joke.

"Hey, go easy on me, gorgeous! It isn't every day a man gets married. I need the Dutch courage."

"Dada!" JJ calls out, chubby arms reaching out for Jake.

"Hey, little man. Come here, I missed you." Jake takes him into his arms, nuzzling his black hair, while JJ's chubby little hands grab at Jake's face, causing Jake to laugh.

Jake's only been away from JJ for the morning. To say he's attached to JJ is putting it mildly, and it goes both ways: JJ adores Jake.

The love Jake has for our son wrecks my heart every single day, in the best possible way.

I love watching them together. It'll never get old. I know just how lucky I am to be here with them both. I treasure every single moment I have with them.

I turn to Stuart, resting my hand on his shoulder. "You ready to go get married?"

He gets to his feet and slings his arm across my shoulder. "Chica, to quote the wise words of our man Jake here... abso-fuckin'-lutely!"

"Language in front of JJ!" Jake chastises.

I can't help but laugh. I never thought I would hear the day Jake would tell someone off for swearing. But he does, regularly.

"Sorry," Stuart apologises, flashing me a "here he goes again" look.

"I saw that," Jake mutters.

"You were meant to," Stuart replies.

They're like a pair of kids at times. And I wouldn't have them any other way.

We take the elevator down and meet Josh outside with Dan, his brother and best man.

The way Stuart and Josh look at each other just melts my heart. I'm so glad Stuart found his someone. He truly deserves to be happy like Jake and I are.

Taking each other's hands, Stuart and Josh enter the room to get married where all our family and friends are waiting inside.

The Mighty Storm family, and what a family we are.

And when our kids grow up and ask about the story of Mummy and Daddy—how we met and how the Mighty Storm came to be—I'll sit them down and tell them the story of how, once upon a long time ago, in Manchester, a girl moved next door to a boy...

ACKNOWLEDGEMENTS

Jenny, we've been on the Storm journey together for a long while now; it's been one hell of a ride, and I have loved every single minute of it! You know I love you, and THANK YOU for everything. Now on to Tom's book!

The biggest thank-you goes to my husband and children. Not only for putting up with the neurotic writer in me, but for allowing me the time to write this book without a word of complaint when I was MIA, which was often. There is not a word in the world to express just how much I love and appreciate the three of you. You have my heart.

My "Brit" girls: Trish, Rachel M., Rachel F., Jenny, and Gitte—I love talking every day with you all. I think if our conversations were ever to be aired, there'd be some real interesting reading in there! And Gitte, thank you for the *WTS* feedback—it meant a ton to me.

Sali Benbow-Powers—no one can make me laugh like you do, and I mean no one! Thank you for the reads and feedback, your opinion is invaluable to me. And I'm officially changing my name to "Spunky Muffin."

Jenn Sterling. I love you. That is all.

Renae Porter at Social Butterfly Creative, thank you for the stunningly beautiful cover for *WTS*! You're crazy talented, girl, and I cannot wait to see the next cover that you create for me.

A big thank-you to all the bloggers who have featured and reviewed *TMS*—

Totally Booked, Aestas Book Blog, Maryse's Book Blog, Angie's Dreamy Reads, Three Chicks and Their Books, Shh Moms Reading, C&C Book Blog, Smardy Pants Book Blog, Love N. Books, Rock Stars of Romance (I'm a million times sorry if I've forgotten to mention anyone). You all work tirelessly, helping indie authors like myself get our books out to the readers. It is truly appreciated. I totally heart you all!

My Tru Bennett on Twitter, you know who you are—thank you so much for all the hard work you put in on a daily basis.

To all the ladies who run and contribute to the Jake groups. The snake lovers! I love popping in and seeing what new talk is going on about Jake and Tru, and the latest Jake pictures that have been posted...which means a separate thank-you to the queen of pictures, America Matthew!

A huge thank-you to my agent Kimberly Whalen at Trident Media. And thanks also to Adrienne Lombardo.

My publisher, Montlake; Kelli Martin for loving *TMS* and writing up a contract in the quickest time known to man! Thank you to my editor, Lindsay Guzzardo, who helped to make *WTS* the best it could be.

And lastly, you. Yes, you, reading this dedication. I wouldn't be writing this now if it wasn't for you buying, reading, and supporting my work. Thank you. Really and truly, thank you from the bottom of my heart.

ABOUT THE AUTHOR

 Samantha Towle began her first novel in 2008 while on maternity leave. She completed the manuscript five months later and hasn't stopped writing since. She is the author of *The Mighty Storm*, *The Bringer*, and the Alexandra Jones series, all penned to tunes of the Killers, Kings of Leon, Adele, the Doors, Oasis, Fleetwood Mac, and more of her favorite musicians. A native of Hull and a graduate of Salford University, she lives with her husband, Craig, in East Yorkshire with their son and daughter.

Don't miss the beginning of Tru and Jake's story!

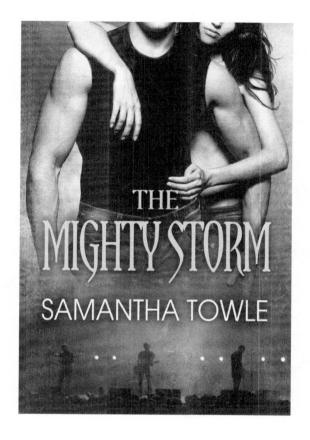